the
MAGNIFICENT
SAVAGES

FRED MUSTARD STEWART

A TOM DOHERTY ASSOCIATES BOOK / NEW YORK

THE MAGNIFICENT SAVAGES

Copyright © 1996 by Fred Mustard Stewart

All rights reserved, including the right to reproduce this book, or portions thereof, in any form.

This book is printed on acid-free paper.

A Forge Book
Published by Tom Doherty Associates, Inc.
175 Fifth Avenue
New York, NY 10010

Forge® is a registered trademark of Tom Doherty Associates, Inc.

Design by Basha Durand

Library of Congress Cataloging-in-Publication Data

Stewart, Fred Mustard, 1932–
    The magnificent savages / by Fred Mustard Stewart.—1st ed.
        p.   cm.
    "A Tom Doherty Associates book."
    ISBN 0-312-86111-7
    1. Americans—Foreign countries—History—19th century—Fiction.
2. China—History—Taiping Rebellion, 1850–1864—Fiction.
3. Family—United States—Fiction.   I. Title.
PS3569.T464M3   1996   95-53162
813'.54—dc20   CIP

First Edition: May 1996

Printed in the United States of America

0   9   8   7   6   5   4   3   2   1

To my wonderful wife, Joan.
And to my agent, Peter Lampack, who is gloriously persistent.

*A*UTHOR'S *N*OTE

Before the adoption of Pinyin by the current Chinese government, there was a confusing variety of spellings in the translation of Chinese into English. The standard translation that emerged was the Wade-Giles system (which translated the capital as "Peking" rather than the Pinyin "Beijing"). I have used the older system because it would have been familiar to the characters in the book.

Each Chinese Emperor, upon ascending the Dragon Throne, was given what was known as a "reign title," different from his real name. Thus the Hsien-feng Emperor, who ascended the throne in 1851, was the "Of Universal Plenty" Emperor. For simplicity's sake, I have used the reign titles in referring to these rulers.

RELATIVE VALUES

$1.00 in 1850 was the equivalent of $35.00 in 1995.
The blue-collar wage in New York was $1.50 to $2.00 per day.
College tuition was $200.00 per year.
A doctor's visit cost $5.00.
Transatlantic fare (one way) cost $60.00.

PART ONE

FIRST LOVE

1   JUSTIN SAVAGE WAS DREAMING OF sailing the ocean in one of his father's famous clipper ships when he was awakened by his plump amah.

"Justin, wake up!" Ah Pin exclaimed. "The *Sea Witch* has been spotted off Sandy Hook!"

The twelve-year-old boy with the red-gold hair bolted upright in his bed, instantly awake. "It's a record!" he exclaimed, throwing off the coverlet and swinging his bare feet to the floor.

"Sylvaner just brought the news," Ah Pin went on, handing him his black trousers, which he pulled on under his nightshirt. "He's downstairs, kowtowing to your father, the son of a snake!"

Ah Pin, which was Cantonese slang for "Flat Nose," spoke to her charge in the language of southern China, which she had been instructed by Justin's father to teach him when Nathaniel Savage had brought her over from Canton on one of his clipper ships to raise the motherless boy. Who Justin's mother was, what had happened to her, and where he had been born, no one knew— including Justin. Only Nathaniel knew, and he wasn't telling. It was one of the great secrets of New York, a source of endless speculation among the rich shipping merchant families that dominated the thriving port in 1850.

"Hurry, boy!" Ah Pin said, taking his nightshirt. His bare, milk-skinned torso was already filling out, pushed by puberty into athletic musculature. "Who knows what Sylvaner may do to your father unless you're there?"

"Ah Pin, Sylvaner is *not* going to murder my father."

"Ai-yee, you think not? I've looked in his eyes many times: there is murder there! If not your father, *you!*"

"You've been reading too many penny dreadfuls," Justin said, pulling on his socks and shoes. His nurse-cum-surrogate-mother handed him a clean white shirt of the finest Egyptian cotton. Justin might be a bastard son, but old Nathaniel Savage lavished his wealth on him, buying him the finest clothes, the best books and education. Everyone whispered the old man was trying to atone for his guilt over the boy's illegitimacy. The betting was she was an actress, because Justin was such a handsome boy, and Nathaniel had always loved the theater. Others said it was the wife of one of Nathaniel's many employees, perhaps even the wife of one of his ship captains. The ships of the Savage Line were at sea months at a time, and who knew what went on ashore? Whatever the truth, the mysterious woman had been the love of Nathaniel's life. And for New Yorkers addicted to gossip, which included the whole city, Nathaniel Savage's secret romance was a mystery everyone ached to solve.

Ah Pin lovingly ran Justin's wooden brushes through his thick hair, then shoved him out his bedroom door on the top floor of the great brick mansion on Washington Square. It was a chilly April morning, but already the trees in the square were budding, and the tulip shoots were pushing through the ground, tempting the resident mice to dig for the bulbs. As Justin raced down the wide, carpeted stair with its heavily carved wooden balustrade from the fifth floor to the second, he caught glimpses of the square from the landing windows. But he wasn't thinking of spring. His young mind was bursting with the wonderful news of the *Sea Witch*'s record voyage from China, an event that would spread through New York like wildfire. The city had become the greatest port in the world, edging out even London as the Black Ball Line set records on the New York–Liverpool run and great shipping houses like A. A. Low and Company and N. Savage & Son bit chunks out of the fabulous China trade that had once been dominated by the English. The new American clipper ships like the *Sea Witch* had become the wonders of the world. Because of their great speed, the clippers could charge twice the rate for cargo that the slower English merchantmen did, and Yankee inventiveness, daring, and seamanship were piling up fortunes for shipowners like Justin's father.

As he reached the second-floor landing, Justin could hear his father's voice through the dark walnut door of his bedroom. The boy knocked on the door. It was opened by Sylvaner Savage.

Justin didn't agree with Ah Pin that Sylvaner wanted to murder him, but he was certainly under no illusions that Sylvaner was fond of him. The tall, black-bearded man in the black frock coat with the thick, curly black hair that many New York debutantes had once swooned over looked down at Justin with anything but friendliness.

"Ah, Justin," he said in his deep voice. "You've heard the news from your amah, I suppose?"

"Yes, and it's terribly exciting."

"Come in, boy," his father called, beckoning to him from his big four-poster bed. Sylvaner stepped back, and Justin hurried into the tall-ceilinged bedroom with its heavy Victorian furniture and brass chandelier. Nathaniel Savage had once been a commanding figure of a man, one of New York's finest sea captains. But he was seventy-four now, and a series of strokes had left him partially paralyzed and bedridden. But his cadaverous face beamed when he saw Justin, which Sylvaner didn't fail to note. He had seen that loving smile many times before. Sylvaner, who was thirty-seven, hated his young half brother.

"A record, boy!" Nathaniel said, opening his arms to hug his son. "By God, think what this means. Canton to New York in one hundred twenty-six days, twelve hours, and forty-two minutes. Think of it! A miracle! Oh, my God. . . ."

He went into a coughing fit. Miss Pry, the Irish nurse, pushed Justin aside so she could pound the old man's back.

"I warned you about too much excitement!" she said. "You've had this cold for weeks. . . ."

"Let me alone, you damned harpie!" he sputtered. "I'll die soon enough without *your* help!"

"Ah, and you're a wicked old man," she shot back. "Haughty and proud— too proud to listen to your doctors, who are tryin' to save you from your grave! They say 'bed rest,' and you, spoutin' like a whale because one of your blasted ships broke a speed record!"

" 'Blasted' ships, you say?" the old man snorted. "You'll speak with respect of the Savage Line ships, or by God I'll send you back to your potato-rotted Ireland where you can starve with the rest of your beggarly race! My ships are the finest in the world, and you'll forget *that* at your peril! The *finest!"*

Miss Pry shrugged, as if she'd heard that before; but Justin, who had also heard it before, swelled with pride because he agreed with what his father had said: the seven beautiful clipper ships that constituted the Savage Line *were* the finest, the fastest, and the most beautiful ships in the world. It was his fondest dream that someday he would be master of one of the Savage Line ships and sail it to the four corners of the globe for adventure and profit. In Justin's mind, the former was vastly more important than the latter. For although Justin knew well the five-story brick offices of N. Savage & Son on John Street between Front and South on the lower East River, the countinghouse where the Savage millions were recorded; and although Justin knew that the lifeblood of American merchant shipping was profit; still, it was the adventure that set his young heart pounding. Justin had crawled over the Savage Line ships, each with a "sea" in its name, so that he knew the sails and the rigging like the back of his hand—although his father had never permitted him actually to climb up the rigging, for fear that he might fall. Justin knew how to box the compass, and he had practiced shooting the sun and the moon out the top-floor window of the Washington Square house, even though he had no true horizon. He had devoured Bowditch, the navigator's bible. The beautiful, mysterious, ever-changing, sometimes lethal sea excited this strapping boy the way a woman's perfume could excite a man a few years older.

"Father," Sylvaner said, standing at the elaborately carved foot of the bed, "Nurse Pry is right: you mustn't excite yourself. We fear for your health."

While Sylvaner was the only legitimate heir, in the tightly knit world of Manhattan's shipping families, it was well known that he and his father didn't get along. It was also well known that Sylvaner, who had run the accounting side of the family business since his father's strokes, had an ugly temper and the brute strength to back it up.

Nathaniel sank back into his big pillows with their lace shams and glared at his son.

"So you fear for my health, Sylvaner?" he said in a mocking tone. "Why don't you tell the truth? You fear my health will *improve,* eh? Let's keep hypocrisy at a minimum. Don't you think I know you and Adelaide can hardly wait to bury me?"

"That's not true, Father!" Sylvaner exclaimed.

"Bilgewater! You've never forgiven me for siring Justin, you damned hypocritical prig! I'd like to have a hundred dollars for every bastard *you've* sired!"

"LIAR!" Sylvaner roared, his darkly handsome face turning red with rage. "I've never betrayed Adelaide—! You, Nurse! Get out!"

Miss Pry, who looked ready to faint, scurried toward the door.

"Don't give orders in *my* house!" Nathaniel yelled. Then he started coughing again.

"If you want to kill the man," Nurse Pry said to Sylvaner, "just keep yellin' at him. He'll be gone in five minutes."

She left the room. Justin hurried to his father's side.

"Father, please," he said. "You must calm down."

"Give me some of the medicine," his father whispered, pointing to a bottle on the bed table. Justin filled a spoon and put it to his father's mouth. Nathaniel swallowed the liquid, made a face, then lay back in his pillows. Sylvaner had managed to get his temper under control.

"Father," he said, "I'm sorry. But it pains me when you cast these aspersions about Adelaide and me. You know we have nothing but the most tender feelings toward you."

"You hate my guts," the old man whispered. "And it would be only fitting if I willed the company to Justin."

Sylvaner's face turned white. *"I'm* the legitimate heir," he said softly.

"Yes, but Justin's the better man. Now get out. Go down to the dock and wait for Captain Whale, then bring him up here so I can hear his report. Go on with you!"

Sylvaner shot Justin a look that left little room to doubt what he thought of him. Then he left the room.

"Well, well," Nathaniel said with a chuckle, "I got his dander up, eh, Justin? And did you see the look on his face when I threatened to leave the company to you? I thought he'd swoon like a maiden."

"Father," asked the boy, "why does Sylvaner hate me so?"

"Ah well," sighed the old man, "I suppose part of it's my fault. It's no secret you're closer to me than he. That damned Sylvaner, every time he sets foot on a ship, he heaves over the taffrail. Some sailor! Now, Justin, dear boy, go over to the highboy and open the top drawer. There's a leather book in it that I want you to bring to me."

Justin obeyed, crossing the flowered Axminster carpet and opening the drawer. He pulled out a small, leather-bound book that was marked "Diary, 1837." The book had a clasped lock. He brought it back to the bed and handed it to his father.

"I've been giving you a lot of thought lately," Nathaniel said, looking at the diary. "Thinking about your future. I'm not long for this world, Justin. At least Doc van Arsdale doesn't bother to lie to me. He says the next stroke will be the last, which is fine by me. It's no pleasure for a man who was as active as I was to be stuck in this bed, day after day. At any rate, what I want to tell you is that I'm going to arrange with Captain Whale for you to ship out on the *Sea Witch* as cabin boy when he returns to China next month."

"Father!" Justin said, his face lighting up.

Nathaniel held out his hand and took Justin's, a smile on his face. "I knew it would bring joy to your heart. You've got the sea in your blood, just like me. That's why we're so close, you and me. And that's probably the real trouble between Sylvaner and me. It's not only that he's deceitful and will cover your stern with spit to get what he wants. It's not only that I'm sure he's cooking the books down at the countinghouse, robbing me blind because he knows I'm too weak to check on him. It's the fact that the damned man don't like the sea! It's not right that a Savage not be loving the sea, you know what I mean? But *you* love it, boy. I've sniffed that in you since you were knee-high. That's why I brought Ah Pin over to raise you and teach you her lingo. Someday you'll be master of a ship, and it'll be a great advantage to you to be able to speak Chinkee. But now, it's time for you to go to sea. It won't be easy, mind. Ichabod Whale works his crews hard, and he won't make things easier for you just because you're my son. But you'll learn the ropes, lad. And I know you'll make me proud of you."

"Oh, Father, I will! You've given me the greatest gift of all!"

"Ah no, Justin," Nathaniel sighed. "No, I cheated you, and it weighs heavy on my soul. I was a foolish old man who fell in love with a beautiful young woman, your mother. I've given you my name. I've legally adopted you, trying to make up for the sadness I caused your mother. But New York knows you're not legitimate, and you'll have to fight that all your life, because we live in a stinking hypocritical world. Someday you'll be a rich man, Justin. As much as I dislike Sylvaner, I can't very well not give him the company because he is the legitimate heir. But after I'm gone, you'll never lack for money. It's just legitimacy I can't give you for what that's worth, and, unhappily, that's worth quite a lot in America."

"Father, may I ask you one question?"

"Of course, son."

"Who was my mother? I know you want to keep it a secret, but it's a terrible thing not knowing who one's mother was."

The old man lifted up the small, red leather diary.

"It's all in here, Justin. The whole story. The day you ship out on the *Sea Witch,* I'll give you this diary and you can read it at sea. You'll be surprised, lad. My heart's in this diary. But I'll tell you one thing: your mother was the sweetest angel of a woman who ever walked this earth. You'll never have to be ashamed one minute of your mother."

There were tears in the boy's eyes. He had heard the rumors of his mother from sniggering schoolmates: how she was a wicked actress, the wife of one of Nathaniel's sea captains . . . the whole pack of gossip that had entertained Manhattan for twelve years.

"Why didn't you tell me that before, sir?" he said. "I've thought all sorts of horrible things. . . ."

"I know, boy, and I'm sorry. But I couldn't let you know the truth until you were old enough to deal with it. When you read the diary, I think you'll understand why. Now run downstairs and have your breakfast. And tell Chin to come sponge me off. I have to look presentable for Captain Whale. And give me a kiss. I fear I'll be in the next world by the time you return from China, and I want you to think well of me when you remember."

Justin put his arms around the old man and kissed his cheek.

"I'll always remember, Father," he said. "And I love you."

He left the bedroom with high spirits. Not only was he going to find out the vexing secret of his parentage, but he was going to sea! For Justin Savage, it was a dream come true.

The house at Number Four Washington Square North was a handsome brick Federal building with a graceful fan window over the white front door. It had been built almost twenty years earlier by Nathaniel and his wife, Charity Stuyvesant Savage, and was considered one of the finest residences in the city. In 1842, when the city brought in water from the upstate Croton system to the Forty-second Street Reservoir on Fifth Avenue, Nathaniel had installed a bathroom on each floor, then an almost unheard-of luxury, and a modern kitchen on the ground floor. And it was into the kitchen a few minutes later that Justin ran, coming up to his amah, who was sitting at the long plank table enjoying her morning coffee, a habit she had picked up after coming to New York from Canton. "Ah Pin," Justin said, speaking in Cantonese, "I'm shipping out as cabin boy on the *Sea Witch!*"

Ah Pin hugged the boy she loved as her own son.

"Ai-yee, I thought this might happen! The Old Big-Nosed One"—which was how she inveterately referred to Nathaniel, even though his proboscis was normal-sized for westerners—"loves you, my golden-haired one, and I knew he would not fail to grant you your dream. When do you sail?"

"Next month. You could come too, Ah Pin! I bet I could talk my father into it, and you could see Canton again, and your family."

Ah Pin's moon face eclipsed.

"Why would I want to see my family?" she asked. "My mother's dead of overwork and childbearing, and my father sold me because he had no use for a woman child. Ah no, my little one. You are kind to think of me, but I'm too old for such a journey. I'll stay here and wait for you. But how proud I'll be of you when you come home! You'll be practically a man!"

She smiled lovingly at him as Miss Pry and Stella, the Irish cook, shot them icy looks from the coal stove where Stella was heating the porridge.

"Damned heathen," Stella whispered, indicating Ah Pin. "If you ask me, the Captain was a fool putting his boy in her care. The lad's more at home in that singsong Chinkee than he is in English. And her, prayin' to her heathen gods and joss sticks on the top floor! It's a sin, that's what it is."

"I couldn't agree with you more," Miss Pry whispered. "And don't she look ridiculous in her western frocks and bonnets! If this were my house, the heathen wouldn't be allowed through the door."

A fact that Miss Pry and Stella chose to ignore was that the vast majority of English-descended New Yorkers said the same thing about the Irish.

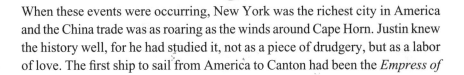

When these events were occurring, New York was the richest city in America and the China trade was as roaring as the winds around Cape Horn. Justin knew the history well, for he had studied it, not as a piece of drudgery, but as a labor of love. The first ship to sail from America to Canton had been the *Empress of*

China, owned by a group of New York merchants. It left New York on Washington's birthday, 1784, saluted the grand battery with thirteen guns, received twelve salutes in return, then passed Sandy Hook off Staten Island to launch its voyage to the distant Orient. Six months later at Macao, having received a "chop" and with a Chinese pilot aboard, the *Empress of China* set sail for Whampoa and Canton. American trade with China was born.

At first, the Americans brought to China such esoterica as bêche-de-mer, or sea slugs, considered a delicacy by the Chinese like bird's nests; ginseng root, considered an aphrodisiac; and especially fur: seal, otter, beaver . . . animals the Chinese had never encountered. The Chinese had tea to sell the Americans, tea in great abundance with names as fragrant as the leaves: Lumking, Mowfoong, Mowfoong Hyson Skin, Lumking Young Hyson, Quichune Young Hyson . . . or names slightly more explosive, such as Wunyen Gunpowder and Loongmow Gunpowder. The British had become addicted to tea, and the habit had spread to America. There was great profit to be made from the tea trade. With auctioneers like Philip Hone or the celebrated Mr. Bell at work, a cargo of tea worth four hundred thousand dollars could be sold in an hour, enriching the shipowners like Nathaniel Savage.

The problem was that after the novelty of sea slugs, ginseng root, and furs had worn off, the Americans had precious little to sell the Chinese, because the great Chinese Empire was largely self-sustaining, the Emperor thinking of trade as "tribute from the barbarians." The British had encountered the same problem years earlier, and they had come up with a solution. They found something they addicted the Chinese to, much as the "barbarians" had become addicted to tea.

Opium.

"He loves him, and he hates me!" Sylvaner Savage said that night as he sat opposite his wife at the dinner table in their elegant house on East Fourth Street. Sylvaner's big, hairy left fist squeezed tight as he went on: "My father loves that bastard, Justin. It's not fair, Adelaide. *I'm* the real Savage!"

"But we've known that for years, Sylvaner," said Adelaide Crowninshield Savage. She was a beautiful woman with rich chestnut hair parted in the middle, then pulled back into a cascade of plunging curls. Her dark brown eyes peered through the silver candelabra at her husband. "All New York has known it for years. It's shocking! To have such a scandal perennially flaunted in the eyes of Society! Justin should have been sent to an orphan asylum or to some farm family upstate, but oh, no, that evil old man had to *adopt* him, and now all of us Savages are tainted. It's shameful."

"If we only knew who the mother was!"

"Dear Sylvaner, can you doubt it was the actress? The one with the red hair who was so popular with the stockbrokers down on Wall Street? I forget her name . . ."

"I never believed that story," Sylvaner interrupted. "Why would Father have made such a mystery out of it? He knew dozens of actresses. My poor mother, God rest her soul, was always complaining about it. No, if the truth ever is known, I wouldn't be surprised if it turns out to be someone totally unexpected, like one of Mr. Poe's mysteries. Someone we might even know."

"Absurd!" Adelaide wiped her thin lips with her linen napkin. "Well, perhaps not in New York. In Salem, of course, such a thing could never happen, and if it did, both parties would automatically become pariahs. But here, in New York . . ." She shrugged her puffed lemon silk sleeves. "Well, dear Sylvaner, you know my views on your hometown. Standards here are scandalously low."

Adelaide was a Crowninshield from Salem, Massachusetts, one of that port's leading shipping dynasties. She had been educated in Paris, where she learned French. She was one of the best-dressed women in New York, a fashion-mad city; but even her few close friends had to admit that Adelaide was a cold, haughty woman, as unforgiving as her husband.

"Yes, I know your views about New York all too well," Sylvaner said, reaching for the etched-glass decanter to refill his crystal wine tumbler. "And I agree with you. In fact, you may be surprised just *how* scandalously low our moral standards can sink."

Adelaide's eyes glistened with interest.

"What do you mean?"

Sylvaner glanced at the door to the butler's pantry to make sure none of the servants was eavesdropping, then looked back at Adelaide. "He's sailing on the *Sea Witch* next month."

"Justin?"

"Yes, as cabin boy. It's not out of the question that Father might change his will," he whispered. "He threatened it today, and he was openly hostile to me."

"Isn't it ever so?"

"Yes, but it occurred to me that Justin's going to sea might present a golden opportunity."

He reached over to refill his wife's glass with the excellent claret. Sylvaner's wine cellar was the envy of New York, and the "young Savage couple," as they were known, were lavish entertainers in a city known for its wining and dining. East Fourth Street was not quite as fashionable as when Sylvaner's house had been built by a prosperous hatter around 1820—the fashion was moving slowly, but inexorably, uptown—but the house was still a beauty, and the dining room, with its brass chandelier over the mahogany table, had been the scene of many festive dinner parties. Adelaide might disapprove of New York's laxity, but she had taken pains early on in her marriage to assert her position as one of the great port's leading hostesses. Being a Crowninshield, she had the lineage; she had the looks; she set a fine table and dressed exquisitely. But most important, she had money: and that had always been the key to the city.

Now her eyes narrowed.

"Tell me more," she whispered.

"You know what we've talked about so often?"

"About Justin? Of course. We've talked, talked, talked. Are you saying that perhaps now is the time for action?"

"I've already taken action. I know, dear Adelaide, that I can trust you . . . ?"

She gestured impatiently. "We two are one. What have you done?"

"I can assure you that Justin Savage will never reach China alive."

A slow smile came over her face.

"An accident?" she whispered. "A member of the crew—?"

"There's no need your knowing the details," Sylvaner said. "Suffice it to say that since Justin so loves the sea, then let him rot in it."

Murder, Adelaide thought, her blood tingling. How often at night, in their big walnut bed, had they toyed with the idea. At first, it had been something of a joke. But as the idea grew . . . she had always suspected her husband might be capable of murder. Now she knew.

"I don't *want* to go to China!" sobbed twelve-year-old Samantha Aspinall as she stuffed a chocolate candy into her pretty mouth. "The Chinese hate women and bind their feet, and they have awful monsters called eunuchs. . . ."

"Samantha!" gasped her mother, Edwina Aspinall. "Wherever did you hear that filthy word?"

"I read it in the book Papa had in his library, the one about China you told me to read."

Edwina had the grace to look embarrassed. She was a handsome woman, despite tipping the scales at 205 solid pounds. She, Samantha, and Doctor the Reverend Ward Aspinall were ensconced in a third-floor suite at Holt's Hotel, Number 127 John Street, a mere block from the South Street seaport and one of the marvels of New York. Holt's had 225 rooms and suites, a dining room that could seat 1,000 people, and New York's first steam-powered elevator, normally used for luggage, but in the case of Edwina, because of her avoirdupois, the lift lifted her along with the bags. Now her massive bosom swelled.

"Surely," she said, "the book didn't explain what a eunuch *was!*"

"Of course it did, Momma. What good would a book be that mentioned something without telling you what it was? The eunuchs guard the Emperor's wives and concubines. . . ."

"Concubines?" Edwina gasped anew. "Oh, my stars! I may have an attack of the vapors!" She sank into a velveteen settee, her voluminous skirts billowing about her like a peacock's tail. "If your father *knew* . . . Dearest Samantha, you must never say these words around your father! Dr. Aspinall would . . . oh! I daren't think *what* he'd . . ."

"Momma, that's beside the point," Samantha interrupted. Reverend Aspinall was a stern man, but Samantha was much less afraid of her father than her mother was. "The point is, I don't want to go to China! It's a horrid place, and I miss Maine, and if we have to go somewhere, why can't it be some pretty place like France or Italy. . . ." She popped another candy into her mouth.

"Samantha, stop eating," her mother huffed. "You'll ruin your appetite. And as we're sailing in the morning on the *Sea Witch,* it's a little late to start complaining that you don't want to go to China. You know we have no choice in the matter. Your father is being sent by the Bishop to Canton to convert the heathens, it's a great honor and a noble calling, and you mustn't carry on . . . STOP EATING!"

Samantha, who had popped yet another candy into her mouth, burst into new tears.

"I can't help it! You know when I'm upset, the only thing that makes me feel better is candy and . . . oh, I'm so miserable! And we'll be months and months on the ship, and we'll probably be drowned in a storm, and . . . I want to go home!"

Edwina opened her arms to her beautiful, if a bit chubby, daughter.

"Dearest Samantha, don't cry. Come here, darling girl. . . ."

Samantha, who was wearing a rather dowdy gingham dress, ran to her mother and snuggled into her expansive lap. Edwina kissed and hugged and petted her.

"Everything's going to be all right," she said. "The *Sea Witch* is a fine ship, and the Good Lord would never allow anything to happen to your father. After all, Dr. Aspinall is . . . well, one might even say he's almost an employee of the Lord, and surely the Lord would not allow one of His employees to be lost at sea."

"I *still* don't want to go," Samantha sniffed. She sat up, wrinkling her nose. "They eat bird's nests!" she said, almost as if she could barely believe the words she uttered. "And thousand-year-old eggs . . . and sharks! It said so in the book! Can you *imagine,* Momma?"

Edwina smoothed her daughter's jet-black hair.

"Well, well," she purred, "perhaps we both can lose some weight, which would be a blessing."

Samantha sighed. More than anything in the world, she wanted to be thin.

"Maybe you're right," she said. "Momma, do you think I'll *ever* lose my baby fat?"

"Not if you keep eating chocolates, and I'm told on reliable authority they have *no* chocolates in China."

"Then maybe this is the Lord's way of making me thin," Samantha said, beginning to cheer up. "Yes, that *surely* must be true! Oh, Momma, maybe it's a good thing we're going to China after all."

"That's better, dear. Now, get up. We have to join Dr. Aspinall downstairs for lunch."

Samantha got to her feet and went to one of the windows to look down at busy John Street three floors below. She saw a boy come out of a brick building across the street. The building had a beautifully lettered sign that read N. SAVAGE & SON. SHIPPING.

What a handsome boy, Samantha thought, admiring Justin Savage's red-gold hair. Samantha was beginning to like boys almost as much as chocolate candy.

2   AT SEVEN-THIRTY ON THE morning of Thursday, May 5, 1850, Nathaniel Savage's elegant carriage pulled up at the Savage Dock where the *Sea Witch* lay moored, its bowsprit jutting with jaunty arrogance over the considerable traffic on South Street. For reasons lost in time, notoriously superstitious sailors never sailed from port on a Friday. Inside the carriage, Ah Pin sat with Justin, who was excitedly looking out the window. It was the day the *Sea Witch* was sailing for Canton, and Justin was reporting aboard for duty.

"Look at her, Ah Pin!" Justin exclaimed. "Isn't she a beauty?"

The sleek hull was painted black, which gave it an even racier look, and the gun strake that carried ten ports to a side was painted white, like a racing stripe around the hull. The three tall masts were slightly raked. The horizontal yards, where now the sails were tightly furled, could carry, Justin knew, as much as twelve thousand yards of canvas. Below the bowsprit, the beautifully carved figurehead glowered, an evil-looking sea witch with a slightly green face, grimacing nastily at the children on the wharf, unnerving them as she was supposed to frighten the demons of the sea. The name and the figurehead had been the inspiration of Adelaide Savage, who, being a native of Salem, knew all about witches. As always when a great ship sailed, a crowd of onlookers was gathering, watching the final loading of the cargo by awesome steam winches. It was a glorious spring day, the sky above the forest of shipmasts along the East River being cloudless, and a number of boys were taking flying dives and cannonballs into the river from the dock pilings. The Cherry Street crimps, who were hired by the shipmasters to round up and, if necessary, shanghai last-minute crew replacements from the dives of Lower Manhattan, had brought the last drunk seaman aboard and gone back to their warren of taverns and bawdy houses where sailors squandered their sixteen-dollar monthly salaries in serious debauchery. From the top of the mainmast, a merry pennant fluttered in the breeze. Justin knew it was called the Moonraker, a name he liked, and it was the shipmaster's challenge to the wind.

"Your father told me to give you this," Ah Pin said, pulling the red leather diary from her drawstring purse. As always since arriving in America, Ah Pin wore western-style clothes and a bonnet. While Justin was used to it, even the most jaded New Yorkers rarely failed to give her startled looks. But Ah Pin had long since grown used to American bigotry. If it hadn't been for her intense love of Justin, whom she considered her son, she might have taken more offense at the anti-Chinese racism she met almost everywhere. As it was, she ignored it, rarely going outside the Washington Square house.

But today, she was losing that son for many months. And the forty-year-old Cantonese woman had forebodings.

"It's Father's diary," Justin said, taking the book.

"No, little one, it's your *mother's* diary."

"My *mother!*" he whispered, starting to open it, but Ah Pin put her hand on his.

"The Old Big-Nosed One said you must not read it till you are at sea," she said.

Justin put the book in his dunnage.

"You're right. But I can hardly wait to find out who my mother was. I'm amazed you don't know, since Father trusted you so much."

"I've known all along."

"Then why didn't you tell me?" Justin said, surprised.

"The Old Big-Nosed One swore me to silence. Besides"—she hesitated, rather embarrassed—"I wanted you to think of *me* as your mother."

Justin smiled.

"You know that I do," he said, and he kissed her cheek. Ah Pin put her heavily shawled arms around him and hugged him. There were tears in her eyes.

"I love you, my golden-haired one," she said. "And I burned joss sticks for you this morning, praying for your safety. You must be careful, my son. I have had bad dreams. It's the gods whispering in my ear that there is danger."

"Of course there's danger. Sailing's a dangerous profession."

"Not the dangers of the sea. Other danger. You must be ever vigilant."

Justin grinned.

"You've been reading those penny dreadfuls again," he said. "Don't worry: I can take care of myself. Good-bye, now. And look after Father. You know more about medicine in your little finger than Doc van Arsdale and Nurse Pry together." He opened the carriage door and blew her a kiss. "I love you," he said.

And he jumped down onto South Street. Putting his sailor's bag with the precious diary in it over one shoulder, he started through the crowd toward the ship's gangway. Several parasol-carrying ladies of the evening out for a morning stroll gave him admiring glances. Justin felt every inch a sailor in his white linen pants, his white open-necked shirt with its loosely tied black cravat, his blue jacket, and his round canvas hat; but he was too young and naive to understand what the ladies were up to.

He spotted several armed guards on the main deck. The *Sea Witch* was carrying valuable cargo, and Captain Whale, or any other captain worth his salt, would not fail to take precautions to guard his ship against the rampant crime on the waterfront.

Justin climbed the gangway to the black-bearded man standing on deck. Justin gave a snappy salute and said, "Permission to come aboard, sir. I'm Justin Savage, reporting for duty as cabin boy."

The man, who carried a revolver in a holster, looked him over with squinty eyes.

"So you're the Savage boy," he said. "The Captain wants to see you in his cabin. Know where it is?"

"Yes, sir," Justin said with a smile. "I've been on this ship many times."

"Bully for you, boy. You'd better not lollygag. The *Tuan* don't take kindly to tardiness."

"The *'Tuan'?*"

"Malay for 'Captain.' Move it, boy! Or do you want my boot in your rudder?"

The many times Justin had been on his father's ships he had been treated with the deference due a Savage. Now he began to realize that as a cabin boy, being a Savage might be more a liability than an asset. As he walked aft, his blue eyes drank in the details of the ship that was to be his home for so many months. The *Sea Witch,* which had been built by Samuel Hall in East Boston, was 183 feet in length, 39 feet in breadth, and 22 feet in depth of hold. Justin knew by heart the lengths of the different sections of her mainmast, starting with the lowest mast: 84 feet, 49 feet, 28 feet, 17 feet, and 13 feet. Her main yard was 78 feet in length. The bowsprit was 30 inches in diameter and extended 35 feet from the bow. The ship's displacement was 1,260 tons. The *Sea Witch* was immaculate, her deck holystoned to a gleaming white, as white as the canvas awning over it to protect from the sun. Her top rails and stanchions, skylights and coamings, were made of mahogany, and the copper and brass— even brass belaying pins—were polished till they reflected the fire from the sun when they weren't protected by the awning. Again, Justin swelled with pride at this thing of beauty that was also the state of the navigational art, the most sophisticated ocean-going machine so far devised by man.

Reaching the companionway just forward of the mizzenmast, he made his way down the ladder to "Officers' Country," then went aft to knock on the Captain's cabin door. When ordered to "Come in," he opened the door and entered the spacious cabin with its red leather bench beneath the aft ports, its great scrolls of mahogany on the bulkheads and door frames, its heavily carved crystal port decanters in their custom bulkhead frames, its chart cabinet and table, its shelves filled with navigational books such as the *Nautical Almanac,* Bowditch's *American Navigator,* Captain Furlong's *American Coast Pilot,* and Dr. Lowe's *Sailor's Guide to Health,* the books protected from pitching out in rough seas by pieces of hemp line, its oil lamps in gimbals. Captain Whale was standing beside his desk, which held his logbook, coastal charts, and tide tables, his British-made Dent sextant with its ivory arc, and a silver-framed daguerreotype of his homely wife and slightly cross-eyed daughter.

Whale might bear the name of a leviathan, but physically he was a shrimp of a man, barely five feet six inches. His left leg had been broken in a fall from the rigging during a storm off the Cape of Good Hope; it had been badly set, and he walked with a slight limp. His clean-shaven face, tanned to leather by years of exposure to the tropical sun, was not unhandsome, though his cold blue eyes were set close together, giving him a rather shifty, beady-eyed look. A large wen on his left cheek, balanced by a lightninglike scar on his right, the result of a lascar's slashing kris during a pirate attack on the *Sea Nymph,* another Savage Line vessel he had served on, added to his rather murderous aspect. The son of a seaman, totally self-taught, Whale had made his way up to the captaincy "through the hawsehole," as the saying went. Due to the rigors of the trade, nearly all sea captains were young, and Whale was no exception. In fact, at thirty-seven, he was ready to retire, not unusual since being master of a ship was no job for a man over forty. With all shipmasters, it was the tradition to dress as a dandy, and again Whale was no exception. He wore a high stock, a broad velvet cravat, and a coat of blue broadcloth with flat pearl buttons designed by one of the many Brooks brothers. His dove-gray pants fitted him closely, and he wore elastic-sided black patent leather gaiters. On the desk beside him was an ebony stick with a gold top and a tall beaver Knox hat. As Justin came into the cabin, Whale gave him a long, searching look.

"You wished to see me, Captain?" Justin said. He had met Whale several times at the house on Washington Square; and while he didn't expect to be offered a seat, still the cold look from Whale's close-set eyes was a bit unsettling.

"I've told your father," the Captain finally said, "that I would take you on this ship only on the condition it be fully understood you would have no special privileges because of your being a Savage, albeit an illegitimate one." Justin's face turned red, but he held his tongue. He knew the insult was meant to demean him. "Is that understood?"

"Yes, sir."

"If you break any of the rules of this ship, you will be punished to the full extent of my power—which, in the case of a serious offense such as mutiny, includes death by hanging. Neither your age nor your family connections would spare you the full force of the law. Is that understood?"

Justin gulped. "Yes, sir."

"On this ship you are one of the four cabin boys, the lowest of the low. I and my officers are to be obeyed without hesitation. Is that understood?"

"Yes, sir."

Whale seated himself at his desk. "Your father tells me you know something about seamanship. What are the names of the masts?"

"The foremast, mainmast, and mizzenmast, sir."

"And the sails in ascending order?"

"On the mainmast, the mainsail, or course, the main topsail, the main topgallant, the main royal, and the main skysail, sir."

"What is the mid watch?"

"Midnight to four A.M., sir."

"The dog watch?"

"Four P.M. to eight P.M., sir."

"How many bells is ten thirty?"

"Five bells, sir."

"Seven thirty?"

"Seven bells, sir."

"What is the futtock shroud?"

"One of the iron rods extending from the futtock plate, used to brace the base of a mast, sir. A seaman should know to scorn the 'lubber's hole' through the mast platform, climbing instead the futtock shrouds outboard of the platform edge."

Was Justin imagining it or did the Captain look a bit impressed?

"I'm assigning you to the port watch. Go to the fo'c'sle and stow your gear. Then report to Mr. Starbuck, the second mate. Dismissed."

Justin saluted and started to leave.

"Oh, and, Savage, one more thing."

"Sir?"

"We have passengers aboard. A Reverend Ward Aspinall and his wife and daughter. The daughter is your age. Her name is Samantha. In your spare time, you might show her around the ship. That will be all."

"Aye aye, Captain."

After he left the cabin, he returned to the main deck and started forward toward the fo'c'sle, thinking rather uncomfortably about the prospect of hanging from one of the yardarms that loomed above him.

"Look, Momma!" said Samantha Aspinall, who had just come aboard with her parents. "It's that boy I saw yesterday from the hotel window—the boy with the red hair! He must be one of the crew."

"I believe," said her father, the Reverend Ward Aspinall, a tall, rather lugubrious gentleman in a black suit and top hat, "that may be the son of the ship's owner, Nathaniel Savage. Captain Whale told me he would be aboard."

"He's *very* handsome," Samantha said. "Oh, Momma, maybe the trip to China will be fun!"

"Samantha," said her father sternly, his salt and pepper beard wiggling as he spoke, "you will remember that you are a Christian and a lady."

Edwina Aspinall was smiling as Justin passed them.

"But he *is* a fine-looking boy," she said. "And if he's Nathaniel Savage's, he must be quite well-to-do."

"Mrs. Aspinall," said her husband, leaning close and whispering in her ear, "the boy is illegitimate."

Edwina Aspinall looked shocked.

Samantha, her eyes on Justin, looked intrigued.

The fo'c'sle of the *Sea Witch* was in the most forward part of the ship, before the foremast—hence the phrase "serving before the mast." It was reached by a companionway abaft the foremast; and when Justin entered it, he was greeted by a tall burly man who was smoking a clay pipe, fouling the air of the low compartment, which was already stifling.

"You be Justin Savage, I wager?" said the man, who had a blond beard.

"That's right."

"That's right, *sir,*" said the man, giving Justin a sharp punch in the chest that sent the boy sprawling back onto the deck. The man stood over him, put his foot on Justin's stomach, and pressed down so hard that Justin gasped. "My name is Mr. Starbuck, and I be the second mate of this vessel. You'll address me as 'sir' or 'Mr. Starbuck, *sir.*' You got that, boy?"

"Yes, sir."

Starbuck removed his foot and stepped back. "You don't get no bunk," he said. "The boys gets hammocks. That's your'n over there." He pointed across the dim, airless compartment with its low overhead to the foremost part where the bulkheads came together to form the ship's bow. Four rope hammocks were strung athwartship.

"When the ship be pitchin' in a storm," Starbuck said, "you'll have a merry time hanging on so you don't fall out. Now get up."

Justin scrambled to his feet, picking up his dunnage.

"There's three other cabin boys," Starbuck went on. "Their names is on that crew list pinned to the door yonder. I don't as a rule much like cabin boys. Do you know anything about sailin' or are you a knucklehead greenhand?"

"I've sailed in small boats, sir."

"Ever climb a riggin' in an ice storm at night?"

"No, sir."

Starbuck removed the clay pipe and grinned at him.

"Well, sonny, the first ice storm we encounter, I'll make it my job to send you aloft. It's mighty fun up there in the dark with the wind howlin' blue blazes and your fingers freezin'. A lot of greenhands lose their grip and fall—a hundred feet or so. When they hit the deck, there's not much left of 'em. They look like a pile of plum duff."

Justin stiffened.

"Are you threatening me, sir?" he said.

Starbuck assumed a look of hurt innocence.

"Naw. Why, how could you ever think that, boy?" He grinned, then scowled. "Report topside in five minutes to the Bosun to help load stores."

Then he left the compartment. Justin went over to inspect the piece of paper pinned to the door. It read, in part:

CREW OF THE *SEA WITCH* SAILING FROM NEW YORK
May 5, 1850

Captain	Ichabod Whale
Chief Mate	Zebulon Horn
Second Mate	Arthur Starbuck
Third Mate	James Whitby
Fourth Mate	Albert Falmouth

Boatswain	Harley Foxx
Carpenter	Rawley Baring
Quartermaster	Roger Dyer
Gunner	Jonathan Winship
Cooper	Fred Handley
Cook	Jimmy Chen
Cabin Steward	Heindrich Anderson
30 Able-Bodied Seamen	
6 Ordinary Seamen	
4 Cabin Boys	Billy Claxton
	Howell Freeman
	Creighton Pruett
	Justin Savage
Ship's Cat	Pyewacket

Justin was glad to see that he at least ranked above the ship's cat.

What he didn't know was that one of the names on the list was the man Sylvaner Savage had paid to be his murderer.

"I wish to welcome you aboard the *Sea Witch,*" Captain Whale said, raising a glass of port, "and let us hope for a pleasant and safe voyage to China."

"Amen to that," said Reverend Aspinall, raising his glass. He, Edwina, and Samantha were in the Captain's cabin as the crew finished loading the ship's cargo.

"The steam tow will arrive at noon," the Captain went on, "and take us out the harbor to Sandy Hook off New Jersey. Then we will hoist sail and get under way. The glass is high, and the wind is from the northwest, so we should make good time for the next few days. Are your quarters satisfactory?"

"Quite nice, thank you," said Ward Aspinall. The Episcopal Bishop of Boston had furnished seven hundred dollars for Ward and his family to buy passage to China; two officers had given up their staterooms for the Aspinalls.

"I believe it will be best if you take your meals here with me in my cabin," Whale went on. "My steward will clean your staterooms each morning and empty your chamber pots, which you will find under your bunks—begging your pardon, ladies, for the indelicacy." The ladies had blushed. "The steward's name is Heindrich Anderson. He's a fine fellow, a Dutchman, and if he proves satisfactory I would suggest you tip him ten dollars at the end of the voyage. I instructed him to buy a portable canvas tub, which he has done. Once a week, weather permitting, Anderson will rig the tub in here, and you can bathe."

"How about laundry?" Edwina asked, ever the practical housewife.

"Anderson would be glad to do that, and he's an excellent ironer. You would have to work out the financial arrangements with him. Now, a word of caution. A ship is a tight-knit little world, and it is a man's world. I have instructed the First Mate, Mr. Horn, to pass word to the men to watch their language when any of you are topside. But you must understand that the average sailor does not come from what one might call a 'genteel' background. In fact, they are a dirty lot of ruffians in general, in some cases a hairbreadth away from the criminal classes. They swear and are sworn at. You may see and hear indelicate things on this voyage, but alas, aside from instructing the men, there's very little else I can do to prevent it."

"We understand, Captain," the Reverend said. "I have already talked to the Lord about this, and He understands also, as of course He understands all things."

"Er, ah . . . yes." Captain Whale looked a bit taken aback by Reverend Aspinall's cozy familiarity with the Almighty. "I'm relieved to hear that. However, I will ask you to limit your time on the main deck, and of course during inclement weather, you will remain in your staterooms. Miss Aspinall"—the Captain turned to Samantha—"there is one member of the crew who comes from a background similar to yours, and that is the cabin boy Justin Savage. As I explained to your father, he is the, um, natural son of the owner of this vessel. I have instructed young Savage to attend to you in his free time, which is of course limited. I fear there is not much opportunity for entertainment on the ship, but I thought you might enjoy the company of someone your own age and class."

"That is very kind of you, Captain," said Reverend Aspinall, "but I have talked to the Lord about that also, and I prefer that my daughter not mingle with the crew."

"Poppa!" Samantha exclaimed.

"As the Captain has mentioned, young Savage is, unfortunately, the offspring of a sinful union not blessed by God. I will not have you consorting with anyone so tainted."

Samantha's green eyes flashed fire.

"I have never heard anything so cruel and unfair!" she said. "For all you know, Justin might be as pure and fine a young man as . . . well, as Thomas Jefferson!"

Her father's eyes glared.

"An unfortunate example," he said, "since Mr. Jefferson was an adulterer.

You will go to your stateroom immediately, Samantha, and stay there until I tell you you may leave. And you will apologize for this unseemly outburst."

"I will *not* apologize!" she said, giving her father a haughty snoot of a look. Then she left the cabin, slamming the door behind her.

"Your daughter seems to have a mind of her own," Captain Whale said, suppressing a smile.

"My daughter has taken leave of her senses, as well as her manners!" Ward Aspinall said, trying to control his rage. "Captain, do our staterooms have locks?"

"Of course."

"Might I have the keys?"

"Dr. Aspinall," said his wife, "you're not planning to—?"

"Until Samantha comes to her senses and apologizes for her outrageous behavior, she will remain locked in her stateroom."

"Oh, my stars!" moaned Edwina, fanning herself with her handkerchief.

But when Reverend Aspinall reached his daughter's stateroom, it was empty. Angrily, he hurried up the ladder to the main deck where he spotted Samantha standing by the port rail. "Samantha," he said, coming up to her. "I have never been so mortified! You will come with me *now. . . ."*

"No! Oh, Poppa, you know I don't want to go to China in the first place, and the one chance I have of having some fun, you deny me for no good reason."

"I have told you the reason, and it is an excellent one!"

"It's so unfair! Look at him. . . ." She pointed midship where Justin and other members of the crew were guiding barrels of rum being lowered through a hatch into the hold. "Did you ever see a face so pure and noble?"

"Have I not often told you that one of the Devil's favorite weapons is handsome features? Now for the last time, come to your stateroom."

"No!"

His left hand grabbed her wrist as his right hand slapped her, hard. Samantha cried out as her father dragged her to the companionway.

Fifty feet away, Justin saw this. Shocked by the cruelty of the slap, his heart went out to the beautiful girl. "Miss Aspinall!" he cried, starting to run to her.

He was grabbed from behind, jerked around, and slugged in the nose by the fist of Mr. Starbuck.

"You'll not abandon your post without permission!" Starbuck roared. "Now, get back there, boy! And when you're through here, you can start polishing brass! By God, you'll learn the rules of this vessel and obey them!"

Justin, blood pouring from his aching nose, started to lunge at this man he was beginning to hate. Then he looked up at the yardarms so far above him and remembered the Captain's warning.

Only a few hours aboard, and he was already beginning to realize that the life at sea he had dreamed of might in fact be a living hell. For a second he considered running down the gangway and going back to Washington Square.

But Justin Savage was not a quitter.

"Aye aye, sir," he said and returned to his work, wiping the blood from his nose on the back of his hand.

His young heart ached for Samantha.

3   SHORTLY BEFORE NOON, THE CLUMSY, high-stacked steam tug arrived at the Savage Dock. A hawser was paid out through the *Sea Witch*'s bow and attached to the tug; the gangway was brought aboard and stowed; the heavy mooring lines were untied from the dock bollards and taken aboard; and as the onlookers at the dock cheered, the *Sea Witch* moved out into the East River and started its journey to the sea.

"What a splendid sight!" said Adelaide Savage, who was sitting in a carriage on South Street beside her husband, Sylvaner.

"Yes, it's a beautiful ship. But sail is doomed, my dear. When I take over the company, which, God willing, will be soon, it will be my sad duty to sell these ships off—probably to some South American navy."

"There will be those who will be sad to see them go," Adelaide remarked. "I include myself. We Crowninshields made our fortune by sail."

"I know, but in business one must be absolutely ruthless."

"Of course, Sylvaner. You are right, as always. You say the end will be soon? What news from Washington Square?"

"Dr. van Arsdale says Father cannot last the month." Sylvaner rapped his walking stick on the carriage roof, signaling the coachman to start up. Then he settled back in the leather seat, taking one last look through the window at the *Sea Witch*. "I suspect," he added, "dear Justin's life expectancy is equally limited."

Adelaide curled her arm around her husband's.

"When will it happen?"

"Soon."

Captain Whale remained in his cabin while his ship was being towed through New York harbor, his absence from the quarterdeck signaling his disdain for being dependent, however briefly, on the hated power of steam. Thus, command of the quarterdeck devolved onto the First Mate, Zebulon Horn, who stood near the wheel admiring the magnificent harbor as it passed by. Horn was a tall, thin man with a narrow, clean-shaven face that was refined and surprisingly gentle for one whose profession was noted for many qualities, none being gentleness. But Horn was well liked by the crews of the Savage Line, which he had served for so many years. The sandy-haired son of an upstate New York farmer, Horn had run away to sea at the age of twelve. Now, fifteen years later, he, like Captain Whale, was "crawling through the hawsehole" to a captaincy, which he hoped might come as soon as his next voyage.

With little to do while under tow, most of the crew were on the main deck enjoying themselves in the splendid weather. Mr. Horn was more than satisfied with the present crew; he had sailed with many of them before, the A.B.'s were skilled, only a few looked hungover, and only four of the ordinary seamen had been recruited by crimps. The average age of able-bodied seamen was twenty-two, and few men lasted for more than a dozen years. By that time, they might have saved enough money to go ashore to start a business, or they might have become hopeless drunks, doomed to spend the rest of their years in sailors' homes. Only men like Horn ambitious enough to become officers might spend as long as twenty years at sea.

As feckless, rough-and-ready, and illiterate as an A.B. might be, Horn still had a respect for them because he knew they carried in their heads a vast amount of sea lore. They could distinguish the first-magnitude stars such as Aldebaran, Capella, Arcturus, and Vega; they could detect land smells when land was still over the horizon; and they had a thorough knowledge of the gales of Capes Horn and Good Hope. They knew all the prominent landmarks of the world: Hatteras and Montauk, St. David's Head, Finisterre, John o' Groat's, Cape Maysi, Makapu, Koko and Diamond Heads, the Farallons, Java Head and Anjer Point, Lintin Island and the Ladrones, as well as dozens more. They could estimate the speed of a ship within a half knot and sense a change of wind even when in their bunks asleep.

But Horn knew they could quickly turn surly, especially over the food, which at the best of times was barely adequate. So in these first pleasant hours of the voyage, Horn relaxed, knowing that he might as well relax now because things would only go downhill.

He spotted Justin polishing brass belaying pins on the port side. Horn of course knew who he was: by now everyone on the ship knew that Nathaniel Savage's bastard was one of the crew. As the *Sea Witch* passed Bedloe's Island to starboard, Horn crossed the deck to Justin.

"Savage, I'm Mr. Horn, the First Mate," he said. Justin turned and saluted, getting his polishing rag in his face.

"Yes, sir."

"Have you been aloft yet?"

"No, sir."

"Have you a fear of heights?"

"I certainly hope not, sir."

"Yes, I hope not also. You won't be much use to us if you do. I'm going to assign you to Dawson, one of the A.B.'s. He'll take you aloft and show you the ropes when we get under way. Meanwhile, perhaps you should go aloft now while we're being towed. You won't be in anyone's way, and you can get the feel of it."

"Aye aye, sir, but Mr. Starbuck told me to polish the brightwork. . . ."

"I'll handle Mr. Starbuck. Go up now. Remember: the first rule is one hand for the ship and one hand for yourself. And never let go one rope until you've firmly gripped the next. Go on, lad. And if you get dizzy, don't be ashamed to come down. We've all had to go up for the first time, and it's a long fall."

Justin put his rag in his pocket and looked up. The three masts with their horizontal yards and their elaborate rigging swayed slowly above him, the sails tightly furled, ready to be let out to catch the wind when they cleared the harbor. Justin felt a certain anxiety. He rubbed his palms against his white pants, then sprang up on the ratlines and started climbing the mainmast.

Justin was tall for his age, just two inches shy of his ultimate height of six feet, and he was of athletic build, good at sports, and well trained as a boxer. Now he scrambled up the rigging with easy agility. Up, up, up. He reached the main yard and looked down. He was eighty-four feet above the deck. The men below looked insignificant, but he noticed many of them were looking up, watching him. They expect me to come down, he thought, but I'll show them. Bastard or no, I'm Nathaniel Savage's son. I'll go all the way to the top. He looked up.

There was still a long way to go.

The gentle swaying of the ship, so much more marked aloft than on deck, created a slight queasiness in his stomach, which he hoped was nervousness. Climbing outboard of the main platform onto the futtock shrouds, thus avoiding the "lubber's hole" and gaining the grudging admiration of the crew below, he started climbing again. Up, up, up, past the topsail yards, up, up until he was at the lower topgallant yard. He was now 161 feet above the deck. As he looked down, the crew were ants. The wind was picking up, the swaying of the ship aloft even more pronounced. He sucked the cool air into his lungs to fight his increasing nausea. Go down! his mind told him. Go up! cried his heart. Go to the very top, to the Moonraker! Show them you're a Savage to be reckoned with!

He climbed past the royal yard to the skysail yard, the highest point on the ship a man could reach. He was now almost 180 feet in the air. The view was awesome. He could see for miles: through the Narrows that separated Staten Island and Brooklyn to the distant Sandy Hook arching north from New Jersey and, to the east, the lush white beaches of Long Island. And, dominating everything, the vast blue expanse of the ocean.

He heard faint cheers from below. He looked down. They're cheering me! he thought. He took off his canvas hat and waved it. I did it! I climbed all the way to the top!

The mast creaked as the ship rolled to port. To Justin's horror, he started to gag. Waves of nausea assaulted him. He opened his mouth and retched to windward. Part of the vomit blew back in his face, spattering his immaculate blouse that Ah Pin had so lovingly ironed the night before. The rest of the puke sailed behind him, fortunately landing in the water rather than on Messrs. Horn and Starbuck, who were, along with the rest of the crew, roaring with laughter.

"Some sailor!" Starbuck guffawed.

"Aye," replied Mr. Horn, "but the lad's got pluck."

Thirty minutes later, the tug threw off the hawser and the crew aloft unfurled the *Sea Witch*'s sails, which billowed in the strong breeze.

Justin, the vomit cleaned from his face, watched with awe as the graceful ship leapt to life, its great white sails flapping as they filled with the wind, its bladelike bow slicing through the water. He was still cringing with embarrassment from his performance aloft.

But he was, at last, at sea.

"Samantha, you *must* eat something! It's been three days!"

Edwina Aspinall had unlocked Samantha's stateroom door and come inside, where her daughter was curled in her bunk, facing the bulkhead. The stateroom, which had a single port for light and, weather permitting, air, was small, with an upper and lower bunk protected by rails, a tiny desk attached to the bulkhead with a reading light in gimbals and a seat bolted to the deck before it, and a washstand holding a basin and pitcher with a small mirror above it.

"I'll eat only when I'm no longer a prisoner," Samantha mumbled.

"You're not a prisoner!"

"Then why is my door locked?"

"Dearest Samantha, your father is stubborn, true, but he's only acting in your better interests. You must believe this!"

Samantha sat up. Her face was pale. She was starving.

"I love and respect my father," she said, "but I will not allow him to treat me like a slave. The only weapon I have against him is my mouth. He can't force me to eat, and I won't eat until he lets me out of here to see whom I please."

"Oh!" Edwina fluttered her ubiquitous handkerchief. "Oh, what can I do . . . ?"

"Tell Father to stop acting like a tyrant."

"But he . . . oh, dear, you may starve to death. . . ."

"At least I'll be thin."

She curled up again, her back to her flustered mother.

"I have some chocolates. . . ."

"No." Her stomach growled.

"My stars, what can I . . . ?"

On the verge of hysteria, the wife of the rector of St. Thomas's Church in Wiscasset, Maine, fluttered out of the stateroom, locking the door behind her. Then she hurried topside to get some fresh air and try to think what her next move could be in this increasingly ugly tug of wills between her daughter and her husband. So far, Reverend Aspinall had remained adamant: either Samantha apologized, or she stayed locked in her stateroom. Samantha's refusing to eat had not moved him. "The girl has the appetite of a horse," he said. "Sooner or later she'll start crying for chocolates."

But she hadn't.

Edwina went to the starboard rail. The weather remained spectacular, with a strong westerly wind, and the Captain had told her at lunch they were averaging so far over 240 nautical miles a day, heading southeast until they were past the Gulf Stream and could, with luck, catch the southeast trade winds to take them down the coast of South America to Cape Horn. So far, aside from Samantha's hunger strike, the voyage had been pleasant, the officers and crew seeming to be in good humor as they worked with quiet efficiency. The ship was clean, her stateroom as comfortable as could be expected, and although her husband had experienced a nasty bout of seasickness the first day out, Edwina's only unpleasant experience had been the sight of a cockroach, which sent her screaming for the cabin steward. The Captain had assured her that the *Sea Witch* had been heavily disinfected with bug powder, but that there was no way a ship could be kept entirely free of vermin, which had calmed her somewhat. What he did not tell her was that the reason for Pyewacket, the ship's fat black cat, was to keep the rat population of the *Sea Witch* at a minimum.

"And how is your daughter?" Captain Whale asked, coming up to her and tipping his beaver hat.

"Alas, dear Captain, she still remains stubborn, as does Reverend Aspinall. I'm at a loss what to do."

"If I might be allowed to comment, madame, it does seem to me to be some-what narrow-minded on your husband's part. Young Savage strikes me as a fine young man. Of course, he's been so seasick since we left New York he hasn't been able to leave the fo'c'sle to perform his duties till this morning. But he seems to be getting his sea legs now. By the way, your husband mentioned to me that all of you have been studying the Chinese language for some time now?"

"Yes, but my husband much longer than either Samantha or I. It has been his most ardent desire since he was a boy to go to China to spread the Good Word, and he has been studying the language for a number of years. Alas, it is an extremely peculiar tongue, what with all its tone inflections, and I fear even my husband still has only a rudimentary grasp of it. He of course hopes to improve his mastery when we arrive in China."

"Did you know that young Savage is fluent in Cantonese?"

Edwina looked surprised. "No."

"His father brought over a Cantonese amah to raise him and she taught him to speak the language. Perhaps your husband might reconsider his opinion of Savage if he knew this. In the long weeks ahead of us, all of you might practice your Chinese with him. Good day."

Tipping his hat again, he walked away.

"My stars!" Edwina muttered to herself. "Perhaps this is the answer!"

The cobblestone street outside the mansion on Washington Square North had been strewn with hay to muffle the passing horses' hooves and carriage wheels so the dying Nathaniel Savage would not be disturbed in his second-floor bedroom. For New Yorkers interested in such things—and there were many—the passing of Nathaniel Savage represented the passing of an era. America was changing with a speed that seemed to increase with each passing week as invention after invention altered the lives first of extraordinary people who could afford such things as bathrooms and central heating, and then later of ordinary people. America was changing from a nation of farms and sailing ships to a nation of factories and steamships. The clipper ship was at the peak of its glory, but already its days were numbered by steam. Nathaniel Savage had loved the sailing ship. When Nathaniel died, people said, the sailing ships would soon follow him.

Upstairs in the house, Sylvaner and Adelaide stood at the foot of the bed participating in that Victorian ritual, the deathbed scene. Dr. van Arsdale sat at one side of the four-poster, feeling Nathaniel's flickering pulse. Beside him stood Nurse Pry, watching life ebb out of the old man in the nightshirt and nightcap. At the other side of the bed stood Ah Pin. The heavy, dark green velvet curtains with their gold fringe had been pulled over the tall windows, shutting out the heat and light of the afternoon and plunging the bedroom into a gloom pierced only by the globed oil lamp by the bed.

"Doctor?" whispered Sylvaner, who looked perhaps a bit too concerned.

The Doctor looked up and shook his head negatively.

Adelaide, who had a bit prematurely put on black, managed to conceal the impatient eagerness she felt. Let the wretched old man die and get it over with, she thought. Out with the old, in with the new, and Sylvaner and I are the new.

Ah Pin watched her. Ah Pin knew.

But Nathaniel wasn't quite dead yet. His eyelids fluttered open like luffing sails. He looked at Ah Pin.

"The diary?" he whispered. "Did Justin get the diary?"

Ah Pin nodded yes.

Nathaniel smiled.

"His mother," he sighed. "My love."

He closed his eyes again and died.

Ten minutes later, downstairs in the front hall, Adelaide came to Ah Pin.

"What diary did he mean?" she asked softly, barely able to conceal her dislike of the Chinese woman.

Ah Pin looked into Adelaide's coldly beautiful face and smiled.

"The diary," she said, "of your sister."

Adelaide's dark brown eyes widened with shock.

"Justin is Constance's son!" Adelaide exclaimed an hour later in the drawing room of the East Fourth Street house. "Do you know what this means?"

"If it's true!" Sylvaner said angrily. "And by God, just because that damned Chinkee woman says it, doesn't make it true!"

Adelaide was nervously pacing back and forth over the fashionable Turkish rug. Above one of the heavily carved Belter horsehair sofas hung a large oil portrait of Nathaniel as a young man, standing tall and handsome in the clothes of forty years before, the painting a mockery of the cadaverous wreck that had just died an hour ago. Again prematurely, Adelaide had already draped black mourning crepe over the gold frame.

"But I think perhaps it *is* true!" she said. "Now that I look back . . . all Constance's maneuverings, which didn't make sense at the time, but now—*now* they begin to make sense! And it explains why that wicked old man kept it a secret all these years! He seduced my sweet sister!"

"Damn it, Adelaide, you're jumping to conclusions!" Sylvaner roared, pouring himself a whiskey. "We don't *know!*"

"But, Sylvaner, if it's true, don't you see what you have done?"

" 'Me'? How about 'us'!?"

"All right, 'we.' " She was on the verge of tears. "We've sent my nephew to his death! Justin is the Crowninshield-Savage heir I've prayed for!" She burst into tears and sank into the horsehair sofa beneath the portrait. "And we've sent him to his death! Oh, my God, what horrible crime have we committed?"

Sylvaner tossed off the whiskey and gave his wife a sardonic look.

"You weren't so worried about Justin before you knew he was a Crowninshield," he remarked. "And you may as well dry your tears, because there's nothing we can do about it now."

Adelaide wiped her eyes with a lace hankie, then looked at her husband as she composed herself.

"You're right," she finally said. "There's nothing we can do about it now." Adelaide Savage was an ultimately practical woman. "And at least no one will ever know about it. My sweet sister's reputation for purity is safe forever." She thought a moment, then frowned. "Except for . . ."

"Except for"—her husband finished her thought—"the Chinkee woman."

4   JUSTIN HAD BEEN TERRIFIED THAT he would be as seasick prone as Sylvaner, thus terminating his maritime career almost before it began; and indeed the first few days of the *Sea Witch*'s voyage he was so wretchedly ill he couldn't get out of his hammock. Mr. Horn, taking pity on him, had assigned another of the cabin boys, Billy Claxton, to tend to Justin. Billy, a big, not overly bright boy from Brooklyn, had dutifully emptied Justin's slop buckets, washing them out in the sea and returning them to the fo'c'sle.

But the morning of the third day, the seasickness went almost as quickly as it had come. Justin, still weak, got out of his hammock onto unsteady legs. Thanking Billy, he went topside and filled his lungs with the sweet ocean air.

Jimmy Chen, the short Cantonese cook, came up to him. "Young Savage feel better chop chop?" he asked in Pidgin, the tortured quasi-language that had grown up over the years to bridge the chasm between English and Chinese.

"I'm not only feeling better," Justin replied in Cantonese, "I'm hungry. Can you give me something to eat?"

Hearing Cantonese spoken by a "roundeye" so amazed the cook, he actually gaped.

As eager as he had been to read his mother's diary, Justin had been too sick to even begin it; besides, the fo'c'sle was no place to read, being ill-lit and smelly. And now, after his recovery, when he was put to work, for the first few days he had no time to read. Besides, he had so much to learn. Gus Dawson, the affable A.B. assigned to teach him the ropes, taught him how to "hand, reef, and steer," that is, how to furl a sail, shorten it, and stand a trick at the wheel. He learned how to mend sails and rigging, how to go aloft with buckets of grease and tar, to slush the spars and tar down the rigging (this last chore having given sailors the name "tars"). He learned to hoist a yard while he and the rest of the crew sang work chanteys:

> *A Yankee ship came down the river,*
> *Blow, boys, blow.*
> *And all her sails they shone like silver,*
> *Blow, my bully boys, blow.*

Life was divided into four-hour watches, four hours on watch, four off. While not on watch, the crew was kept hard at work at various chores, so that sleep was something to snatch when one could. The rhythms of the ship's routine were set up by the ship's bell, which was struck as the sandglass was "capsized" every half hour: one bell at 12:30 A.M., two bells at 1:00 A.M. . . . up to eight bells at four, when the sequence began again for the next four hours.

By the end of his fifth day aboard the *Sea Witch,* Justin was sore all over, exhausted, and his hands were blistered and raw from climbing the rigging.

But hellish as the living conditions were, he found that life at sea, despite the risks and intrinsic boredom of the routine, was somehow wonderful. He didn't know if it was his imagination, but he was feeling bigger and taller and stronger.

His father had given him a razor before he sailed. He thought he might soon have to use it.

"We have a serious crisis," said Reverend Ward Aspinall that night in the Captain's cabin, where Justin had been summoned. "My daughter is starving herself to death."

Justin remembered the sight of the tall clergyman slapping his beautiful daughter the day they sailed, and he was not disposed to like the dour-looking man with the Maine accent. Right now, the Reverend was looking nervous, as was his fat wife.

"Why, sir?" Justin asked. He was standing in the center of the cabin, his canvas hat in hand. Captain Whale was seated at his desk, smoking a pipe.

"It involves you, in a way," the Reverend said uncomfortably. He had never dreamed that Samantha's willpower would prove to be so indomitable, but the fact was that she continued to refuse to eat, and it was the sixth day. Edwina was frantic. As much as Ward Aspinall hated to back down about Justin, he had no choice.

"How, sir?" Justin asked.

"This perhaps is my fault," the Reverend said, hating every moment of what he considered a recantation. "I forbade my daughter to . . . to mingle with the crew. You in particular."

"Me, sir? Why me?"

"It was all a mistake!" Edwina exclaimed impatiently, wringing her hands. "Dr. Aspinall meant no disrespect to you, young man. . . ."

"Mrs. Aspinall, I will do the talking!" said her husband.

"Yes, you've done all the talking, and look what a pretty pickle we're in, with poor Samantha at death's door!" Edwina spat out at her husband with unusual forcefulness. She turned back to Justin. "The plain fact is, my husband forbade Samantha to talk to you because you are Nathaniel Savage's natural son, which was grossly unfair—"

"The Bible says—" her husband interrupted.

"I don't care what the Bible says!" Edwina snapped. The Reverend Aspinall looked so shocked, he sat down in a chair. "Now, we're going to start all over," she went on to Justin. "I hope you can be enough of a Christian to forgive all of us. And I beg you to take this key"—she held out the key to the stateroom— "unlock Samantha's door, tell her she can talk to you until the cows come home—and get her to *eat something!*"

A slightly stunned Justin took the key.

"Yes, ma'am," he said. "And I certainly do forgive you. And"—he glanced at the Captain, who had a bemused look on his face—"and I'm sorry I'm a bastard."

He hurried out of the cabin as Reverend Aspinall groaned.

A minute later Justin unlocked the stateroom door and went in.

"Miss Aspinall?" he said. The room was dark.

"Go away."

"It's me—Justin Savage. Your parents sent me to get you to eat something."

There was a moment's silence. Then she said, "Could you light the lamp, please? I'm a little . . . weak."

Justin's eyes were adapting to the darkness, and there was enough light from the passageway lantern that he could make out the lamp in the gimbal above the small desk. He lit the lamp and looked at the bunk. Samantha was sitting up. She was wearing a rumpled black dress. Her face was pale and thinner than he remembered. Her thick black hair was unbrushed. She looked a bit of a mess, but Justin thought he had never seen anyone so beautiful.

"I guess this means I've won," she said.

"Yes, I think so. Your mother was very short with your father. He looked a bit shocked. You must be terribly hungry. May I get you something from the galley? Some soup, perhaps? Jimmy Chen, he's the cook, and he made a pretty good fish soup for dinner. He said it was the last we'll have for some time unless we catch something . . . Miss Aspinall!"

She had fallen back into her pillows. Justin hurried to her, taking her right hand and patting it.

"Are you all right?"

"I just . . . felt a little dizzy. . . ."

"Samantha!" It was her mother at the door. "My stars, she's dying—!"
She hurried in.

"Momma, don't fuss. I'll be all right. Justin's going to get me some soup."

Her eyes were devouring his face. I've won! she thought triumphantly. And Justin Savage is a god, an absolute god!

Someday, he's going to be mine.

"This is my mother's diary," Justin said to Samantha four days later, showing her the red leather book. They were standing on the deck as the *Sea Witch* raced before a stiff following wind. Samantha had recovered her strength and was eating regularly, although her loss of weight during her hunger strike (as well as the fact that the food in the Captain's cabin was becoming increasingly unappetizing) had inspired her to lose even more weight to achieve her dream of svelteness. "I haven't had a chance to read it yet," Justin went on. "And there's so little light in the fo'c'sle, I can't read it there. Besides, the crew is always snoring and the place stinks to high heaven."

"Sounds charming," Samantha said.

"It isn't, believe me. The crew's always complaining about something. They call their mattresses 'donkeys' breakfasts,' for instance. And the food! They never stop complaining about that—and I don't blame them. I'm so sick of lobscouse, daddy funk, and plum duff, I think I'll . . . well, I won't say what I'm thinking."

Samantha laughed as the wind tried to tear the white and blue bonnet off her head. "I know what you're thinking, because I think the same thing. This voyage is going to do wonderful things for my figure. For the first time in my life, I don't mind not eating."

"I think your figure's just fine, Miss Aspinall."

"Why, thank you, Justin. And I hope you'll call me Samantha."

He looked into her lively green eyes and felt a most unusual sensation. He had no idea what it was.

"Yes, Samantha. Your father won't think it forward of me if I call you that? I am, after all, a bastard son."

"Surely you know by now that Poppa was completely unjustified in what he said and did."

"He has yet to apologize to me."

"He will in time. Poppa's just stubborn. And Momma is trying to arrange for all of us to practice our Chinese with you."

"That would be difficult, as I don't have much free time."

"Momma's going to talk to the Captain about getting you some time off. But you were saying about your mother's diary?"

"Yes, um . . . what I was going to ask you, might I use your desk and reading light from time to time to read this diary? It would mean a great deal to me."

"Of course, Justin. You could use it tonight, when you come off watch."

"Your father wouldn't mind?"

"He'd probably explode, but what he doesn't know won't hurt him, and he's a sound sleeper. Besides, it will be a sort of payment to you for improving our Chinese."

"You could practice with Jimmy Chen too. He's from Canton."

She put her hand on the back of her bonnet as a gust of wind caused the ship to rise on a wave and, simultaneously, roll to starboard.

"I'd much rather practice with you!" Samantha yelled as the ship crested the wave and plunged into the trough, sending a wall of spray over the bow. Justin grabbed her hand.

"It's getting rough!" he yelled. "You'd better go below!"

"Come to my stateroom tonight," she said as they hurried across the sea-swirling deck toward the companionway. "Knock on my door once. I'll be expecting you."

She gave him her most enchanting smile before disappearing down the ladder.

Again, Justin felt that unusual sensation. His heart was beating faster, and his whole young body tingled.

What in the world *is* it? he wondered. Am I catching the ague?

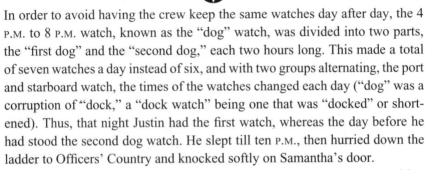

In order to avoid having the crew keep the same watches day after day, the 4 P.M. to 8 P.M. watch, known as the "dog" watch, was divided into two parts, the "first dog" and the "second dog," each two hours long. This made a total of seven watches a day instead of six, and with two groups alternating, the port and starboard watch, the times of the watches changed each day ("dog" was a corruption of "dock," a "dock watch" being one that was "docked" or shortened). Thus, that night Justin had the first watch, whereas the day before he had stood the second dog watch. He slept till ten P.M., then hurried down the ladder to Officers' Country and knocked softly on Samantha's door.

After a moment, she opened it. She was in a blue dressing gown, and her hair, which she generally wore in curls, she had now brushed out so that it fell to her shoulders in a black cloud. She put her finger to her lips and beckoned him inside. He tiptoed in and she closed the door.

"Father's already snoring," she whispered. "I hear him between the ship's creaking. Sit down."

He sat in the desk chair and put the leather diary on the desk. He pulled the small brass key from his pocket and fitted it in the clasp lock. He turned it, then opened the book. The first page had printed on it in elegant copperplate:

DIARY
For the Year 1837 A.D.
This Diary is the Property of:

Written in ink on the next line was:

Constance Crowninshield.

Justin was amazed. He turned to Samantha and whispered, "My mother was a Crowninshield!"

"From Salem?" Samantha looked impressed.

"Yes. I remember hearing about her. She died years ago in a sanitarium . . . they said she had a weak heart and was an invalid most of her life . . . Then this means I'm Adelaide's nephew!"

"Who's Adelaide?"

"Sylvaner's wife . . . Oh, you wouldn't understand, it's complicated. But this is incredible!" He turned to the first page.

"Read it to me," Samantha whispered, standing beside him as the oil lamp swayed in its gimbal.

" 'January 1, 1837,' " Justin began. " 'The new year starts with heavy snow, but I have met the most interesting man who has brought a touch of spring into our dreary winter days. His name is Nathaniel Savage, and he is to be my sister's father-in-law, for Adelaide is marrying Sylvaner Savage, a member of the wealthy New York shipping family. The match is looked down on by some of our friends because the Savages are considered somewhat *arriviste*—Nathaniel Savage made the family fortune himself—and besides, of course, dear Adelaide, who is so beautiful and talented, has always been considered a desirable "catch" by the local beaux and for her to marry outside Salem has not gone down well with many. But Sylvaner seems presentable and is most dashing, with curly black hair and dark eyes. He was graduated from Harvard two years ago. He and Adelaide met at a regatta last summer, and my sister told me it was "love at first sight." How very romantic!

" 'But handsome as Sylvaner is, I for some reason think his father is even more attractive. Strange that I would find such an older man so appealing, but he seems to have a warmth to him that Sylvaner lacks. Of course, I am judging by the most superficial of first impressions, but still sometimes first impressions tell the truth. Yes, the more I think of it, the more I think Sylvaner is rather cold and stuck on himself, while his father has a sweetness that appeals to me. Of course, being an invalid, I can only dream of having a true romance. But I think if I were healthy, like Adelaide, I could quite lose my heart to Nathaniel Savage even though he is three times my age. Ah, but what wicked thoughts for me to pen; I should be ashamed. After all, Mr. Savage is happily married, and has been for years. But still, to you, dear diary, I can open my heart.' "

Justin finished the first entry.

"Oh, how sad," Samantha sighed. "Your poor mother . . ."

"But obviously she *did* have a romance, because I'm here!" Justin said.

"Yes, that's true." And thank heaven for it, Samantha thought. "Read some more." Oh, what beautiful hair he has!

There was a knock at the door. Justin froze. Samantha pointed to a corner behind the door, and he silently hurried to it as she opened the door.

"Yes, Momma?" he heard her say.

"Is someone in here with you?" Edwina said.

"Of course not."

"But I heard voices. . . ."

"I was reading to myself."

"Oh. Well, it's late, dear. You should be in bed. The Captain tells me the glass is falling, and he expects rough weather."

"Yes, Momma."

"Good night."

Justin, crouching behind the door, heard Edwina kiss her daughter. Then the door closed. Samantha held up her finger to her lips. Then she opened her leather writing kit, took a pencil, and scribbled the following note on a piece of pad paper:

> *Momma's ears are better than I thought. Let me keep the*
> *diary. I'll read it and tell you later.*

She tore it off and gave it to Justin, who read it and nodded.

They looked at each other a moment. Then she opened the door and he hurried out.

They looked at each other again as he slowly closed the door.

He hurried up the ladder, emerging topside just as the *Sea Witch* took a heavy roll to port. Seawater rushed across the deck as Justin ran forward to the fo'c'sle.

Yes, he thought, I'm definitely catching the ague. Or *something*. Every time I look at her, I feel so very odd. . . .

5   JUSTIN WAS UNABLE TO LEARN more about his mother for a while because the *Sea Witch* was soon wallowing in a fierce Atlantic storm, confining the Aspinalls to their staterooms and keeping the crew up almost around the clock as Captain Whale ordered the two acres of sail to be reefed. Toward evening, the sky, which had been darkening all afternoon, turned back and the wind began to pick up force as rain began coming in great sheets.

"Take in your jib-tops'l and kites, Mr. Horn," Captain Whale bellowed through his brass voice trumpet. He was standing on the quarterdeck beside the wheel and binnacle that housed the compass.

"Take in the jib-tops'l and kites, sir!" Mr. Horn bellowed back. It was a matter of pride as well as practicality to leave the sails unfurled till the last moment, because without the sails the ship lost its propelling force. But now that the wind was at fifty knots, with gusts to hurricane strength, leaving the sails up meant risking losing them—or the masts. Now the crew ran forward on the pitching deck as the bow plunged into forty-five-foot seas. The sail was hauled down, and then the flying jib was furled and the gaff-topsails were clewed up.

"You, Savage!" Mr. Starbuck yelled at Justin. "I told you I'd get you aloft in our first storm! Well, get your ass up the rigging! We're reefin' the tops'l next!"

Justin, dripping wet from the rain and the spray, jumped up on the bucking ratlines and began climbing. It was almost dark now, the sun having set fifteen minutes before. His hands were blistered and sore. Even though he had his sea legs, this was his first major storm and he was afraid: he would have been a fool if he weren't. The rest of the crew, being more practiced, were already on the cross-trees before Justin was halfway up. He found he was holding tighter the higher he went, clinging to the topmast shrouds while the huge sails flapped about in front of him. The wind came in gusts, stronger and stronger with the rising sea, and the *Sea Witch* was heeling over to an angle of 45 degrees. He could feel the mast bending under the strain as he inched out on the footlines, hanging over the yard. The windward roll and the forward pitch of the ship threw the topsail full of wind. But rising on top of the next wave, the sail was whipped forward of the mast and around Justin's head. The next roll carried the sail back, scraping his face and pulling the cap from his head. It circled high above the sail, then it was caught by the howling wind that swept it far away to leeward where it finally dropped into the white-capped waves.

By pulling and hauling on the sail, he nearly succeeded in spilling the wind from it when a big sea carried the ship high in the air. A gust of wind tore the sail from his grasp. Justin let go and the whole sail blew out to leeward again.

Justin had been brought up to speak like a gentleman and avoid swearing. But he had quickly learned the lingo of the fo'c'sle. Now he was so furious he roared, "SHIT!"

The rain was making the sail even more difficult to handle and the rigging harder to hang on to. Being over a hundred feet above the deck, Justin knew he was one slip from death. He was further unnerved by the cracking of the jaws of the foregaff below him as it swung around the mast that itself was quivering, vibrated by the wind as it whistled through the rigging. He made another attempt to get the sail, which was vibrating strangely. Another dip to leeward and he saw the reason why. The Captain was keeping the ship into the wind as best he could and thus shivering the leech of the foresail, which flapped back and forth with loud cracks when too near the wind.

Justin climbed up the ratlines of the topmast shrouds where he could use his weight against the sail. Then, taking a turn around the sail with the gasket, he gradually smothered the wind from it and tied it fast to the masthead.

Returning to the deck, vastly relieved to have finally succeeded, he was ordered by Mr. Starbuck to help lower the mainsail. This done, the jib was reefed and the foresail close-reefed. Justin watched Starbuck while he passed the weather earing. The man might have been a bit of a monster, but he knew his seamanship. All hands pulled away on the reef-points to leeward to stretch the band along the boom as much as possible while the earing was passed through the cringle in the leech of the sail and around the boom-end. Then Justin helped knot the reef-points. This being done, the crew hoisted the reefed foresail.

By now it was two bells and Starbuck, as wet as the rest of the crew, said, to Justin's surprise, "Well done, boy. Now go below and get some rest. You've got the mid watch."

He was too exhausted to feel elated. Going to the dimly lit fo'c'sle, which was rolling crazily, he took off his soaked clothes, hung them on hooks to dry, then, naked, crawled into his swinging hammock and tried to get some sleep. His last thought before drifting off was that for the first time he felt at home on the ship; and that he thought he now had the confidence to handle any contingency that might arise in the future.

"It was a little scary last night," Samantha said the next morning. The storm had passed, and while the sea was still rough, the sun was shining brightly in a clear sky. "I was almost thrown out of my bunk. Were you frightened?"

"Nah," Justin said. He was feeling cocky. "I had a little trouble up in the rigging, but . . ." He shrugged. He was polishing brightwork on the main deck.

"You weren't a *little* scared?" Samantha insisted.

He grinned sheepishly. "Well, maybe a little."

"Uh-huh. I thought so. Anyway, I finished your mother's diary. Oh, Justin, it's such a beautiful story! And so sad. You see, her mother—your grandmother—thought Constance, your mother, was much sicker than she really was. I mean, she *did* have a weak heart, but there was no reason she had to be treated as an invalid. Her mother kept her in bed or on a chaise longue all the time, and she hardly ever could even leave their house on Chestnut Street in Salem. But your mother was very beautiful, sort of like Marguerite in Monsieur Dumas's novel *La Dame aux Camélias* . . . did you ever read it?"

"Um, no. I don't read many novels."

"Oh, I *love* novels, especially French ones because so often they're about love and romance, and I just *love* love and romance, don't you?"

"Well, I'm not sure what love *is*. . . ."

"You'll know when it happens to you," she said firmly. Just as I'm in love with you, she thought. "Anyway, where was I? Oh, yes. So your father, that is, Nathaniel Savage of course, had come to Salem for the wedding of Sylvaner and Adelaide—and now I know who they are. And that's when your father met Constance. He took one look at her lying on the chaise longue, and he fell madly in love with her! That's what she said in her diary that he told her. Isn't that wonderful?"

"Yes, I expect it is."

"Well, of *course* it is. But naturally, they had to keep their love a secret because Nathaniel's wife was there with him, and then there was Constance's mother who had told her she'd die if she ever got overexcited. But Constance told her diary she couldn't help but be excited because she was so much in love . . . her heart was palpitating. Just think, she could have keeled over at any moment, dead because of love! It's so sad!"

"It's sort of morbid too."

"Oh, pooh, I can see you haven't a romantic bone in your body. Or are you hiding it? Are you a *teeny* bit romantic, Justin?"

He got red in the face. "Well, maybe."

Oh, I do hope so! she thought. I want you to hold me in your arms and cover my face with passionate kisses! "Well, I think you're *very* romantic, Justin. But where was I? Oh, yes. After Sylvaner and Adelaide's wedding, Nathaniel and his wife went back to New York. But a week later, Nathaniel came back to Salem and rented a house on Chestnut Street just five houses away from Constance. He had lied to his wife and used a false name when he rented the house so that no one in Salem would know who he was. Isn't that wonderfully romantic?"

Justin was impressed. "Yes, I think that really *is.*" He tried to imagine his bedridden father involving himself in such an ornate subterfuge, but it was difficult. It occurred to him that this thing called "love," whatever it was, must be a terribly powerful force. "And then what happened?"

"Constance had a maid named Flora who became the go-between. She delivered the love letters between the two by hand, down Chestnut Street. And then, three days after Nathaniel had returned to Salem, Constance told her mother she wanted to get out of the house—it was a lovely day for January, and she hadn't been out of the house since before Christmas. So the carriage was brought around, and Constance was carried out of the house by the coachman. He put her in the coach and off they went down Chestnut Street. But Flora had arranged it all with the coachman, who was her boyfriend, and the carriage stopped at Nathaniel's house. Constance went inside on her own, because she really *could* walk, it was just that her mother had told her she shouldn't because it would strain her heart. And she and Nathaniel spent the entire afternoon making love. Isn't it wonderful?"

Justin frowned. "But what does 'making love' *mean?*"

Samantha looked a little troubled. "Actually, I'm not quite sure myself," she said. "But Constance wrote in her diary that she had never known such ecstasy, even though her heart was palpitating."

"It certainly *sounds* nice."

"Yes, but she was feeling terribly guilty about it, so I expect it wasn't quite proper, whatever it was. Anyway, they did the same thing three more times over the next ten days. And then, Nathaniel had to go back to New York."

"Good morning, Mr. Savage," said Edwina Aspinall, who had just come on deck to get some air.

"Good morning, Mrs. Aspinall."

"My stars, wasn't that a terrible storm last night? Dr. Aspinall and I were praying to the Good Lord for delivery from the maelstrom, and obviously the Good Lord heard our prayers, for here we are, safe and sound. Samantha, have you mentioned to dear Mr. Savage the possibility of his improving our Chinese?"

"Oh, yes, Justin," Samantha said, "it would be such a wonderful thing if you could help us. The Captain said we could use his cabin on Sundays from two to four if the weather permits, and he'd arrange for you to have time off. Would you?"

Justin looked at the beautiful girl. It's not the ague, you ninny, he thought. I'm falling in love with her! Just like my father fell in love with my mother! I'm in love with Samantha!

"I'd be delighted to," he said.

"Of course, we'd pay you," Edwina said. "Would a dollar a lesson sound right to you?"

"I'd be glad to do it for free." He smiled. "There's no use for money out here anyway."

"Well then, we'll take you to dinner at a nice restaurant when we get to Canton."

"They may not have restaurants in Canton, Momma," Samantha said.

Edwina looked shocked. "They may be heathens," she said, "but surely they have restaurants. No one could be *that* barbaric!"

"I hate to tell you this, Mrs. Aspinall," Justin said, "but the Chinese think *we* are the barbarians. They had a refined civilization when the English were painting their bodies blue and worshiping the sunrise."

"Ah, but that was before Jesus saved the English, as well as the rest of us," Edwina said. "And now, *we* must save the poor Chinese."

"With restaurants, Momma?" Samantha said, a mischievous twinkle in her green eyes.

Her mother looked indignant. "Of course not. With your father's inspired sermons, naturally. Come along, Samantha. Take a turn on the deck with me. We mustn't waste too much of Mr. Savage's valuable time."

"More later," Samantha whispered to Justin as she joined her mother.

Justin was thinking, I'm going to have to ask someone in the fo'c'sle just what "making love" entails. I'm sure they'll know. I have an odd feeling it has something to do with my penis.

On another part of the deck, Justin's paid assassin was watching his prey. The boy, he thought, is about to be fish food.

When Nathaniel Savage's will was read, Sylvaner and Adelaide became one of the richest young couples in America. Sylvaner inherited all the stock in the shipping company, which was privately held and estimated to be worth around two million dollars. He also inherited the house on Washington Square and stocks, bonds, and cash worth in excess of one million dollars. Ah Pin was given a pension of ten thousand dollars a year for the rest of her life in return for her "services" to the family, which made the plump amah an heiress. And Justin was bequeathed a half-million-dollar trust fund.

Suddenly, rolling in "filthy lucre," Adelaide, a passionate shopper to begin with, went on a world-class shopping spree. At the time, Broadway was Manhattan's worthy rival to London's Regent Street and Paris's rue Faubourg St. Honoré. Although at night Broadway was a hunting ground for what an inspired contemporary called the "peripatetic whorearchy"—the bejeweled ladies of the night working the streets in front of the gas-lit theaters or working out of the many busy concert saloons, luring their hooked clients a block west to the elegant brothels of Green and Mercer streets, red lights twinkling merrily over their front doors—by day, Broadway was a passing parade of New York's shopping-addicted middle- and upper-class women. That a country founded a few decades before upon egalitarian principles could produce a citizenry so hell-bent on expenditure and ostentatious display never failed to confound foreigners and dismay puritanical natives. But New York women were known for their passion for jewelry and clothes, and Adelaide, although a New Yorker only by marriage, was no exception. She reluctantly agreed to wear mourning for a month after her father-in-law's demise; but within three days after the funeral, she was in her carriage heading for 271 Broadway, where the city's leading jeweler, Tiffany & Co., had opened its new doors three years before across the street from New York's first, and biggest, department store, A. T. Stewart and Company.

Adelaide warmed the hearts of the Tiffany salesmen by buying a thousand-dollar diamond bracelet, a nine-hundred-dollar diamond and sapphire brooch, and a complete silver service, handmade in the Tiffany factory on Centre Street, all to be delivered to Number 4 Washington Square North, which Adelaide was in the process of moving into (first getting rid of many of what she considered Nathaniel's "hideous" pieces of furniture—as well as Ah Pin, who moved out after the funeral).

Anything but sated—in fact, her shopping lust merely whetted—she crossed Broadway, dodging the incredibly heavy traffic, aiming for A. T. Stewart's. Streams of scarlet and yellow omnibuses, racing in the more open parts of the thoroughfare, and locking each other's wheels in the narrower, vied for leeway with loaded stages hurrying to and from the huge hotels, with the carts and wagons laden with merchandise, with the elegant private carriages and the fast-trotting horses of the "young set" to make Broadway a considerable challenge for the pedestrian. The shouts and curses of the drivers, the rumble and rattle of the wheels, the clip-clop of the horses' hooves, combined to create an "Anvil Chorus" that inspired Walt Whitman to describe New York as "noisy, roaring, rumbling, tumbling, bustling, stormy, and turbulent." He might have added "smelly and dirty," for although Broadway itself was kept clean by the storeowners, who hired private trash collectors to sweep the gutters and sidewalks, the side streets were filled with garbage, in which wild pigs rooted and rats gamboled.

But none of this could deter a committed shopper like Adelaide. Dodging the traffic, lifting her voluminous black skirts to avoid the mud puddles, she barged into A. T. Stewart's and delighted the clerks by ordering an entire new Jacobean-style dining-room suite for the Washington Square house, the suite being a reproduction carved in North Carolina. Then she repaired to the second-floor boutique of Madame Marie de Paris, who was really de Québec; but such was the French capital's reputation for chic that anything marked "Paris" could fetch twice the price, even if it had been made on Spring Street. Adelaide ordered two new ball gowns from Madame Marie, at two hundred dollars apiece—certainly top dollar, but hardly unheard of in big-spending New York—and three shawls at fifty dollars each. She bought five new bonnets at twenty dollars apiece, two hundred dollars' worth of lingerie handmade, allegedly, by Belgian nuns, then went to the first-floor Salon des Chaussures to drop yet another two hundred dollars on shoes and boots. She finished her orgy by buying a five-ounce bottle of the "shocking" new perfume from Paris called Nuit d'Extase, which the local Episcopal clergy had tried to ban from the country, but which, of course, in true American fashion, had only made it a huge seller.

Then, sated at last, she left the huge white marble department store, got in her carriage, and drove to 365 Broadway, at the corner of Franklin Street, to lunch with a friend at the city's biggest and most extravagant restaurant, a mecca for rich lady shoppers, Taylor's.

In an age of excess, Taylor's was overkill. According to a guidebook, just a glance inside the place was "bewildering." The fifty-by-hundred-foot grand saloon was "a perfect blaze of decoration . . . a complete maze of frescoes, mirrors, carving, gilding and marble," according to the *Daily Tribune.* Nine richly curtained windows overlooked Franklin Street. The opposite wall was all mirrors. Corinthian columns, painted crimson with gilt trim, rose to the frescoes and gilt ceiling twenty-two feet above. A stained-glass window preened on the back wall, flanked by two fountains. Adelaide, who was well known by the maître d', was immediately taken to one of the hundred black walnut tables, eliciting envious glares from the ladies waiting in line. But, as always, maître d's had their fingers on the social pulse of the city, and this one knew that *this* Mrs. Savage was important and was probably soon going to be *very* important.

As Adelaide ordered champagne from one of the uniformed waiters, the decorative triumph of Taylor's, a twenty-one-foot-high crystal fountain, tinkled merrily, the six glass dolphins in its marble basin spouting streams of water from their snouts. To some, Taylor's would be viewed as an overdecorated horror. But to Adelaide, sipping her champagne, her shopping lust in temporary abeyance, her black veil pulled up around her black hat, Taylor's was heaven.

"Darling!" said Francesca Stuyvesant Bruce, a cousin of Sylvaner's and one of New York's smartest young hostesses, who hurried to her table, "I'm sorry I'm late, but the traffic is dreadful, as usual."

"Yes, it's terrible today."

The two women kissed, and Francesca sat down opposite Adelaide, removing her gloves. "How wonderful to see you out after your bereavement," she said. "But don't you think it's perhaps a bit indelicate for you to be shopping so soon after Sylvaner's father's death, poor man?"

A slow smile came over Adelaide's face. "No," she said.

"My dear, you shock me." Fran smiled. Actually, she was intrigued.

"Dear Fran," Adelaide said, "I'm probably going to shock you much much more. Some champagne?"

Adelaide might have complained about the laxity of New York's moral standards, but that was only when she was grumbling about Justin. Also, while Nathaniel was alive, she felt it wise to keep a certain restraint on her behavior. But now, she was determined to do what she pleased, at least to the point of not outraging public opinion. And public opinion, which once would have frowned on women lunching in public, much less drinking, now accepted both, as was evident by the fast-gossiping, wine-sipping female crowd at Taylor's. Adelaide signaled to a waiter, who brought Fran a glass and filled it with champagne.

"How's Tony?" Adelaide asked, referring to Tony Bruce, Fran's stockbroker husband.

"Oh, fine. He has a sniffle, but he'll survive."

"And the children?"

"Both in school, complaining about homework, as usual."

"When Sylvaner and I are moved into the Washington Square house, we're going to give a ball. I haven't sent out the invitations yet, but it will be the fifteenth of next month. Save the date. It wouldn't be any fun without you two."

Fran, who was a very attractive blonde, smiled. "That's sweet of you, Adelaide, and we wouldn't miss it for the world."

"Good. Well, cheers!"

She raised her champagne glass. The two ladies clicked, then sipped.

Adelaide had plans for Tony Bruce.

The *Sea Witch*'s course from New York had been east-southeast. The ship had made excellent time until it hit the Horse Latitudes at 30 degrees North, but even here, in a place notorious for weak winds, the ship made better-than-average time and the crew were talking about a new record. However, when in the third week the ship arrived in the Equatorial Doldrums, the winds stopped entirely, the sea became flat, and a burning sun in a copper sky caused the crew to move like zombies in the fierce heat.

"There's nothing we can do," Captain Whale told the Aspinalls in his cabin, "except wait for a squall. They come along from time to time. Once we're past the Equator, things will pick up again."

Samantha had told Justin the rest of his mother's tragic story, as related in her diary. How Constance had become "in the family way," as she primly wrote. How Nathaniel, terrified that his ardor might cost her her life, had tried to arrange an abortion by Madame Restell, New York's leading "Society" abortionist, who, it was said, inspired Poe to write of the death of Marie Roget. But Constance adamantly refused, saying she didn't care if the child would be illegitimate, she wanted to bear it even if it cost her her life. And all the while, the desperately elaborate stratagems to keep the affaire a secret, for if the truth had become known in Salem, Constance would have been "ruined."

Nathaniel, agonized by the trouble he had caused, fearful for his beloved's safety, had arranged for an eminent Manhattan heart specialist, a Dr. Forbes, to visit Salem, ostensibly to test Constance's heart and suggest she spend several months at his sanitarium near Poughkeepsie to undergo a new "treatment" he had developed that might cure her. The reality was that Nathaniel had paid him a small fortune to get Constance away from Salem so she could have her baby.

The miracle was that this scheme worked. Constance's family bought the whole package and rejoiced that this "invalid" might be restored to health. Constance was taken to the sanitarium in a horse-drawn ambulance before anyone even suspected she was pregnant. And there, at Shady Lawn, six months later, with Nathaniel at her side, she gave birth to a healthy, seven-pound boy.

"Her last entry in the diary was written the day after you were born," Samantha told Justin, tears in her eyes. "It's so beautiful, I have to read it to you."

She opened the red leather diary. They were on the main deck of the ship on a gray, blustery day before they reached the Horse Latitudes.

" 'September 29, 1837. Nathaniel and I have decided to name our beautiful boy Justin,' " she began, " 'a name we both like and is found in both our families. He is such a beautiful baby, with the sweetest blue eyes, that I know in my poor heart he will grow up to be a fine-looking man and a credit to his parents. Alas, I fear I won't live to see it happen, though. I am already so weak I can barely write these lines, and the fearful look in my poor darling Nathaniel's eyes as he sits next to my bed, holding my hand, tells the story so well. The irony is that my mother was right after all: I am too weak to bear a child, and my sin—though I can't consider it that—will cost me my life. But what would twenty more years of lying in bed have been worth compared to the joy I have known these past few brief months? For I have loved and been loved. And I have my darling Justin. Surely, the length of life is not as important as the quality of life lived. For in the end, we are all dead, whether we have lived eight years or eighty; and I go to my grave fulfilled and happy. I regret nothing. And I have told my sweetest Nathaniel to love and protect our child. . . .' " Samantha looked up. "And that's the end of the diary," she said. "Your father wrote at the bottom of the page: 'My darling love died at eight bells in the evening. I was with her at the end. I will do my utmost to raise and protect our child, Justin, though his parentage must be kept a secret. But oh, my heart is so sad, for I loved Constance as I have never loved anyone. She was an angel on earth, and I know she is now one in Heaven. [Signed] Nathaniel Savage.' "

There were tears in Justin's eyes as he listened. "I only wish I could have known her," he said. "She sounds so different from her sister, Adelaide, who is so cold and proud." He sighed. "But I can see why my father felt so guilty. I suppose, in a way, he murdered her with his love."

"Oh, Justin, I don't believe that. I think they loved each other so much they didn't think of the consequences. Or maybe, they *did* think about them, but didn't care. I think it's very beautiful. Sad, but beautiful."

"Perhaps." Justin looked at the horizon with bloodshot eyes. He had learned from the crew what "making love" entailed, a lesson taught with many lewd sniggers, gestures, and remarks like "Wait till we get you on one of the 'flower boats' in Canton, lad. You'll learn what it's all about soon enough there." "Flower boats," they had explained, were floating brothels. There was much talk of different "positions," and how the Chinese gave poetic names to each of them: "The White Tiger Leaps" (woman taken from behind), "The Dragon Turns" (missionary position), "The Jade Girl Playing the Flute" (fellatio). He had concluded that he indeed had much to learn about the mysteries of love and sex.

But if his father had so loved his mother that he killed her by sex, was love, then, all good, or did it have an evil side, like most human things?

He looked again at Samantha. Now he knew that he loved her. His rapidly maturing body also desired her. Was this good, or bad? Or both?

He sighed. It was all very confusing.

At least half a dozen sharks were lazily circling the *Sea Witch,* which was drifting in a flat sea.

"Jimmy Chen was trying to catch one," Justin told Samantha, who was standing at the port rail watching the fins slice the water, "because shark meat is very healthy to eat. He put a piece of hardtack on a thick steel hook and threw it in the water last night. One of the sharks bit the steel hook in half."

Samantha, who was protecting herself from a fierce equatorial sun with a parasol, shuddered.

"I don't think I want to fall overboard," she said.

"Definitely a bad idea."

"It's too bad, because the water looks so cool, and this heat is so ghastly. My stateroom's so hot I can hardly sleep."

"You ought to try the fo'c'sle. It's an oven. The crew is really angry because the Captain won't let us sleep on the deck where we could get some fresh air. But he says it's bad for ship's discipline, which I think is crazy. At least I'm lucky tonight, because I've got the mid watch and can be topside."

"If I asked the Captain if I could sleep on the deck, do you think he might say 'yes'?"

"He might. Ask him."

"Yes, I think I will." Then we could be together, she thought. Together in the moonlight.

The Captain politely, but firmly, said no. He didn't want anyone on deck at night except the watch, which, because of the Doldrums, he had reduced to one officer and one crewman. The risk of an accident at night was too great.

It had seemed overly cautious to Samantha, but he was the Captain and his word was law at sea. But that night, as she tossed and turned in her airless stateroom, where the temperature was a sizzling 93 degrees, she mentally cursed the Captain for his lack of consideration.

She got off her bunk and went to her port to stick her face out and get some air. In the moonlight, she could see the shark fins slowly circling the ship, as if the ravenous creatures were waiting. . . .

She closed her eyes a moment. Just a few feet above her was Justin.

She *had* to get some fresh air.

Putting on a robe, she went to the door and let herself out. The ship creaked as it rolled slowly in the slight sea. She went up the ladder and looked out. The ship was eerily beautiful in the moonlight, its great white sails luffing listlessly as the canvas waited in vain for a breath of wind.

At first, she thought the deck was empty. Then she saw Justin leaning on the port rail, looking at the water.

She started out of the companionway when she saw something that made her stop.

A man had stepped out of the shadow of the mainsail. He was coming up behind Justin. She saw that he had a belaying pin in his right hand.

Now he raised it to hit Justin over the head.

"Justin!" she screamed. "Watch out!"

Justin turned around, raising his arm to deflect the blow. Mr. Horn, the First Mate, crashed the belaying pin down on Justin's shoulder. He raised it to hit again, but Justin ducked and plowed his head into Horn's stomach. Then Justin righted himself and punched Horn's jaw with his right fist. Horn grunted and fell back against the rail. He threw the belaying pin at Justin's head, but Justin ducked as Horn charged him. Justin hit him again, landing a right to his nose. Again, Horn fell back against the rail, but this time with such force he stumbled backward and pitched overboard. He screamed as he fell, then there was a loud splash.

"Man overboard!" Justin yelled, running for a line.

There was the most horrible scream Samantha had ever heard.

And then, silence, except for the splashing of water.

Justin ran to the rail and threw a line. But the sharks were roiling the water in a feeding frenzy. It was too late.

Mr. Horn had been bitten in two.

6   "I TELL YOU, YOU CAN'T hang Justin!" Samantha exclaimed the next morning in the Captain's cabin.

"He murdered my First Mate," roared Captain Whale, "and by God . . ."

"He did no such thing! I saw it all! The First Mate tried to murder Justin. He came up behind him with one of those pins and started to smash it down on Justin's head until I yelled at him!"

The Captain glared at her. Justin, his wrists manacled, was standing by the door guarded by Mr. Starbuck. Justin looked apprehensive, as well he might. The Captain had ordered a hangman's noose to be tied to the main yardarm.

"Why," the Captain finally said, "would Mr. Horn want to kill Justin Savage?"

"I have no idea," Samantha snapped, "but I saw it happen. . . ."

"What were you doing on deck?"

"Getting some fresh air."

"I expressly ordered you, Miss Aspinall, to stay in your stateroom. . . ."

"I realize that, Captain, but I was becoming sick from the heat. I'll add that if the crew had been allowed to sleep on the deck, which would have been only humane in this terrible heat, none of this would have happened last night. It's almost as if things had been arranged so that Justin would be up there alone, an easy prey for Mr. Horn!"

"And what are you implying by that?"

"Only that it all seems *rather* peculiar. But at any rate, I saw that dreadful Mr. Horn come up behind Justin to attack him. Justin is completely innocent of anything, and if you hang him, I will make it my personal crusade when I get home to have you tried for murder! I might add that my father is not without influence in Washington and is a personal acquaintance of the President, Mr. Fillmore."

Captain Whale gave her a murderous look, but seemed to back down somewhat. He looked at Reverend Aspinall, who was standing beside his daughter.

"Samantha," Dr. Aspinall said, "try to compose yourself. Captain, I apologize for my daughter's indecorous behavior, but I fear I must, in this case, back her up. My daughter has faults, but she doesn't lie. And if you hang this young man, believe me, sir, I, too, will do everything in my power to bring you before a court of law."

Whale took a deep breath.

"Very well," he finally said, "I won't hang him." Justin looked understandably relieved. "But the fact remains that Mr. Horn met a horrible death under mysterious circumstances, and for that there has to be some accounting. Mr. Starbuck, put Savage in the brig. He will be deprived of his liberty until we return to New York, at which point I'll turn the matter over to the Federal authorities. In the meantime, I want all of you *out* of here! We're finally getting a breeze, and I have a ship to command."

As Samantha passed Justin on her way out of the cabin, he whispered, "Thank you. I'll never forget this."

"Oh, Justin, you don't have to thank me. I'd . . ."

"By God!" roared the Captain. "None of this mush in *my* cabin! And I'll hang *myself* before I allow a damned meddling female on one of my ships again!"

Samantha turned to shoot him a haughty glare. Then she left the cabin.

Professor Rastrelli, conductor of the Rastrelli Society Orchestra, raised his baton, then brought it down to begin a lively polka. The double drawing room of the first floor of Number 4 Washington Square North, was filled with what the city's reporters referred to as "the cream of New York's upper crust," a ridiculous culinary metaphor. Sylvaner and Adelaide were throwing a housewarming party for themselves, and they were sparing no expense to do it first class—a disregard for economizing that would later earn them the half-mocking sobriquet, the "Magnificent" Savages. White-gloved waiters were passing glasses of Veuve Clicquot champagne, while in the library brandy punch was being dispensed as well as the finest Scotch single malt whiskeys, Maryland rye, and Kentucky bourbons for the more bibulous guests. The dancers romping around the parlors were sending the temperatures soaring, not only because it was a warm June evening to begin with, but because the gas lights and many candles were hotting things up further. But no one seemed to mind, and the ladies had fans. They also had gossip to take their minds off the heat, and there was much to gossip about: Adelaide's scarlet ball gown, for one thing, which was showing every square inch of her shoulders and breasts that decency allowed, and perhaps even a bit more. Her new Tiffany diamond bracelet and brooch, the cost of which had caused a firestorm of speculation. Her redecoration of the Federal mansion in the latest "Renaissance Revival" style, featuring orgies of overcarving.

"It's all so *vulgar,*" said Florence Rhinelander to her twin sister, Floribel.

They were sitting on gilt chairs at one side of the parlor watching the dancers swirl by. The Misses Florence and Floribel, known to New York Society as the "Cash Flo's" because of their hefty trust funds, were confirmed old maids, both of whom resembled middle-aged birds with their hawk noses and many egret plumes. "One would never think Adelaide was a Crowninshield the way she's throwing money around. I have no idea whom she's trying to impress."

"They say she paid two thousand dollars for the bracelet," Floribel said, gossip having doubled the actual price. Floribel was the more timid of the two.

"Revolting, when there are beggars in the streets—along with pigs. And this awful furniture! 'Renaissance Revival' indeed. If this is what the Renaissance looked like, it shouldn't be revived." She raised her lorgnette to peer at Adelaide, who was dancing with a tall young man. "Is that Tony Bruce she's dancing with?"

"Yes, dear Florence," Floribel sighed. "Isn't he handsome? I love his curly hair."

"Probably uses a curling iron," snorted Florence. "A bit of a fop, if you ask me. And I hear that his business affairs are not in order."

"Tell me, Florence!" Floribel sounded eager for dirt.

"Speculation," Florence said, spitting out all four syllables. "Short sales, bear raids—the usual tomfoolery on Wall Street. They're all a bunch of swindlers down there."

Her twin looked shocked. "But, Florence, dear Father was on Wall Street!" Her sister glared at her. *"Then* it was honest. *Now* it's a den of thieves."

What fascinated New Yorkers was money, sex . . . and real estate.

"I'm thinking of buying a lot way uptown at Fifth Avenue and Twenty-third Street," Adelaide was saying to Tony Bruce. "I realize that's practically in the wilderness, but everyone does seem to be moving north of Fourteenth Street. You're so smart about real estate and business, Tony. Could I possibly lure you uptown to take a look at it?"

Tony Bruce, who was over six feet tall and was tremendously proud of his sweeping mustache and luxuriant chestnut curls that had so intrigued Floribel Rhinelander, looked into Adelaide's dark eyes and wondered what she was up to. Though Tony's wife, Fran, was one of Adelaide's best friends, Adelaide had always been somewhat off-putting with him, almost as if she didn't quite approve. But now? It all seemed sugar water and roses. But what did he care what she was up to? She and Sylvaner had inherited a fortune, and they didn't, as far as he knew, have a personal stockbroker. It might pay him to be attentive.

"I'd be delighted to, Adelaide," he said aloud. "What are the owners asking for the property?"

"Five thousand."

"That seems a bit high for that far north. But of course, you're right. The city *is* pushing north. No other way to go."

"That's so kind of you, Tony. I don't want to rush things, but might you be free tomorrow? There's somebody else interested in the property, and I'd hate to lose it."

"Tomorrow would be fine. Shall I pick you up at, say, noon? We could have lunch."

"Better yet, I'll have a picnic basket prepared and we can have a picnic on the property."

"People may talk," Tony said with a mischievous smile.

"No they won't." Adelaide seemed quite serious. She looked across the room. "Then it's set. Now, we should dance with our spouses before people *do* talk."

She led him across the room through the dancers to Sylvaner and Fran, who had been polkaing.

"Fran, I tried to kidnap your husband," Adelaide said with a smile, "and I succeeded. He's going to take me up to see more property on Fifth Avenue tomorrow. We're going to picnic: would you like to join us?"

Fran looked at her husband a moment. She knew Tony had been unfaithful to her—several times, in fact. But she didn't think he would try anything with Adelaide. He told her often he found her cold and not particularly attractive, despite her beauty.

"That sounds like such fun," she said with a smile, "but I told you I have a luncheon engagement tomorrow at Taylor's."

"Of course," Adelaide said. "I forgot." Which was a lie.

"So you two have fun."

Oh, thought Adelaide, we will indeed.

When Florence Rhinelander referred to Tony Bruce as a "fop" she wasn't slurring his masculinity. He might not have been Daniel Boone, but he was *muy macho*. He had a peacock's fascination with his clothes and appearance because he was enormously vain, for he was one of the best-looking men in New York. He had a snobbish desire to be in the latest fashion, to have the finest-cut trousers, the finest broadcloth, the most elegant patent leather boots, the best beaver hat—a tradition that derived from the English "exquisites" like Beau Brummel and not uncommon in New York Society. There were young men known as Bowery dandies who went much further, taking self-absorption to the point of lunacy; but they were no more or less silly and narcissistic than the young of any generation. And it would be unfair to lump Tony with them, since Tony was a hardworking stockbroker—albeit a crooked and inept one.

The next day at quarter past noon—Tony always made a point of being fashionably late—he pulled up in front of Number 4 Washington Square North, in his shiny brougham, driven by Jules, his coachman, whose pay was four weeks in arrears. Tony got out and went to the front door to ring. While he was waiting, he reviewed in his mind the articles that had appeared that morning in the penny press describing Sylvaner and Adelaide's ball the night before. Although reporters were never invited to private parties, it was rumored that some members of "Society" supplemented their incomes by selling items about the doings of New York's gratin to the members of the press whose job was to titillate the public through the city's fourteen dailies and eight semiweeklies, forerunners of today's tabloids and gossip columns. From what Tony had read that morning, it was obvious there had been an informer at Adelaide's the night before, because the description in the *Herald* had been right on the mark. Adelaide had not gotten good press in that newspaper. The article had contained a number of thinly veiled hints about "vulgar excess," leading Tony to wonder, not for the first time, whether the *Herald*'s informer might not be one, or both, of the "Cash Flo's." He knew that the Rhinelander trusts, considered so conservative and secure, had taken a few hits lately in the volatile stock market.

But so had Tony.

The door was opened by Sheffield, the Savages' new English butler.

"Mr. Bruce to see Mrs. Savage."

"Ah, Tony, there you are, late as usual." It was Adelaide, coming up behind the butler. She was dressed in the height of fashion, more suitable for a lunch at Taylor's than a picnic in the wilderness of Twenty-third Street; but Tony had never thought of Adelaide as a country type. "Sheffield, have the picnic hamper brought to Mr. Bruce's carriage."

"Yes, madame."

"You don't look at all tired," Tony said, accompanying her to the sidewalk.

"Why should I be?"

"You *did* have a few people over last night."

"Tony, in case you haven't noticed, I'm not the swoony type. If there's one thing I have plenty of, it's energy." She climbed in the carriage as Jules held the black lacquer door. Tony climbed in beside her.

"I thought your party was a triumph, but it got rather mixed reviews in the press," he said as they waited for the picnic hamper.

"I pay no attention to the press," she said, which was a lie. She had read every paper.

"The *Herald* seemed rather hostile. It implied you were trying to buy your way into New York Society."

"That's ridiculous. I'm already in it. And for that matter, who hasn't bought his way into New York Society? Let's be honest. This city is all about money."

The carriage started up.

"Then what is it you're after?"

She didn't answer while the carriage turned up Fifth Avenue, which, to many people's surprise, was beginning to show signs of being *the* avenue of the future instead of the cowpath it had seemed to be until recently.

"Perhaps," she said, "I'm after nothing. Perhaps I'm after everything." She turned to look at him. "What are *you* after, Tony?"

He folded his gloved hands over the top of his walking stick. "I'm much easier than you," he said with a smile. "I'm after everything."

"The lot is probably a good buy," he said a half hour later as they sat on the blanket chewing on cold chicken and sipping a chilled Chablis. Although Fifth Avenue had been paved, as were most of the crosstown streets, they were picknicking in a field with a few scruffy trees and shrubs and only a few buildings in sight. "But if I were you, I wouldn't buy it."

"Why?" Adelaide watched him as she sipped her wine from a crystal goblet. She had bought the wicker hamper with its silver, crystal, and china from Ball, Black & Co., New York's second jewelry store after Tiffany's.

Tony waved a horsefly away from his patrician nose. It was a pleasant June day with great cumulus clouds sailing across the sky like an armada.

"How old are you, Adelaide?" he asked.

"Twenty-nine."

He shot her a knowing look.

"All right. You have world enough and time, as the poet says. I'd go a mile farther north and buy a farm. In ten years you'd be as rich as the Goelets, and in fifteen years as rich as the Astors. This lot would be a nice little investment, but New York's a giant in toddler's clothes. I'd go for the brass ring."

She wiped her lips on the linen napkin.

"Yes, I've already come to the same conclusion," she said. "Except I may buy both. I've put a bid in on the Callahan farm. Thirty-five acres with five hundred feet footage on the East River."

"Then why did you ask me up here for my real estate expertise?"

"Because for one thing I wanted to see if you had any brains behind that pretty face."

"And for another thing?"

Adelaide pulled a chicken thigh from the hamper and bit in.

"You don't tell Fran much about your business, do you?" she asked.

"No. Why should I?"

"Don't you think your wife deserves to know that you're so in debt you'll probably be bankrupt in a month?"

He shrugged. "You've heard those ridiculous rumors," he said. "But that's all they are: rumors."

"Sylvaner says differently. My husband has his faults, but he has a good head for business and he knows what goes on in this town. He says you're up to your ears in debt. He says you might even go to jail." She looked at him over the chicken. "Ugly stories about how you've taken money from your clients' accounts without bothering to tell them? That sounds a lot like embezzlement to me."

Tony took his hat off the ground and stood up.

"I think I'll terminate this conversation," he said. "I have an appointment downtown. . . ."

"With whom? The police? Sit down, Tony, and don't be so pompous. I'm trying to save you. More wine?"

He hesitated, then obeyed.

"What do you want?" he asked as she refilled their glasses.

"I want an heir," she said. "Sylvaner is infertile. He *must* be! I've been to the best doctors, and there's nothing wrong with *me*. But we try and try and nothing happens. I'll pay your debts up to thirty thousand dollars if you give me a child."

He stared at her.

"You're insane."

"Not at all. It's the best solution, and I don't want to adopt a baby. I want to know exactly what I'm getting."

"But . . . everything else aside . . . what about Sylvaner?"

"He would never know. The child would be the Savage-Crowninshield heir. And if you ever told, I'd ruin you."

"But"—he drank more wine—"why me?"

"Because for all your character faults, which are legion, you come from one of New York's finest families. You're good stock, Tony. And you look enough like Sylvaner that the child, with any luck, could pass as his own. Besides, I know I can buy and control you."

He finished his wine.

"What a cold-blooded witch you are," he said softly.

"I come from Salem." She smiled. "Do we have a deal?"

He didn't even hesitate.

"Of course."

7 THE *SEA WITCH* PITCHED AND rolled in another Atlantic storm as Samantha made her way to the tween decks where the ship's brig was located. It was the fourth day of Justin's incarceration, and he was looking dirty and tired when she came up to the heavy wooden door of the cell, which had a two-foot-square barred window in it, just enough for her to see his face and shoulders. The cell was only seven feet by four, barely big enough to allow him to lie down and sleep. When he saw her come down the ladder, his face brightened.

"Samantha!"

"Justin," she said, putting her hands on his, which were gripping the bars. "Something strange has happened. The Captain has changed his course."

"What do you mean?"

"He told my parents this morning that the winds have been so unfavorable, he's going around Africa to China across the Indian Ocean instead of around South America across the Pacific."

"That's crazy." Justin frowned, thinking. "There must be some other reason. . . ."

"Can he do that? I mean, can he go any way he wishes?"

"Yes. Generally, captains are supposed to follow the wishes of the owners, but they have wide discretion to do what they want. But this thing about the winds doesn't make sense. Except for when we were becalmed in the Doldrums, we've been making excellent time."

He fell silent, thinking, and she examined his face. She was terribly worried about his health. The tiny cell was built into the starboard side of the small compartment, which had no ports, the only air and light coming from the companionway above. The space was hot. He had taken off his shirt, but even so he was drenched in sweat. She knew they let him out once a day for a fifteen-minute turn about the deck, but otherwise he was caged like an animal.

"Are they feeding you enough?" she asked.

He came out of his reverie. "I get the same food as the rest of the crew, which isn't saying much."

"Jimmy Chen told me he's making some biscuits this afternoon for us and the Captain. I'll save you mine. Jimmy says it's the last of the flour. He had to throw the rest overboard because it got maggots."

"If I eat any more of that lobscouse, *I'll* get maggots."

"Isn't it awful?" She made a face. Lobscouse was a concoction of dried potatoes and peas mashed together with salt beef, hardtack, and water all cooked to an unappetizing mush. As the food supplies dwindled, lobscouse was becoming the mainstay of the menu. Although the crew knew this was inevitable, the grumbling was growing as the meals shrank. "The only good thing coming out of all this is that I'm finally losing my baby fat. In fact, I'm becoming skin and bones."

He gave her a tired smile. "You look awfully good to me, Samantha. You look like an angel. I get so lonely down here. . . ."

She could see the pain and suffering on his face, and her heart ached for him.

"My poor Justin," she said, softly rubbing her fingers over his. "This is all so wrong and unfair. I can't imagine why the Captain is being so cruel to you—or, for that matter, why Mr. Horn tried to kill you."

"Well, I've pretty much figured that out. Someone wanted me dead and paid Horn to do it for him."

"But who—?"

"Who would want me dead? Sylvaner, who else? He's always hated me, and he's terrified my father would disinherit him for me. Murder's simple on the high seas. A little push in the middle of the night, and it's good-bye, Justin. And Horn wanted to be made a captain—I'll bet that was part of the deal. But what you just told me makes me wonder about the Captain too."

"What do you mean?"

"As you pointed out, it was awfully peculiar that he wouldn't allow anyone to sleep on deck that night, and that he reduced the night watch to two men. I mean, he made it awfully easy for Horn to try to kill me. And then when it didn't work—thanks to you—the Captain was mighty eager to hang me as quickly as possible. Once again, you messed things up for him. I owe you my life twice, and I won't forget it."

"Dear Justin, you owe me nothing but your friendship." And love, she thought. I hope. "Then you think Sylvaner paid the Captain too?"

"Maybe. But changing the route to China sort of makes me wonder if it might be something else. Something much bigger than a payoff."

"What?"

"What country will we pass going around Africa that we wouldn't going around South America?"

"India?"

"Exactly."

"So?"

"What could Captain Whale pick up in India that he could sell for a fortune in China? Something my father would never allow, but Sylvaner might be more than glad to get a cut of, since he has the morals of a rattlesnake?"

"What?"

Justin lowered his voice to a whisper.

"Opium."

Samantha was shocked.

"Opium?" she repeated. The word carried with it all the dreaded implications of vice, madness, opium dens, and violence. To Samantha, whose parents were, except for an occasional glass of port, teetotalers, and whose father regularly delivered thundering sermons on the evils of alcohol from his Wiscasset pulpit, opium made whiskey seem like lemonade. "But don't the Chinese prohibit the opium trade?"

"They say they do, but they take bribes and look the other way. There's too much money in it for everyone—the Chinese, the English, and now us Americans. I know Sylvaner was working on my father for years to get in the trade, but he always refused. Look: I'm sure Captain Whale, and probably all the other captains of the Savage Line, have been picking up opium in Batavia and selling it in Canton for years. There's no way my father could prevent them, because the captains have what they call a five-ton 'privilege,' which is a cargo allowance for their own private use. But if you fill a whole ship with opium—particularly the top chop Malwa Indian opium, which is what Sylvaner always wanted my father to trade—you're talking about a profit of millions. This is Whale's last voyage before he retires, and I'll bet anything he and Sylvaner cooked the whole thing up, banking on the probability my father would die before the *Sea Witch* gets back to New York. And part of the deal was getting rid of one inconvenient bastard son—namely, me."

"But"—Samantha gulped—"that means . . . that means this ship is in the drug trade!"

"That's exactly what it means, if I'm right. And I bet I am."

"Oh, Justin, this is terrible! I mean, my father, for all his faults, is a minister of the Lord! He'll have conniptions when I tell him!"

Justin reached through the bars and grabbed her wrists.

"Listen to me," he whispered. "If you breathe a word of this to your parents, we'll all be dead. Because if the Captain finds out we know, he'll make sure *none* of us gets home alive. I'm telling you, it's too easy to murder out here! Out here, he's God. Both you and your father threatened to blow the whistle on him if he hanged me, and that stopped him. But if your father started sermonizing to him about the evils of the opium trade, he'd find a way to shut us all up, if not on the ship, then somewhere else. In India or China, assassins are a dime a dozen. So please, my darling Samantha, whom I love with all my heart, keep your pretty mouth shut."

Samantha smiled.

"Say it again," she whispered. "Say you love me with all your heart."

"I do. That's the only thing that keeps me from going crazy in this stinking cell. That and one other thing."

Samantha frowned.

"What other thing? There's not someone else?"

Justin's young face became icy.

"Yes there is," he said softly. "There's Sylvaner. Someday I'm going to pay him back for what he's done to me. Someday I'll have my revenge."

The look of hate in his blue eyes chilled her.

"Justin, I can understand how you feel, but my father has delivered sermons on the evils of revenge. He says 'revenge is the Lord's.' "

"I don't care what your father says, or the Bible, or anyone else. *This* revenge is going to be mine, and it's going to be *sweet.* Someday I'm going to kill Sylvaner Savage."

As much as she loved Justin, Samantha knew that now she had to save him from someone besides Captain Whale or Mr. Horn.

She had to save him from himself.

Swede Larsen slowly and silently raised the bedroom window at the back of the rooming house on Perry Street in Greenwich Village, then stuck one leg over the sill to climb inside. It was a chilly September night. He was an ex-sailor, hired by Sylvaner Savage to track down and murder the amah, Ah Pin, for which he had been paid five hundred dollars down, five hundred on execution of the contract. It had taken him almost three months to track her down, because Ah Pin had known she might well become a target of Sylvaner and Adelaide and she had covered her trail well, first getting a solemn oath from Nathaniel's lawyer not to reveal her whereabouts. Ah Pin's fears had not been paranoia. She had seen the look in Adelaide's eyes when she was told by Ah Pin that Justin's mother was her sister. Ah Pin had grown up in China, where murders were as common as decapitations by the Manchu, or Tartar, rulers of the Ch'ing Dynasty who had ruled China by terror and intimidation since they overthrew the Mings in 1644. Ah Pin knew that Sylvaner and Adelaide might pose as respectable churchgoers, but their hearts were as ruthless as Malay pirates.

The killer carried a .36-caliber Old Model Navy pistol in his right hand and a safety match in his left. Now he held up the match and scratched it on the wall. It flared. The bedroom was small, plainly furnished, and neat.

It was also empty.

He was confused. Swede Larsen had spent twelve years in the China trade with both English and American companies. He had connections in New York's burgeoning Chinese community, which was one reason Sylvaner had hired him. Still, it had taken him three months to find a Chinese who knew where Ah Pin was living and who would talk. He gave Swede the Perry Street address, and the killer had staked out the house. He had seen Ah Pin go inside that evening. He knew she had the back room on the ground floor.

But now, nothing.

He lit a lamp with the match and went to the bureau. The drawers were empty. The closet was empty.

He saw a note pinned to the door. He tore it off and read:

> *Tell Sylvaner Savage he will never find me. But one day I will find him.*
>
> > *Ah Pin.*

With her ten-thousand-dollar annuity from Nathaniel, Ah Pin had become wealthy enough to buy protection from the rulers of the fledgling triads of New York's Chinatown.

"Dear Sylvaner, I have the most glorious news," Adelaide said the next evening as she dined with her husband in the dining room of the Washington Square house. "I am with child."

Adelaide might have been a murderess, but she was a genteel one. When it came to bodily functions, Adelaide was very much a product of her time and class. While she wouldn't go to the ludicrous lengths of prudery like many of her contemporaries, who called legs "limbs," draped piano legs with shawls, and segregated books by male and female authors to different shelves, still she was eminently Victorian.

Sylvaner's face lit up.

"My dearest Adelaide, is it true?"

"Yes. Dr. MacLeod confirmed it this morning. We are to have an heir. An heir to the Savages and the Crowninshields."

Well, not *quite,* she thought, since the father was Tony Bruce.

Sylvaner got up from the table and came to his wife to kiss her.

"You've made me the happiest of husbands," he said. "When can we expect the blessed event?"

"Dr. MacLeod said sometime in the spring, perhaps April."

"You must be careful, my angel, and get lots of rest."

"Oh, pooh. I'm healthy as a horse. But it *is* exciting, isn't it? We've waited for so many years. I'll have to start searching for a nanny. Amanda Prynne had an excellent one, perhaps I'll talk to her."

"Speaking of nannies," Sylvaner said, "Ah Pin has disappeared."

"Yes, I know, dear. And good riddance, I say. I never could stand the woman."

"No, you don't understand. I hired an ex-sailor to find out where she had gone, which he finally did. But somehow she found out he was looking for her, and she left the house on Perry Street."

Adelaide frowned at him. "I don't quite understand. You hired an ex-sailor to track her down . . . ?"

"That's right."

"But why?"

Sylvaner lowered his voice. "To kill her, of course. As you pointed out, she's the only person who knows Justin's mother was your sister. So the best way to shut her up was to hire an assassin to kill her."

The color drained from Adelaide's face. "Sylvaner, this is terrible news . . . I don't quite know what to say. . . ."

"But I assumed that's what you wanted?"

She started rubbing her hands together, nervously. "Sylvaner, this is getting to be a rather bad habit of yours. I mean, this is New York, it's not Renaissance Italy or ancient Rome. It's one thing to hire someone to push a young man overboard at sea—although the Good Lord knows I would never have consented to that scheme if I'd known Justin was my nephew—but now you're hiring ruffians to murder Ah Pin? Really, darling, you're going too far!"

"It would have been perfectly safe! No one would have known."

"Obviously, Ah Pin knew, or she wouldn't have left. No, this has gotten entirely out of hand. You must swear to me you'll never do anything like this again."

"But what if Ah Pin tells about your sister?"

"Let her! I don't care! It's not worth *murdering* for. Oh, yes, once the idea of murder excited me, but now . . . now I'm about to be a mother! I don't want to be Lady Macbeth, and I don't want you in jail. Swear to me you'll never do this again."

Sylvaner gave her a cool look. "All right, I swear. But I must say, Adelaide, your moral squeamishness is coming a bit late in the day. You once said we were one: I trust you haven't changed your mind about *that?* After all, I wouldn't like to think that one day my wife might accuse me of murdering Justin Savage."

She took his hand. "That was different," she said. "You were afraid old Nathaniel might disinherit you. But this: well, perhaps it's not so different after all. But we must remember we are Savages with a capital 'S,' not a small one. We are quality."

"Mmm. You're an interesting woman, Adelaide. You never fail to surprise me." He raised her hand to his lips and kissed it. "Very well: no more murder."

"And you know I would *never* betray you, darling. I mean, about Justin."

"Yes, of course. I trust you."

I think.

8 JUSTIN HAD BEEN IN MANY ways prescient about the voyage of the *Sea Witch.* In the ten weeks since his incarceration, the ship had rounded the Cape of Good Hope, encountering the expected storms, landed at Isle de France in the Indian Ocean to take on much-needed stores and water, for the crew was beginning to show signs of scurvy; then it had crossed the Indian Ocean, landing at Bombay, where three fourths of the cargo was off-loaded and sold at a handsome profit.

Then the crew began taking aboard chests of opium, the best Malwa from north of Bombay, whose poppy was grown by Indian chiefs and rajahs. In one particular, Justin had been overly alarmist, which he now realized. There was no way Captain Whale could keep the loading of so much opium a secret from the crew or anyone else, and Justin now saw that his own rather naive idealism about the role of the Savage clipper ships had misled him. In fact, there was no need to keep the loading of opium a secret, if Sylvaner had approved the move. The opium trade was perfectly legal with the British in India, and they had fought a war to make it so. They were soon to fight another one.

At the heart of the problem was one of the great, if glacial, historical movements: the interaction of China, the most populous nation on earth, with the western world.

In the seventeenth and eighteenth centuries, notably under the great Ch'ien Lung Emperor, China had been one of the richest countries in the world, its territories including Burma, Annam, Laos, Siam, Nepal, Korea, Manchuria, and Turkestan, as well as China. Over the years, a number of Jesuit priests had come to the imperial court in Peking, where they had been tolerated and even had their brains picked about certain European customs—for example, the great Summer Palace west of Peking, the Yuan Ming Yuan, built by the Ch'ien Lung Emperor, was based loosely on the idea of Versailles. But mostly, the Chinese mandarins, secure in their power and glory, ignored the "barbarians," about whom they knew little and cared less. And when, in 1793, the English sent an embassy to Peking under Lord Macartney in the hope of obtaining trading concessions, the Emperor dismissed the "barbarians" out of hand. They had nothing the Celestial Kingdom wanted or needed.

Except opium, which by the nineteenth century the Chinese both wanted and needed because two million of them had become addicted by the English trade. By now, the power of the great Ch'ing Dynasty emperors was fading, enfeebled by their own success and debauched lifestyles. At the end of the eighteenth century, the Ch'ien Lung Emperor was succeeded by his son, the Ch'ia-Ching Emperor, who was not at all the equal of his father in talent or brains, and who was haughty and stubborn to boot. His reign was plagued by rebellions, as was the reign of his son, the Tao-Kuang Emperor, who came to the Dragon Throne in 1821 after his father was struck by lightning. This was considered a sign that the gods were unhappy, and the Ch'ing Emperors were losing the "Mandate of Heaven," which was their commonly acknowledged Confucian reason for ruling.

The Tao-Kuang Emperor was not without talent and courage, but the Celestial Empire was beginning to unravel for a number of reasons, not the least of which was the enormous corruption in the imperial system. But rather than address the cancer that was gnawing at the entrails of the Ch'ing Dynasty, the Emperor became obsessed by the ever-increasing incursions of the western powers. Particularly irritating was the increasing opium trade, which was forbidden by Peking. And in December of 1838, he ordered the Viceroy at Canton to strike at the English and suppress the opium trade, dispatching his commissioner, Lin Tse-hsu, to enforce the order. Lin confiscated millions of pounds' worth of English opium. The English, furious and determined to protect their profitable trade, fought back. English warships were sent; the antique cannons of the Chinese didn't have a chance against the state-of-the-art gunnery of the barbarians, and the Chinese were brought to their knees. In 1842, at the Treaty of Nanking, Hong Kong was ceded to the British, the Chinese paid six million dollars in reparations for the confiscated opium, and five so-called "Treaty Ports"—Canton, Amoy, Foochow, Ningpo, and Shanghai—were opened to foreign trade, and British merchants were allowed to live in them with their families along with their own consuls to represent their interests. Nothing was mentioned in the treaty about the opium trade, which was tacitly agreed to be permitted to continue. And the Americans, with their new clipper ships able to transport the trade faster than the English, were eager to get in on the action. Many of the great shipping fortunes in Boston, New York, and Philadelphia, such as the Cushings and Delanos, were built on opium, which was considered much less distasteful a traffic than the slave trade, which had made the fortunes of the Brown family in Providence, among others. Only a few abstained from it on moral grounds. Old Nathaniel, Justin knew, had abstained on practical grounds, because the opium trade was fraught with danger, and a quarter of the ships involved with it disappeared without a trace.

The reason was that there were others beside the English and American shippers who sniffed the huge profits to be made from opium: namely, pirates. And Justin realized that by taking on a huge cargo of opium, Captain Whale was turning the *Sea Witch* into a floating magnet for every murderous pirate in the China Sea. The opium trade was as dangerous as war, its dangers multiplied by the poor charts of both China Seas, and the possibility of the three "devil winds": *Mausim,* Chinese for "Monsoon"; *Taifung*—the "Typhoon," which could blow the great pine masts from a ship; and *Teet Kiey,* which meant "iron whirlwind." In the case of the pirates, Justin assumed Captain Whale was depending on the ten Long Tom cannons, made of brass and capable of great range, on each broadside of the ship, as well as pivot and swivel guns at the *Sea Witch*'s bows and quarters to repel them, but it was still a risky business. Justin thought Whale's greed had overpowered his prudence, and he knew that his father would be outraged if he knew what was happening with his beloved *Sea Witch.*

In the event, there was nothing Justin could do about it. Three months of imprisonment had left him twenty pounds skinnier, depressed, and bitter. Only his beloved Samantha had saved him from sinking into the blackest despair. She came to the brig every day, often two or three times, talking to him, doing everything to cheer him up, sneaking whatever few snacks she could procure from the galley for him, trying out her rudimentary Cantonese on him. The greatest difficulty for Samantha, as for all "foreign devils," was the Chinese system of tones, which gave the language its singsong quality. "Oh," she exclaimed with exasperation, "I'll never get it right."

"It's hard, I know," Justin said. "But you *have* to get it right if you ever want to speak it. For instance, you could say 'I know the Chinese people.' But if you use the wrong tone, you'll be saying 'I eat the Chinese people,' which I think you'll admit is a bit different."

Samantha giggled. The bond of love being forged between these two adolescents under such unusual circumstances was as intense as that of Romeo and Juliet; and whereas family rivalries had kept those adolescents of an earlier day apart, it was Justin's thick wooden cell door that prevented him from embracing his Juliet.

Oddly, Justin had found another friend aboard the *Sea Witch:* none other than Mr. Starbuck, now the First Mate, having replaced Horn. Starbuck, who had seemed so hostile at first, now was taking an interest in Justin, moved by his plight. He had convinced the Captain to increase Justin's time topside to a half hour a day, which was a great boon, as Justin hated the confines of his cell. And Starbuck came down to visit him from time to time, keeping him abreast of events. It was Starbuck who told him about the fifty chests of opium being brought aboard by the crew, each chest costing 450 rupees plus 125 rupees duty to the British Government. Each chest weighed a *picul,* which meant 1331 1/2 pounds. "The ship's gonna be ridin' low," he told Justin, "and we'll be losin' speed and maneuverability because of it. But the crew don't give a damn because the Cap'n has promised all of us three percent of the profit, split by seniority. So those bilge billies are lickin' their chops, as am I, I'll confess. But it's a rum business."

"And not exactly a great day of glory for the Savage Line," Justin said sourly.

"Aye, that be true. I can see why you'd be bitter, lad."

"How is the opium packed?"

"It's made up into balls about the size of a thirty-two-pounder shot, and wrapped and packed in dry leaves. It don't smell none that I can notice, but I wager the Devil's in them balls. I've seen opium dens filled with addicts suckin' their pipes. Them poor creatures is nothin' but zombies, more dead than alive. Well, well, I suppose it don't make no matter as long as we all make a few bucks, eh?"

"I wouldn't touch the money if it were offered to me, which it won't because I'm not one of the crew anymore."

"Well, you're a fine lad, with more quality than most. I admire you for it, Justin. But don't be blamin' me for bein' a bit greedy. I've got my retirement to be thinkin' of."

Justin sighed. "No, I don't blame you."

I blame Sylvaner, he thought.

That pig.

As frustrated as he inevitably was by his confinement, Justin's spirits began to pick up as the *Sea Witch,* laden with its thirty-plus tons of opium, set sail from Bombay, rounded India, and headed east across the Bay of Bengal to pass between the Andaman and Nicobar Islands across the Andaman Sea into the Strait of Malacca between Sumatra and the Malay Peninsula. Then the ship sailed through Singapore Strait and headed north into the South China Sea.

China. The Orient. Justin was a prisoner, true. But every mile brought him closer to the China he had dreamed of, the China that somehow he had felt since his childhood was part of his special destiny.

And yet, would he not even be able to get a glimpse of China in his cell with no port?

Late in October, in the middle of the night, he was awakened by shouts, then gunfire. Getting to his feet, he put his face to the barred window in his door, straining his neck and eyes to see through the companionway that afforded him a partial glimpse of the deck above. He saw what looked like flaming flares sailing through the dark night sky. More shots.

Then the *Sea Witch* shook as the Long Tom cannons began firing from the port side. More shouts, yells . . . a hubbub. . . . He heard Starbuck's voice: "They're boarding! Repel the bastards! Repel them!"

Pirates! His fears were being realized. The fool! he thought as he grabbed his tin mess dish off the deck. Whale's greed may cost us all our lives!

"Let me out!" he yelled, banging the dish against his bars. "Let me fight! Let me out!"

He knew they probably couldn't hear him. Samantha! Was she safe? Could she possibly be safe? Were any of them safe?

The cannons kept booming, shaking the ship's timbers, but now a new sight and sound became evident. The sky was lighting like noon, and an ominous snapping and cracking could be heard above the shouting and gunfire. He knew that the pirates' main weapon—crude, perhaps, but effective—were stinkpots, big clay jars filled with gunpowder and inflammable oil, which they would catapult from their junks onto the barbarian clipper ships or merchantmen. Those were the flaming flares he had seen moments before, and they had done their work. The great sails of the *Sea Witch* were on fire!

"Let me out!" he kept yelling, banging his mess kit. He could hear the pirates now, yelling and shouting as they exchanged gunfire with the crew. He could even see some of them as they ran past the companionway above him. How many of them were there? he wondered.

He could see the roiling smoke of the sails now. Cries of "Man the pumps!" amid the gunfire. He saw the spray of water as part of the crew managed to start hosing down the flaming sails, but Justin wondered if it would be possible to save the ship.

A sinewy, half-naked Malay scrambled down the ladder, screaming. He was spattered with blood and carried a bamboo spear in one hand and an ominous kris in the other—a Malay sword with a wave-shaped blade.

Seeing Justin's face in the window of the cell door, he ran up to him and stared.

To Justin's amazement, he grinned. Tugging at his own black hair, he then pointed at Justin's red-gold hair that had grown to shoulder length during his imprisonment. Justin knew no Malay, but he intuited that the pirate thought his red hair was funny.

"Gnaw cee may kork yun," Justin said. *"Nay wooee kgong chung mun ma?"* "I am an American. Do you speak Cantonese?"

He thought there might be the off chance the pirate did, but he obviously didn't. He kept laughing for a moment. Then he raised his kris and banged it down on the cell door's lock, breaking it in two. He tugged open the door and beckoned Justin to come out, still grinning.

Justin came out of the cell, unsure whether the man was going to kill him or show him off as some sideshow freak. The pirate grabbed his left arm and shoved him toward the ladder, pointing upward.

Justin scrambled topside to see a scene of unparalleled confusion. The royals and skysails were ablaze, although the lower sails had been wetted down: they were still smoking and more than half burned, but their fires had been extinguished. The deck was swarming with Malay pirates, some still fighting with crew members. But there could be no doubt that the ship had been taken over: most of the crew were huddled on the quarterdeck surrounded by sweaty pirates armed with pistols, muskets, and spears, who were yelling at them. To Justin's amazement, the *Sea Witch* was surrounded by a dozen war junks. The *Sea Witch*'s crew had been outnumbered by at least four to one, which, combined with the element of surprise and the crippling effect of the fiery stinkpots, had offset the advantage of the clipper ship's superior gunnery.

"Justin!"

He turned to see Samantha coming out of the companionway leading to Officers' Country. Her hands were tied behind her back: behind her were two burly Malays who pushed her out onto the deck.

"Samantha!"

"They killed Captain Whale!" she cried with a sob. "They shot him in his cabin. . . ."

One of the pirates yelled at her and pushed her facedown on the deck.

"You bastard!" Justin cried, running toward them.

Something hit him on the back of his head, and everything went blank.

When he recovered consciousness, his head throbbing with pain from where the pirate had hit him, he found he was lying on a bunk in a small cabin, his wrists and ankles securely tied with hemp rope. It was daylight now, and he

THE MAGNIFICENT SAVAGES 77

managed to sit upright. The cabin was small, and judging from what he could see through the Chinese-style ports, it was at the stern of what he figured was one of the pirate war junks. He could see the junk was under way. The cabin had richly carved fretwork around the bulkheads, which were painted vermillion with gold trim. On the deck was a beautiful Chinese rug, and beneath the stern ports was a small, built-in altar, with joss sticks on top and a wooden statuette of Tien Mu Hou, the patron goddess of sailors.

The cabin door opened and a man came in. He was different from the Malays: Justin thought he was Chinese. He was dressed in a white shirt, with baggy black pants and high leather boots, the toes curled in the Manchu fashion. On his head was a pointed leather Manchu helmet. He was short and rather delicate-looking. Justin thought the man looked almost beautiful.

"Chur see der gnaw shurt nay lung kwong chung mun," the man said, and Justin realized from the voice that he was a she. *"Whyee sum mor?"* "The cook tells me you speak our language. Why?"

"Who are you?" Justin asked.

"My name is Madame Ching, and I am the master of this fleet."

"A woman pirate?" Justin gawked.

"Does that surprise you?"

"Yes."

She came closer to him. "My late husband was the great pirate Ching-yeh. When he was killed by the barbarians, I took over his fleet. My men have learned to respect me. *You* will learn to respect me, my pretty one."

Justin gulped. He was wearing nothing but his ragged trousers, his shirt and socks having been long since abandoned because of their stench. His skin was filthy, and he hadn't bathed in weeks so he stank to high heaven. His cheeks and chin were covered with fuzz that was quickly turning to whiskers, so he felt anything but "pretty." But Madame Ching was looking at him hungrily. "You haven't answered my question. Why do you speak our language?"

"I . . . I had an amah from Canton," he said. "She taught me."

"I see. The cook also told me you are the bastard son of the owner of the *Sea Witch.*"

"That's right. Where is the *Sea Witch?* Is it safe?"

Madame Ching put her hands on her slim hips and laughed.

"Oh, yes. It's very safe. No pirates will ever board it again, unless they can swim like fish. We removed the cargo, killed the crew, and sank it to the bottom of the China Sea."

Justin felt a pang pierce his chest. "You *sank* it? Why?"

"Why not? Now no one will ever know what happened to it except you and me and my crew."

"But why did you kill the crew?"

She shrugged. "They were of no value, and we would have to feed them. They're better off dead. Why were you being held prisoner?"

"Because of Captain Whale. He wanted to murder me. . . ."

"So what the miserable cook said about you was true: you are the bastard son, and your family wanted to get rid of you. That's perfectly understandable, like getting rid of an unwanted dog. But it's unfortunate for you, because you have no ransom value, like the missionaries."

Samantha! He tried to remain calm. "Where's Samantha?"

"Who?"

"Miss Aspinall, the missionaries' daughter."

"She and her ridiculous parents are on one of my junks. They'll be taken to the mainland where we'll hold them for ransom from the roundeyes. Make the cursed Christians cough up something besides that seditious gibberish from their Bibles."

"Then she's all right?" He sounded relieved.

Madame Ching's eyes narrowed.

"Do you care?" she asked.

"Of course I care!"

She leaned down close to his face. Her breath reeked, not unpleasantly, of cloves. "Do you like the roundeye girl?" she asked. "Do you find her pretty?"

Justin pushed back away from her into the cushions of the bunk. "Yes."

"Do you find her prettier than me?"

Again, Justin gulped.

"I . . . uh . . ."

She pulled off her peaked helmet and threw it on the deck. She shook out her long black hair, which fell over her shoulders. She ran one of her hands through it and gave him a sultry look. He figured she might be twenty.

"You're different," he said diplomatically.

She glared at him a moment, then straightened and laughed.

"A very wise answer," she said. "They say the barbarians are stupid and pig-headed, but I think you may be different yourself. I'm going to keep you for a while to be my toy, like the Emperor's Pekinese dogs. You can tell me about the life of the roundeyes. And then, when you become a man"—she smiled and chucked him under the chin—"which will be soon, judging from the cat fuzz on your face . . . I see why they call you barbarians the hairy ones . . . I think you'll fetch a fine price in the capital. I can think of several noble families in the court who would find it amusing to have a pretty roundeye as their slave."

Justin's eyes widened.

"Slave?" he said in wonderment. "I'm a *slave?*"

Madame Ching took a kris off the bulkhead and placed its blade against his throat. She smiled and said, "Yes, you're my slave. If I could get ransom from your family, that would be another matter. But since they have already tried to get rid of you, they obviously wouldn't pay a Mexican dollar for you. So you will be my slave till you're old enough to be sold. And meanwhile"—she put her lips close to his—"I will teach you all the refinements of the art of love. And if you continue to prefer this Samantha creature to me," she smiled and said simply, "I'll kill her."

PART TWO

BARBARIAN LOVE

9   SHE WAS ONLY FIVE FEET high, but when she put on her pearl- and stone-encrusted clogged shoes with their raised central wedge, she was five feet six. She was fifteen years old and well trained in the arts of cosmetics. Since she was a Manchu, and not Chinese, her feet had not been bound and were therefore normal, well shaped, and naturally small. The Manchus, who had swept down from Asia in 1644 and toppled the Chinese Ming Dynasty, had forbidden their women to bind their feet, but Lan Kuei (Little Orchid) secretly wished her feet had been bound. Even though the binding horribly deformed the foot, forcing highborn Chinese girls to hobble in the famous "Lily Walk," Chinese men found it maddeningly and irresistibly erotic. And Lan Kuei dreamed of reducing men to quivering jellies of desire.

She was destined to make men quiver, but not always from desire.

She was not a natural beauty, though her mother had trained her how to make the best of her looks. On this autumn day in 1851, she was attired in the finest robes her family could buy—or borrow, for her father, Hui-cheng, a Manchu minor noble of the Yehe Nara clan, was not rich. Lan Kuei lived with her father, mother, two brothers, and sister in a house in Pewter Lane, Hsi-la-hu-tung, a side street on the east side of Peking, and neither the house nor the neighborhood was particularly grand, though it was not far from the high, purple walls of the Imperial City. Her father was a government official, though not a powerful one.

But today, his future was perhaps brighter. For today, his daughter was to be taken to the Forbidden City, the home of the all-powerful Son of Heaven, the twenty-year-old Hsien-feng Emperor, perhaps to become one of his concubines. Hsien-feng's father, the Tao-Kuang Emperor, had died, embittered by his defeat by the barbarians during the Opium War. It was said the new Emperor was frail, but Lan Kuei didn't care. If she could become his concubine— and being summoned to the Forbidden City did not necessarily mean she would pass the various inspections—she might win his love, and then her future would be full of infinite possibilities.

But she knew the chances of this happening were slim. It was even possible she could be chosen as a concubine, yet never be called to the Emperor's bed—or even, for that matter, meet him. There were dozens of concubines in the Forbidden City, and once in they could never return home. Even when the Son of Heaven died, his concubines remained prisoners, living to an old age in the warrens of the imperial palace, forgotten relics of forgotten reigns. Lan Kuei knew she was throwing away the possibility of finding a rich and loving husband outside the Forbidden City. But she had no choice. In China, a daughter did what she was told. She had been one of sixty Manchu girls selected for possible service in the palace, and she must go.

As the imperial couriers rolled into Pewter Lane in their yellow carts, preceded by heralds, to take her to the Forbidden City, Lan Kuei knew she was taking the gamble of a lifetime, and the stakes were enormous.

She would either win the love of the Emperor, or die in obscurity.

Two hours later, sitting cross-legged in a sedan chair, she joined the procession of other would-be concubines, all of whom were carried across the gray-green moat into the Imperial City. It was a bright, cold day, the sky above Peking an intense autumnal blue, and the rectangular-shaped Imperial City seemed a magic place with its pavilions, gardens, and temples. Then the procession entered a side gate next to the T'ien An Men, the Gate of Heavenly Peace, which was the southern entrance of the palace. South was the direction of the sun, which was the source of the Emperor's celestial energy. Any city he entered, he did so through the southern gate. His throne in the Forbidden City faced south, and when he died the Emperor turned his face to the south. Conversely, the symbol of the Forbidden City was the North Star around which it seemed to the Chinese that the cosmos revolved. Somewhat confusingly, the North Star was the homophone of the character for "purple," which was the color of the walls of the Forbidden City.

Inside the purple walls, the Forbidden City was a serene expanse of the white Yunning marble and yellow-tile-roofed vermillion pavilions, each set on its own raised marble terrace surrounded by graceful carved marble balustrades. The procession crossed one of the five parallel white marble bridges arching the bow-shaped Golden Stream that snaked across the cobble courtyards. Lan Kuei drank all this splendor in with thirsty eyes; for her and the other girls, this was the center of the universe.

The procession was taken to the Nei Wu Fu, the offices of the Imperial Household Department, where they waited for the Empress Dowager to arrive, accompanied by the Chief Eunuch. For the prospective concubines would be inspected not by the Emperor, whose sexual appetites they would presumably whet and satisfy, but rather by his stepmother and a man whose sexual organs had been cut off by a knife at the age of twelve.

The Emperor himself was not even in the Forbidden City. He and his cousin, Prince I, accompanied by bodyguards and all in disguise, had spent the past twelve hours in an opium den in the Tartar City in the north of Peking, smoking opium pipes and watching pornographic peep shows.

There were several good reasons why the power of the once-mighty Ch'ing Emperors was seriously on the wane. And why absolute power in the final decades of the Chinese Empire would be wielded by a person alternately reviled and revered by the Chinese: a woman. Namely, the Dowager Empress Tz'u-hsi, who on the autumn day in 1851 was still known as Lan Kuei. Yet, for the next twenty years she would be known by her other name, Yehenala.

1 0   "BUT, MOMMA, I DON'T *WANT* to marry Mr. Partridge!" Samantha exclaimed angrily. "I've told you that a hundred times! I'm not in love with him, I don't like his name—he sounds more like a bird than a man—and I'm in love with Justin Savage!"

Edwina Aspinall threw up her hands.

"My stars, Samantha, why can't you get it through your head that Justin is dead and has been for five years?"

Samantha, who was now seventeen and had blossomed into a stunning beauty, stamped her foot.

"He's *not* dead! At least, no one knows for sure. And until someone can prove to me what happened to him, I'm not going to marry anyone else. Especially Mr. Percy Partridge who, among other things, has bad breath!"

Her mother groaned. They were in the living room of their comfortable bungalow in the American "concession" of Shanghai across Soochow Creek from the British concession. Madame Ching had put a ransom of ten thousand Mexican silver dollars, a favorite international currency, on the Aspinall family after she had captured and sunk the *Sea Witch*. While she held them in surprisingly pleasant conditions in one of her secret hideouts on the mainland, the French, British, and especially the Americans railed against the Imperial Chinese authorities over this "outrageous" kidnapping. The authorities, in the person of the Viceroy of the Two Provinces, Prince I, a cousin of the Emperor, listened to their complaints politely and publicly decried the "heinous deeds" of the Chinese and Malay pirates. But privately, the Viceroy had been pleased, because any attack on the hated barbarians was agreeable to him. Besides, he knew Madame Ching well and was "on the take." Unbeknownst to the barbarians, Prince I would receive a healthy five percent of the Aspinall ransom money, as he received five percent of all Madame Ching's earnings, which were considerable. This was how the female pirate operated without fear of interference from the imperial authorities: she bought them off with "squeeze"—i.e. bribes—that was more than a way of life in China. Squeeze was the way the entire corrupt imperial system worked.

The various European and American missionaries in China pooled their resources to pay the ransom (they were later paid back by the Episcopal Bishop in Boston) so that the Aspinalls were released unharmed after a mere three weeks and taken by boat to Canton. There, Samantha had desperately tried to find out what had happened to her beloved Justin. But none of her kidnappers, or no one else in Canton for that matter, knew anything or, if they knew, were too afraid of the wrath of Madame Ching to tell. The Episcopal authorities, worried about the possibility of another attack on the Aspinalls, moved them up the coast from Canton to Shanghai.

Shanghai was already becoming known as a "sin city." It wasn't as fashionable as nearby Soochow, with its lovely canals; nor was it as important a commercial center as Canton. But it was rapidly catching up because of its situation near the mouth of the mighty Yangtze River, making it a natural gateway to the interior of China. After the first Opium War, the imperial authorities had been pressed into granting "concessions" to the British and later the French and Americans, the "concessions" being grants of land along the Huangpu River and Soochow Creek. And it was here that the Aspinalls spent the next five years mingling socially with the growing foreign colony, dominated by the British, Samantha finishing her education in a private school run by a Madame Dulage from Paris, clinging desperately to her hope that one day she would hear news about Justin.

But as the years passed, her hopes began to seem like a dream. And to her mother, they began to take on the uglier aspects of an obsession.

"Samantha, you're behaving in an impossible manner—certainly not for the first time," her mother returned to the attack. "Mr. Partridge is an eminently desirable catch for you. He has a brilliant future in the English diplomatic service, his uncle is an earl, he's rich and quite good-looking, and he's mad for you. He has asked your father permission to make you an honorable proposal, and we will both be highly displeased if you say no to him."

"But don't you understand? I don't love him!"

"Piffle and tosh. You don't know what love is."

"I *do!* Love is what I feel for Justin—I felt it practically the first time I saw him back in New York!"

"Dear child, Justin is dead!"

"He's not! Oh, I'm so miserable. . . ."

Samantha sank into one of the overstuffed chairs her father had imported from America and began to sob. Her mother came over and stroked her hair.

"If Justin were alive," she said more softly, "don't you think somehow he would have gotten word to us?"

"Maybe he can't. Maybe he's a prisoner somewhere. . . ."

"But that's unlikely. Dearest Samantha, I know how you loved him, but you can't throw away your life loving a ghost. You must be practical. Mr. Partridge is a fine young man who is devoted to you and who will give you a rich, full life. Please try to open your mind and give him a chance to prove his love."

Samantha wiped her eyes and sighed.

"All right, I'll think about it," she said. "When is he planning to propose to me?"

"Tonight at the ball at Government House. You have your beautiful new ivory silk gown to wear, and I know you're going to be the most beautiful girl at the ball."

"In Shanghai, that's not saying much."

"You're aware, of course, that Mr. Partridge is about to be reassigned to the British Embassy at Paris? His uncle, Lord Saxmundham, is arranging it through the Foreign Office, where he has a great deal of influence. I know you don't like Shanghai, and it does have a miserable climate, I agree. But just think, my dear: Paris! What a brilliant future could lie before you if you just said one little word: 'yes'!"

Edwina clasped her hands and a rhapsodic look came over her plump face. Edwina was no snob, being the plain-living wife of a New England missionary. But when Mr. Partridge started showing unmistakable signs of infatuation with Samantha, she found her mind wandering while her husband, Reverend Aspinall, gave his nightly readings from the Good Book. It was common knowledge around the close-knit Foreign Settlement in Shanghai that Percival Montague Marmaduke Partridge, who was twenty-six, was the heir to the Earldom of Saxmundham; his uncle, the present Earl, being a confirmed bachelor. With the earldom came fifteen thousand acres of rich Suffolk farmland and the rent roll of several blocks of expensive real estate in the West End of London. Plus a stately home near the sea and Saxmundham House on Saxmundham Square in London. Percy Partridge was almost ostentatiously eligible, and the thought that her daughter, Samantha, might one day be an English countess had erased whatever foolish resentment Edwina might still harbor against the Red-coats her grandfather had fought during the American Revolution. After all, it was 1855, the great Victorian Empire was blazing toward its zenith, the En-glish were beating the Russians in the Crimea and picking up colonies all over the globe with such speed that Lord Palmerston, the Foreign Secretary, had complained about "having to look the damned places up on the map." What could any good, red-blooded, democratic American mother desire more for her daughter than a titled English husband? If *only* Samantha would cooperate and forget Justin who was, after all, an illegitimate son!

She reminded herself to hint gracefully to Mr. Partridge that it might be a good idea to sweeten his breath that night by gargling with eau de cologne.

As for Samantha, she had to admit that the thought of Paris was alluring. She found Shanghai tedious, the climate was horrible, and all of China was in an uproar, seething with rebellion against the Manchus who, in turn, were fu-rious at the westerners.

Perhaps, she mused, Percy Partridge wasn't *all* that bad. They had met at a reception at Government House, which was the slightly pretentious name given the home of the British Consul, Thomas Taylor Meadows, a noted China ex-pert and Percy's superior. They had seen more of each other at teas and at the racetrack, which had been one of the first structures the British had put up in Shanghai and which was the center of social life for the small Foreign Settle-ment. Percy had asked to take Samantha riding in his two-seated gig, for the center of the racetrack was used as a private "Rotten Row" when the track was not in use, and Samantha had accepted. Percy seemed nice, and she had to admit he was good-looking. Not anywhere near as handsome as Justin, of course. But still . . . not bad.

Justin! Was her mother right? Was he dead after all? She remembered the last time she had seen him, when that terrible Malay pirate had hit him over the head with the belaying pin. Had they thrown him into the shark-infested sea as they had thrown the rest of the *Sea Witch*'s crew?

Perhaps the question was not whether Justin was alive, but rather: how, after five years, could he possibly not be dead?

"May I have the pleasure of the opening quadrille, Miss Aspinall?" asked Percy that night at Government House.

"I would be delighted, Mr. Partridge," Samantha answered, giving him her gloved hand and standing up. Tonight, she was looking at him in a different, more searching light. After all, the man was going to propose to her. She had better begin looking beneath the surface, and admittedly the surface was pleasing. Percy was tall, thin, and elegant with thick, curly blond hair. He had big blue eyes rather like a cocker spaniel begging to be liked. For a man destined to inherit a fortune, he wasn't in the least overbearing like so many of the Europeans she had met in the Foreign Settlement. In fact, the only unpleasant thing she had noticed about him so far was his condescending attitude toward the "natives," but then this was something shared by all the whites in Shanghai, most of the Americans included. The Aspinalls were different in that Reverend Ward Aspinall had inculcated into his wife and daughter the conviction that all human beings were "God's children" and therefore equal. Which was why the Aspinalls were confirmed Abolitionists and why Samantha, even though she disliked Shanghai, had come to love the Chinese people she came in contact with.

Samantha was looking ravishing in her new ivory ball gown Madame Dulage had created, using out-of-date fashion magazines from Paris as her inspiration and Chinese seamstresses as her expert fingers. Madame Dulage not only ran her private school, but had a thriving dress business on the side, an immense success with the shopping-starved ladies of the Foreign Settlement. The dress had a full skirt with three layers of lace flounces and off-the-shoulder sleeves that her mother thought were too "daring" but which Madame Dulage had assured her were *comme il faut* in Paris. In her hair she wore little sprigs of white flowers. Percy's heart was thumping as he led her onto the dance floor and began the quadrille, the music being played by the local military band of the British forces in China, commanded by General Sir John Michel. Samantha went through the elaborate "positions" of the quadrille, which was an ancestor of the Virginia reel; but she thought the ancient dance a bit of a bore and longed for a waltz, which even now had a slightly "racy" reputation. Government House was a large, two-story bungalow facing both the Huangpu River and Soochow Creek. The so-called ballroom did hold a few appurtenances of the imperial style: a life-size oil portrait of Queen Victoria at one end of the room and a crystal chandelier. But otherwise, the room was rather plain, and the dance floor couldn't hold more than a dozen couples at a time.

Finally, the quadrille ended and the band struck up a waltz. Percy took her in his arms and began twirling her: she had to admit he was a good dancer. Part of the "racy" reputation of the waltz was that it allowed couples to dance intimately and, if so inclined, to converse—which was impossible in the more formal gyrations of the quadrilles and minuets. Now Percy took the opportunity of this intimacy to ask: "Miss Aspinall, might I take the liberty of calling you Samantha?"

She wanted to giggle: the stuffy formality of the British was amusing to her, an American.

"I thought you'd never ask, Percy. I *may* call you Percy?"

"Oh, yes, please, I say, your dress is an absolute stunner."

"Why, thank you."

"I hope my breath isn't offensive to you? Your mother suggested I gargle with eau de cologne, which I did. I know it's the cigars I occasionally smoke that give it an unpleasant odor, but I'd be more than glad to give cigars up for good, if that would please you."

Mother! I could kill her! Samantha thought. But his breath *is* sweet tonight. I wonder what being the Countess of Saxmundham would be like? It does have a nice ring to it. Of course, the English put so much importance on their silly titles, but . . . And, after all, Justin is dead.

Isn't he?

"We received a dispatch from Lord Palmerston, the Foreign Secretary, today," Percy went on. "He says the time may come soon when we'll have to teach the Chinese a lesson. The cheeky beggars in Peking aren't living up to their treaty obligations. Of course, what can one expect from heathens?"

"We must remember that they think of us as barbarians," Samantha said, remembering when Justin had told her on the *Sea Witch*. Justin! Am I betraying him? But he's dead. . . .

"Yes, I know. It's a bit of a joke, isn't it? You know, the T'ien Wang, or so-called 'Heavenly King,' has the cheek to call himself the brother of Jesus Christ! He obviously is a madman, but his rebel army, they say, is posing a great threat to the Manchus in Peking. The Heavenly King might even pose a threat to Shanghai one day. It might come to be rather dangerous here."

"Yes, Papa had become quite nervous lately. He talks of sending Mama and me to Canton for our safety's sake, which of course neither of us would do."

"Would you come to Paris with me? Paris and Saxmundham Castle?"

She looked at him with surprise.

"Why, Percy, whatever are you talking about?"

"Please . . . would you come out to the veranda with me for a moment?"

Dear God, he's going to propose to me! . . . Now.

"All right. It *is* a bit warm in here."

He took her hand and practically tugged her through the open doors onto the terrace overlooking the Huangpu River. On the other side, a few lights burned in Pootung, before which a number of junks were berthed, bobbing in the water. He led her to the balustrade and took both her hands.

"I haven't been exactly truthful with you," he began. "The fact is, I am engaged to Lady Hermione Fawn, a neighbor of my uncle's in Suffolk, someone I've known since childhood. We became betrothed before I came out to China. But the fuh-fact is . . . excuse me, I used to have a terrible stammer when I was a boy, and when I become excited, as I am now, sometimes it comes back. . . . Where was I? Oh, yes, the fact is that since I met you, my dearest Samantha, if I may be so bold as to address you in such an intimate fashion, I haven't given one thought to Hermione. For all my thoughts have been of you. I wish I were better at expressing myself in a romantic way, like the blasted French, but . . . what I'm trying to say is, this morning I sent a letter to Hermione breaking off our engagement. I told her I had met the sweetest angel in the world who has captured my heart. Dearest Samantha, that angel is you."

"Percy, please . . . we hardly know each other. . . ."

"Let me finish. You know that Shanghai is dangerous. I'm sailing Wednesday next for London, and then, after the new year, I'm to be posted to the embassy in Paris. Nothing would please me more than to have you at my side as my beautiful bride." He raised her hands to his lips and kissed her gloves. His eyes implored her like a puppy. "Say yes, Samantha. Please say yes. Fill my heart with happiness as I vow I shall try to fill yours."

She looked at him, thinking . . . if only he were Justin!

But Justin is dead. . . .

The twelve Chinese prisoners, stripped to the waist, were marched into the Field of Executions outside Canton by the troop of Bannermen. Each criminal wore a *cangue* around his neck, a square wooden stock in which his hands were locked. Each wore on his back a placard on which his crime had been painted: in ten cases, the crime was piracy. A crowd of Cantonese surrounded the field, the men, women, and children giggling at the plight of the condemned, most of them hawking and spitting in the hot sunlight: the Chinese propensity for spitting being one thing the "foreign devils" found so revolting about the residents of the Celestial Kingdom.

The Bannerman Captain shouted an order, and the *cangues* were unlocked and removed from the prisoners' necks. Then the twelve men were lined up in two rows of six each and forced to their knees.

A man carrying a heavy sword appeared from the crowd and walked toward the condemned. He was the imperial executioner. His imminent victims eyed him with looks of terror tempered with resignation.

Now the crowd became silent, even the hawking and spitting stopped. To the rear of the crowd, a man stepped out of a rickshaw pulled by a sweating coolie. Though the man wore a black silk long-gown embossed with gold *fu,* prosperity, ideograms, he was not Chinese. He was a foreign devil with tanned skin and red-gold hair beneath a round black hat. Being taller than the Chinese by almost a foot, he could watch what was happening on the Field of Executions

over the heads of the spectators. The Bannerman Captain spotted him and muttered to his lieutenant: "It's the white pirate. He should be kneeling with these
poor devils, but the Viceroy protects him." And he spat on the ground.

Three of the Bannermen grabbed the first of the condemned, two pulling his
arms behind him, the third grabbing his pigtail and forcing his head down and
forward, exposing the nape of his sweating neck.

The executioner stepped up and raised his sword above his head with both
hands. Its blade flashed in the sun.

"The prisoners in the back row," the Bannerman Captain announced in a loud
voice, "will have the privilege of seeing how cleanly the executioner's sword
cuts off the heads of the prisoners in the front row. You all have been condemned to death by the Son of Heaven for your miserable crimes, but the Emperor does not lack compassion. You will see that your deaths will be swift
and painless. Proceed with the executions."

As the crowd watched in silence, the executioner's sword swung down,
neatly lopping off the head of the first condemned. Blood squirted from the
trunk as it collapsed to the ground. The Bannerman holding the head by its
queue now held it up in the air and swung it around like a ball on a chain as
the decapitated trunk jerked like a fish out of water. Then it lay still.

The executioner moved on to the second of the condemned and raised his
bloody sword again.

But Justin Savage had seen enough. He climbed back in the rickshaw and
told the coolie, "Take me to Pink Jade Road."

The coolie picked up the shafts of his rickshaw and began the run back into
Canton. Justin had seen many executions in the past five years, but repetition
had not dulled their gruesomeness. He felt sick to his stomach. Like the Bannerman Captain, Justin knew that if it weren't for the squeeze Chang-mei—
for such was Madame Ching's name—paid the Viceroy, he might well have
been one of those miserable pirates kneeling on the ground waiting for the executioner's sword to dispatch him to the next world. True, Justin did not consider himself a pirate; all he did was steer Chang-mei's war junk, and he had
never taken part in the attacks on the other ships. But without the protection of
the Viceroy, Prince I, he knew that the imperial authorities would laugh at his
fine distinction.

Now the coolie ran the rickshaw through the gate of the Chinese City and
Justin entered the dirty, smelly, but fascinating world he had called home for
the past five years. The sandals of the rickshaw coolie slapped on the cobblestones of the narrow street lined with vegetable stalls and dark, cavelike shops.
Open drains and stagnant canals with liverish water stank with refuse, but Justin
was used to the smells. He had come to enjoy the humanity that thronged the

streets and rutted alleys of Canton, the coolies with their long, jiggling bamboo carrying poles, the women bent over with their heavy loads on their backs, the ubiquitous peddlers hawking their wares—fresh crabs, sprouting beans, iced bitter-prune soup, almond tea—the playing children, the hungry dogs, the whining beggars holding up their deformed babies to try to shame coins from the passersby, playing on the guilt of the better off. They were professional beggars, Justin knew, but some of them were so pitiful he could hardly not give them money. One man, both legs cut off above the knees, their stumps covered with leather patches, could only maneuver himself by his arms, dragging his mutilated body behind him. Justin had seen him many times and knew he would receive no thanks for his money. But he tossed him a Mexican silver dollar anyway, which the beggar grabbed with the speed of a cormorant diving into the sea for a fish. Justin might not be as rich as Chang-mei or Prince I—far from it. But compared to the wretched poor of Canton, he was Croesus.

The rickshaw turned into Pink Jade Road, one of the better *hutungs* of the city.

"The house at the end of the lane," Justin ordered.

Although he had first been appalled at the sight of human beings playing the same role as horses did in western society, he had become used to it. He knew that if some benevolent Manchu official—almost an oxymoron—were to banish rickshaws on humanitarian grounds, literally millions of Chinese would be thrown out of work and reduced to starvation. Rickshaw coolies might not be "nice" in western terms, but the profession was preferable to death.

The panting coolie pulled up at a high brick wall at the end of the street and Justin climbed out, paying the man two Mexican dollars, tip included. Then he walked to the round moon gate in the wall. This was the *cha-lan-men,* or barrier gate, made of solid wood painted a faded rose color. Justin entered through one half of the double gate, coming into a tiny court where there was a second wall with another gate. He went through that into a courtyard, first stepping around a wooden "devil screen" put up to keep out bad spirits. As Justin had become used to the smells of Canton, the brutality of the Manchus, the beggars and rickshaw coolies, he had also become used to the incredibly complicated maze of Chinese superstitions. The Chinese enjoyed one of the most ancient civilizations on earth that was, in many ways, also the most refined. But when it came to their endless devils, demons and dragons, the Chinese were almost like children. Not that Justin looked down upon them, as most foreign devils did. He was a "guest man," which was the courteous way the Chinese referred to foreigners. And as a guest man, he respected the manners of the country. More than respect: with time he had come to take pleasure in the parade of Chinese life: the feast days, the colorful processions with their banging firecrackers, the endless intricacies of "face" and "squeeze." He came to know the paradoxes of the Chinese character: their sensitiveness and their crass materialism; their awareness of beauty and their greed; their immense courtesy, and yet their unfailing conviction, shared by the most wretched coolie in rags, of the innate superiority of the Chinese over the rest of the world.

Justin came round the devil screen into a lovely courtyard, dominated by a big linden tree, a lotus pond, and around all four sides big earthen pots planted with oleanders, pomegranates, flowers, and fig trees. The main house faced south, as did all proper Chinese dwellings, with two pavilions on the east and west side, one housing the servants and the other the kitchen. These constituted three sides of the courtyard, with the second, inner, brick wall providing the fourth, this wall on the inside being covered with white plaster. The courtyard was the focal point of the house, and the arched veranda that ran along the front of the main house was where Justin had spent many a pleasant evening sitting and watching the moon rise over the gently sloping tile roofs of the house and then over the branches of the linden tree. It was during these moments that the serenity of Chinese life seemed sweetest, and he could almost forget the hustle of his former life in New York. But he never completely forgot. Sylvaner was as firmly lodged in his memory as a tumor, never to be dislodged until accounts were settled. And although he had not personally enriched himself, already in these past five years Justin had begun to even the score with his half brother.

He started across the courtyard toward the veranda of the main house, where he was met by Ah Ling, his newly hired baby amah.

"How is my wife?" he asked, taking off his black hat and handing it to her.

"Tai-tai is feeding the baby," Ah Ling replied, *Tai-tai* meaning "madame." The baby amah bowed as she took the hat and yet again marveled at the hair of the tall foreign devil. Ah Ling still found it hard to believe that men could have blue eyes and red hair and white skin that turned brown from the sun. Although the house had a bathing chamber, sometimes on hot days Justin bathed himself in the courtyard. She had seen him and, again, could hardly believe that foreign devils had hair on their chests and legs, and penises that seemed absurdly long. But she accepted these facts as part of the mysterious divine scheme of things, secure in the knowledge that she was superior to her barbarian master. And yet, she had to admit that, for a barbarian, Justin was extremely gentle and kind. And she knew that her mistress found him, strange as he looked, irresistibly handsome.

But of course, Madame Ching was different in almost every way. A genuine heroine to the poor of China for her amazing career as a pirate, she shocked and infuriated the rich—particularly the rich men—by her flaunting of all the traditional Chinese values. Women were definitely subordinate to men; but Madame Ching had not only had a career—something unheard of in China— she had made millions at it. Half the time, she even dressed like a man. Madame Ching made her own rules, which was a dangerous game to play in China.

Thus, when Madame Ching's "toy" barbarian, Justin, had matured and she had taken him on as her lover, no one was surprised: besides, what decent Chinese man could possibly want someone so wildly unconventional? What had caused a good deal of gossip, though, was when, one month before, Madame Ching had actually married the foreign devil in a Buddhist ceremony in Saigon. And then, a few weeks later, Chang-mei had given birth to a baby girl. True, the mother had been severely disappointed. But to Ah Ling's surprise, Justin had been delighted and was as much in love with the child as if she had been a son. Ah Ling wrote this off as another peculiarity of the foreign devils. The rivers and canals of China were filled with the bloated bodies of unwanted girl babies. The Chinese peasants wanted sons to help them in their endless struggle to make a living.

"And how is Julie?" Justin asked. Julie was the name Chang-mei had given the child, taking the name from a hat shop in Canton that she liked called "Miss Julie." Ah Ling also knew that Chang-mei was not taking to motherhood, that she was restless and unhappy and was already voicing doubts about the wisdom of having a child by a foreign devil.

"The first-born is fine," the baby amah said.

"But I can hear her bawling. Is something wrong?"

"No, Master. *Tai-tai* is breast-feeding her. It will be her last day. I have found a wet nurse."

"Good."

Justin went into the combination living-dining room of the house with its brick floor covered with matting, its potbellied brass Chinese stove and its handsome furniture made of hardwood so dense it was said to sink in water. Beautifully traceried windows admitted light to the airy room. He crossed the room to the bedroom door, opening it and going inside. There, his wife lay on her *k'ang* beneath which, in cold weather, a fire could be lit to warm the room. Now, beneath the bed lay a knife to frighten away bad spirits—a precaution Ah Ling had pooh-poohed on the grounds that bad spirits would never be interested in harming a useless girl baby. On the thin straw mattress that Justin had never grown used to lay his wife, holding Julie at her breast. By the system of counting used by the Chinese, the baby had been one year old the day she was born. Justin came to the bed and smiled at his bawling daughter.

"Hello, firstborn," he said, leaning down to kiss the top of her head. "And how's my beautiful bride?"

"How do you expect?" said Chang-mei. "Bored. Thank heavens Ah Ling has found me a wet nurse for this half-breed girl child."

"You know, Chang-mei, you're a wonderful pirate, but you're turning out to be a rotten mother."

"I didn't want the child! *You* were the one who wanted her. I should have gone to the old ladies in Willow Lane and gotten rid of it—and I certainly would have if I'd known it was going to be a girl. Ah Ling!" she yelled. The baby amah appeared in the doorway. "Take Julie." She removed her nipple from the baby's mouth and handed Julie to the amah, who took her out of the room.

"I don't understand you," Justin said. "I don't understand how you can't love your own child."

"Love! There's that word again! You're always talking about love, and I don't even know what it means. You barbarians are so strange! In China, a man doesn't have time to 'love' his wife. He can't afford to."

"Don't you love me?"

"I desire you. I enjoy you—at times. At other times, you annoy me. I don't know if I love you because I don't know what your 'love' is. You say in America young men fall in love with young women, but they can't touch each other so they 'love' each other instead—it doesn't make any sense to me. I think you're all crazy. Do you 'love' me?"

"Of course—I'm your husband."

"When I captured the *Sea Witch,* you were in love with the missionary's daughter—what was her strange name, Samantha?"

"Yes, I was. But I'll never see her again, because if I go home, they'll hang me as a pirate."

Chang-mei laughed. "So much for love. I don't think I'll ever understand you. Why was it so important to you that we got married?"

"I told you: I didn't want my child to be illegitimate, like I was."

"My poor Justin. You're worse than one of the roundeye missionaries, trying to bring 'Christian' virtues to China. What a foolish waste of time. Anyway, my red-haired lover, if it makes you feel better to hear me say it, then I will: I love you. Now sit down and tell me the news."

She spread her beautiful black hair over the hard porcelain pillow—another Chinese custom Justin had never quite grown used to—as he sat on the edge of the *k'ang.*

"The *Sea Goddess* is on its way to Canton from Bombay. The word is that it's Sylvaner's last voyage under sail, and the ship is carrying over two million dollars' worth of opium."

Chang-mei's dark eyes lit up.

"Then we'll take it!" she exclaimed. "Two million—that will be our biggest take this year!"

Justin didn't answer for a moment. In his heart, he had mixed emotions. The *Sea Goddess* was a thing of beauty, as the *Sea Witch* had been and the four other Savage Line clipper ships he and Chang-mei had attacked in the past five years, along with innumerable other European and American ships. It went against Justin's grain to attack these beautiful creations, even though they carried cargoes of opium. But he had made a deal with Chang-mei. He would captain the *Eastern Dragon,* the flagship of her present fleet of fourteen war junks, thus giving her the use of his expert seamanship and knowledge of European and American thinking—of invaluable aid to her. But he would remain a noncombatant. And there was one other condition: she could not murder the crews of the captured ships. Chang-mei had raged against this stipulation, because sparing the crews meant letting them spread the word to the European authorities about who had attacked them, whereas sinking the ships and murdering the crews conveniently ensured the silence of a watery grave. But Justin remembered Mr. Starbuck and Jimmy Chen and his other friends on the *Sea Witch* who had gone to their deaths. Justin would go along with confiscating the opium cargoes, especially the ones of the Savage Line ships. But he would not condone murder.

Chang-mei had finally given in to him because despite the fact that Chang-mei pooh-poohed the idea of "love," Justin suspected she was more in love with him than she knew. With motherhood, Chang-mei had been forcibly retired from pirating, and Justin was hoping she would never go back. After all, Chang-mei was now one of the richest women in China, for piracy paid. By selling the opium she stole from the clipper ships, she had piled up an immense fortune, always being careful to pay off Prince I, Viceroy of the Two Provinces. She had told Justin she had over seven million dollars in silver in the vaults of a bank in Macao. Even though the money wasn't Justin's—and Chang-mei was as tightfisted as Scrooge—it gave him satisfaction anyway, because at least half of those millions were Sylvaner's.

But the birth of Julie was changing everything. Perhaps it was time to get out of the piracy racket entirely. He had even toyed with the idea of not telling Chang-mei about the *Sea Goddess,* but he knew she would have found out eventually. And now, the old look of excitement and greed in her eyes was back.

"Maybe we shouldn't take it," he finally said.

"Are you mad? Two million dollars?"

"You're in no condition to go back to sea."

"I'm as strong as a water buffalo. And now that I have a wet nurse, I can get out of this damned bed and have some fun."

"I saw the executions a while ago. Ten pirates had their heads chopped off. You know there's only one man standing between us and the Field of Executions."

"Of course. Prince I. I've paid him millions. Why would he ever withdraw his protection? You're talking like an old woman. I'm going to get dressed, then we'll go down to the ship and start buying stores. I'm ready for a little action."

She got up.

"We're making a mistake," Justin said.

She removed her white robe, exposing her beautiful naked body. As wild as Chang-mei was, Justin never tired of looking at her firm breasts, her tiny waist, and her extraordinary legs. She blew him a kiss.

"You let *me* run the business," she said. "You say this is Sylvaner's last run under sail? Well then, maybe this *will* be our last job—at least until we can buy a steamer. You certainly couldn't resist this one last time to steal your half brother's opium? And then maybe we'll talk about retiring."

"Uh-huh. Until you can buy a steamer."

She laughed as she came over to kiss him.

"You Americans are so funny, always worrying. Why don't you admit you've had the time of your life these past five years being a pirate with me?"

"I'm no pirate."

"Oh, yes, I forgot. You just steer the junk. Well, anyway, my husband with the fire between the legs, we'll retire temporarily, at least. That I'll guarantee you. So stop worrying. And meanwhile, we'll have one final fling. Two million dollars! I can hardly wait!"

"There it is!" Chang-mei said three nights later as she stood next to Justin who was manning the steering oar of the *Eastern Dragon*. "The *Sea Goddess!* She's a beauty."

It was one A.M., the hour of the rat. Though they preferred operating in darkness, tonight there was a full moon that had just come out from behind clouds, turning the China Sea into a mass of shimmering silver and revealing the three-masted clipper ship on the horizon.

"She's low in the water," Justin said. "It's the opium. Sylvaner's so greedy, he's sacrificed his greatest asset, his speed."

"We'll take his opium and give him back his speed," Chang-mei said cheerfully. "Bring us five degrees to port."

Justin pushed the oar, which was attached to a mammoth teak rudder, so big that there were four diamond-shaped holes in it to allow some water through, else it would have been impossible to move. The big junk turned to port. It was then Chang-mei saw the clipper ship also turn to port. "They've spotted us! Give the signal to fire!"

"But, *Tuan,*" said Paou, her Malay first mate, "we're not close enough for the stinkpots." Paou was a wiry man, a fisherman's son who had been picked up at sea while fishing by Ching-yeh, Chang-mei's first husband.

"I don't mean the stinkpots, you idiot! I mean the Forest guns. Commence firing!"

While Justin had remained a noncombatant, he had strongly recommended to Chang-mei that she use some of her immense profits to buy up-to-date guns for the junks. She had agreed and bought a number of quick-firing Forest guns from an arms dealer in Macao. Justin had assured her the Forest guns were at least the equal of Sylvaner's on the *Sea Goddess.* Now the junk trembled as the bow gun fired, the other junks beginning to fire also. The junks had an advantage over the clipper ships in that their guns were placed in the bows while the clipper ships had to come broadside to fire. Thus Chang-mei had a brief advantage while the *Sea Goddess* was turning.

The bow guns roared over and over again. Now the *Sea Goddess* fired. There was a strong southwest wind, and the junks were closing rapidly on the clipper ship. The *Sea Goddess*'s fire missed the flotilla of junks, but one of the junks' balls hit the mizzenmast of the *Sea Goddess.*

"A hit!" Chang-mei yelled. "A hit!"

The *Sea Goddess* stopped firing. One dividend from Justin's insistence that Chang-mei not murder the crews was that ships tended not to fight when they saw the fourteen junks descending on them, preferring to give up the cargoes rather than fighting against such overwhelming odds. Now the crew of the *Eastern Dragon* began cheering as Chang-mei gave the order to cease fire. "They're giving up!" she cried, throwing her arms around Justin and kissing him. "We've done it again!"

"You've done it," he said, laughing.

"But it was you who told me to buy the guns! Aiyee, will we celebrate when we get back to Canton! Two million! Maybe even that fat snob, Prince I, will condescend to invite me to his palace."

Justin didn't say anything, because he doubted that would ever happen. To the Chinese, wives were chattel, not considered worthy to dine with or mingle socially with men. The Viceroy might be a scoundrel, but he was rigidly conservative in terms of traditional Chinese mores. He would never invite Chang-mei to his palace, a fact she knew and gnawed like a bone. Chang-mei, the daughter of a farmer who had run away to sea when she was fourteen, was a rebel hell-bent on turning upside down the traditional male-dominated Chinese society. That she had succeeded as a pirate—the only path open to Chinese women with the exception of concubinage—was a testimony to her strength of character. But the Viceroy would never ask her to dine. It was a fact that chagrined Justin as much as his wife. Chinese attitudes toward women were one aspect of the Celestial Kingdom Justin definitely did not admire.

The Captain of the *Sea Goddess* stood on the quarterdeck of his beautiful ship watching the war junks approach. "Damned pirates," he said to his first mate, who was supervising the cutting away of the mizzenmast. "Mr. Savage is going to be fit to be tied when he hears of this. Every one of his ships has been taken. It's almost as if it's a goddamned plot against the Savage Line."

It was then he spotted the handsome young couple on the deck of the *Eastern Dragon*. He wondered what in the world a white man was doing on board a pirate war junk in the China Sea.

During her first few years in the Forbidden City, Yehenala, the former Lan Kuei from Pewter Lane, was ignored by the other concubines, who considered themselves better born than the daughter of the minor Manchu official who had never achieved any higher government rank than that of *taotai*. Even more discouraging, she was never summoned to the Emperor's bed by the Chief Eunuch, who wielded immense power in the palace and, like all eunuchs, wore an orange and green robe embroidered with the five-clawed imperial dragon, indicating he was one of His Majesty's personal attendants. Yehenala began to despair of winning the great gamble and to fear that she would end up a toothless old lady haunting the minor pavilions of the palace.

Nor was she invited to join in the simple pleasures of the harem. These consisted chiefly of inspecting fabrics for gowns brought to the palace by the eunuchs: shopping. And playing games devised by the ubiquitous eunuchs, who were called "crows" behind their backs by the tittering concubines because of their high-pitched voices. (The eunuchs were extremely sensitive about their unusual physical condition. The sight of a teapot with a broken stem could send them into hysterics.)

Yehenala might not have been having much fun, but she was smart enough not to waste her time. The Forbidden City had well-stocked libraries of ancient scrolls and fabulous collections of art. She practiced calligraphy and learned about art, refining her tastes. She studied the histories of the Twenty-four Dynasties and read the *Analects* of Confucius and the writings of Mencius.

She began to understand the philosophical underpinnings of Chinese society, which was so incomprehensible to most of the barbarian missionaries. The agnostic universe of Confucius was one that was based on harmony and order, the same harmony that kept the planets moving around the sun. China was, theoretically, one big harmonious family, each individual family based on the concept of ancestor worship and the paying of filial respect to the parents. The family, in turn, paid homage to the Emperor, who was the focus of all authority. Yehenala could understand how the concept of Christianity being proselytized by the western missionaries with its ideas of individual liberty and free will and its, to Chinese, incredible story of God's son being raised from the dead was so diametrically opposed to the hierarchic society outlined by Confucius.

Yehenala also studied the ancient manuals of eroticism: *The Manual of Lady Mystery, The Secret Codes of the Jade Room,* and *The Art of the Bedchamber.* As Chang-mei had taught Justin all the various positions and how to achieve maximum pleasure during the time of "clouds and rain," as the Chinese poetically named the sex act, Yehenala learned by reading the ancient scrolls. Surrounded by hundreds of eunuchs, she had no opportunity to practice firsthand what a peasant girl learned on her wedding night. Still a virgin, she read and waited and prayed that her chance might come. More practically, she was solicitous of every wish of the Emperor's stepmother, and it was this that finally paid off.

One night in 1855, at the double hour of the pig, the Chief Eunuch appeared at her apartment. "Slave of the Emperor," he announced in his squeaky voice, "the son of Heaven has chosen your ivory plaque from the jade casket. Prepare yourself for divinity."

Yehenala thrilled that the great moment had come and her plaque, with her name carved in Chinese ideograms as well as square Manchu script, had been picked. Helped by the Chief Eunuch, she stripped herself, bathed, anointed herself with ointments, and then was rolled in a scarlet silk rug and carried to the Emperor's chamber. There, as dictated by custom, she was unrolled from the rug. She crawled to the foot of the Emperor's wide bed.

The Hsien-feng Emperor was twenty-four, but already one of his legs was swollen from excessive drinking of rice wine and kumiss, the Manchu drink made of fermented mare's milk. He was soft and flabby, like a eunuch she thought; although his blunt-nosed face was pocked by the *tien-hua ping,* the heavenly flower disease or smallpox that disfigured so many Chinese, she noticed that his body had not been marked. Now she crawled across the floor with her buttocks provocatively raised, it being common knowledge in the harem that the Emperor's whimsical masculinity could often be aroused by signs of self-abnegation. Behind the imperial bed was a huge orange lacquer screen decorated with a great gilt double-joy ideogram that symbolized physical love. As she kissed the imperial toes, the Emperor said, "Our stepmother tells Us you will please Us."

"This slave will try, Majesty," Yehenala said. "Although she is unworthy."

"This *Kua . . .*" the Emperor went on, using the petulant word for "orphan" because the Emperor was by custom supposedly fatherless. "This Orphan wishes to produce an heir, but We have been"—he paused to consider the proper word—"overindulged by the flower girls and catamites of the Flower Quarter. The carmine smiles of the ladies of the golden lilies have sapped Our virility. You must use your arts to arouse Us."

"This slave will do her utmost," Yehenala said, forced by custom to use the almost ludicrously stilted dialogue of imperial concubines. "Would the Son of Heaven perhaps be pleased if the jade girl played the flute?"

"An excellent idea."

Crawling into the bed, she performed "The Jade Girl Playing the Flute" as the Chief Eunuch watched in the recesses of a dark corner. When Yehenala was finished, the Chief Eunuch stepped forward and bowed.

"Does Your Majesty wish me to return the jade girl to her chamber?" he asked.

Hsien-feng was panting. "No," he whispered, "the orchid girl has performed well. Our stepmother was right. Leave her. We will try for more clouds and rain."

At dawn, the Chief Eunuch marked her name and the date on the jade tablet, a sort of calendar of the harem that would ensure the Emperor's paternity in case Yehenala became pregnant. Then he rolled her up in the silk rug and carried her back to her chamber.

Six weeks later, the court was ablaze with gossip. Yehenala was carrying the child of the Son of Heaven! If it turned out to be a man child, the daughter of the minor Manchu noble would ascend to a position of paramount importance in the court.

1 1   "YOU'RE A REMARKABLE YOUNG MAN," said Prince I. "You're not yet seventeen, and you're already a multimillionaire. . . ."

"My wife is," Justin corrected politely. He was having dinner with the Viceroy in his summer palace in the White Cloud Hills overlooking the city below and the Pearl River. Chang-mei had not been invited and had to stay in the house on Pink Jade Road. Her exclusion from the dinner had not come as a surprise to her, but it had nevertheless infuriated her. "The money is all Chang-mei's," Justin went on, "and believe me, she doles out little driblets to me, mainly to pay household expenses."

Prince I smiled. Though not yet forty, his Lucullan appetite had swelled his girth to over three hundred pounds.

"You may speak Chinese and wear Chinese clothes, my friend," the Prince said, "but your mind is still western. We Chinese men own everything. But tell me: Is what she wrote me in the note yesterday true? Has she really decided to retire from pirating?"

"Yes, it's true—at least for the time being. Our capture of the *Sea Goddess* was our finale. I finally convinced her that, with our baby, it is time to come home. In fact, we are looking at some property here in the White Cloud Hills with the thought of building a house."

"Excellent: you will be my neighbors. But I can't say I welcome the news. Chang-mei's pirating was very profitable to me—very. As you know, only yesterday she deposited one hundred thousand taels in my Macao bank account. I will miss these little donations." Three taels, the basic unit of Chinese currency, equaled five dollars American.

Justin took a sip of the excellent Montrachet. Prince I had acquired a liking for European wines from the French and English in Canton. "By the way," he said, "if it would not be presumptuous on my part, my wife asked me to convey to you a message. She would like a favor from you."

"Ah, anything for Chang-mei."

"She was very upset that she was not invited here tonight. She would like some time soon—at your convenience, of course—to be invited here perhaps for tea. She would very much like to see the inside of your palace."

The Prince's fat face remained impassive as he helped himself to more Cantonese pan-fried noodles and pork. The Prince's chef was one of the best in China. "That, of course, would cause a minor revolution," he said, "and China is having enough revolutions as it is. However, perhaps someday it can be arranged. I am aware that your wife is—how to put it politely?—something of a revolutionary in her own right. She dresses like a man, at times, and has the temenity to think herself an equal of all men. And, in marrying you, a foreigner, she also has broken the ancient rules of conduct. In fact, Chang-mei makes me a bit nervous, even though we have had so many successful business transactions."

Justin was amused by the Viceroy's euphemisms. The squeeze he had extracted from Chang-mei had made him one of the richest men in China—some said even richer than his cousin, the Emperor.

"She would be flattered to hear that, my lord. She would be flattered to think she makes the powerful Prince I nervous."

The Viceroy chuckled. He had once been a handsome man, but gluttony had wreathed his face in chins. A long mustache drooped from his upper lip, his head was completely shaven, a style that was adopted by many of the higher Manchu nobles; the Manchus forced all Chinese men over fourteen to shave their heads except for a queue, or pigtail, which was worn as a sign of subservience to the Ch'ing Dynasty. His tunic was woven with gold thread and highly ornamented with mythic symbols and peacocks.

"She makes me nervous," the Prince said, "but I'll survive. However, I'm beginning to wonder if the Dragon Throne will survive. What makes me much more nervous than your wife is the state of China. You know that our history has always been cyclical, in terms of the dynasties. The first generation is clean, the second is less so, and the third and fourth are corrupt and degenerate. That is happening in Peking today. My cousin, the Emperor, is a libertine who is becoming totally the creation of the concubine, Yehenala. In fact, I can tell you confidentially, there is talk that he may one day soon make her the Empress, particularly now that she has borne him a son. I know you think me corrupt, my friend, and I freely admit that I am. Everyone in China is corrupt: the question is not whether a man is corrupt, but rather the degree of his corruption. The problem is that if the Dragon Throne falls and the Emperor loses the Mandate of Heaven, the party for me is over. Which is why I am nervous about the situation in Peking. And which is why I invited you here tonight to dinner." Justin looked surprised. The Prince, whose fingernails were extremely long to indicate he did not have to do manual labor—an important status symbol in status-crazed China—put down his chopsticks. "Now that you are a retired pirate," he went on, "what are your plans?"

"Well, if I were in America, by now I'd be ready to enter college. So what I'd like to do is try to learn something besides how to rob clipper ships."

Prince I looked amused. "As to that, you've learned from an expert. Chang-mei's living habits may make me nervous, but I have nothing but admiration for her abilities as a pirate. Tell me, my friend: Are you serious about Chang-mei? Or is this some adventure on your part?"

"I beg your pardon, my lord. Why would you think me not serious?"

"You are a foreigner. I know what you westerners think of us Chinese. As we think of you as barbarians, you think of us as a backward race. Is this not true? And you think of our women as pretty flowers to be plucked, but not to marry. Is this not true?"

"It may be true of some westerners, but it's not of me."

"Then you love Chang-mei in the way you westerners speak of love—a concept I've never quite understood."

"Of course."

"There is no other, western woman in your heart?"

Justin shifted uncomfortably. "I will not lie to you, my lord. There is a western girl I was in love with. But that was many years ago, and I will never see her again."

The Viceroy studied his face. "But if you did see her again," he said, "how would you choose between her and Chang-mei?"

Again, Justin squirmed uncomfortably. "I would hope the decision would never have to be made," he said.

"But if it did?" the Prince persisted.

"My lord is asking me unpleasant questions."

"There is a reason for my asking."

"My first duty would be to my wife and child."

"Then do you think of yourself as more a Chinese than a westerner?"

"I think of myself as both."

"Do you love China?"

"Yes, very much. With all its faults. But I also love America, with all its faults."

"You say you want an education. I have a proposition that may interest you." He signaled to the servant kneeling in the corner to refill the wine goblets. "You know that China is in great turmoil. The Taiping rebels are firmly entrenched in Nanking and will try again to take the capital. My cousin, the Emperor, is weak-willed and dissolute. As I said, he is more and more coming under the influence of Yehenala, who is as strong-willed as your wife, Chang-mei."

"Is Yehenala intelligent?"

"Very. But she knows nothing of the west, and the barbarians—excuse me, dear friend—the westerners are as great a threat to China as the Taiping rebels. Each year the power of the English grows, and instead of learning their ways so as to be able to fight them on an equal footing, the court relies on the ancient ways of the Manchus—perfectly fine in the sixteenth century, but woefully inadequate today. I think you would agree to that?"

"Absolutely."

"You say you love China. Do you love it enough to try to help it?"

Justin shrugged. "If I could, of course. But I'm a nobody. . . ."

"You are too modest. You are the great white pirate who knows the ways of the sea. You know how to lead men. You are young and strong. You were smart enough to equip your war junks with modern weaponry. You could be a great help to China."

"But how?"

"Have you heard of Sandhurst?"

"England's West Point."

"You say you want an education. What if I arranged for you to enter Sandhurst next year?"

"My lord, are you serious?"

"Very. China needs a warrior who knows the modern ways. If you went to Sandhurst, you would get the education you desire. Then you would come back to China and train our armies. And in return, China would make you rich beyond your wildest dreams. Are you interested?"

Justin stared at him, his mind reeling.

"But . . . aside from everything else, if I went to England and they found out who I am, they'd hang me for piracy."

"Why would they ever find out who you are? You never boarded any of the ships you attacked, and only a handful of European sailors ever saw you. Besides, the person I'm thinking of who could get you into Sandhurst is very powerful in the English government. On the remote possibility that there might be any trouble, he could protect you."

"Who's that?"

"The Earl of Saxmundham. As a young man, he made a fortune in the China trade, and he was a great friend of my father. His nephew, who's a diplomat, just married an American girl and left Shanghai. You'd have powerful protection in England. Of course, we wouldn't tell Lord Saxmundham *why* we're sending you to Sandhurst. We must be, as the westerners never tire to label us, inscrutable. So: that's my proposal. What do you think of it?"

"The idea of getting an education is very tempting. But what about Chang-mei and Julie? I don't think it would be very practical to bring them to England with me."

"Very impractical, my friend. And I'm not sure Lord Saxmundham would extend his patronage and protection to a Chinese girl who has sent dozens of English ships to the bottom of the sea."

The hangman's noose. Justin shuddered slightly.

"You see," Prince I went on, "I originally had this idea for my son. I thought if I could educate him in England, he could return to China and help us. But unfortunately, my son has inherited the less admirable traits of our clan. He is lazy and self-indulgent. He drinks with the Emperor and smokes opium. At times, I have thought the gods are paying me back for the great wealth I have made out of the opium trade by turning my son into an addict. At any rate, my son will never help China. And it occurred to me that you might—with the added advantage, of course, that you speak English."

Justin looked at the Prince. He had heard stories of his son, who was one of the wildest libertines in the Emperor's court, a drinking companion of Hsien-feng who also accompanied the Emperor incognito into the gamier fleshpots of Peking.

"You honor me," he said.

"Then you will consider it? The financing of the entire enterprise would be taken care of by me."

Justin knew it was a golden opportunity to acquire the education he wanted so desperately. "My lord, I accept. Although I think my wife is not going to be very happy with me."

"You son of a monkey!" Chang-mei screamed three hours later, throwing a pewter mug across the cabin at his head. He ducked and it hit the vermillion bulkhead, clanging to the deck. "You make me a mother, you talk me into re-tiring, then you leave me for four years? I'll kill you!"

She ran to grab the kris from the bulkhead, but Justin was there first.

"Chang-mei, listen to me! Prince I says if I do this for him and China, the Emperor will give us a pardon. . . ."

"Why do I need a pardon? I've already paid off the Viceroy . . . let go of me, damn you . . . !"

They were wrestling in the cabin of the *Eastern Dragon,* which alternated with the house on Pink Jade Road as their home.

"Chang-mei!" he shouted. "Stop fighting and listen!"

Little Julie woke up and started crying in the cradle custom-made for her by the ship's carpenter. Chang-mei simmered down. She flopped on her bunk and looked at him angrily.

"I hate men," she said in a sour tone.

"But you're stuck with us. We have everything to gain by this, and nothing to lose. . . ."

"Why can't Julie and I come with you?"

"Because a Chinese woman will stand out like a sore thumb in England, and you're a rather famous pirate, in case you've forgotten. They could hang you. . . ."

"But they'll hang *you!"*

"No one knows who I am." He sat beside her and put his arm around her. "You stay here and build us our house. The time will go by quickly, and when I come home Prince I says the Emperor will give me a fourth-rank mandarin-ate with a peacock feather."

Chang-mei looked impressed. To become a mandarin for the Chinese was an honor equivalent to a peerage for an Englishman.

"A mandarin," she said in an awed tone. Then a look of skepticism came over her beautiful face. "The Emperor doesn't give out mandarinates for nothing."

"Well, I'd have to win a few victories for him first," Justin said with a grin, "which should be easy. And when I become a general, you can shine my boots."

She gave him a shove: "Son of a monkey: you'll shine *my* boots!"

He put his arms around her and kissed her. "We'll shine each other's boots—with nothing else on."

"Mm," she purred. "My beautiful roundeye. I'll miss you. Will you miss me?"

"As the tides miss the moon."

She pushed him off and sat up.

"I'll take a lover," she said. "I'll take ten. I'm beautiful, young, and rich. I could have any man in China!"

"You're absolutely right."

"You wouldn't be jealous?"

"Of course I would. When I come home and find you with your lovers, I'll take that kris and chop all your heads off."

She frowned. "Sometimes I think when you make love to me that your mind is somewhere else. With another woman . . . that missionary's daughter, who was plain as yak milk. Though I don't understand what your 'love' is, do you still 'love' her?"

"Why do you care, since you don't love me?"

"You haven't answered me. Do you still love her?"

"Be practical. She's long since forgotten me. She probably has a husband and ten children and is fat as a pig."

She eyed him suspiciously for a moment. Then she got off the bunk and went to the small altar to light a joss stick.

"What are you doing?" he asked.

"Since you won't give me a straight answer about the missionary's daughter, I'm praying to the gods to save our love—whatever it is. And to keep me from going crazy with boredom while you're gone. You *do* amuse me, my round-eyed husband."

"You won't be bored. You'll have Julie and the house. . . ."

She turned and looked at him. "Even if I build the grandest house in China, do you think anyone will come to visit me? Of course not. The westerners hate me because I'm Chinese, and the Chinese hate me because I'm a woman—and a low-born one, with regular feet instead of bound ones. Why do you think I became a pirate? Because in this horrible world, it was the only way I could become someone of importance. I was born with everything against me, and I became what I am because I was willing to fight my fate." She paused. "Maybe I *do* love you after all. And why do I? Because you're a westerner who doesn't hate me because I'm a Chinese, and a man who doesn't hate me for being a woman. Don't forget me, Justin. Don't break my heart."

He came to her, took her in his arms, and kissed her. "I could never forget you," he whispered.

12   "I HAVE REASON TO BELIEVE Justin Savage is alive."

The remark, made quietly by Sylvaner in the dining room of the Washington Square mansion in New York, caused Adelaide to look up from her jellied consommé.

"Are you mad?" she said to her husband. "He was killed years ago on the *Sea Witch.*"

"Yes, we've assumed that. But how do you know for certain? The *Sea Witch* vanished. It's certainly possible that Justin's still alive, because we don't know how he died. I spoke to Captain Forbes of the *Sea Goddess* today, which just arrived. I didn't want to break the news to you, but . . ."

"Not *another* one?" Adelaide said, alarmed.

"Yes. Pirates again. They took the entire cargo of opium."

"Dearest God, that's the fifth ship that's been attacked!"

"The sixth if you count the *Sea Witch,* and I've thought all along that it was probably sunk by pirates. There's been a pattern here: it's as if someone was purposely attacking our ships. All ships are at risk from the damned pirates, but it seems bizarre that every one of ours has been hit. It's cost us a fortune, an absolute fortune! And as you know, I haven't been able to insure the last two ships, so the cargo of the *Sea Goddess* is a total loss."

Adelaide asked nervously, "Then are we in trouble, financially?"

"Well, I can't say this has been a banner year for the Savage Line. But I'm sure I can sell the clipper ships to Argentina for a good price, and then we're out of the damned China trade, and good riddance. But something the Captain told me today has stuck in my mind."

"What?"

"He said he saw a white man on one of the pirate junks. He didn't come aboard the *Sea Goddess* with the Malays, but he was watching from the junk. He was perhaps twenty years old and he had red hair. Now, what would a twenty-year-old white man with red hair be doing on a Chinese junk filled with Malay pirates?"

"Justin would only be eighteen. . . ."

"But he might look twenty. I'm telling you, I feel in my bones that it's Justin! And that *he's* been behind these attacks on our ships."

"But, Sylvaner, how could he possibly have survived when everyone else on the *Sea Witch* was killed?"

"Ah, but everyone *wasn't* killed. I remembered that a missionary family named Aspinall had booked passage on the *Sea Witch*. On a hunch, I went to the Archdiocese of New York this afternoon and talked to the Bishop. He knows all about the Aspinalls. They were held for ransom by the pirates, and the Church paid the ransom. They were set free and ended up in Shanghai. So it turns out there *is* someone who knows what happened to the *Sea Witch*. And there is someone who could tell us if Justin is alive."

"But surely you're not thinking of going to Shanghai to find out?"

"I won't have to. The Aspinalls' daughter just married the nephew of the Earl of Saxmundham, and they're on their way back to England for their honeymoon. We're going to London next month for business. I think we should pay a call on Mrs. Partridge. That's her name: Samantha Aspinall Partridge."

"Yes, and meeting Lord Saxmundham would be a useful contact. I've read that he's quite powerful in the Tory party. But what if we find out that Justin is alive? What could we do?"

"If I'm right, my dear half brother has cost me over three million dollars in losses. If I can get my hands on him, I'll have him hung for piracy. And *this* time, he won't escape!"

"Excuse me, Mrs. Savage."

Adelaide turned to look at the Irish nanny who was standing in the entrance to the hallway.

"Yes, what is it, Geraldine? And I've spoken to you before about sneaking up on us!"

"I wasn't sneakin', ma'am, and I'm sorry if I startled you. It's Master Francis. His cough is gettin' worse, and I think he has a fever. Should we be sendin' for Dr. MacLeod?"

Adelaide sighed.

"Yes, I suppose we should. I'm sure it's only a cold, but if he has a fever, the Doctor should look at him. I'll send for him. Thank you, Geraldine."

The nanny curtsied and went back upstairs. Adelaide rang her silver bell for the butler.

Sylvaner stood up. "When did Francis catch cold?" he asked.

"He had the sniffles this morning. It's really nothing to be alarmed about."

But Sylvaner was alarmed. He left the dining room to hurry up the dark wooden stairs to the second floor, where four-year-old Francis had his bedroom next to his parents'. Sylvaner adored his much-longed-for son.

What he didn't know was that Francis's biological father, Tony Bruce, was already in financial trouble again.

"You'll find that Uncle Algernon is a bit eccentric," Percy said as he and Samantha drove through the foggy fields of Suffolk in Lord Saxmundham's dark blue–lacquered carriage, which had picked them up when they landed in London from France. It was a chilly October day, and the heavy fog that had rolled in from the English Channel gave Samantha the feeling she was in a dream.

"How so?" she asked. She was wearing a green velvet traveling suit with a smart green hat, part of the lavish wardrobe Percy had bought her in Paris. Whatever faults she had discovered in her new husband, lack of generosity was not one of them.

"He's only interested in two things: politics and astronomy. He built an observatory next to Saxmundham Castle, and when the weather's good he stays up all night looking at the stars through his telescope."

"I don't find that eccentric. It sounds very interesting."

"Well, he sleeps all day to stay up all night."

"I suppose *that's* a bit eccentric. Oh, Percy, do you think your uncle will like me?"

Percy smiled and squeezed her gloved hand, the glove custom-made in Paris of the finest kid. Shopping in Paris was a far cry from shopping at Madame Dulage's in Shanghai. Samantha had been in seventh heaven.

"How could he not like you?" Percy said. "You're so beautiful."

She smiled nervously at him. She could think of quite a few reasons why Lord Saxmundham wouldn't like her. She had seen enough of the English to realize how ingrained was their social snobbery. It was a tight little closed world she was moving into. It was also a very grand world. She had known that Percy's family was rich, but she had no idea *how* rich they were until she and Percy got to Paris, where he spent money with abandon. And now, the carriage with the coat of arms on the door, the beautiful horses, the coachmen on the box seat in their green jackets, tan breeches, shiny boots, and top hats . . . It was far removed from the plain-living world of Wiscasset, Maine, that she had grown up in, and she was naturally apprehensive. Samantha was a well-brought-up girl, well educated by the standards of her time when most girls' education was limited to a little piano, a little embroidery, a little history and "culture," and not much else. But Samantha had a sharp, inquiring mind. She was well read, fluent in French, thanks to Madame Dulage, and she could get along in Cantonese.

But she was still nervous.

"There it is," Percy said. "Saxmundham Castle. Of course, properly speaking it shouldn't be called a 'castle' at all, since it was built only thirty years ago. But Uncle Algernon's a bit of a romantic . . . about buildings, that is."

She looked out the window of the carriage. To the right she could barely make out the Channel, its waves slapping the rocks at the bottom of the bluff the carriage was driving on. But to the left, a castle was emerging from the fog. It might not have been a "real" castle, but it certainly looked real. And rather forbidding, with its crenellated roof, its heavy stone walls, and the tall round towers at both ends. Samantha didn't know if it was the brooding look of the place, the dank fog, her apprehensions, or all three that gave her a sudden sense of depression. But far from being exhilarated by the sight of Saxmundham Castle, she felt as if somehow something terrible was going to happen to her.

But these thoughts dissipated as the carriage stopped and the door was opened. She stepped out, pulling the sable cape Percy had bought her around her shoulders, for the fog was chilling. Liveried footmen were taking the luggage being handed down by the coachmen. Percy took her arm and led her up the broad stone steps flanked by crouching stone lions to the veranda where they were greeted by a solemn butler Percy introduced as Despard. Then they went into the great stone entrance hall with its stone staircase and its suits of armor and displays of fanned spears and swords on the walls.

"Uncle Algernon bought the armor and spears," Percy explained. "He's passionately fond of the Gothic Revival style, and when he built the castle he thought he had to have some weaponry to make it look authentic."

"His Lordship is expecting you in the library, sir," Despard said. He led the young couple across the hall to a carved wooden door, which he opened. He bowed as they passed through. Inside was a room of heavy magnificence, more reminiscent of a sixteenth-century French château than a medieval castle. The walls were carved Circassian walnut, and there was a tall marble fireplace carved with hunting scenes that had in fact once stood in a sixteenth-century French château. Standing in front of the fire was an elderly man with a long white beard. His shoulders were slightly stooped with age. Yet, there was a certain decaying elegance to the old man, and Samantha thought he must once have been handsome. She wondered why he had never married.

"Uncle Algernon, this is my beloved Samantha," Percy said, leading her across the room to him.

Lord Saxmundham turned his cold blue eyes on Samantha, who gave him a curtsy.

"I'm honored to meet you, Uncle Algernon," she said, giving him her prettiest smile.

"I wasn't aware I had given you permission to call me 'Uncle Algernon,' " said the old man.

Samantha reddened. "Well, I . . . No, you hadn't. . . ."

"Then you will wait until I do. In the meantime, you will call me 'Lord Saxmundham.' When I received Percival's letter, in which he informed me that he was marrying you in Shanghai, I was most displeased. I will speak plainly, madame. I care little for Americans, and Percival behaved rashly, in my opinion, marrying you when he could have found a far more suitable match here in England."

"But, Uncle Algernon, I love Samantha!" Percy blurted out.

His uncle shot him a cool look. "Love, as I have told you often, has little to do with marriage. However"—he turned back to Samantha—"the damage is done. You are now a member of the family and the wife of my heir. Perhaps things will work out for the best. But I warn you: I will judge you by the highest, strictest standards. I intend for Percival to reach high office in this land, and the wife of a politician or diplomat must be above reproach. If you do not disappoint me, then perhaps we can become friends."

Samantha was burning with anger. "And if I *do* disappoint you?" she asked.

"Then we will become enemies. And I warn you, madame: I can be a most implacable enemy."

"Thank you for the warm reception, Lord Saxmundham," she said, seething. She turned to Percy and snapped, "I'm tired from the journey. If you will both excuse me."

She walked across the Persian rug and slammed out of the room. Percy looked nervously aghast. He turned to his uncle and said, "She's really very suh-sweet, Uncle Algernon," Percy said, his stammer creeping back.

His uncle glared at him. "She's going to be trouble," he said. "You were a fool to marry her, but then you've never thought things out. You let a pretty face turn your head, you young ass. Women are a trap—a lesson I learned years ago. Now, obviously, you're going to have to learn it for yourself. She's proud, I can see that. And headstrong. But if she crosses me, she'll pay dearly, pretty face or no. Now leave me alone. I have some correspondence to finish. Oh, and, Percival."

"Sir?"

"Welcome home."

"I have *never* been so insulted!" Samantha said five minutes later as Percy came into their bedroom overlooking the sea. "Even the Malay pirates treated me better than your uncle!"

Percy hurried across the big room and put his hands on her arms.

"I told you Uncle Algernon is eccentric. . . ."

"Eccentric? He's *rude!* He never even gave me a chance—he prejudged me! In America, a person is supposed to be innocent until proved guilty, but not here! Oh, no! I'm the trashy American who's going to ruin your career. . . ."

"I'm sure he didn't mean that!"

"Oh, but he *did!*" She started sobbing. "I'm your wife! I deserve to be treated with a little respect and dignity, not like some . . . some monster! Your uncle is nothing but a rotten old snob."

She threw herself down on the enormous Jacobean bed with its plumed canopy supported by four carved black walnut posters. The room was richly paneled, its walls hung with family portraits. The mullioned windows overlooking the sea were draped with red velvet curtains. A fire burned in the enormous grate, sending sparks flying up the chimney.

Percy knelt beside her on the bed and leaned over to kiss her ear.

"I suppose I should have warned you," he said, "but I didn't want to make you apprehensive."

"Warned me of what?" she said, turning to him.

"Uncle Algernon is a bit of a misogynist. He really doesn't like women."

"That's fairly obvious."

"Well, you see, Uncle Algernon was supposed to be married when he was twenty-one. He was very much in love with Lady Alicia Cholmondely, who was very beautiful. But the night before the wedding, Lady Alicia ran off with one of her cousins. It caused a great scandal, and broke Uncle Algernon's heart. Which is why he never married and why he doesn't like women. So you shouldn't take what happened downstairs personally."

She sat up, sniffing. "It's rather hard not to."

"If you'll just give him time, I know he'll come to see how sweet and wonderful you are."

"You think so?"

"Oh, yes."

"Do you think I'm sweet and wonderful?"

"You know I do."

He took her in his arms and kissed her. Then, slowly, he laid her back down on the bed, kissing her with increasing ardor. Samantha had come to enjoy sex after a near disaster of a wedding night, which was hardly surprising since she had been totally ignorant of the facts of life and had about fainted when she saw what Percy had between his legs. The problem was, he liked to do it at every available moment.

"Oh, Percy," she sighed, "I do hope things will work out. But I have this odd feeling . . ."

"Everything will be fine," he said, unbuttoning the top of her dress. "Let's take our clothes off and have a roll before supper."

"Percy, you're a . . ."

"I know. A rabbit."

Unlike the vast majority of stately English homes at the time, Saxmundham Castle had indoor plumbing. And an hour later, Samantha lolled in her tub having her back sponged by her maid, Wendy, who was pert and pretty with a snub nose and pink cheeks.

"Oh, His Lordship's terribly snarly," Wendy was saying. "He don't like women at all, never so much as growled at me, and I've worked here three year now. And poor Master Percival's mother, who lives in the next county and is an invalid, poor dear, and very frail. But I don't think His Lordship's gone to see her once since I been here, and she's his sister-in-law. But I'm sure His Lordship will grow to like you in time, ma'am. Why, how could he not, you bein' so pretty?"

"That's sweet of you, Wendy. But I don't think I bowled His Lordship over."

"Ah well, these things take time. Now, I got all your things unpacked—such beautiful gowns you have! It gives me pleasure just to run my hands over them! But what is that band that's sewn inside the hems of the skirts?"

"That's something new they've thought up in Paris. Those hems are called 'balayeuses,' or 'broom-sweepers.' They brush up all the dirt when I'm walking, and you can remove the 'balayeuses' and clean them. It saves the garments."

"Those Frenchies are clever, you have to give them that! And what would you be likin' to wear this evening?"

"The blue taffeta, I think. Tell me, whatever happened to Lady Alicia Cholmondely?"

"The lady who broke His Lordship's heart? Ah well, that was long before my time. But she was killed a few years later, that is, after she run away and left His Lordship standin' at the altar, so to speak. Fell off a horse and broke her neck, poor dear. They say that on moonlit nights, you can see her ghost walkin' the battlements of the castle. And she moans and cries and gibbers and rattles her chains because she's ashamed of breakin' Lord Saxmundham's heart and turnin' him into a mean old man."

"Do you believe that, Wendy?"

"About the ghost? Well now, I'm no more or less superstitious than the next. But if you knew the history of the Partridge family, you'd believe about anything. No disrespect, mind you, but they're a bunch of crazy loons, startin' with old Hugo Partridge, the one whose portrait's hangin' in the dining room. Took an ax to his wife and chopped her to pieces, he did."

"Good Heavens! When was that?"

"Back in sixteen ninety somethin'-or-other. Black Hugo, they call him, and he founded the family fortune. But he's hardly the only one. There's not been a generation of that family that hasn't had a bad one . . . be it a drunk, or gambler or suicide, or doin' unspeakable crimes. It's a miracle they're not *all* walkin' the battlements, gibberin' and clankin' their chains."

Samantha laughed. "Well, I'll listen for the moans and gibbering."

"No tellin' what *he* might do," Wendy went on, lowering her voice. "Lord Saxmundham, I mean. He's as queer as they come, sittin' in his observatory all night long, waitin' for the clouds to go away so he can look at his stars. They say he's waitin' to avenge himself on a woman. That's what they say."

Samantha looked at her.

"Are you trying to tell me something, Wendy?" she asked.

Wendy's face became a mask.

"Why, ma'am, I have no idea what you're talkin' about."

"Is there a family history where I can read about my colorful in-laws?"

"Why, yes, ma'am. Down in the library. A big black book called *A History of the Partridge Family of Suffolk.* It's heavy goin', they tell me, but maybe you should take a look at it."

"Yes, I intend to."

Wendy was right: in psychiatric terms, the Partridge family history was a mother lode. After her bath, Samantha went downstairs to the library and pulled out the heavy tome. Placing it on the reading table, she lit the gas lamp and began. She learned that the family fortunes were founded in the seventeenth century by the "Black Hugo" Wendy had mentioned, a soldier of fortune who fought on the King's side during the time of Oliver Cromwell and was rewarded by Charles II when he returned to the throne with a barony and large landholdings in Suffolk. Hugo had an unfortunate habit of raping the local maidens. He also was a heavy drinker who took a dislike to his wife, Lady Margaret Partridge, whom he hacked to pieces with an ax, for which he was hanged in 1694. His son, not surprisingly, went mad and hanged himself. The third baron was a drunkard, as was his son, the fourth baron, who was also a gambler who squandered what was left of the family fortune on the gaming tables of London and had a "peculiar" relationship with his male valet, whom he later murdered. Being a member of the House of Lords, the fourth baron was eligible to be hung with a silken rope, a privilege he exercised. The fifth baron, Algernon's father, was a recluse who took to chicken farming and didn't speak to his wife for twenty years.

Thus, Algernon's inheritance was anything but normal; and if Samantha had known about genetics, she would probably have thought twice before marrying Algernon's nephew.

To revive the family's failing fortunes, Algernon had gone into the China trade where he made millions, legally if immorally, off opium. He contributed heavily to the Tory party and was rewarded by being upgraded to a viscountcy and, later, an earldom. But Algernon could not escape his twisted genes. He, too, was a recluse and eccentric.

After a month at Saxmundham Castle, Samantha began to think she might go mad herself with boredom and loneliness. Every attempt on her part to make conversation with Lord Saxmundham was rebuffed by the crusty old man, whom she rarely saw anyway. As for Percy, he was away all day hunting. And when he came home at night, he began making serious inroads on his uncle's wine cellar, reminding Samantha rather ominously of the family's fondness for alcohol.

"Why can't we have someone over for tea?" she asked at dinner one night. "I've been here a month and haven't met anyone. Can't we have a dinner party or something?"

"Uncle Algernon would never permit it," Percy said, refilling his wineglass with the excellent Pommery '47. "He hates entertaining."

"Yes, as he hates women. Charming. I have no one to talk to except Wendy and the other servants. And Despard has hinted to me rather broadly that he prefers I don't speak to the servants at all."

"And quite right he is. You're the lady of the house. You're not supposed to talk to the servants, and Despard would consider it an interference with his duties if you did. Things are very stratified here. The servants have their pecking order, and it shouldn't be trifled with. I know that may be hard for you to understand, being an American, but please try."

"But I'm lonely!"

"We'll be going to London next month. . . ."

"Why can't we go now? I'm dying to see London."

"We can't leave the country now. It's the hunting season. Nobody goes to London till near Christmas and the opening of Parliament. It's simply not done. But I'll send a message over to the Grange and ask Lady Hermione Fawn to pay you a visit. She's interesting to talk to."

"Isn't she the woman you were engaged to?"

"Yes.'

"I have an odd feeling she's not going to become my bosom friend. Percy, dear, I *do* wish you'd slow down on the wine."

"Why? It's an excellent wine, meant to be drunk."

"But not all at once! And *you* certainly aren't meant to be drunk—which you have been all too often recently."

Percy leaned forward, a dark look coming over his handsome face. He stared down the long table with its gleaming silver at his wife. They were in the dining room of the castle, with its life-size portrait of a murderous-looking Black Hugo dominating everything. A great bay window behind Percy looked out on the sea, which on this night was stormy. Black clouds scudded across a gibbous moon.

"Dear Samantha," Percy said softly, "I hope you're not going to become a scold. A nagging wife is so very unattractive. I wouldn't like that at all."

Samantha glanced up at the portrait of Black Hugo, the ax murderer. Then she looked back at Percy, sipping the wine. He looked so boyish, she couldn't believe there was an ugly side to him.

Two mornings later a carriage drove up to Saxmundham Castle shortly after Percy had left to go hunting. Samantha, hearing the horses, hurried to the window of her bedroom to look out. It was an unusually pleasant day. She saw a beautiful woman step out of the carriage.

"Wendy, who's this?" she asked the maid, who was making the bed. Wendy hurried over and looked out.

"Oh, that's Lady Hermione Fawn. She lives over in the Grange, the daughter of Lord Roderick Fawn. She was ever so eager to marry Master Percival before he went out to China."

"Yes, I know they were engaged."

"He was lucky to get out of it, if you ask me. She's a fortune-hunter, that one. Out after Master Percival's money, she was. I'd watch my back, if I were you."

"Thank you."

Samantha hurried out of the room. Coming down the great stone staircase of the entrance hall, she saw Lady Hermione talking to the butler. She had a big hat on, and under her cloak she was wearing a gray silk dress with a bolero jacket. She turned to look up at Samantha. She was a honey blond with beautiful skin. She smiled and extended her hand as Samantha reached the bottom of the stairs.

"How do you do? I'm Lady Hermione Fawn, your neighbor. Percy sent over a note asking me to pay a call. I've been so anxious to meet his American bride. Percy and I were engaged, you know."

"Yes, he told me." Samantha felt extremely uncomfortable.

"And then he went off to China, met you, and forgot all about me. The wicked boy! Of course, there are no hard feelings." She smiled, and Samantha got the definite impression there *were* hard feelings.

"Would you care for some tea?" Samantha asked, gesturing toward the drawing room.

"In the morning?" Lady Hermione's well-bred voice dripped condescension. "What a quaint idea. Do people take tea in the morning in America?"

"We actually drink coffee in the morning."

"I see. You must tell me all about life in America. The Indians, and all that. It must be terribly exciting. But I really can't stay. I wanted to invite you and Percy to a small soirée my father and I are giving Tuesday next. It will give you an opportunity to meet the county. Of course, we're terribly provincial here, nothing like London or what I'm sure you're used to. Percy tells me you come from a place called Wiscasset? Is that an Indian name?"

"Yes, it is."

"How terribly interesting. Does one dance in Wiscasset?"

"Oh, yes. We do square dancing and reels."

"We'll have a small ensemble playing at the soirée. Nothing grand, of course, but I hope you will find it amusing. I know how reclusive Lord Saxmundham is, and I'm sure you're feeling rather lonely in this"—she looked around, then smiled—"rather forbidding place."

"I'm feeling *terribly* lonely," Samantha said truthfully. "And I can assure you I'm not used to anything grand at all. I'd love to come."

"How nice. Then we shall see you Tuesday. Eight o'clock précis, as the French say. Good day, my dear." She started toward the door. "Despard, how are your wife's teeth?"

"Still hurting, milady."

"Tell her to put some oil of cloves on them."

"I will, milady."

As Despard closed the door, Samantha told herself she must *try* to like Lady Hermione. But it would not be easy.

"Lady Hermione Fawn was here today," she said that night as she and Percy ate dinner in the dining room. As usual, Lord Saxmundham was in his observatory.

"Yes, I know."

"How?"

"Because she told me, of course."

"But . . . when did you see her?"

"This afternoon. I see her practically every day. I hunt with her father, Lord Roderick."

"Oh? You never told me."

"Slipped my mind, I suppose."

"She's quite beautiful."

"Hermione? Yes, she is. Poor as a church mouse, though."

"Well, I'm sure with her looks she'll find a well-off husband one day."

"Perhaps. Not many around here, though. I asked her to give a dinner party next week so you could meet some people."

"Oh, that was sweet of you, Percy!" She smiled. "She told me she was giving a soirée next Tuesday. I'll be so looking forward to it."

"Good. I want you to be happy, my dear. By the way, Uncle Algernon told me we're having a visitor tomorrow. A chap from China."

"China? What's he doing here?"

"Uncle Algernon is arranging to have him tutored to get into Sandhurst. He's doing it for Prince I, who's the Viceroy of Canton. His father was an old friend of Uncle Algernon's."

"Is this person Chinese?"

"I suppose. Uncle Algernon is letting him stay in the crofter's cottage while he is being tutored. So we can both practice our Chinese with him. Must say mine's getting a bit rusty, not that I ever could speak the blasted lingo."

Samantha dipped her heavy silver spoon into the soup, wondering who in the world the mysterious Chinese visitor was.

At least, she thought, it will be someone I can talk to beside Wendy.

13   THE NEXT MORNING SAMANTHA WAS coming down the stone stairs of the entrance hall when she saw a tall man in a black suit and top hat examining one of the displays of fanned spears on the wall. His back was to her, but she could see his hair beneath his hat. The hair hung to his shoulders and looked vaguely familiar.

"Good morning," she said. "May I help you?"

The man turned around and looked up at her. He was extremely handsome, about her age. She stopped, grabbing the banister, her heart thumping wildly.

"Oh, my God . . ." she said. "It's not possible . . . Justin?"

They both looked as if they were seeing ghosts.

"Samantha?" he said, his voice as disbelieving as hers. "Samantha Aspinall? You're the American who married Percival Partridge?"

"Yes, I . . ."

He ran up the stairs two at a time. She was starting to lose her balance. She literally fell into his arms.

When she regained consciousness a few minutes later, she was lying on one of the gilt French divans in the semicircular drawing room of the castle. He was kneeling beside her, holding one of her hands while his other hand smoothed her brow.

"Justin," she whispered. "Is it really you?"

"Yes, it's I. My dearest Samantha. In my wildest dreams, I never thought I'd see you here . . . or anywhere, for that matter."

"This must be a dream. You're dead, aren't you?"

"I'm very much alive. More alive this moment than I have been for five years. You were a girl then, and now you're a woman. The most beautiful woman in the world."

She looked up at his face and was assaulted by incredible emotions, a firestorm had been lit in her soul.

"Are you . . . the man from China?"

"Yes. I just arrived from London a few minutes ago. The butler is going to take me to the cottage where I'm staying."

"Percy . . . did you meet him?"

"The butler told me he's out hunting."

With some difficulty, she stood up and went over to the curved windows of the great semicircular bay to look out at the sea a moment. Then she turned to look back at Justin. He had gotten to his feet.

"Why didn't you get word to me?" she asked, bitterness creeping into her voice. "If only I'd known, I would never have married Percy. And now it's too late . . . I waited years to hear from you. . . . Why?"

He came to her and took her hands in his.

"For the simple reason that for almost a year I was Chang-mei's prisoner, and then she and I . . . well, we became, as they say, partners in crime. Not to put too fine a point on it, I became a pirate. That's to be kept our secret, by the way."

"A *pirate?*" She stared at him. "Who's Chang-mei?"

"My wife."

Her eyes widened.

"You're married too?"

"That's right. She's staying in China with our daughter."

She stared at him, trembling. Then she yanked her hand from his and slapped him, hard.

"Damn you!" she cried. "Damn you to hell, Justin Savage! You've ruined my life!"

She ran out of the room. Justin, holding his cheek, watched her go with amazement. Then he ran after her.

"Samantha, stop!" he cried, running into the hall. She was hurrying up the stairs. "What's wrong?"

She stopped, looking down at him, her face furious.

"What's wrong?" she exclaimed. *"Everything's* wrong! I'm married, you're married . . . it's an impossible situation! Go away! Go away from this house! I never want to see you again!" She started crying. "I'd almost forgotten you, and now you're back and everything's ruined. . . . Go away, go away. . . ." She started up the stairs again, slowly now, her heart breaking. "Please go away. . . . Oh, God, I can't stand it. . . . I wanted you for so long, and now I can't have you. . . . Oh, God, God . . . how could You have done this to me? Go away. . . ."

She reached the top of the stairs and took one last look at him.

"If you knew how I've wanted you," she said, "how I dreamed of you when I slept and thought of you when I was awake . . . If you only knew! And now . . . Oh, God, I wish I were dead!"

She ran down the upstairs hall out of his sight. Justin, standing at the foot of the stairs, was in shock.

"If you're ready, sir," said a voice behind him, "I can take you to the cottage."

Justin turned around to see the butler standing behind him. He wondered how much the man had heard.

The crofter's cottage was a charming one-story, thatched-roof structure overlooking the sea about one hundred yards from the castle. An hour later Justin was unpacking his suitcase in the small bedroom when Samantha appeared in the door. She had thrown a shawl over her shoulders, for it was a windy day promising to become more windy. She looked more composed.

"Justin, I want to apologize," she said. "It was such a shock seeing you, but I had no business acting like a schoolgirl. I certainly had no business telling you to go away. Will you forgive me?"

Justin closed the bureau drawer into which he had been putting his shirts.

"There's nothing to forgive. We were both shocked. Didn't Lord Saxmundham tell you I was coming?"

"Yes, but he didn't say who you were. He told Percy it was a man from China, and we both assumed it would be a Chinese. And it turned out to be *you*. . . . Besides, Lord Saxmundham barely speaks to me. I married into a family of maniacs."

"Is your husband . . . ?"

"Well, he's sane, I suppose."

"Do you love him?"

"Yes. He's nice enough, and he adores me. . . . Oh, Justin, I can't lie to you. I married Percy because Mother was pushing me to marry him, and he's rich and will have a title someday and I thought you were dead! And now . . ." She sighed. "Well, there's no reason for you to go just because I became hysterical. Percy and I will be leaving for London in a few weeks, and after the first of the year, we'll be in Paris where Percy's going to be First Secretary at the embassy. If I can keep my head, there's no reason everything can't work out smoothly here. However, I don't think we should let Percy or his uncle know that we . . . well, that we had been close before, as children."

"I don't know how much the butler heard a while ago, but if he heard much, he's going to know that we were more than playmates."

"Yes, we were, weren't we? Even though I didn't know much about, well, the physical side of marriage, I was in love with you then."

"So was I. I still am."

"It doesn't seem to have prevented you from marrying someone else."

"I was a bastard. I didn't want my child to go through the same hell I have."

"What's her name?"

"Julie."

"But you say her mother is Chinese?"

"Yes, but Chang-mei hates Chinese society because it's so cruel to women. She wanted our daughter to have a western name. There's a hat shop in Canton called Miss Julie, and . . ." He shrugged.

"Do you love Chang-mei?"

"Yes." He heard in his mind the voice of Chang-mei: "Don't forget me, Justin. Don't break my heart." It had been four months since he left Canton, and he hadn't forgotten either Chang-mei or Julie. But Samantha! This changed everything so radically. . . .

"You say you love Chang-mei, but you also still love me. You can't have it both ways, Justin."

"You dreamed of me, but don't you think I dreamed of you? You were my first love, and that's the most precious love there is. Yes, I married another woman. You married another man. Circumstances fooled us both. But that doesn't mean we don't love each other. Whatever happens to us, we'll love each other till the day we die."

She closed her eyes for a moment. Then she opened them.

"Justin, I won't pretend I don't love hearing you say these things. I do. But under the circumstances, you're just pouring salt in the wound. Since we can't be lovers, we'll have to pretend to be friends. . . ."

He came to her, took her in his arms, and kissed her. For a moment she tried to push him away. But then she relaxed. The firestorm within her rekindled.

"Oh, God," she whispered as he held her. "We mustn't do this. . . ."

"I can't help myself."

"I have to think of Percy. . . ."

"To hell with Percy."

He kissed her again, even harder. This time she pushed him away. She was panting. She put her hand through her hair.

"We have to use our heads," she whispered. "I'm afraid of Lord Saxmundham. He doesn't like me, and if he became suspicious, it would be ruinous for me. . . ."

"It wouldn't help me, either. He has to get me into Sandhurst."

"We'll have to play a game. We'll have to pretend the . . . well, the truth. That we came to China on the same boat, nothing more, nothing less. I must go now. If they see me here . . ."

He took her hand.

"Samantha, I'll play the game, as best I can. But I won't play any game with you. I love my wife. But I adore you."

Slowly he raised her hand to his lips and kissed it. She looked at him with frightened eyes.

"Oh, God," she whispered, "what hell are we letting ourselves in for?"

When she got back to the castle, the front door was opened by Despard. She came into the great hall, telling herself to remain calm, but burning with curiosity as to how much the butler had seen or heard.

"Lord Saxmundham will be dining with you tonight," Despard said. "A gale is blowing up, thereby precluding any celestial observations tonight. And His Lordship is eager to hear the latest news from China from Mr. Savage. His Lordship asked me to show you the menu for your approval."

This was certainly a first. Since arriving, Samantha had been excluded from the running of the castle. While the meals were excellent, she had had no say in their planning, the inference that she drew being that she was considered a guest rather than, as Percy had said, "the lady of the house." Now she took the menu from the butler and looked at it. It read, bilingually:

Turtle Soup.
Turbot with Lobster Sauce.
Suprême de volaille aux truffes.
Ris de veau au jus.
Fricandeau à l'oseille.
Venaison à la jardinière.
Turkey poult.
Plovers' eggs in aspic jelly.
Macédoine de fruits.
Meringues à la crème.
Pineapple ice.

Sherry; hock and claret; port and Burgundy; Madeira.

"That should get us through till breakfast," she said, handing the menu back to Despard and marveling at the excessive food, although she knew this was not uncommon among the upper classes who gorged themselves while the poor considered themselves lucky to have meat once a month.

She hurried upstairs to her bedroom where she lay down to try to compose herself. Her emotions were tearing her apart. Justin's reentry into her life—and a mature Justin, no longer a boy, but a glorious man—had turned her world upside down. She was fully aware of the consequences if she made love to Justin and they were caught. Divorce was practically an impossibility—it required an act of Parliament—and a "ruined" woman ran the risk of becoming an outcast. Endless novels were published about the dire fate awaiting "fallen women." Serious art portrayed scene after scene of domestic tragedy: "The Wife Who Strayed, the Husband Betrayed." Of course, there was a vicious double standard. The husband could, and did, sleep around, and if the wife found out, she "suffered in silence." But if the wife "strayed," she was worse than a whore. Whatever Percy's faults, and no matter how peculiar his family, she was still securely fixed in the top ranks of Society. The business with the menu suggested that even the odious Lord Saxmundham was beginning to melt a bit. If she played her cards right, everything deemed desirable lay in her future: social success, wealth, probably motherhood, and domesticity.

But she wanted Justin. She ached for him. He set her on fire. His kiss had been catnip. She wanted him to love her and make love to her.

"Oh, God," she groaned. "What am I to do?"

She sat up. Whatever happened, she decided, she was going to look irresistible that night for dinner.

She got off the bed and hurried to her closet to look through the many dresses Percy had bought her in Paris. She stopped at the red satin gown created by Mr. Worth.

"Tell me about this Chinese rebel who claims to be the elder brother of Jesus Christ," said Lord Saxmundham that evening at seven as he, Percy, and Justin waited in the drawing room of the castle for Samantha to come down. Outside, the wind of a fierce Channel storm howled around the battlements and swooshed down the chimneys causing the fire in the hearth to flicker and the many beeswax candles to sputter.

"Actually, my lord," Justin said, "he claims to be Jesus Christ's *younger* brother."

"Damned cheeky of him to claim to be related at *all,*" Percy said. He was impatient for Samantha to come down not only because he was anxious to see her, but because he was eager to get to the dining room and have some wine, the cocktail hour not having yet been thought up.

"Well, it's an improbable story," Justin went on, "which is why it's so interesting."

"Well put," Lord Saxmundham said. "After all, the Bible is improbable."

"I'm sure it's no news to you that the Manchus are corrupt and the millions of Chinese peasants, their subjects, live in terrible poverty. There have been a number of rebellions over the years, so the real surprise of this one is that so far it seems to be succeeding."

"But who *is* this so-called 'Heavenly King'?" Lord Saxmundham persisted. He was seated before the fire.

"His name is Hung Hsiu-ch'üan, and he was born a peasant in a small village north of Canton. About twenty years ago he tried to pass the entrance examinations of the Chinese civil service, but he failed four times. As you know, the civil service is about the only way a Chinese male can rise to any position of power.

"Hung's failure to pass threw him into a terrible illness—exactly what the illness was, I'm not sure, but some people say it was epilepsy. He had a high fever and became delirious. He had a dream that he ascended to Heaven, where he was split open and his internal organs replaced, so that he became reborn. An old man with a golden beard came to him and gave him a sword, telling him to bring the world back to the one true faith. Hung then went through the heavens killing evil spirits with his sword in the company of an older man. When he came out of the delirium, he was shrieking, 'Slay the demons! Slay the demons!' "

"Extraordinary," said Lord Saxmundham. "But who was the man with the golden beard, and who was the older man who went with him to slay the demons?"

"I'm coming to that, my lord. Apparently, Hung remained inactive for the next six years. In the meanwhile, the English defeated the Chinese in the Opium War, and the corruption of the court—as well as the misery of the people—increased dramatically. Then, about twelve years ago, Hung read a book called *Good Words to Exhort the Age,* written by a Chinese who had converted to Christianity. The book is a somewhat muddled rendering of Bible stories mixed with Chinese folk wisdom. But to Hung, the book was a revelation. Because he now understood the dream he had had when he was delirious.

"The man with the golden beard was the Christian God, who was his father. And the man who went with him slaying demons was his older brother, Jesus Christ."

"Blasphemous!" snorted Lord Saxmundham.

"Perhaps to you, my lord. But if you're a starving Chinese peasant hating the Manchu court—and remember, the Chinese consider the Manchus to be foreign invaders from the north, which they are—what is blasphemy to us could sound like revelation."

"Then he began preaching insurrection against the Manchus?"

"Not at first. First he went to Canton to study Christianity with an American Baptist from Tennessee named Reverend Roberts. Roberts was impressed with Hung, and further interpreted his strange dream. Then Hung returned home and started preaching. He rapidly became what we would call a cult leader.

"He began mixing politics with religion, delivering harangues against the Manchus. This proved wildly popular, and he attracted more and more followers, whom he began training as a militia. Four years ago, on his thirty-eighth birthday, Hung proclaimed the Heavenly Kingdom of Great Peace, or *T'ai-ping t'ien-kuo,* with Hung as its leader, or Heavenly King—*T'ien Wang.* He now had a nomadic army of a hundred and twenty thousand fanatical followers who, incidentally, were forbidden to indulge in sex on pain of death."

"They would *have* to be fanatical," Percy said.

"He began to take over China, village by village. The Manchu armies, riddled with corruption, seemed unable to stop him. Two years ago he captured Nanking, China's second most important city, where he threatens to launch attacks against Peking and Shanghai. The Emperor and his advisers are becoming frantic."

"But this Heavenly King must be a maniac!" Lord Saxmundham exclaimed. "Calling himself the son of God—preposterous!"

"I'm sure, my lord, there were those who said the same thing about Jesus Christ."

"Point well made. But then, if Hung and his followers are Christians, shouldn't we be supporting him?"

"The problem is, Hung's success has gone to his head. He has taken on all the trappings of the imperial court, he surrounds himself with concubines while he forbids his followers to indulge in sex, his court is riddled with nepotism . . . in short, he's become the problem instead of the solution. Bad as the Manchus are, it's difficult to see that the Taipings, who are stealing everything they can get their hands on, are much better. And at least the Manchus are the established authority, as legitimate as anything can be in China."

"Good evening, gentlemen."

Justin turned to see a vision of his own: Samantha had just come into the drawing room in her red satin gown. The great bell-shaped skirt with its large bows was held out by a steel hoop Wendy had helped her into, padded by several crinolines, the new fashion craze supported by the French Empress Eugénie to help sell more French fabrics. The bodice was tight-fitting with extreme décolletage that displayed Samantha's gorgeous shoulders and the upper cleavage of her magnificent breasts. She had put on a diamond necklace and matching earrings, wedding presents from Percy; and Wendy had pulled her hair back into a sunburst of curls, pinned by four diamond stars. She had pinched her cheeks pink, but otherwise her beautiful skin and features were as God had made them.

"I say," Percy exclaimed, coming to his wife to kiss her hand. "You won't have to go to your observatory tonight to see a star, Uncle Algernon. One just came in the room."

She's breathtaking, Justin thought. Breathtaking.

"My dear, I want you to meet our new neighbor in the cottage. Mr. Justin Savage, this is my wife, Samantha."

"I have had the privilege," Justin said, bowing, "to have made the acquaintance of your wife a number of years ago when we both took the same ship out to China. Of course, then we were only children. You can imagine what a surprise it was for both of us this morning when our paths crossed in this most unlikely part of the world—unlikely for two Americans, I hasten to add."

"Oh?" Percy said. "So you two knew each other. Capital!"

"Yes," Samantha said, curling her arm around her husband's, "and you will find, Percy, that Justin is a most agreeable fellow—for an American, that is."

They all laughed except Lord Saxmundham, who was watching Samantha and Justin. Despard told me, he thought, that she almost became hysterical this morning when she saw him in the entrance hall. She's trouble, that one. He seems pleasant enough, but who can tell with Americans? They'll both bear watching.

1 4   "MY SOLICITOR SENT THE FOLLOWING note to Lord Sax-mundham today," Sylvaner said to Adelaide. They were in their suite in Claridge's Hotel. Through the windows, a thick, yellowish London fog was swirling. "This is a copy."

"Read it to me," Adelaide said.

" 'November 17, 1855. My Lord: I have the honor of representing the British interests of the Savage Shipping Company of New York. The company's President, Mr. Sylvaner Savage, has just arrived in London with his wife. Mr. Savage is searching for information about the fate of his half brother, a certain Justin Savage. If the latter is alive, my client wishes to bring criminal charges against him under various Piracy Acts in the United Kingdom (8 George I, c. 24; 18 George II, c. 30) or in the United States under the act of Congress, April 30, 1790. My client has reason to believe your niece, Samantha Aspinall Partridge, may have information that would be helpful in his search. Therefore, I am taking the liberty to inquire if you would be agreeable to my client interviewing Mrs. Partridge at Saxmundham Castle. My client and I will be most grateful for any assistance you may offer us. I am, your most obedient servant, et cetera, [signed] Sir Charles Hawtrey.' " Sylvaner looked up. "He sent it by personal messenger with instructions to wait for a reply. We should have an answer in the morning. Sir Charles knows Lord Saxmundham, so he has every reason to believe he will agree to the interview."

Adelaide, who was knitting a scarf for Master Francis, said, "Wouldn't it be extraordinary if Justin were alive?"

"Perhaps not so extraordinary."

"But then, dear Sylvaner, what would you do about his half-million-dollar trust? Give it back?"

Sylvaner smiled.

"Gladly. The morning they hang him."

✦

Percy was snoring drunkenly when Samantha lifted off her duvet and carefully got out of their bed. He had driven her to see his mother that afternoon. The woman was biologically only fifty-five, but the ravages of consumption had left her a wreck, looking distinctly old. The sight of his mother had so unnerved him that when they returned to Saxmundham Castle, Percy had proceeded to get quite drunk. She had put him to bed at ten, where he passed out. It was now midnight.

Quietly, in the dark, she put on a pair of boots, then tied a cloak over her nightgown. It was cold but clear, not an auspicious night for an excursion, particularly one so potentially dangerous, but she couldn't help herself any longer.

She had to see Justin. It had been three days since his arrival at the castle. She had controlled herself, not going to the cottage, trying to keep her thoughts off him. But it was impossible. She had to see him.

She had a plan.

Opening the bedroom door, she let herself out into the cold upstairs hall, then softly closed the door behind her. Ahead, dim light from the entrance hall was visible. She knew that a night porter was sitting by the front door of the castle, probably asleep in his chair. She hurried in the opposite direction, to the stairs leading to the servants' hall. She hurried down the stairs, which were winding, and listened a moment at the bottom.

Silence. Saxmundham Castle had a staff of twenty-five servants, all under the supervision of Despard, the butler, and Mrs. Eustace, the housekeeper. Most of the housemaids, including Wendy, slept in small rooms in the attic of the castle, whereas the unmarried male servants—grooms, porters, and groundsmen—slept about the stables, not unsubtly being grouped with the animals. The married servants, who were in the minority, lived in the nearby village of Brandon-super-Mare. It was a dark night, and Samantha figured the chances of her being seen were slim.

She hurried across the servants' hall, through the kitchen, the buttery larder, the scullery, and the laundry to the back door. This she unlatched and let herself outside. A cold wind was blowing from the west, and the black velvet sky was strewn with stars. She hurried away from the castle, running along the cliff toward the cottage. Below her, the sea swirled, its foam glowing with phosphorescence in the dark.

Arriving at the cottage, she knocked on the door. After a moment a light came on. She waited impatiently until Justin opened the door.

"Samantha!"

"I must see you," she said, squeezing by him into the living room.

"Where's your husband?" Justin said, closing the door.

"Asleep. He got drunk as a hoot owl tonight."

She went to the hearth, where the remnants of a fire were burning, to warm her hands. Justin, who was barefoot, wearing a white flannel nightgown, watched her. After a moment she turned to him.

"My marriage was all right, I suppose, until you came here. But now, it's all wrong. I'm an American, and the English will never really accept me as one of their own. But the point is, I'm in love with you, and I'm miserable without you. It was one thing when I thought you were dead, but now . . . What I'm leading up to is, will you run away with me? We could go back to America and start all over again. I know: you're married, I'm married . . . but if you really meant what you said, that we'll love each other till we die, then it's wrong for us not to be together. And I also know I'm being terribly selfish, but I don't care." She hesitated, watching him, waiting for some sort of reaction. "I suppose you think I'm a terrible person," she added. "The missionary's daughter who turns out to be a total sybarite. Actually, it's sort of a bad joke." She waited again. "Well? Can't you say something? Here I've stripped away every shred of decency from myself, shown myself to be a complete hussy . . . for God's sake, Justin, say something!"

"What can I say? I mean, yes, part of me says, that's a wonderful, romantic idea! But I can't very well throw away all my obligations to my family, as well as to Prince I, who has invested a lot of money in me. . . ."

"Why?"

"I can't spell out the details, but he wants me to return to China after getting my education. Listen: he may have put his faith in the wrong man, but the point is, he's done it. I can't betray him."

She sighed.

"I know," she said. "I was wrong to ask it of you and a fool to have come here. I wish I didn't love you so. I wish I had ice in my veins and a heart of stone so I could say to hell with the entire male sex! To hell with love and romance and entanglements. All I want is a little peace."

He came across the room to her and took her hands, kissing them.

"You're trying to plan your entire life," he whispered. "Why don't you settle for one night?"

"Oh, God, I wish I could. One night of love . . . it sounds like a French farce. If it were only that simple! But I'm trapped—I realize that now. Trapped by marriage and society. You say your wife hates Chinese society because of the way they treat women. Well, I'm beginning to hate *our* society for the same thing! Do you realize for me to divorce Percy I'd have to get an act of Parliament? Just because I made a mistake and married the wrong man, I have to pay for this the rest of my life? It's unconscionable! That's the reason I just want to run away from it all, but I know: I can't. I might as well be a prisoner! It's all so totally *wrong!* Why should I be punished because I was born a woman?"

"You're getting hysterical. . . ."

"Why shouldn't I? The one thing I want in life—you!—I can't have because a bunch of men a thousand years ago wrote the rules of the game! And don't think I don't know why he married me. He says he's in love with me, and I suppose by his standards he is. But if I were plain, he wouldn't give a hoot about me. Because I happen to be attractive, he can parade me around and show off his 'beautiful wife.' "

"Samantha, *stop* it!"

"I don't care!" She burst into tears. "I'm angry, don't you understand? Angry! And I'm trapped. . . . It's all so *wrong. . . .*"

She was sobbing. He put his mouth against hers and kissed her.

"Oh, Justin," she cried, "hold me! Make love to me! If we can only have each other for one night, then I'll take the one night!"

"My darling Samantha. . . ." He picked her up in his arms. She put her arms around his neck as he kissed her forehead, her eyes, her nose, her lips. "Let's forget tomorrow and live for tonight. It's the sins we *don't* commit that we'll regret when we're eighty."

He started for the bedroom.

"That's a convenient philosophy for a philanderer," said a voice at the front door.

They both looked to see Lord Saxmundham standing in the open door, a fur-collared black coat covering his tall, stooped body. Justin put Samantha down as the old man came into the cottage, closing the door behind him.

"How did you—?" Samantha gasped.

"Know you were here? You forget, madame, that I sleep by day and stay up by night, observing the stars. Tonight is an exceptional night for astronomy. The sky is clear and Venus is ascendant in the heavens. Venus is obviously ascendant here on earth too. While brewing a cup of tea in my observatory, I saw you hurrying toward this cottage. It didn't take the genius of the divine Galileo to infer that you were hell-bent on a shameful amorous tryst."

"I came here to talk to Justin—!"

"Do you usually carry on a conversation in a man's arms? You will return to the castle, madame. As I suspected, it has taken you a very short while to betray your husband and bring dishonor to this family."

"Dishonor? To *this* family? Surely you're joking! You're a bunch of maniacs and criminals! Founded by an ax murderer with generations of drunks, wastrels, catamites, and murderers . . . you made your money supplying opium to poor, starving Chinese peasants. . . . You have the nerve to speak to me of dishonor? I suppose the 'dishonor' I bring to the great Partridge family is that the only crime I was contemplating was the pedestrian one of adultery! Excuse me, my lord, for not being more original in my depravity!"

The old man was red in the face.

"Get out of here, you American bitch," he snarled.

"Yes, I'll leave. But I can see through you now. You can't stand the thought of two people being in love because you were jilted by a woman who probably realized what a dried-up prune of a man you are! You can love a star, because that's a million miles away. But you can't love a human being here on earth, because that requires a bit of heart, something you are woefully lacking!"

"Damn you!" he howled, rushing toward her. She screamed as he grabbed her throat with both hands, starting to choke her. Justin pulled him away and threw him across the room against a wall, roaring, "Don't you dare touch her!"

The old man started coughing violently. Justin turned. "Go back to the castle, Samantha," he panted.

"No! Let's go, Justin! Let's run away together! Let's forget these awful people. . . ."

Lord Saxmundham's coughing had stopped, though he was still wheezing. "I think," he said, "before you try that, you should listen to what I have to say. Yesterday, a messenger brought me a note from a friend of mine, Sir Charles Hawtrey, the well-known solicitor. He represents Mr. Sylvaner Savage, who is in London. Does that name ring a bell, young man? A *ship's* bell, perhaps?"

"Sylvaner?" Justin said softly. "In London?"

"Yes, looking for information about your whereabouts. It seems he believes my niece could enlighten him. He wants to bring criminal charges against you, young man. Charges of piracy."

Samantha turned pale as the old man smiled. "Justin. . . ." She took his hand.

"I replied to Sylvaner Savage he needn't interview my niece, because you are here. I expect Mr. Savage will arrive sometime tomorrow in the company of an inspector from Scotland Yard with a warrant for your arrest."

"No!" Samantha cried. "You despicable man . . ."

"If you run away with Justin Savage," Lord Saxmundham continued, "you will become an outlaw, subject to criminal prosecution. So, madame, I recommend you return to your bed. And you, sir"—he turned to Justin—"I was willing to help you because of my friendship with Prince I's father. But you have betrayed my hospitality. Because I wish to avoid a scandal, you may take one of my horses. I would advise you to start for London at once, and be out of this country within twenty-four hours. In case you're not aware of English law, if convicted of piracy, you will hang."

"I'd rather be an outlaw with Justin than an in-law with you!" Samantha spat out.

The old man shrugged.

"That, of course, is up to you. I would advise you both to make a swift decision. In the meantime, good night."

He left the cottage, closing the door. Justin turned to Samantha and said, "He's right. Go back to the castle. I have to get out of here. . . ."

"Justin, fight them! How can they prove you were a pirate? Where are their witnesses?"

"If Sylvaner's found out it was me attacking his ships, he must have a witness."

"Then take me with you—!"

"No! Forget me, Samantha. I'll bring you nothing but trouble. Your first instincts were right: I should have left here the moment I saw you. And if you go with me, you'll end up in jail, for which I'd never forgive myself. Lord Saxmundham is powerful. God knows what he could do to us. . . ."

"I don't care!"

"Care! Maybe everything is all wrong, and society or fate or whatever has dealt us a bad hand, but it's not for us to make the world right."

"Not even one tiny corner?"

"Not even one tiny corner. Now give me one last kiss, my love."

He took her in his arms and kissed her, hungrily.

"Justin," she whispered, "will I never see you again?"

"If not in this world, perhaps in the next. Perhaps it's better this way. We'll never fight, we'll never grow old together, we'll never watch each other's youth fade into bitterness. Our love will be a dream. And perhaps that's the only perfect love."

She was almost in a daze, tears in her eyes. "Perhaps everything is a dream. I'll never forget you, Justin. You've been the perfect dream, the sweetest dream. And now"—she looked at the door—"I suppose it's time for me to wake up."

"Samantha?"

"Yes?"

"I'll always love you."

She went to the door and opened it. Then she looked back at him with a sad smile.

"And I'll always love you, Justin."

"Milord, Mr. Savage has gone."

It was the next morning. Sylvaner and Inspector Oswald Charteris from Scotland Yard were standing in the drawing room of Saxmundham Castle along with Lord Saxmundham and Percy, the latter looking bloodshot and woefully hungover. Despard had just come in to make the announcement.

"Gone?" Sylvaner exclaimed. "Gone where?"

"I have no idea, sir. But he took most of his clothes and toiletries. And a horse is missing from the stable, milord."

Lord Saxmundham shook his head.

"Shocking," he said. "I offer the man my hospitality, and the blackguard steals a horse."

"Someone must have tipped him off," Sylvaner said to Inspector Charteris. "What do we do now?"

Oswald Charteris—thirty-six, a heavyset, red-faced man in a bowler and tweed cape—said, "We'll send out a dragnet and hunt him down like a fox. Milord."

He tipped his hat respectfully to Lord Saxmundham, then hurried out of the room, followed by Sylvaner.

"Uncle Algernon," said Percy, "what in the world happened?"

"We've got rid of one villain," Lord Saxmundham said in a raspy voice, "and now we're going to get rid of another."

Percy looked confused.

"Your wife. You young fool, I told you she was trouble! Last night, while you were hog-snarling drunk, she was out in the cottage with Savage."

"Savage? I don't believe it! She loves me."

"You conceited ass, I was there. I saw them."

"Blast! How could she—?"

"Easily. Now, here's what we're going to do. And you'll keep your mouth shut and obey me. Understand?"

Percy could hardly swallow the fact that his beautiful Samantha had cheated on him behind his back. It rocked his self-esteem.

"I uh-uh-understand."

15   As Sylvaner and Inspector Charteris came into the entrance hall of the castle, Despard said, "Excuse me, sir. I have some information that may be of use."

The Inspector looked at the butler. "What's that?"

"I live in Brandon-super-Mare, a mile up the road. It's a fishing village. Last night, someone stole a fishing boat."

The Inspector, who had broken veins in his cheeks, looked interested. "Does this happen often?"

"Never, sir."

"The Channel," Sylvaner said. "Justin's a sailor: he must have stolen the boat and sailed to France."

"Thank you, Despard," the Inspector said, taking Sylvaner's arm and heading for the door. "I'll send a cable to the Sûreté to watch all the Channel ports, and have the Admiralty send out cutters to search the Channel. Let's go to Brandon and take a look around before we head back to London. The next train's not till one-thirty."

Outside, they climbed in a two-horse coach they had rented in Ely, where the London train terminated. The coach lumbered northward toward Brandon.

"He's fled to the Continent," Sylvaner said to Adelaide that night after he returned to Claridge's in London.

"Then it wasn't a hoax? Justin really is alive?"

"Very much so. He rode to a fishing village named Brandon, stole a boat, and took off. The Inspector and I went to Brandon and asked around. A boy who lives near the docks said he had heard a horse whinnying about two in the morning, so we presume that was the horse he stole from Lord Saxmundham."

"But how would he have known you were coming?"

"As to that, one can only speculate. But I think it might well have been Lord Saxmundham himself. Inspector Charteris told me he's well known about dreading even a breath of scandal—presumably because there have been several murderers in the family."

"Charming. So what happens now?"

"We wait. Charteris has notified the French police. When they capture Justin, he'll be extradited to London to stand trial in the Old Bailey. Captain Forbes's testimony will put the noose around his neck, and the business we started five years ago will finally be terminated."

"This all supposes they capture him."

"They will. The French Sûreté is the finest police force in the world."

"But how long will we have to wait here in London?"

"As long as it takes to catch Justin."

"But, darling, we'll miss the Christmas season in New York. Poor Francis will be alone for Christmas, which will be a shame, and we'll miss the Rhinelanders' ball. Besides, in my delicate condition, the longer we wait the worse the weather will be for the return crossing."

Sylvaner, who had been standing by one of the windows watching the snow fall on London, came over to her chair, leaned down, and kissed her forehead.

"Dear Adelaide," he said, "what joy fills my heart when I think you are going to have a second blessed event, a brother or sister for young Francis. It's what I've prayed for. If you wish to return home, I can arrange passage for you immediately. But I hope you can appreciate that under the circumstances I must remain in London until Scotland Yard and the Sûreté catch Justin. I'll miss you, of course."

"And I'll miss you. But I think perhaps I should go back."

"I'll book passage on the first ship. I believe the Cunard Line has a ship leaving the day after tomorrow."

"Thank you, dear. I think this is for the best. By the way, I'll need an extra ten thousand dollars from the office."

Sylvaner straightened, a look of surprise on his face.

"Ten thousand? What in the world for? I gave you ten thousand before we left."

She smiled at him.

"But, my dear, surely you wouldn't begrudge me a new wardrobe for Christmas? And I want to buy a sleigh for Francis, and I have to redo the nursery."

And I have to make the final payment to Tony Bruce for making this second "blessed event" possible, you ninny. If you want children, you have to pay for them.

"Dear Samantha, how lovely you look!"

The speaker was Lady Hermione Fawn, who was standing in the small foyer of the Grange, a stone house on a low hill about a half mile from the Saxmundham Castle. Hermione was wearing a pale peach silk ball gown that Samantha knew, from her recent shopping in Paris, was more than a little out-of-date. However, she looked lovely with a necklace of jet and matching earrings.

"Thank you," Samantha said, giving her sable cloak to the butler. She was wearing a blue gown, another of Mr. Worth's creations.

"And, Percy, you look dashing, as always."

Percy kissed her gloved hand.

"Thank you, Hermione."

"Do come in. It's frightfully cold, isn't it? But I'm so looking forward to hearing about all the excitement at the castle last week. I hear that you actually *knew* this Mr. Savage, Samantha, and that he was a pirate? How terribly thrilling! I've always wanted to know a pirate, especially one so dashingly handsome as I hear this Mr. Savage is. But you must have been terrified he would ravish you, my dear? I'm filled with frissons just thinking about it!"

Samantha shot Percy a cold look, then turned back to Hermione and smiled.

"Fortunately, Mr. Savage is a very well-mannered pirate," she said. "But I agree with you, Hermione. I had my share of frissons."

"Ah, well, it's so dull here in the country, we should hire pirates to raid us periodically, as in the old days when the Vikings came to Brandon and carried off all the virgins in their long boats."

Percy, who had a rudimentary sense of humor, guffawed.

"Oh, I say, Hermione—a lovely idea! However, from what I hear from the servants, there are precious few virgins in Brandon these days."

Hermione smiled as she took Samantha's arm to lead her into the drawing room. "Yes, despite the earnest efforts of the clergy, I fear the morals of the lower orders are becoming increasingly lax. As per capita income goes down, the birth rate goes up. I'm sure there's a useful lesson to be derived from such depressing statistics, though what it is, I have no idea. Ah: and here's another of our neighbors, Colonel Crawford de Pugh and his wife, Laetitia. This is Percy's new wife from America, Samantha."

Colonel de Pugh, a beanpole of a man who had lost an arm at Waterloo, raised Samantha's hand with his remaining arm to kiss it.

"Delighted, dear lady," he said. "So you're from the colonies?"

"America is a *former* colony," Samantha said. "We *did* win the Revolution."

"Yes, of course. Damned ungrateful of you, I've always thought, but there you have it."

"Pay no mind to my husband," Mrs. de Pugh said with a smile. "He's hopelessly patriotic. Welcome to the country, my dear. I've been so looking forward to meeting you. We live in such a remote part of the world, we hardly ever meet foreigners. You must tell us all about America! Have you been to the South? I hear the plantations are lovely, with their charming slaves."

Dear God, she thought, they all hate me. And I hate them. I want to go home to Maine.

" 'Charming' is hardly the word I'd use to describe the slaves," Samantha said, aloud. " 'Pitiful' is more like it."

"Oh? But I've read they sing—what do they call them?—spirituals?"

"Yes, they call them that. They also sing sad songs about their home, Africa, where they were enslaved and brought to America by English traders. Just as English opium traders"—she looked at her husband, whose face was turning red—"have enslaved millions of Chinese by turning them into addicts."

The drawing room, which was filled with guests who had been gossiping, now became silent as everyone turned to stare at Samantha. Colonel de Pugh said, in the coolest possible tone, "If we English so offend you, Mrs. Partridge, why don't you return to America?"

Samantha gave him her coolest smile.

"Nothing," she said, "would please me more."

Percy's face went from red to scarlet.

"*Damn* you!" he exploded two hours later as they returned to Saxmundham Castle in the carriage. "You made a spectacle of yourself!"

"Oh?" Samantha said, sitting next to him. "I suppose I besmirched the famous Partridge family honor again?"

"How could you have said those things about us English? Don't you realize you've made enemies of half the county?"

"What I said about the English happens to be true. And if I've made enemies, so what? Bunch of stuffy bores anyway. 'Dear' Hermione would stab me in the back for a plug nickel."

"At least Hermione wouldn't cheat on her husband!"

Samantha sighed.

"Look, Percy. I'm not going to defend my actions that night. I didn't go to bed with Justin, but yes, I *would* have if your uncle hadn't barged in. So you're right: I'm a terrible wife. Thus, it makes no sense for us to stay together, does it? So why don't I go back to America? Wouldn't that solve everything?"

"No. It wouldn't solve anything. I want a wife who will be an asset instead of the liability you're becoming. I need a wife for my career, which would be ruined by a divorce. I need someone to love and who will love me. You never loved me. I can see that now. All along you were in love with that damned pirate."

"*If* I had known he was alive, I wouldn't have married you. I've told you that dozens of times. Oh, Percy, there's no point in our fighting and making each other miserable. Neither of us deserves that. Surely with all your uncle's power, he could get us a divorce in Parliament?"

"I've told you a divorce would ruin my career. Divorced diplomats just don't exist! Besides, my uncle wants to avoid scandal, and a divorce would be a scandal."

"Good God, your family has had every scandal in the book! Ax murders, suicides, drunks . . . what's a little divorce compared to that?"

"That's why my uncle doesn't want another scandal. This pirate business has already caused enough publicity in the trashy press, and he wants no more." He took her hand. "Samantha, I duh . . . duh . . . do love you, you know that. We must *try* to make our marriage work. Won't you cooperate?"

She sighed.

"Your uncle hates me. How can our marriage ever work?"

"You're not married to my uncle, you're married to me."

"Yes, but, Percy, every time your uncle says hop, you hop. Look: since you refuse to let me go home, I'll try my best to make things go smoothly between us. But I'll ask you to try and stand up to your uncle a bit and keep him from interfering with our marriage. It's the only way it's ever going to work for us."

Percy released her hand and sat back. She's right, he thought. But could I ever stand up to Uncle Algernon?

"Mr. Savage, there's a note for you," said the bellboy, who had brought the letter up to Sylvaner's suite on a silver tray.

"Thank you."

Sylvaner tipped him a shilling, took the letter, closed the door, and went into the living room of the suite. It was ten days after Adelaide had sailed for New York, and to Sylvaner's distress, Inspector Charteris still had no news from the Sûreté. Sylvaner couldn't believe that the Sûreté, which had been founded by an ex-galley slave named Vidocq who knew every criminal in Napoleonic France, couldn't track down an ex-pirate like Justin.

But still no word. He had celebrated Thanksgiving by himself, and he was feeling lonely, restless, and irritable.

He opened the letter.

"Sir:" it began. "If you would like to find out where Justin Savage has gone in France, bring fifty pounds in cash to Bygrave Manor, Hampstead Heath, tonight at midnight. Do not tell the police, or I will never tell what I know. Come alone. You will not be disappointed. [Signed] Eleanor Waterville."

"Who the hell is Eleanor Waterville?" he mumbled to himself.

His first thought was that it was a hoax.

His second thought was that since neither the Sûreté nor Scotland Yard had been able to locate Justin, he probably had nothing to lose to go talk to Eleanor Waterville.

Just why the London fog was yellow no one was sure. But at certain times of the year—November being the worst month—the entire city was enveloped in a suffocating yellowness, so much so that lamps had to be lit indoors during the day. It was undoubtedly caused in part by coal stoves. By eight in the morning, the sky began to turn black as thousands of fires warming bedrooms and cooking breakfasts were lit, and the fog lasted the rest of the day, becoming at times so thick that people fell into the Thames by mistake and drowned.

Such a fog was choking the city that night as Sylvaner's hansom cab took him to Hampstead. Gas streetlights emerged eerily from the fog, resembling the globs of paint by the Impressionists just beginning their movement in France. The horse's hooves clopped on slimy cobblestones, and the sound echoed in the mist.

Then the sound stopped. The horse whinnied.

"Bygrave Manor, Guvnor," said the driver. "Want me to wait? You won't find many cabs round 'ere this time o' night."

Sylvaner climbed out. He looked around. The fog was so thick, the houses were barely visible. But he could make out a brick wall in front of him. It had a dull brass plaque proclaiming "Bygrave Manor."

"Yes, wait," he said, starting toward the iron gate.

It squeaked on rusty hinges as he pushed it open and went into a weed-choked garden, evidently untended for many seasons. He walked up a brick path, his heels clicking. Sylvaner was not a nervous man, but there was something about Bygrave Manor that was unnerving. He wondered if he had been a fool not to tell Inspector Charteris. The story of "the Suffolk Pirate" had been trumpeted by London's penny press tabloids, and the sensation-hungry public had eaten it up. Was he possibly being entrapped by a gang out after the fifty pounds he had in his pocket? Was Eleanor Waterville a fake name? On the other hand, if she was real and could tell him where to find Justin, it would be well worth the fifty pounds. And he had bought a gun that afternoon: a small derringer that he had inside his jacket. It hadn't much range, but at ten feet it could put a hole the size of a quarter through a man.

Now the house was appearing out of the fog. A rather handsome two-story dark brick structure that was in the Regency style of a half century before. It was umbrellaed by two overarching oak trees, their bare branches stirring slightly, fingers scratching softly at the dark paned windows of the second floor. Sylvaner thought that it might once have been the residence of a rich merchant, perhaps, but that it had been abandoned for some years.

He came to the front door, surmounted by a brick pediment, and banged the brass knocker. After a moment he saw a soft glow through the paned lights on either side of the door. The glow increased. Then the door squeaked open.

"You are Sylvaner Savage?" asked a gray-haired woman who held an oil lamp in one hand. She was slightly stooped with age and wore a fringed shawl over her black bombazine dress.

"I am. Are you Eleanor Waterville?"

"Aye. Come in, sir."

She held the door. Sylvaner started in when the horse on the street whinnied.

"What's that?" whispered the woman.

"The horse of my cab. I told the driver to wait."

"I instructed you to come alone. Send him away."

"But how will I get back to the hotel?"

"That's your problem. Do as I say."

"How do I know your information is correct?"

"You don't. Do as I say."

Sylvaner stared at her. Her voice was husky with age. He wondered who in God's name she could be.

"Wait."

He hurried back down the walk to the cab, pulling some bills from his wallet.

"Here's three pounds," he said to the cabbie. "Keep the change and don't wait."

"Right-o, Guv. It's your funeral."

With that cheery remark, he snapped his whip and the horse clip-clopped off into the fog. Sylvaner started back to the house.

"That's better," said Eleanor Waterville. "Come in, dearie. Follow me down the hall."

He obeyed, closing the door behind him. The house smelled musty, and the hall, at least, was devoid of furniture. Faded, grimy wallpaper had lighter squares and ovals where pictures once had hung.

"Whose house is this?" he asked, following the woman.

"None of your business, dearie. In here, please."

She turned right and went into what, judging from the empty bookshelves, had once been a library. In the center of the room stood the only furniture: a wooden desk with a pen, inkwell, and writing paper, and a chair. Eleanor Waterville went to the desk and set the oil lamp on it. Then she came back to the door.

"Wait here," she said.

"Wait? For what? You said you knew where Justin Savage is. . . ."

"Yes. He's here," said a voice from the hall. Justin, holding a gun, came into the room. Sylvaner reached into his jacket and pulled his derringer, aiming it at Justin, who fired, blasting it out of his hand. Sylvaner howled with fright as Eleanor Waterville slipped into the hall. Justin came up to Sylvaner and hit him so hard in the face that he fell back against the desk, knocking over the oil lamp, then falling on the floor.

"Don't kill me!" he cried.

"I always suspected you were a coward," Justin said, picking up the oil lamp and putting it back on the desk. "Cowardice being another of your admirable qualities. God knows what our family has done in the past to come up with a beauty like you."

Sylvaner sat up, sucking the blood from his hand where the bullet had grazed him. "I'm wounded," he said.

"Ah Pin, give him this handkerchief." Justin, still aiming the gun at Sylvaner, stepped back and handed the amah his handkerchief. Ah Pin had just come in from the hall.

"We meet again, Mr. Savage," she said, taking the handkerchief from Justin and going over to Sylvaner. "You've put on a bit of weight. I suppose life can be very fat when you steal my son's half-million-dollar trust fund."

"Where did *you* come from?" Sylvaner asked, truly confused as he wrapped the handkerchief around his hand.

"When you sent that incompetent Swede to murder me," Ah Pin said, "I decided to move to London for my health."

"And when I came to London," Justin said, picking up the derringer from the floor, "after stealing the boat in Brandon and sinking it so you'd think I'd gone to France, I went to Limehouse where I heard about her. Being able to speak Chinese can be a great advantage in London's Chinatown. Now sit down at the desk, Sylvaner. You're going to write us a nice, long letter."

"What is this—? And who is Eleanor Waterville?" Sylvaner asked, getting to his feet. He was shaking with fright.

"Eleanor Waterville is a charming lady from Gin Lane whom I hired to lure you here to this house, which I rented for a week. Sit down, Sylvaner." He pointed at the desk with his gun. Sylvaner obeyed. "Now, my dear half brother," Justin continued, "I want to comment on the monstrous crime you tried to commit."

"What crime? What are you talking about?"

"The crime of attempted murder. Don't waste time playing innocent. Do you know who my mother was? Constance Crowninshield, your wife's sister. You're scum, Sylvaner. Rotten scum. And now you're going to confess to the world just how scummy you are. Take the pen."

"This is preposterous! I never tried to murder anyone!"

"Liar!" Ah Pin exclaimed hotly. "You tried to murder me and you tried to murder Justin!"

"Take the pen," Justin repeated. "Or I'll blow your brains out. And believe me, nothing would give me greater pleasure."

Sylvaner, mumbling to himself, took the pen.

"Now start writing what I dictate," Justin said. " 'December 1, 1855. To the Commissioner of Police, New York City. I, Sylvaner Savage of New York, New York, do confess that I hired Zebulon Horn, late first mate of the clipper ship *Sea Witch,* to murder my half brother, Justin Savage.' "

"Not true," Sylvaner sputtered as he wrote.

" 'I also hired the late Captain Ichabod Whale, master of the *Sea Witch,* to facilitate the murder in whatever fashion he saw fit, said murder to be performed at sea. I fully admit to masterminding this heinous crime. And, on the assumption that villainous plot had succeeded, I misused my powers as trustee and executor of the estate of Nathaniel Savage to claim the half-million-dollar trust that had been willed to Justin Savage.' "

"This will never hold up in court!"

"I think otherwise. Keep writing. 'Furthermore, while it is true the selfsame Justin Savage was aboard various pirate ships in the China Sea, I have no evidence that Justin Savage committed any acts of piracy or that he boarded any ships attacked by the pirate junks. I swear the above statement to be the truth, the whole truth, and nothing but the truth, so help me God.' Now, sign it."

"I'll sign. But there isn't any judge in the land that won't laugh this so-called 'confession' signed at gunpoint out of court."

"Who'll tell the judge it was signed at gunpoint?"

"I will, of course."

"But you won't be alive."

Sylvaner looked up, his face turning white in the pale lamplight. Justin took the confession from him and read it.

"Justin," Sylvaner said, "you wouldn't kill me?"

"Why not?"

"But I'm your half brother!"

"Mm. Yes, you are, aren't you? And I'm yours. Which didn't seem to stop you from trying to kill me. Here, Ah Pin. Keep this interesting little document for the police, who won't find it so laughable." He gave her the confession and his gun, then pulled three pieces of rope from the pocket of his black jacket.

"Put your hands behind your back," he ordered.

"Justin, in the name of the Lord, I'm the father of a son. . . ."

"And I'm the father of a daughter. Do what I say, half brother, or Ah Pin will shoot you through your crooked heart. She'd love nothing better—right, Ah Pin?"

"Right."

Whimpering with fear, beads of sweat oozing from his forehead, Sylvaner put his hands behind the chair. Quickly, expertly, Justin tied his wrists.

"One dividend of a life at sea—that is, if you don't get murdered—is that you learn about knots," Justin said. "You won't be able to wriggle out of *these* knots, dear half brother. And now, your feet."

Stooping down, he quickly tied each of Sylvaner's ankles to the chair legs.

"There, now," he said, standing up. "A package of joy, to be delivered soon to the Heavenly Choir. Or, in your case, Sylvaner, more likely the fiery pit. Just think: within minutes, you will know the answer to all the world's major religions. Unfortunately, you won't be able to let us in on the secret."

"Justin . . . dear God, whatever evil I did to you, you can't kill me in cold blood! It's not Christian!"

"I converted to Buddhism."

Justin pulled the wallet from Sylvaner's jacket and extracted five ten-pound notes. "Since you found out the whereabouts of Justin Savage, I'll deliver the fifty pounds to Eleanor Waterville." He stuck the wallet back in Sylvaner's jacket, then took a handkerchief from his own and tied it around Sylvaner's mouth.

"There, now," Justin said, stepping back and admiring his handiwork. "Sylvaner Savage, prominent New York businessman. I should take a picture of you and send it to the newspapers." Sylvaner grunted as Ah Pin handed Justin his gun. "Just beneath you, Sylvaner, in the basement, is a barrel of gunpowder with a timed fuse. In exactly"—he pulled a gold watch from his trousers and checked the time—"forty-five minutes, the gunpowder will explode and you will get a lovely bird's-eye view of London. Good-bye, Sylvaner, you rotten bastard. Or should I say: good night, foul prince and flights of devils sing thee to thy rest? Come on, Ah Pin. This room has an unpleasant stench."

He walked out of the room with Ah Pin, leaving Sylvaner twitching and grunting with terror.

As they hurried through the rear garden and climbed into the carriage waiting behind the house, Justin chuckled. "I think Sylvaner is going to have a very unpleasant forty-five minutes waiting to be blown up. Now he'll know how I felt waiting to be hanged on the *Sea Witch.*"

"You're too soft-hearted, my son. You *should* put gunpowder in the basement and blow that snake up."

"I can't do it, Ah Pin. When everything's said and done, he's still my father's son."

"You'll live to regret your kindness."

"Probably." He held the carriage door for his amah, who climbed in. "But if you insist," she said, "I'll send a note to Scotland Yard tomorrow telling them where they can find him. By then I'll be on my way to New York with his confession."

Justin climbed in beside her and signaled the Chinese driver to start the carriage.

"Put it in a bank vault. I don't know whether it will stand up in court or not, but at least it's enough to scare Sylvaner."

"And what will happen to you, my son? You can't keep running forever."

"I know, but I still have an obligation to Prince I. Of course I can't go to Sandhurst now, so I've decided to get my military education somewhere else, with the greatest general in the world."

"And who's that?"

"Giuseppe Garibaldi."

"Him?" Ah Pin sniffed condescendingly. "That ragtag rebel? With his so-called army of red-shirted hooligans?"

"Those hooligans have scared the wits out of half of Europe. And you're wrong about Garibaldi. He's been my hero since I was a kid. I'm going to find him and ask him if I can enlist with his soldiers. I can't think of a better way to learn to be a warrior."

"But how will you get to him? He's somewhere over in Italy, isn't he? In exile?"

"I've read he's on an island off Sardinia called Caprera."

"You'll need money." She opened her purse. "Here: let me give you some. . . ."

He put his hand on hers. "You've already given me more than you should have, Ah Pin. I'll take no more of your money. I'll get there on my wits, and the fifty pounds I took from Sylvaner."

"But this money comes from your father! You can pay me back someday."

He smiled and kissed her cheek.

"Dear Ah Pin," he said. "If only everyone in the world were as good and kind as you, this would be a perfect planet."

"Don't think I'm *too* good and kind," she said harshly. "If I had my way, that snake, Sylvaner, would be food for the vultures."

16   SAMANTHA SAW THE WOMAN IN white on the cliff two days after the London tabloids had trumpeted the headline: AMERICAN MILLIONAIRE FOUND BOUND AND GAGGED IN MYSTERY MANSION! SYLVANER SAVAGE CLAIMS HE WAS ROBBED BY MASKED GANG! SCOTLAND YARD BAFFLED!

Samantha had wondered if Justin had had something to do with the "masked gang." She figured he probably did, and that somehow he had frightened Sylvaner sufficiently that the latter would be afraid to include his half brother in the "attackers." She was glad that Justin had so far escaped the police, but this brought him no closer to her. She told herself over and over that what he had said was right: they must forget each other, their love must remain a dream. Easy to say, perhaps, but hard to live with.

After his plea to her to "cooperate" to make their marriage work, Percy had become somewhat removed from her and rather jumpy, as if he were afraid of something. He spent much of his time during the day away hunting. And at night, he often drank too much and went to bed early, snoring his way into a drunken reverie. Whenever she tried to make a conversation with him, he would either change the subject or leave the room. She didn't think it was so much his being hostile to her as it was that he was afraid of something: he was nervous.

It was an unpleasant way to live; and in her unhappiness, she reverted to her childhood habits: she began to overeat. The svelte figure she had dreamed of as a girl and had maintained as a woman by careful eating habits she now ignored. Eating was the only thing that gave her any pleasure in this remote and dreary castle. So at the silent dinners in the dining room overlooking the sea, instead of talking to her husband she stuffed herself. Rich puddings, cheeses, sweetmeats, roasts, poultry, plovers' eggs . . . she ate with abandon, and inevitably, she began putting on weight. Wendy scolded her, but Samantha didn't care. Eating was an act of revenge against her nervous, silent husband. Perhaps it was silly and self-destructive, but it made her feel good.

And then she saw the woman on the cliff.

Percy had sat silent through the dinner, as usual, drinking too much wine, also as usual. Then, mumbling "Good night" to his wife, he went upstairs after dinner and put himself to bed. Samantha read for a few hours in the library; then she, too, went upstairs. Putting on her nightgown, she slipped in bed beside Percy, who was snoring peacefully. She turned out the light and tried to go to sleep. Another symptom of her unhappiness was insomnia: she found it more and more difficult to sleep. But on this night, she eventually drifted off.

She was dreaming of being held in Justin's arms when she heard a distant voice call, "Samantha."

She sat up, awake. Percy was still snoring. She thought the voice must have been part of her dream when she heard it again.

"Samantha."

She looked at the windows. One of them was open. It was a cold, snowy night, and she remembered distinctly that the windows had been closed when she went to bed, the curtains pulled over them—a habit of Percy's, who had a European dislike of fresh air at night.

But now, the curtains were open and one of the mullioned windows was ajar, snowflakes swirling through it into the room.

"Samantha." The voice had a distant, cooing quality, going up on the middle syllable and then down again, so that it sounded like "Sa-MAN-tha."

She got out of bed and went to the open window, shivering in the cold. She looked out. A woman in a gauzy white dress was standing in front of the castle on the cliff overlooking the sea. It was a dark night and difficult to see through the snowflakes, but Samantha could perceive that the veils of the woman's dress fluttered around her in the wind, almost like shrouds. The woman was looking up at her.

Samantha leaned out the window and called, "Who are you? What do you want?"

The woman remained silent.

"What is it? Why are you calling me?"

Silence.

"Samantha, whom are you talking to? And why is that blasted window open?"

She turned to see Percy sitting up in bed. He lit the bed lamp.

"There's a woman on the cliff," Samantha said. "She's calling to me."

"What woman? And close that window. It's freezing in here."

"I didn't open it! And come here and look for yourself. I have no idea who it could be."

"Damned nuisance. . . ."

He got out of bed and came to the window.

"What woman?"

"That one."

She pointed out the window.

But the woman was gone.

"Well, she *was* there a moment ago. I saw her! And I heard her!"

She turned back to her husband.

He was looking at her oddly.

When she woke up the next morning, Percy was gone, and Wendy was opening the curtains.

"Good morning, ma'am," the maid said cheerily. "Terrible night, wasn't it? Cold and snowy . . . we about froze in the attic."

"Good morning, Wendy." She sat up, rubbing her eyes. Then she remembered the woman on the cliff. "Did you hear anything last night?"

"Ma'am?"

"Did you hear a woman calling my name last night? It must have been around midnight."

"A woman, ma'am? Who would that be?"

"I don't know who it was. She was standing on the cliff."

"Outside on a night like that? She must be barmy. And she was calling you?"

"Yes. Did you hear her?"

"No, ma'am. Are you ready for your breakfast tray?"

"Yes, thank you. You're sure?"

"Sure about what, ma'am?"

"You're sure you didn't hear anything?"

"No, ma'am. I'm sorry."

She left the room.

It was all very queer.

After breakfast, she got dressed, put on a cloak and boots, and went outside the castle. Almost three inches of snow had fallen the night before, and the castle grounds were a vision of pristine beauty. The cobblestone courtyard had been shoveled and swept. She walked across it to the edge of the cliff where the woman had been standing the night before.

There were no shoe prints in the snow.

Of course, she told herself, the wind and snow might have drifted over them. But still, it was peculiar.

Had she been dreaming? Or was there some other, more ominous explanation?

She returned to the castle, sorely troubled. Going to the morning room, she rang for the housekeeper, who appeared a few minutes later.

"You rang, madame?"

Mrs. Eustace—and Samantha didn't know her Christian name—was a short, plump woman whose gray hair was tucked into a white lace cap and who always wore black bombazine. Samantha sat down at her desk.

"Yes, Mrs. Eustace. I wondered if any of the servants had heard a woman calling outside the castle last night?"

"Not that I am aware of, madame."

Is it possible? she thought. Am I the only person who heard her? And yet she was *there!*

Wasn't she?

"Is there anything else, madame?"

Samantha snapped out of her reverie.

"Oh . . . uh, no. Thank you, Mrs. Eustace."

The housekeeper started to go, then stopped. An odd look came over her face.

"You say you heard a woman, madame? Did you see her?"

"Yes. I looked out the window of our room."

"Was she by any chance standing by the cliff?"

"Yes! That was where she was."

"Did she have black hair?"

"Yes."

"And she was wearing a white, filmy gown?"

"That's right. With a sort of gauzy cape that swirled around her in the wind."

Mrs. Eustace's pleasant face looked troubled.

"Then it must be she," she said to herself. "She's returned!"

"Who?"

"Lady Alicia Cholmondely! She hasn't been seen for many years—not since the death of Lord Saxmundham's mother, poor woman."

"What are you talking about?"

"The ghost of Lady Alicia Cholmondely, the woman who broke His Lordship's heart. His Lordship's mother claimed to have seen her ghost on the cliff and up on the battlements of the castle. Lord preserve us, she's back!" She crossed herself.

"Come now, Mrs. Eustace. I love a ghost story as much as the next person, but I don't believe them."

"Ah well, madame, you can believe them or not, that's your privilege. But it sounds to me as if you've seen your first ghost, and I wouldn't take it so lightly. His Lordship's mother saw the ghost and you know what happened to her."

"She fell off the cliff. At least, that's what it said in the book about the Partridge family."

"Fell? Aye, that's what they said, because there's been so many suicides in the family. But those who worked here at the time say the poor woman went mad and jumped."

Samantha's eyes widened.

"Jumped?" she repeated.

"That's what they say, madame. Now, if you'll excuse me, I have to check the laundry."

"Yes, of course."

Jumped? she thought as Mrs. Eustace left the room. Ghosts? Madness?

She stood up from the desk and told herself to come to her senses. Ghost stories were fun, but she couldn't allow herself to start believing a lot of Gothic Revival poppycock. Besides, she had important news for Percy, and it had nothing to do with the dead.

She went to the library to find a good book.

Two hours later Despard came into the library where Samantha was reading Mrs. Gaskell's popular novel *Cranford.*

"Madame," he said, "Lady Hermione Fawn is in the drawing room."

"She is? Whatever for?"

"She said you had asked her to come by."

Samantha put down the book and stood up.

"There must be some mistake."

She was somewhat annoyed, as Lady Hermione was not her favorite person by a long shot. She left the library and crossed the entrance hall to the drawing room, where her neighbor from the Grange was standing at one of the curved windows looking out at the sea. Hearing Samantha come in the room, she turned. She was wearing a green velvet riding habit with a black top hat.

"I've always admired the view from this room," she said. "I have a passion for the sea. Its waters swirling, pounding on the rocks . . . terribly dramatic, don't you think? It makes one have profound thoughts of the timelessness of nature, of life and death. We insignificant mortals are born, we lead our tawdry little lives and die, but the sea goes on forever. How sublime is eternity!" She paused, rather hammily, then she smiled. "That was the second act curtain speech of a terrible play I once acted in for charity. How are you, my dear? Am I wrong, or is it possible you've put on a little weight?"

"Unfortunately, you're right. I've been eating like a pig, and I must stop it. I have an unfortunate habit of eating when I'm upset."

"Oh? And are you upset?"

"I don't think it's any secret that Percy and I are not getting along. He's never forgiven me for what I said at your party."

"Well, Percy has no sense of humor. I thought you were quite amusing, although I wouldn't deny that most of my guests found your behavior a bit . . . peculiar. You sent for me, my dear?"

"No."

"No? But one of your grooms brought over a letter this morning. You asked me to drop by."

"But I never wrote a letter."

"You didn't? But it was on the castle stationery."

"Might I see it?"

"I'm afraid I threw it in the fire. I didn't think it had any importance."

Samantha was becoming annoyed. She went to the wall and tugged the bell pull. "Do you remember which groom brought you the letter?" she asked.

"Let me think. Yes, of course. It was Wilson, the boy with the buck teeth. He said Despard had given it to him and told him to bring it to the Grange."

"You rang, madame?"

Despard had appeared in the doorway.

"Yes. Did you give Wilson a letter this morning to take over to the Grange?"

"Yes, madame."

"Who gave you the note?"

"You did, madame."

Samantha stared at him.

"When?" she finally said.

"Shortly after you came inside, madame. You had come downstairs after your breakfast and went outside. You walked over to the cliff for a few moments, then you came back inside and went into the library. A few minutes later you rang for me and handed me the letter, telling me to send it over to the Grange, which I did. Did I do something wrong, madame?"

"You're lying!" she shouted. "You're making this up! I wrote no such letter, and I furiously resent this! I shall speak to my husband about this . . . this monstrous lie!"

She stormed out of the room. Lady Hermione Fawn and the silver-haired butler exchanged looks.

"Despard is very upset," Percy said that evening as he sat down at the dining-room table. "He said you accused him of lying about a letter you gave him."

"I *didn't* give him any letter," she said, sitting at the opposite end of the table. "And I can't imagine why he would say I did."

"But Hermione received a note from you. She told me this afternoon after her father and I returned from the hunt. She said you screamed at Despard, which was embarrassing to her. You know, Despard has worked for Uncle Algernon for fifteen years. It's unconscionable to accuse him of lying and treat him as you did. . . ."

"He *lied!*" she interrupted. "I'm sorry if I wounded his feelings, but he lied. If you want to take the servant's side instead of your wife's, fine. It's what I've come to expect of you. Now, I don't quite understand what's going on around here with these lies. Perhaps I saw a ghost last night, I don't know. But I'm warning you, Percy: you had better start treating me as a human being unless you want your child to have a nervous wreck for a mother."

Percy looked startled.

"My child—?"

"I have reason to believe I am with child."

Percy put down his fork.

"She's in the family way," Percy said an hour later to his uncle. He was pacing back and forth in the observatory as Lord Saxmundham sat at his ten-foot-long telescope that was aimed at the Crab Nebula through an opening in the roof. "I hadn't cuh-counted on this. We must stop everything."

"How do you know she's not lying?" said his uncle, his eye glued to the state-of-the-art instrument.

"She's missed her monthly. I'm sending her to Dr. Jeffries in the morning to have her examined."

"How do we know the child is yours?"

Percy stopped his pacing.

"I'm sure of it, Uncle," he said. "Whatever faults she has, Samantha doesn't lie. I believe her when she says she didn't go to bed with Savage. And there's been no one else. Of that I'm sure. No, the child is mine."

There was a long pause. Then his uncle said, his eye still on the telescope, "Very well. We'll stop everything until the child is born. But then we'll start again. The woman is to be gotten rid of."

"But Uncle Algernon, I stuh . . . stuh . . . still love Samantha! I don't want to harm her, puh . . . particularly if she's bearing my child! It would be cruel to send her to an asylum."

"You young fool," his uncle said, "my God, to think you're my heir, that some day you'll inherit everything. Don't you understand that to drive her insane is the *only* way we can get rid of her, short of murdering the woman? Divorce is absolutely out of the question. And if we allow her to go back to America, as she says she wants, she'll still be your wife. You'll be unable to marry again. Is that what you want?"

"Nuh . . . no."

"Then we'll proceed with my little charade, after the child is born. Fortunately, there's a history of eccentricity in the family and that ridiculous ghost story . . . it's enough to suggest she's insane. The servants have all been paid to cooperate, and Hermione Fawn will do anything we ask her with the hope of bagging you as a husband. We'll have Samantha declared insane, she'll spend a few years in the asylum, and then she can go wherever she wishes—back to America, or to the Devil, as far as I'm concerned. Meanwhile we can have your marriage annulled on grounds of insanity and you can marry a proper wife—an *English* woman who will help your career. I rather fancy it's an original scheme with a certain elegance to it. Are we agreed?"

Percy looked at his uncle, of whom he had been terrified most of his life. He's old, he thought. He doesn't have long to live. I *have* to stand up to him! I'm the future of the family. . . .

"No!" he blurted out. "We're not agreed! It's cruel to try and make her think she's crazy, and I won't stand for it. Samantha's my wife, the mother of my child, and I won't have her sent to an asylum!"

He slammed out of the observatory as his uncle gaped.

For the first time in his life, Percy realized, he had not stammered when he was excited.

Five minutes later he came into his bedchamber. Samantha was sitting up in bed reading, her long black hair hanging to her shoulders. He closed the door softly, marveling yet again at her beauty. He came to her bed as Samantha put down her copy of *David Copperfield.*

"Samantha," he said, sitting on the side of the bed, "I owe you an apology. I've done you a terrible disservice, and I hope you'll see your way to forgiving me."

"What disservice, Percy? Trying to convince me I'm mad?"

He nodded. "It was Uncle Algernon's idea."

"He hates me that much?"

"I told you he hates all women. He bullied and bribed the servants to go through with this silly charade, but I've told him I won't allow it."

"Why? Because I'm bearing your child? Before it didn't matter what happened to me, but *now* . . . now your blood is mingling with mine, so it's not such a good idea to pack me off to Bedlam?"

He turned red.

"I don't blame you for thinking that, and perhaps it's true to a certain extent. I've always been so afraid of Uncle Algernon . . ." he hesitated. Then, his back straightened. "But now I'm not afraid of him anymore." He took her hand. "I know you love Justin Savage, but I beg you to give me a second chance. Now that I've finally stood up to Uncle Algernon, I'll keep him from bothering you again. In my heart I truly love you."

He raised her hand to his mouth and kissed it.

I believe he's sincere, she thought. Perhaps he has truly repented for his terrible behaviour.

"Percy, Justin told me I should forget him. If you mean what you say about loving me, then I will do my best to be a good wife to you. Let's both forget the past, what you did and whom I loved. Let's try and make this marriage work, not only for our sake but for the sake of the child I'm carrying. Perhaps, if we work at it, our love will grow and we'll both find happiness."

"That would make me the happiest of men."

Oh, Justin, my lost love, I'll never forget you, she thought, but this surely is the best way.

1 7   THE GILDED PALANQUIN OF PRINCE I, carried by eight grunting porters, weaved its way into the front yard of what was undoubtedly the most peculiar residence in China—at least to Chinese eyes. It was a two-story, mid-Victorian house with a mansard roof, a central tower topped by wrought-iron filigree, and enough carved wooden gingerbread to gag a dragon. The Viceroy of the Two Provinces stared in wonderment at the house, which he had not seen but which was the talk of Canton. He knew that Chang-mei had hired a young English architect from Hong Kong to design her a house in the "very latest European fashion." The result was this absurd monstrosity, which might have looked less absurd in a suburb of Manchester, Liverpool, or Albany, but in the hills above Canton it looked downright laughable. The Viceroy, who had a refined eye for Chinese art and architecture, had no idea what to make of this strange building as he heaved his bulk out of the sedan chair that the porters had set on the ground. As his bodyguard of twenty mounted Bannermen of the top-ranking White Banner dismounted from their white horses, the Viceroy waddled to the covered porch that girdled the front of the house.

Chang-mei was waiting for him, wearing well-cut white slacks, boots, and a white silk blouse open at the throat. On her head she wore a black brimmed hat that gave her the look of a South American gaucho, though she had bought it in the Philippines. She was smoking a Manila cheroot. Prince I, who had heard of her beauty and her eccentric dress style, thought she was as peculiar as her house. But he also thought there was something surprisingly erotic about this youthful, trim Chinese woman in the clothes of a western man.

The Prince knew that in her rebellion against all things Chinese it was possible Chang-mei might refuse to render him the obeisance due him as a member of the imperial family. If this happened, to save face before his Bannermen the Prince knew that Chang-mei would have to be punished by decapitation, a fate he earnestly wished to avoid, since she was Justin's wife. When he had sent her the note advising her of his intended visit, he had strongly hinted that

she would be expected to "respect the formalities due his rank." But he needn't
have worried. Chang-mei might have outraged convention by frequently wearing men's clothes and when wearing women's clothes insisting on European
styles rather than traditional Chinese robes, but she was not so foolish as to insult a man as powerful as the Viceroy of the Two Provinces. When Prince I's
chief Bannerman barked the traditional order: *"Kuei hsia!"* Chang-mei threw
away her cheroot, knelt, and made the obeisance.

"My humble house is honored by your presence, O Lord," she said as the
Prince huffed his way up the steps of the porch. Despite the warm weather, he
wore a heavy brocaded dragon robe of gold and cerulean blue.

"Rise, Chang-mei," he said. "And your house is anything but humble. In fact,
it's almost as big as my palace. It would not have been wise for you to have
made it bigger."

Chang-mei rose and smiled at him. She guessed that he was intrigued.

"I would never have been so presumptuous," she said. "Please come inside,
my lord."

She led him into the entrance hall of the house, which was paneled in dark
wood like a suburban villa and had a staircase. The Prince looked around.

"So this is how the English live," he said. "Strange. You of course consulted
the astrologers before you built this place?"

"Oh, yes, my lord. And they told us the day to begin and judged the *feng
shui.*" The spirits of wind and water. Chang-mei was not defying *all* Chinese
conventions.

"Is the house comfortable?"

"Yes, my lord. I thought it might amuse you to be served an English tea,
which my architect taught me how to do."

"That should be interesting."

"You see, my lord, I have tried to take the best of both cultures, Chinese
and western. I like to think of myself as a breath of fresh air in our ancient
kingdom."

"Fresh air, or the breath of the dragon?" said Prince I, coolly. "However,
serve me your tea. I have a letter for you from your husband, which is one reason I came. And frankly, out of curiosity to see your house. Rumor has it, it
cost you one million taels. Could this be true?"

"Actually, it was a bit more. We had to import so much from England."

She led him into the drawing room that was decorated with department-store
furniture from Maples in London. She gestured toward an overstuffed horsehair sofa.

"If you'll sit here, my lord? My English architect tells me this is all the rage
in London. He says Queen Victoria has a sofa like this in Buckingham Palace."

"Really? Most interesting." He pulled a letter from the sleeve of his robe. "By the way, here's the letter from Justin."

"Thank you."

She took it and placed it on the mantel as the Prince sat on the sofa. Then she sat in a wing chair next to a table holding a silver tea service.

"You don't wish to open the letter from your husband?" the Prince asked.

"It can wait till later. The English put sugar and milk into their tea, or sometimes lemon. Which would you prefer, my lord?"

"I now understand why they are called barbarians. But the lemon sounds interesting."

Chang-mei poured the tea into a Staffordshire cup, then handed it to a young Chinese servant who took it to the Prince, bowing. The Prince examined the cup.

"The cup is Chinese?" he asked.

"English, my lord. They copy our patterns. The English make sandwiches out of cucumbers. They are rather delicious."

The servant presented a tray with the cucumber sandwiches. The Prince took one and popped it in his mouth. He chewed it, smiled, and took three more.

"You're right: they are tasty."

Chang-mei dismissed the servant with her eyes as she poured her own tea.

"Why," said the Prince, "are you not more eager to hear news of your husband? He's been gone for over a year. Has your desire for Justin cooled?"

She set down her cup. "My husband is a son of a sea snake!" she exclaimed. "In his last letter, he told me he had seen the missionary's daughter, that monkey-faced strumpet with skin like yak's milk! I *knew* he would do it!"

"He told me what happened at Saxmundham Castle, but he swore he did not make clouds and rain with the missionary's daughter."

"Pardon, my lord, but if you think I believe *that!* For all their talk of romantic love, the moment they get away from their wives, they are sniffing after other women. The barbarians are as bad as Chinese men—begging your pardon, my lord. But we women are treated like the scum of the earth by both barbarians and Chinese."

"I can see you feel strongly on the subject. Is that why you sometimes dress like a man?"

"Exactly."

"Still, you married a western man, you built a western house, you wear western clothes, and you drink western tea. You realize that the way you live is a provocation against the ancient wisdom of Confucius, who taught us to honor the father as we honor the Emperor."

"Yes, my lord. I realize that. But I have always been a rebel, ever since I was a girl. I feel, in my heart, that I must express disagreement with the ancient wisdom."

"I find it curious that Justin, your husband, has gone to Europe to learn the western ways of warfare to protect China. While you, his wife, are leading a life that makes a mockery of all we Chinese hold sacred. The Celestial Kingdom does not take rebels lightly. The Emperor has heard of you and has sent me a memorial. He has instructed me to tell you to revert to Chinese ways or suffer the consequences."

Chang-mei's face turned to ice.

"Is that a threat, my lord?"

"No. It is an order." He put down his teacup. "China is going through a great ordeal. We are attacked from within by the Taiping rebels and from without by the barbarians. Any Chinese who does not follow the path of righteous honor will suffer the Death of a Thousand Cuts." He stood up. "Use your head, Chang-mei. Or you may well lose it."

She bowed as he started out of the room.

"You know," the Prince said, "that Justin is studying warfare with the great Italian General Garibaldi. A most interesting idea. Your husband is a fine man, Chang-mei, and he is my friend. Don't force me to punish the wife of my friend. Do I have your word?"

He stopped at the door to the entrance hall and looked at her, his many chins jiggling as he turned, his slanted eyes peering into hers. She bowed.

"You have my word, my lord."

"Good. And thank you for the tea. It was interesting, but I prefer the Chinese style."

She watched as he waddled out of the house onto the porch. His bearers, who had been squatting on the ground, jumped to their feet as the Bannermen remounted their horses, shouting, *"Zhuyi! Gau kuai!"* The red-robed bearers bowed as the Viceroy of the Two Provinces climbed into his palanquin. Then the bearers hoisted the elaborate gold chair, surmounted by a gold roof and enclosed from the public view by green and gold paper panels, to their shoulders and started the stately procession back to Canton.

"What did he want?" asked the young man, coming up beside Chang-mei and putting his hand on her shoulder. The man, whose name was Li-shan, was tall, athletic, with a striking, hawklike face. Unlike most Chinese men, he had cut off his pigtail and let his hair grow to his shoulders as a sign of rebellion against the Manchus. Thus, he was given the nickname Chang-mao, or "long-haired rebel."

"He told me to stop wearing western clothes or be put to death."

"And you said?" Li-shan kissed her ear. He was a Taiping, the son of the

Chung Wang, or "Faithful King," who was second in command to the leader of the Taiping Rebellion, the T'ien Wang or "Heavenly King"—the man who claimed to be the younger brother of Jesus Christ.

"I told him I would obey him," Chang-mei said.

Li-shan frowned. "Surely you won't give in so easily?"

She turned around and put her arms around him, kissing him hotly. "You have sworn to me that the Heavenly King preaches equality between the sexes. You have sworn to me that if I join the great rebellion, I will no longer have to bow to you or any other man. Is that true, Li-shan?"

"It is true."

"Then tonight," she said with a smile, "we set sail to your father in Nanking."

"With the silver?"

"With the silver. Let the Manchus rot. I will mount the fiery tiger and join your rebellion."

Li-shan smiled.

"What a beautiful baby! What's her name?" asked Tony Bruce, who was admiring the baby being held in the arms of the Irish nanny.

"Georgiana," said the nanny, Geraldine, smiling proudly at her charge. "Isn't it a lovely name for a lovely child? Mrs. Savage dreamed it up, she did. Oh, and the baby has the disposition of an angel!"

"Does she?" Tony glanced at Adelaide, who was seated in a chair in the drawing room of the Washington Square mansion, doing petit point. "She must take after her mother," he said with a smile.

Adelaide shot him a look, then said to the nanny, "Thank you, Geraldine. You may take her back to the nursery now."

"Yes, ma'am."

The nanny curtsied, then took the three-week-old baby out of the room. It was a warm morning in June. Tony, dressed as always in the height of fashion, came over to sit in a chair opposite Adelaide.

"Well," he said softly, "now we have two: a boy and a girl. Quite a little family we're raising."

"*I'm* raising, Tony," Adelaide said. "The children are mine and Sylvaner's, bought and paid for. Don't get any ideas."

"Well, it's difficult for me not to get ideas. In fact, my head is always filled with ideas. About money. About Wall Street. Such a fascinating place, Wall Street. It's always filled with rumors. I suppose there's something about the place that encourages rumors. Most of us are speculators, after all, and speculation is fed by rumor. Stocks going up, stocks going down. . . ."

"What *are* you nattering on about, Tony?"

He smiled and leaned forward toward her.

"There's a rumor going around the Street that what Sylvaner told the press in London wasn't *quite* the truth. There's a rumor that a certain dashing former pirate, who received so many headlines in England as 'the Suffolk Pirate'— a delicious conceit—was actually the man who lured Sylvaner to the 'mystery mansion' in Hampstead. And that he forced Sylvaner to sign a confession."

"What a lurid mind you have, Tony," Adelaide said, continuing her petit point. "You really should write for the *Tribune.*"

"Ah yes: murders! Gang wars! Crime and corruption! All the things people love to read about, mainly because they happen. And the sophisticated smile condescendingly and say 'trash.' But to return to this alleged confession your husband signed. Apparently there are some lurid revelations in it. How Sylvaner had plotted to have his half brother murdered at sea. How he hired a professional killer to murder Justin's amah, who knew too much to stay alive. And how it all backfired."

"You should write this all down, Tony. It would make a wonderful novel."

"Ah, but Sylvaner already wrote it down. And the amah, Ah Pin, brought the confession to New York where it is now in the safe of a certain lawyer. Where it will remain as long as Sylvaner does not pursue the charges of piracy against his half brother. Of course, as I said, it's just rumor. But if it were true, it would paint an interesting portrait of your husband, wouldn't it? It would make the 'magnificent Savages' look not quite so magnificent, wouldn't it?"

"I suppose. You begin to bore me."

"Do I? Sorry."

"We're leaving for Newport in three days. I have to supervise the packing." She put her petit point in a bag. "If you'll excuse me . . ."

"Sit down. I'm not finished."

His tone turned slightly less silky and urbane. She had started to get out of her chair. Now, slowly, she sat back down.

"I'm sure you've heard I'm in financial trouble again," he said.

"Yes. It's hardly news. You're always in financial trouble, Tony. Have you ever thought of another profession besides stockbrokering? Perhaps house painting?"

"But I like stockbrokering. The thrill of the gamble. The possibilities of great fortunes made on the turn of a stock instead of a card. Exciting stuff. My problem has been that I've never had enough capital to be a player of the first magnitude. I hear the tips. I have the sources. I just don't have the money. I'd like to change that."

"I'm sure you would."

"I'm putting together a pool of one million dollars."

"That's a lot of money."

"Not anymore. It would be an investment pool, which I would direct. The word on the Street is that there's bound to be a war over the slavery issue sooner or later. Wars provide fantastic opportunities to make vast fortunes."

"I never realized you were such an idealist, Tony."

"I'm not rich enough to be an idealist. I want you and Sylvaner to invest in my pool. If you invest, it will give the whole operation legitimacy."

"How much are you talking about?"

"Perhaps a quarter million. Perhaps more."

"Why in the world should we give you a quarter million dollars to invest in stock speculation?"

Tony got up and placed his hands on the arms of her chair, leaning down until his face was inches from hers.

"Because if you don't," he said softly, "I'll tell Sylvaner who is the real father of his children."

"I knew you would try this sooner or later. It was the chance I had to take. You know this is called blackmail?"

"I couldn't care less."

"How would you prove this ridiculous assertion?"

"Do you remember where we met to bring about the second blessed event? Shall I refresh your memory? It was in room 403 at the St. Nicholas Hotel. We met there on four occasions. Each time I made sure there was a friend of mine in the adjacent room, 404. A friend of mine who is definitely not a friend of yours. She made notations as to the time and date of each of our trysts. If such an unpleasant proof should be needed, there would be no doubt at all as to the parentage of that lovely baby upstairs in the nursery, Georgiana Savage."

Adelaide stared at him, her face white.

"You swine!" she whispered. "Who is this 'friend' of yours?"

Tony's smile was sheer insolence. He straightened and clapped his hands.

Geraldine, the red-haired Irish nanny, came back into the room. She smiled at Tony.

"You darlin' man," she said to him. Then she turned to Adelaide and her smile vanished. "It's all true, Mrs. Savage. We've got the goods on you. You'd best be doin' what Tony says."

"You Irish bitch!" Adelaide snarled. "I knew you were a sneak, but . . ."

"I'll thank you not to be insultin' me, but I suppose this means you won't be givin' me a reference? Just for the record, though, I'm givin' you notice. I'll be leavin' this house now." Again, she smiled at Tony. "Such a fine-lookin' man, isn't he? Someday we should compare notes about his lovemakin'."

On New Year's Day two years before, the biggest, grandest, and most extravagant hotel in America had opened its doors to the public. The St. Nicholas Hotel ran a hundred feet along Broadway and two hundred feet through to Mercer Street. But the initial success of the hotel was so overwhelming that a year later the owners opened a south wing running down Broadway to the southwest corner of Spring Street. The six-story, marble-fronted hotel contained 600 rooms, 150 of them family suites, and had all the modern conveniences that were making America the talk of the world. There were two miles of halls, all lavishly decorated and carpeted, and thirty miles of piping for heat and plumbing.

On entering the porticoed main entrance on Broadway, one came into a broad marble-floored hallway lined with settees covered with the skins of wild animals. Off this great hall were the "gentlemen's parlor," a reading room with a richly ornamented dome, the main washroom, and the bar. Next to the reception desk at the end of the hall was the grand staircase, built of white oak, which led to what the *New York Herald* described as the "brilliant surprise" of the second floor.

Here, a hall two hundred feet long, lined with mirrors and illuminated by great gilt gas chandeliers and wall sconces, led from Broadway all the way to the rear of the hotel on Mercer Street. This hall was the "peacock alley" of its day where stylish New Yorkers paraded in all their finery, displaying their considerable wealth. Off this great hall was the "ladies parlor" facing Broadway, decorated with an Axminster carpet in a medallion pattern and gold-colored brocade satin damask window curtains, interwoven with bouquets of flowers, which an awestruck reporter had discovered cost seven hundred dollars a window.

Also on the second floor was the grandest room of the St. Nicholas, the main dining room, fifty by a hundred feet of breath-snatching magnificence. Gilt pier mirrors marched down the walls interspaced with twenty-four pilasters that soared twenty feet to the frescoed ceiling. A huge staff of low-paid Irish immigrants filled the dining room and kitchens, such newly patented contrivances as dumbwaiters, steam tables, and steam-driven roasting spits easing somewhat their job of serving five meals a day: breakfast from five to noon, lunch from one-thirty to three, a dinner in one sitting at five, tea from six to eight, and a late supper from eight to midnight. The menus were all in French, confounding most of the American guests. And one greatly admired "gimmick" of the waiters was for each of them to reach over the shoulder of the seated guest, grasp the handle of the silver cover of the main course, and then, at a given signal from the maître d', lift all the covers off at the same moment, eliciting whoops and gasps from the diners. Men may come and go, but pretension lives forever.

Another innovation on the second floor was the bridal suite, a "newly invented institution of the hotel profession." Here the walls were covered with white satin, the same material being used for the curtains. Elaborately carved woodwork, a ton of gilt, imported French furniture, and four crystal chandeliers made the suite so "scandalously splendid," according to one magazine, that "timid brides are said to shrink aghast at its marvels."

Geraldine O'Brian was no "timid bride," nor was she a virgin. But two nights after she left the employ of the Sylvaner Savages, where she had served as nanny, she was disporting herself naked in the arms of Tony Bruce in the massive rosewood bed of the suite, which was covered with white lace and satin.

"Ah, Tony, me darlin'," she sighed as he kissed her full white breasts, "I'll never forget the look on Mrs. Savage's face when I walked into her parlor the other day. I thought the mean bitch would have a stroke."

"Yes, it was quite a lovely scene." Tony chuckled, sitting up to scratch his hairy chest and light a cigar. "You played your part magnificently, I might add. Have you ever thought of going on the stage? You surely have the looks."

"Ah, don't be plantin' foolish ideas in me head. I'm just a simple girl from Tralee with no education or breedin'. The only parts I could play would be servin' girls or maids. All the star parts are for great ladies or duchesses."

"You could be taught to play a duchess. We could hire you a speech coach and in a matter of weeks you could sound like the English Ambassador's wife."

"But coaches cost money. I'm flat broke, and you, you wicked man, are up to your ears in debt. God knows how you're goin' to pay for this bridal suite."

"But tonight is a celebration, my chickadee. My little blackmail scam has paid off handsomely. I received a note this afternoon from Sylvaner Savage—the great man himself! He's agreed to invest three hundred thousand dollars in my investment pool. We're rich, Gerry. Stinking rich."

"You devil! Why didn't you tell me?"

"I thought a nice surprise would put some zip into your sexual performance."

"But we just did it!"

"For what this suite is costing, once is definitely not enough . . . what the hell?"

The door to the suite had opened and a man in a black suit and bowler hat had come in, followed by Adelaide and a young man who was rapidly making pencil sketches in a pad.

"Good evening, Mr. Bruce," the man said, tipping his hat. "Pray let me introduce myself. My name is Frank Tippet, and I am the house detective here at the St. Nicholas Hotel—a caravansary known for its high moral tone, I might add. This distinguished lady you know, I believe?" He indicated Adelaide, who smiled.

"Good evening, Tony," she purred. "And dear, sweet Geraldine. What *could* you two be discussing? Politics? The weather? Ah, but of course: religion. But don't let us stop you."

Tony, a murderous look on his face, sucked his cigar. "All right, Adelaide," he said. "Tit for tat. I get it. Except it won't work."

"Oh, but I think it will. And this young gentleman," Adelaide continued, indicating the man with the sketch pad, "is Mr. Edward Delaney, a quick-sketch artist who freelances for several leading metropolitan newspapers. He is recording this immortal scene for posterity."

"Miss O'Brian," the house detective said to Geraldine, who was cowering behind the sheets, "I will give you"—he pulled out his gold pocket watch— "exactly eight minutes to get dressed. Then I'm taking you to the local police station where you'll be booked for prostitution. . . ."

"I'm no whore!" she cried.

"Lewdness, immoral acts in a public place, and whatever else I can think of. It should be enough to deport you back to the Old Sod."

"No! Oh, Tony"—she threw her arms around her lover—"don't let them do this to me! I don't want to go back. . . ." She started sobbing.

"I'll get a lawyer," Tony said. "They're just trying to scare you."

"They're succeedin'!" she wailed.

"You have seven minutes," announced the detective, looking at his watch.

"Adelaide," Tony said, "I'm sure you think this is very clever, but it's not going to do you any good. It doesn't change anything between us—I mean, as far as the intimate knowledge I have of the parentage of certain children you know is concerned. This won't shut me up."

"Oh, yes it will," Adelaide said. "Since your chief witness, *dear* Geraldine, might have a credibility problem with jurors if this were taken to court—which is exactly where I would take it if you decided to be so foolish as to push me any further. But of course, neither of us wants bad publicity, do we? Foremost in your twisted little brain is a desire to succeed with your investment pool—am I not right? And neither I nor any other prospective investor would want to place money with a man who commits adultery with an aging nanny in the most expensive hotel suite in New York."

"I'm not 'aging'!" Geraldine yelled.

"You have six minutes," announced the detective.

"Think about it, Tony," Adelaide said with the sweetest of smiles. "In this case, silence is indeed golden. And publicity will ruin you forever. Come, Mr. Delaney. I'm sure you have enough sketches."

"Yes, ma'am, and they're sizzlin' hot!"

As Adelaide and the artist left the room, the detective said, "You have five and a half minutes."

"Oh, shut up!" Geraldine growled, getting out of the bed as Tony sucked pensively on his cigar.

18 CHANG-MEI PLACED HER DAUGHTER, JULIE, in her cradle as Li-shan came into the main cabin of the war junk *Eastern Dragon*.

"There's a ship off the port quarter," he said. "It's one of the imperial fleet. The Captain is signaling us to come to—he wants to inspect us."

Chang-mei, who was wearing her usual shipboard outfit of white blouse, black pants, and boots, straightened from the cradle.

"Which ship?" she asked.

"The *Yellow Lotus*."

"That leaky tub," she said scornfully. "The master is an opium addict and only has his job because of bribes. But Prince I must have been told that I took all my silver out of the bank of Macao."

"What should we do? If they find the silver, they'll take it, won't they?"

"Of course. They won't even need an excuse, because Prince I has probably already guessed what I'm up to. And when he finds out you're aboard, we'll both be candidates for the executioner. I'll come topside."

She crossed the cabin, pausing a moment beside Li-shan to run her fingers over his naked shoulders, for it was hot and he was shirtless. Li-shan had begun training in the martial arts when he was twelve. Now, in his twenty-fourth year, his body was a superb machine, his torso sculpted, each muscle defined. Every time she looked at him, Chang-mei tingled with desire.

She kissed him quickly, then hurried out of the cabin and went up on deck, followed by Li-shan.

"Lower the sails," she shouted. "Let the *Yellow Lotus* come alongside. Raise the flag of compliance."

"Are you going to let them aboard?" Li-shan asked.

She smiled. "You'll see." She turned to her chief gunner. "Load the Forest guns. Be ready to fire at my signal."

"You're going to engage the imperial fleet?" Li-shan asked, marveling at the daring of this young peasant's daughter turned pirate.

"I'm going to sink it," she said matter-of-factly. "The cannons on that tub are forty years out-of-date. Thanks to Justin, my guns have twice the range."

"If you sink it, we automatically become traitors."

Chang-mei laughed as the wind blew her thick black hair.

"It's a little late to worry about that," she said.

It was a clear, bright day, the sun blazing in the sky. They were twenty miles off Hong Kong, heading north with a following wind. Now, with the sails lowered, the war junk wallowed clumsily in the light sea. Li-shan knew little about warships, but even his untutored eye could tell that the government junk was rundown, the gaudy yellow paint on its hull peeling, its sails patched. The crew, most of them shirtless like Li-shan in the scorching midday heat, were hanging from the rigging or standing on deck. Li-shan might have been a rebel against the Manchu government, but he was a Chinese. His stomach wrenched at this shabby spectacle that called itself the Chinese Imperial Navy. Tales of corruption in the court at Peking whirled in his mind, particularly stories of the now nearly all-powerful concubine, Yehenala, the girl from Pewter Lane, who, it was said, sucked money from the naval funds to buy herself jade and finery.

"Fire!" Chang-mei yelled. The cannons of the *Eastern Dragon* roared, belching fire and smoke. The mainmast of the *Yellow Lotus* was hit, its sail collapsing on the deck.

"Fire!" Chang-mei yelled again.

This time, the hull was hit in three places. Li-shan could hear the distant screams of the crew, some of whom were beginning to jump into the shark-infested waters of the China Sea.

"Fire!" Chang-mei yelled a third time.

One of the balls hit the ship's magazine, and the *Yellow Lotus* became a fireball.

Chang-mei ran to Li-shan, throwing her arms around his waist, her eyes ablaze with excitement.

"That's my answer to Prince I!" she exclaimed with a triumphant grin. "The *Eastern Dragon* has breathed fire, and look at the result! To hell with the Manchus!"

"To hell with the Manchus!" Li-shan echoed. "And you, my jade girl, are stronger than the Topaz Tree! Together with the Heavenly King, we will soon take Peking!"

And he kissed her as the crew of the junk cheered.

"What is this strange thing the barbarians call 'love'?" Li-shan asked that night as he lay beside Chang-mei on the bunk in the main cabin of the war junk. They were in "The Fish Eye-to-Eye" position of the ancient manuals of erotic love, their stomachs touching. "You tell me Justin often spoke of it to you."

"Yes, especially just before we made clouds and rain."

"Did Justin love you?"

"No. He lied. He desired me, and there was an excitement between us. After all, we both were exotic to each other. But his heart lies with the accursed missionary's daughter."

"But what does that mean? What does 'love' mean? I'm curious. Is it what my father feels for his concubines?"

"I think not—exactly. Justin told me that in America when men and women desire each other and want to make clouds and rain, they are not permitted to do so."

"Why?"

"That part I never quite understood."

"The Heavenly King forbids clouds and rain except at certain specified times. He says it takes energy away from other pursuits—although he allows himself and the other kings to have concubines, as my father has."

"I thought you told me that in the Heavenly Kingdom men and women are equal?"

"They are, but there are rules. None will apply to us, of course, because I am the son of the Chung Wang. But to get back to this 'love': if men and women in America can't make clouds and rain, how are there any children?"

"They can make clouds and rain after they are married. But until then, they are in love."

"This love must be very uncomfortable. When I want to make clouds and rain and I can't, it's agonizing. So is this 'love' agonizing?"

"Apparently it is. That's part of the pleasure of it, Justin said."

"How curious. Then after marriage, when the man and woman can make clouds and rain, there is no longer any need for love?"

"I never quite understood that, either," Chang-mei said. "Although Justin did say once that when people got married, they were supposed to live happily ever after. Now I know he spoke with a double tongue, because after he married me he ran away to his missionary's daughter. Ah, what a snake." She sighed. "But a charming one."

"Do you miss him?"

She didn't answer for a moment. Then: "Yes, I cannot lie. As angry as I am at him, I do miss him."

"Does it put you in agony?"

"Yes, a little."

"Then you must be in love with him."

She sat up, looking at him in wonderment. "Could it be possible?" she said. "Is *that* what he was talking about? Is what I'm feeling about him 'love'?"

Li-shan's face was icy with jealousy. He grabbed her and pulled her down into his arms, kissing her hotly on the mouth. "You tell me he is handsome, but I have never seen a roundeye who was handsome."

"Nor I. Except for him."

"Is he as handsome as I?"

"He's different. He has gold hair."

"Is he as strong as I?"

"Your muscles are harder."

"Then you will stop loving him and start loving me!"

"How can I love you? We've already made clouds and rain—many times! According to Justin . . ."

He pushed her angrily away. "I know: no clouds and rain. It makes no sense."

Chang-mei put her head back on her pillow and smiled rather dreamily. "Yes, it doesn't make sense. But I'm beginning to understand why the barbarians make such a fuss over love. It's really rather a pleasant sensation."

Li-shan climbed over her out of the bunk and pulled on his pants.

"Where are you going?" Chang-mei asked.

"Up on deck. It's hot in here."

Chang-mei smiled. "You're angry that I'm in love with Justin."

"Damned women!" he snorted. "Damned barbarians! Damned love!"

He slammed out of the cabin. Chang-mei smiled to herself, remembering Justin, her former "toy" who had turned out to be such a passionate maker of clouds and rain but who had been so amusingly "missionary-ish" about marriage. How confusing the barbarians were! But how exciting, in a way. After all her anger, was she in love with Justin? Was anger part of love? She *did* miss him.

She turned on her side, thinking of the excitement that afternoon when they had sunk the imperial war junk. Li-shan was the son of the Chung Wang and therefore rich and powerful; but he was an outlaw to the Manchus, as was she after sinking the *Yellow Lotus*. If they were ever caught, their heads would be sliced off in the Field of Executions. Or, even worse, the excruciating Death of a Thousand Cuts, when criminals were slowly skinned alive. It was a sobering thought. She wondered if she had been insane to rush off with Li-shan to join the Taiping Rebellion?

Li-shan came back into the cabin and slammed the door. "I have decided," he said, "that when we get to Nanking, you will be my concubine."

"I don't want to be anyone's concubine," Chang-mei said. "I keep telling you one of the main reasons I'm joining the rebellion is that you told me men and women were equal in the Heavenly Kingdom."

"All right, then be my wife."

She laughed. "I'm already married."

"The Heavenly King is all-powerful: he can divorce you from the barbarian."

"But we're not in love!"

He glowered at her a moment. Then he came to the bunk, climbed on, and shook her angrily. "You will love *me,* you understand? *Me!*"

"But, Li-shan," she said with a smile, "you don't know what love is—remember?"

"It is nothing more than a barbarian way of talking about clouds and rain! I'll show you what love is!"

Almost fiercely, he executed "The Monkey Wrestles," "The Seagull Hovers," and finally "The Rooster Descends on the Ring." When he had finished this exhaustingly athletic exercise in classic Chinese sex play, he lay beside her, panting.

"That's what love is!" he puffed.

"No it isn't," Chang-mei said, smiling.

"Damn you! Then what *is* it?"

"You'll have to find out for yourself."

Li-shan groaned with frustration.

He had appeared in her life a month before in the middle of the night. She had been asleep in her new mansion outside Canton when she heard a horse ride up. Running to the window, she had looked out to see in the moonlight a warrior dismounting from a white charger. He went up on the porch and banged on her door. Not knowing what to expect, Chang-mei had hurried downstairs. She opened the door to see Li-shan. She knew from his long hair that he was a Taiping, but for some reason she was not afraid. He told her he had an important message for her from the Heavenly King.

Curious, she admitted him, lighting the lamps. When she saw his face, with its high cheekbones and hawk nose, she felt a tingle she hadn't experienced since she had first seen Justin.

Li-shan explained that he was the son of the great rebel general, the Chung Wang, and that the Heavenly King had sent him south to try to convince Chang-mei to back the rebel cause with her great fortune in the Macao bank. Chang-mei had reflected that the Heavenly King was not without sophisticated guile to send this handsome warrior to try to enroll her in the cause. But she was also aware of the dangers involved, for the Taiping Rebellion was the greatest threat to the Manchu Throne in Peking since the Manchus had founded the Ch'ing Dynasty two hundred years before, and the Manchus were taking no prisoners.

She toyed with him, as he toyed with her. She told him she must think such an enormous and risky step over; and meanwhile, if he wished, he could stay with her in her house. He accepted readily enough: outside the dominions of the Heavenly King, he was a wanted criminal.

By the second night, they had become lovers. Meanwhile, he was telling her of the advantages that would accrue to her if she backed the Taipings. When the Heavenly King overthrew the Manchus, Chang-mei would be brought to the court in Peking where anything she wished would be granted her. Since it was so well known that she herself was a rebel against the ancient Confucian subordination of women, the Heavenly King promised that he would establish new decrees that would empower Chinese women, lifting the yoke of male domination that had existed for thousands of years in the Celestial Kingdom.

For Chang-mei, this was heady stuff. And when Prince I had come to her house threatening her with death if she did not revert to traditional Chinese ways, she had made the decision to throw in her lot with the rebels.

But now, as she lay next to Li-shan, she marveled at the risks she was taking. If the Heavenly King *didn't* win . . . if, more immediately, she and Li-shan were caught by the imperial forces . . .

She thought of the Death of a Thousand Cuts, and as brave as she was, she couldn't help but shudder with fear. The Manchus might fight progress and be considered by the rest of the world as hopelessly backward, but there was one thing in which they led the world.

Cruelty.

Though there was considerable risk in sailing the *Eastern Dragon* up the Yangtze River to Nanking, Li-shan convinced Chang-mei that there would be far greater risk trying to transport the twenty heavy chests filled with silver taels and Mexican silver dollars across land (the Mexican currency being preferred by the foreign traders). Imperial troops, known as "demon imps," controlled Shanghai and its environs. Aside from that danger, inevitably word would spread that this enormous fortune was being moved across land, and bandits from all over China would descend on them like flies to honey. Li-shan assured Chang-mei that once past Shanghai, the towns on the Yangtze were in control of the Taiping rebels. And if they entered the Yangtze by sailing north of Ch'ungming Island, they would be out of sight of Shanghai, which was not on the Yangtze but slightly inland on the Huangpu River.

To this Chang-mei agreed. They entered the Yangtze at night and proceeded up the great river to the west where, some two hundred miles inland, lay Nanking, the second city of the Chinese Empire and the capital of the Heavenly King, who had renamed it Tienking, the Heavenly Capital. Navigating the relatively narrow channel of the Yangtze north of Ch'ungming Island by night was tricky. By dawn, they had passed Ch'ungming Island, and they turned to port to seek out the deeper water of the middle river. Here, in the delta, the Yangtze looked more like the open sea. The great waterway, known to the Chinese as the "Long River," was so wide that neither shore could be seen. Progress was slow, as both the wind and the current were against them; however, they were still affected by the ocean tides so that when the tide was coming in they gained an advantage. Otherwise, they were forced to tack continuously to grasp what breeze they could. But by night they had reached the Lang-shan crossing, the most difficult navigation of the river. Li-shan, who knew the river well and was manning the steering oar, recommended they anchor for the night because gales were known to spring up suddenly at this point of the Yangtze. Chang-mei agreed. And after setting an armed watch, for the Yangtze swarmed with pirates as well as imperial river patrols, she and Li-shan went to her cabin to eat supper. Ah Ling, the baby amah, had fed Julie and put her to bed. Now Chang-mei and Li-shan sat down to a delicious meal of *tang-li yü*, crisp-fried eels.

As they ate, he told her more about his father, the mighty Chung Wang, or "Faithful King."

"He's only fifteen years older than I am," he said, "since he began soldiering at a very young age and decided he must have a son in case he was killed."

"That seems practical," Chang-mei said, biting her beautiful white teeth into an eel.

"Oh, my honorable father is very practical and very brave. He's from Kwangsi Province, which is where the bravest men in China come from."

"You told me his real name is Li Hsiu-ch'eng, and he was once a poor mountain farmer?"

"Yes, but now he is the second ranking noble in the Heavenly Kingdom. He commands an army of hundreds of thousands of soldiers, and his personal bodyguard is five thousand strong, all from the Maoutze, or aboriginal mountaineers. They have never been conquered by the Manchus, so their hair has never been cut and it falls to their feet. It's quite wonderful to see."

"Are you bragging?"

He smiled. "Of course."

Julie woke up and started crying. Li-shan rose from the table and went over to her bed. He took her in his arms and cradled her, humming a Chinese lullaby. Chang-mei watched as her and Justin's daughter stopped crying and went back to sleep. Then Li-shan gently replaced her in her bed.

When he returned to the table, Chang-mei said, "You really love children, don't you?"

"Of course. I want some of my own—preferably by you."

"I can't believe you haven't had clouds and rain with other women."

"I have slept with flower girls."

"But the Heavenly King forbids intercourse?"

"Yes. But not to his kings and their sons."

"You're very privileged."

"I'm a prince," he said matter-of-factly. "A heavenly prince to the Heavenly King."

Yes, he *is* a prince, she thought, looking at him rather dreamily. And he certainly is heavenly to look at. Also he is of my blood, my people. I, who so rashly married Justin to become the wife of a roundeye, should I not now wed one of my own kind? And a handsome prince, at that?

I have cast my lot with the Taiping rebels, I have gambled all on their cause. Perhaps I *should* become the wife of Li-shan, son of the great Chung Wang.

In the morning they found that the current had dragged them a half mile downstream. They raised anchor, hoisted their sails, and started upstream again. Reaching the Lang-shan crossing a second time, they navigated the sharp turn, avoiding with difficulty the numerous mud flats about the Lang-shan hills on the right bank. The river scenery was for the greater part flat, the surrounding countryside a low, alluvial soil. However, the cultivated fields were embedded among luxuriant foliage that added beauty to the scene. There were thickets of bamboo along the bank and lovely bowers of weeping willows. Chang-mei was enchanted by what she saw, although they passed several pagodas that had been burned by the Taipings. Li-shan explained that the Heavenly King wanted to replace all the pagodas in China with Christian churches.

"Are you a Christian?" she asked, standing next to him on the poop deck.

"Of course. And you will become one too when you marry me."

Chang-mei snorted. "I've always thought the stories I've heard of Christianity were silly. Why would the Jews kill Jesus when he was a Jew? And how can a man die and then come to life again? It doesn't make any sense."

"It will all come clear when you speak to the Heavenly King," Li-shan said calmly.

"Maybe, but you might as well know I'm skeptical. I believe in what I can see and touch, like the twenty chests of silver in the hold. If you're rich enough, you can buy your way into Heaven—if there *is* a Heaven."

Li-shan laughed. "It will be perhaps the Heavenly King's greatest task to convert you," he said in a pleasant tone. "However," he added, "if you refuse to be converted, he will decapitate you. It's surprising how the threat of execution helps people see the beauty and truth of the Christian religion."

Chang-mei stared at him.

"In the first place, Li-shan," she said, "I haven't said I would marry you, and your threatening to have me decapitated if I don't become a Christian is not making me eager to say yes to you. And in the second place, we're not in love with each other."

"Love," he snorted. "I've thought about that and come to the conclusion it isn't Chinese. I think you can only know what this 'love' is if you have clouds and rain with a barbarian, as you did."

"You may be right. But it's a wonderful thing. You should find a barbarian, as I did."

Maybe someday, he thought. I must admit I'm curious to know what she's talking about.

19   IN THE GARDEN OF CRYSTAL Rivulets in the Summer Palace west of Peking, Yehenala, who had been raised to the third rank of Ping concubine after bearing a son for the Hsien-feng Emperor, filled a peony-painted porcelain wine cup for her master, the seventh emperor of the Ta Ching Chao, the Great Pure Dynasty. The sun was setting over the Western

Hills as the two sat on a terrace of the Pavilion of Auspicious Twilight. Before them lay the seventeen arches of the bridge to South Lake Island; beyond that rose the Mount of Myriad Longevity. They were in the fabled Yuan Ming Yuan, the Park of Radiant Perfection, which had been laid out a century earlier by Jesuits for the pleasure of the greatest of the Ch'ing Emperors, the Ch'ien Lung Emperor. Now his great-grandson, the alcoholic Hsien-feng Emperor, accepted his wine cup from Yehenala and burped.

"This Orphan is sad," he said, sipping the wine. Yehenala knew that when he referred to himself as *"Kua,"* it meant he was in a tricky mood. "We have received a memorial from Our cousin Prince I, the Viceroy of the Two Provinces. He tells Us that Our finest war junk, the *Yellow Lotus,* was blown up by that daughter of a bitch turtle, the pirate Chang-mei."

"She is the peasant girl who wears men's clothes, built an English house, and married the red-haired foreign devil?"

"The very same. Prince I tells Us that she has taken her entire treasure out of the Bank of Macao and is presumably defecting to the accursed rebels. There is a rumor going around Canton that she has been lured into defecting by a Taiping prince, a certain Li-shan, the son of the Chung Wang."

"This slave has heard of him," Yehenala said, using the elaborately demeaning archaic language of the court. "It is said he is young, handsome, and brave."

"The sea bitch has undoubtedly coupled with him for clouds and rain."

"If this slave could be so presumptuous as to offer a suggestion to Your Majesty, whose wisdom extends beyond the heavens, it would seem to be wise to punish this Chang-mei, who has committed an abomination by presuming to rebel against the Son of Heaven."

A flock of birds rose past the crimson pillars of the Tower of Buddha's Fragrance, frightened by a little lion dog, one of Yehenala's pets. The Yuan Ming Yuan covered several hundred square miles in total, all for the enjoyment of one man, the Son of Heaven. It was undoubtedly one of the most exquisite marriages of nature and man's artifice anywhere on earth. Hsien-feng, who was wearing an imperial yellow silk robe embroidered with five gold-thread writhing dragons, held out his wine cup for a refill.

"You do not speak unwisely, Nala," he said, using her informal name. "We have put a reward of fifty thousand taels on her head, and if caught she will suffer the Death of a Thousand Cuts. We will also confiscate her treasure and estates, which Prince I assures Us exceeds millions of barbarian dollars. Of course, Our cousin, the great fat whale, has undoubtedly lined his purse with the woman's squeeze over the years. We do not begrudge a viceroy taking bribes—after all, it spares Us paying them excessively—but Prince I is a pig, both physically and mentally. Alas, We are not well served." He sighed and took the refilled wine cup.

"Did this slave hear correctly, O Lord of Ten Thousand Years?" Yehenala said as wind chimes tinkled in the evening breeze. "Did Your Majesty say 'if' she is caught? Can there be any doubt?"

"Alas, Our generals are incompetent," the Emperor moaned, tragically, sipping the wine. "Our mandarins are greedy and treacherous—what curse has befallen this Orphan? We are supposed to control the lower Yangtze, but Chenkiang, Our river fort, has fallen to the rebels. It is no certainty that the daughter of the bitch turtle will be caught by Our forces. Ah, Our life is not auspicious, Nala. If only We could see some way to"—again, he burped—"to breathe the fire of the dragon into Our generals!"

Yehenala, who was sitting on a stool at the feet of the Emperor, looked up at the Son of Heaven and her heart filled with scorn. If you would stop drinking, you sot! she longed to say. If you would lead your armies like your warrior ancestors instead of listening to the twitterings of your army of eunuchs, who think of nothing but how to steal from you and cheat you. If you would be a man instead of a worm, China might be saved! Someday, she thought, I will have the power. And then I, Yehenala, the girl from Pewter Lane, will crush the rebels and purge the hated foreign devils.

But all she dared say was: "If this slave might be so presumptuous . . . ?"

"Yes, yes, speak, Nala. You have a good head on your shoulders. We listen to your advice."

"Perhaps, Majesty, a new general?"

"Yes, yes, yes, but who?" he said petulantly. "Who?"

Yehenala knew who. It was a certain rich governor of one of the provinces. She insinuated his name into the Emperor's wine-ringing ear. The Governor in question had paid her a small fortune in slipper-shaped silver taels to mention his name to the Emperor.

Yehenala might dream of saving China. But she wasn't about to change the age-old system of squeeze.

"We will consider your suggestion," sighed the Emperor, who by now was half-drunk. "Perhaps it has merit. Look, Nala: the moon rises over the Western Hills!" He pointed over South Lake Island where a full moon was ballooning into the purple crepuscular sky. "We think perhaps We are like the great poet, Li Po, who, in the eighth century, got drunk, leaned out of his boat on the Yangtze, and tried to kiss the moon's reflection in the water so as to capture the impossible beauty. Like Li Po, We are reaching for the impossible: a happy China. And, like Li Po"—the Emperor drained his wine and sighed—"We may fall out of the boat and drown."

"There is Silver Island," Li-shan said to Chang-mei on the morning of their fourth day on the Yangtze. They were approaching the city of Chen-kiang, the former imperial fortress that had recently been captured by the Tai-pings.

"It's beautiful," Chang-mei said in awe as she looked at the heavily treed island that rose dramatically out of the river and soared to four hundred feet. The current had become so strong that an earlier attempt to pass the south end of the island had been abandoned and they were now passing to the north. "Tell me about it, Li-shan."

"One of the most important joss houses in the Empire is that temple over there—see it?" He pointed to a sloped-eaved building at the foot of the island-hill. "Inside are images of every devil and god in the Chinese religious calendar. Needless to say, the Heavenly King has vowed to destroy it one day. The monks also have a menagerie of every animal found in China."

"Fascinating."

"Isn't it? See that pagoda on top of the island?"

"Yes."

"Do you hear the drums?"

"Who couldn't?"

"The monks beat the oxhide drums around the clock every day of the year."

"Why? They must go deaf."

"The monks beat the drums to soothe the great 'Joss' fish that they believe carries the world on its back. If the drums stop and the 'Joss' fish can't hear the beating, it wriggles and causes earthquakes."

Chang-mei laughed. "That's almost as silly as Christ rising from the dead."

Li-shan shot her a cold look. "I would advise you," he said, "to curb your tongue about Christianity. We are now in the realm of the Heavenly King, and he does not take kindly to those who ridicule our religion."

It was the second time he had warned her, and a new fear began to fill her. She had gambled everything to join the Taiping rebels, but it had never occurred to her they were religious fanatics. In fact, almost everything she knew about the rebels was what Li-shan had told her. Had he sugar-coated the pill, hiding the ugly truth? Just what was she getting into?

She was soon to see even more ugliness. As they passed Chenkiang, she began to see scenes of appalling devastation: burned villages, burned fields, bloated bodies floating downstream past the junk.

"What is it?" Chang-mei asked Li-shan as they stood at the rail of the ship. "I thought you said the villages on the river were in control of the rebel forces?"

Li-shan looked troubled.

"They are," he said. "But these towns have been fought over for years. The town of Wuchang, for example, has changed hands three times. And while my father, the Chung Wang, practices Christian mercy, the other rebel generals don't. Some of the Taiping soldiers steal and burn and rape."

A bitterness had crept into his voice. "Then how are they any better than the imperial forces?" Chang-mei asked.

"In many ways, they're not."

"Why didn't you tell me this before?" she said angrily. "Why didn't you tell me the Heavenly King is a religious fanatic who will chop my head off if I don't convert to Christianity?"

He turned and took her hands. "I couldn't tell you everything because you would never have come with me," he said.

"You lied, you son of a sea snake!" she shouted, jerking her hands away. "Why should I finance this man? He's as bad as the Emperor!"

"Chang-mei, calm down! Nothing is perfect, and certainly the Heavenly King isn't. My father does not like what he sees happening to him. His success has gone to his head, and in ways he is becoming as cruel as the Emperor."

"Then why should I finance him?"

"Because the Heavenly King, for all his faults, is one of us: Chinese. The Emperor is a Manchu. And the Heavenly King is our best hope of ridding our country of these foreign bloodsuckers. I realize I wasn't completely truthful with you, but your support is vital to the rebellion."

Chang-mei curbed her anger, but she was still sulking. "When your blood is being sucked," she said, "I'm not sure it makes much difference whether the sucker is a foreigner or your next-door neighbor."

Li-shan said nothing. But in his heart, he wondered if she might not be right.

An hour later they passed another town on the north bank of the river. This town, like the others, had been burned. But here, there were the living: crowds of people standing on the riverbank, many of them half-naked, waving their arms and shouting.

"Who are they?" Chang-mei asked.

"Refugees, I expect," Li-shan answered.

"We must go ashore and help them."

"How? What can we give them? We're low on food ourselves."

"We can give them money."

"But the money is for the Heavenly King!"

"If the Heavenly King has caused all this destruction, he has to pay for it. Besides, it's *my* money and this is *my* ship. Helmsman! Take us ashore."

As the *Eastern Dragon* neared the bank, Chang-mei looked at the skeletal people and thought of her own childhood on the tiny farm in Kwangtung Province, the province of Canton. She remembered being miserably poor and dirty. She remembered her father, who had tried to sell her because she was an unwanted girl child. But just as seared in her memory was hunger. There was never enough to eat: she hadn't tasted meat until she was twelve, and then it made her sick. These are my people, she thought, looking at the wretches on the shore. I must help them. I have clawed my way out of their terrible poverty, I have killed, burned ships, stolen opium, and sold it. Now I am rich, I owe a debt. But not to the Heavenly King. To hell with him. Now that I am beginning to see his true face, why should I give my millions to him? I can't go back because I have burned my bridges and lost the protection of Prince I. But if I give my silver to the Heavenly King, it will never trickle down to these poor wretches.

I must be careful with Li-shan. I have yet to gauge his true feelings toward the Heavenly King. . . .

"Look: soldiers!" Li-shan exclaimed, shielding his eyes from the boiling sun to better make out the dozen horsemen he had just spotted riding toward the village, the horses sending up clouds of dust.

"Demon imps?" Chang-mei asked, rather anxiously.

"No, rebels. A detachment from the Bamboo Company, one of my father's. Good: there'll be news."

By now, the junk was close enough to the riverbank that a gangway was able to be put out. Chang-mei ordered her crew to bring up from the hold one of the chests of silver taels as she and Li-shan went ashore. Chang-mei was instantly surrounded by the refugees, who were wailing and begging, their voices a chorus of woe.

"My home was burned!" cried one old woman, who was in rags. "They killed my husband and two sons and stole everything, my pig, my chickens . . ."

"They killed my father," wailed a boy, tears streaming down his dirty cheeks. "I haven't eaten in a week! Please, kind lady, whoever you are . . . some food . . . please. . . ."

Chang-mei, profoundly affected by this tide of sorrow and misery, held up her hands for silence.

"Please, my friends," she said, "I have no food to give you. But I have money: twenty silver taels for each of you."

The people looked dumbfounded. Twenty silver taels, approximately thirty dollars, was almost a year's income for a peasant. A *successful* peasant.

"Now," Chang-mei went on, "if you'll queue up by the gangway, I'll distribute the money. And when I get to the court of the Heavenly King, I will tell him of your plight and do everything in my power to restore your homes. Unhappily, I can't bring back the dead, but we can rebuild what has been burned, we can give you seed for new crops, we can provide you with new pigs and chickens. I know you have seen the terrible dragon of war, but a new and better China can rise out of all this misery. So take heart, my friends. I, Chang-mei, swear to you I will do everything in my power to sway the Heavenly King to help you. And now: the money."

"My lady," said one old woman, touching her arm and pointing to the rebel soldiers who were dismounting a short way down the river, "is this a trap? Will the soldiers kill us if we take the money?"

Chang-mei looked. To her surprise, she saw the rebel soldiers bowing to Li-shan. She knew that her young warrior lover was a heavenly prince, but all his talk about democracy and equality in the Heavenly Kingdom had led her to believe that such feudal posturings as bowing and kowtowing would have been eliminated. Obviously, she was wrong. She looked back at the old woman.

"You have nothing to fear," she said. "My friend, Li-shan, is the son of the great Chung Wang. He will protect you. Open the silver chest."

As she returned to the ship, one of the crew obeyed, lifting the heavy leather-bound and brass-clasped lid.

The refugees gasped as the sun reflected off the pile of silver coins in the chest. Then, screaming, they surged on to the gangway, as if the treasure was a mirage that might at any moment vanish like the morning mist on the hills.

"Who is she, my lord?" asked Tang Shumei, the Captain of the company as he pointed at Chang-mei. "Is she the famous woman pirate?"

"Yes," Li-shan replied. "I convinced her to bring her treasure and join the rebellion. I'd wager there is more silver on that junk than there is in the Emperor's treasury in Peking. Did my father send you to ride guard for us?"

"Yes, my lord. Our scouts spotted your junk two days ago."

"Are there demon imps nearby?"

"Not as far as we know, my lord. But if the wind holds, you should be in Nanking by tomorrow. By the way, our spies in Shanghai tell us that the Emperor has placed a bounty of fifty thousand taels on the head of the woman pirate. Word reached the court that she had the temerity to blow up one of the imperial war junks. Is this true?"

"It's true."

"What kind of woman is this who can wage war like a man? Is she possessed by demons?"

"Perhaps. Perhaps the demon was the barbarian she now claims she loves. Now tell me: what news is there from Nanking?"

Tang Shumei hesitated. Then he lowered his voice.

"The news is very bad, my lord," he said. "The Heavenly King is showing signs of madness."

20 "YOU GAVE AWAY OVER FIVE hundred taels!" Li-shan exclaimed after he returned to the junk. They had once again set sail, moving along as close to the north bank of the river as was practical while Tang Shumei's company of soldiers rode along the shore to protect them from demon imps.

"So what?" Chang-mei said. She was in her cabin, brushing her long black hair. "It's my money, and those people were starving—thanks to the great and merciful armies of the Heavenly King." She put down her brush and turned to him. "I can't tell you how betrayed I feel, Li-shan. You painted this wonderful picture of the Heavenly King and his Heavenly Kingdom, where everyone was equal and there was no corruption and people practiced compassion and humility. And what am I seeing? Your soldiers bowing to you, which is not exactly my idea of equality. And the Taipings murdering and burning and stealing—they make the Manchus look like amateurs! And it turns out that far from men and women being equal, the Heavenly King and your father have concubines, just like the Emperor! And if I don't convert to Christianity, I'll be executed! Some paradise! It sounds an awful lot like China to me."

He came across the room to her. "I warned you not to mock Christianity," he said, "but you don't have to believe in it. My father can protect you as long as you conform to the outward appearances."

"Conform?" she snorted. "The last thing in the world I am is a conformist! Why do you think I was attracted to what you told me about the Heavenly Kingdom in the first place? Because you led me to believe it was a place where people could be free to do and be what they wanted. Now you're telling me I have to conform. I would have been better off staying in Canton!"

"You seem to forget that Prince I told you to conform or die?"

"Well? Aren't you telling me the same thing? I have desired you, Li-shan.

There are many things about you I find exciting. But unless you can offer me something better than conforming to a *new* set of rules, I could easily come to hate you." He started to take her hand, but she pulled it away. "Don't touch me," she warned. "There will be no more clouds and rain until we've straightened this out. And I'm having serious second thoughts about handing over my treasure to the Heavenly King. If I give to anyone, it will be to people like those poor wretches today."

"Don't be a fool, Chang-mei. If you don't give the treasure to the Heavenly King, he'll *take* it! And all of your bargaining power would be gone. Even my father couldn't protect you."

She stared at him. "Are you telling me I am a prisoner?"

"No, of course not. . . ."

"Then what *am* I? Is it *my* money, or the Heavenly King's?"

Li-shan was agonizing. "You said you'd give it to him—!"

"But I'm changing my mind!"

"You *can't!*" he shouted, letting out the anger that had been building in him. "Don't you understand? The Heavenly King is another Emperor trying to found a new dynasty, a *Chinese* dynasty! This has happened over and over again in Chinese history: one dynasty becomes corrupt and perverted, it loses the Mandate of Heaven, and a new, vigorous dynasty replaces it. That's what we're involved with. The Heavenly King may preach compassion and equality, which he believed in once—"

"But no more?" she interrupted.

"I don't know." He didn't want to tell her what Tang Shumei had told him about the Heavenly King's incipient madness. Chang-mei's doubts were bad enough as it was. "But I do know this: the Heavenly King is not about to give up any of his power—nor is my father, nor, for that matter, am I! Now, if you go along, if you conform, everything will work out beautifully. We will be married, and you will be a princess in the new dynasty. But if you *don't* go along and conform, neither I nor my father will be able to save you. It's that simple."

"What a fool I've been," she finally said. "What a blind fool. As always, I've allowed my lust for a man's body to cloud my brain. If I could only wrest that lust out of my mind, I'd do it. But I can't."

"Chang-mei," he said tenderly, "you speak of lust. I don't understand what this 'love' you speak of is, but I do know I admire you and want you. Perhaps that is love. . . ."

"Love," she said coldly. "I'm beginning to think love is a word men made up to enslave women. Every time Justin told me he loved me, what he really wanted was clouds and rain."

"But you said you thought you loved him now?"

"Yes, I do. In ways it's quite wonderful. But in other ways, it makes you a prisoner. Just as, apparently, I am with you."

"Your anger will pass. You'll see that everything will be auspicious—as long as you do what I tell you."

She laughed. "Oh, what a lovely joke! I thought I could change China, and how do I end up? The loving woman who will be petted and fed—as long as I do what you tell me. All right, Li-shan. I'll conform. Everything will work out—you don't have to worry. If nothing else, I owe you the moon for the lesson you've taught me: when everything seems to change, it turns out nothing has changed at all."

He smiled and spread his hands. "Is that so bad? We have each other."

"Yes, so we do. Well: it seems that I am now a *former* rebel."

"That's what I like to hear." He took her in his arms. She put up no resistance. But she knew what she had to do.

The great stone walls of Nanking loomed above the junk the next morning, a brilliant, warm day of cloudless blue sky. The walls were fifty feet high at their lowest point and were nineteen miles in circumference. They had been built by the first Ming Emperor in the fifteenth century to protect his Southern Capital. The saying went that it would take a full day to ride around them on horseback, and as Chang-mei looked up at them from the deck of the *Eastern Dragon,* she could easily believe it. She, Li-shan, and Ah Ling holding little Julie were on deck as the junk tied up at the wharf before the huge northeast gate of the city. A cheering crowd had gathered to greet the son of the Chung Wang and the notorious "Queen of the Pirates," as Chang-mei had come to be known. The story had spread like wildfire through the Heavenly Capital that Li-shan was bringing home the great pirate treasure after having sunk an imperial war junk in the China Sea—none of the Taipings could believe that the *Yellow Lotus* had been sunk by Chang-mei, a woman—and the crowd was giving him a hero's welcome. Tang Shumei was there with his company that had been augmented by fifty other soldiers to guard the treasure as it was carried to the palace of the Chung Wang where, that night, at a festive celebration, the twenty trunks of silver would be unlocked and formally presented to the Heavenly King himself.

Li-shan took Chang-mei's hand and led her off the ship to a gilded sedan chair, into which she climbed. Then, as Li-shan mounted a white stallion, eight bearers picked up the sedan chair and Chang-mei began her procession into the city, first transiting the wall through three high gates in a tunnel one hundred feet long. She was naturally curious to see how the Heavenly King's version of "theocratic communism" actually worked (Li-shan had heard of the new word that Karl Marx had coined when he was special correspondent for the New York *Tribune* in London). Had Li-shan's glowing descriptions of the peaceful Heavenly Kingdom been all lies, concealing the truth of the Heavenly King's despotism?

Her first impressions were favorable. Nanking lay on the southern bank of the Yangtze, and the northern part of the city was given over to fields of grain, interspersed with gardens, small villages, and detached houses. Li-shan, riding beside her sedan chair, said, "The fields and gardens are in this part of the city so they can be irrigated by the river during droughts. Everything belongs to the city. The fields and gardens are tended by volunteers, and the produce is distributed free to the populace. This way, no one goes hungry. Of course, there are also markets where you can buy food if you want to."

After a half hour, they came to the southern part of the city, which was thickly populated. By any standards, the wide streets were clean. But by Chinese standards, they were remarkably so. Chang-mei, used to the filth of Canton, could hardly believe how clean and free of beggars and cripples Nanking was. The people were well dressed, the typical costume of both men and women consisting of loose black trousers, with a sash at the waist, and a short, tight-fitting jacket, usually red. Moreover, the inhabitants of the city, all of whom cheered the procession as it passed, seemed to have a free and happy bearing, the reverse of the cringing and humbled appearance of so many of the Chinese under the rule of the cruel Manchus. Many palaces and handsome official buildings occupied prominent positions; and Chang-mei began to wonder, with a sinking feeling, if perhaps she had misjudged the Heavenly King. Then she remembered the horrors she had seen along the riverbank, and her determination returned. She also saw that most of the men carried guns and knives in their sashes, so while Nanking might look like a paradise, obviously there was at least some trouble in paradise.

They passed the great palace of the Heavenly King, which was surrounded by a high yellow wall crowned with minarets with green, scarlet, and golden roofs. Li-shan told her the palace had been constructed with stones taken from the old palace of the Ming Emperors, which the Heavenly King had ordered destroyed—something Chang-mei considered bordering on the criminal, as well as wildly wasteful, but which didn't seem to bother Li-shan in the slightest. By the most conservative estimates, over ten million Chinese had already lost their lives in this bloodiest of rebellions against the Manchus; and while communal gardens were all very fine, to lavish wealth on grandiose palaces seemed shameful under the circumstances of such widespread suffering. When she mentioned this to Li-shan, he shrugged and said, "The only way to rule the

Chinese is to impress them." While there was a nugget of cynical truth in this observation, nevertheless Chang-mei didn't like hearing it.

But when the procession reached the palace of Li-shan's father, the Chung Wang, Chang-mei was bowled over by the size and magnificence of the place, which made Prince I's palace in Canton seem puny in comparison. They entered through an immense archway, supported by beautifully sculptured granite columns, which led to a large courtyard. Passing through this, the covered way next led to the grand entrance of the palace with its carved and gilded columns and roof covered with a brilliant representation of Chinese mythology. Over the principal door was a board with a gilded inscription saying the palace was dedicated "to the Glory of the Faithful King," a sentiment that struck Chang-mei as somewhat lacking in democratic humility. The door itself was covered with huge painted dragons and opened upon yet another court fronting the Chung Wang's tribunal—Li-shan explaining that his father often acted as judge in criminal cases. On either side of the grand entrance stood a gigantic drum; the drums were sounded whenever the Chung Wang held court or for purposes of assembly or alarm.

Here, Chang-mei descended from her sedan chair as Li-shan dismounted from his horse. They proceeded on foot, followed by Ah Ling holding Julie, passing into the courtyard that was planted with miniature weeping willows, peach trees, acacias, sweet-smelling magnolias, delicately hued camellias, sensitive mimosas along with tiny lakes filled with silver and gold fish. The Hall of Justice itself was crowned by two immense domes, one in silver, the other in gold, supported by brilliantly decorated columns twined by serpents. As Chang-mei drank all this splendor in, she began to understand the Heavenly King's hunger for her treasure, and she was even more certain that it would never reach those starving peasants in the countryside. And this was the Chung Wang's palace, not the Heavenly King's! How much grander must his be?

After the Hall of Justice, they passed through an area containing a number of offices for secretaries, then another open court was reached where an orchestra was playing, celebrating the return of Li-shan, the prince and heir apparent of all this lavish display. Then an Audience Chamber was entered, then the apartments of the palace officials, then another open court and finally the Heavenly Hall, which was a private chapel for the Chung Wang and his family.

And here, finally, was the Chung Wang himself, the mighty general whose troops had routed some of the most seasoned soldiers of the Chinese Empire. Li-shan hurried to him, bowed, then embraced his father, who was standing before a gilded altar.

"Honorable father," Li-shan then said, turning to Chang-mei, "I want to present Chang-mei, the topaz tree of my desire."

Chang-mei stepped forward and made an obeisance. The Chung Wang was an imposingly handsome man in his late thirties, tall like his son, and dressed in the most extraordinary regalia. His state robe was a gorgeous affair, reaching almost to his feet, of beautifully embroidered yellow satin, stiff with gold bosses and dragons worked in gold, silver, and scarlet threads. Yellow embroidered trousers and boots of yellow satin completed his outfit. In his hand he carried a jade scepter, or "yu-i," carved at each end and covered with sapphires, pearls, garnets, and amethysts. On his head he wore a crown made of gold. The metal was beaten thin into beautiful filigree work and leaves, and formed into the figure of a tiger, the eyes being large rubies and the teeth rows of pearls. At each side was an eagle with outstretched wings, and on the top was a phoenix. The whole crown was decorated with large jewels set into the gold, while pearls, sapphires, and other gems hung all around on thin gold chains.

"Welcome to the Heavenly Capital of the Heavenly Kingdom," the Chung Wang said, his sharp eyes examining her. "I see that my son has chosen a lotus of rare beauty."

"You honor me, my lord," she said, furious at all the pomp and display. For *this* she was supposed to give up the treasure she had worked years to accumulate?

"And what are your first impressions of the Heavenly Kingdom?" the Chung Wang asked her in a friendly tone.

"It is not what I expected," she said.

2 1 "YOU HAVE DISPLEASED MY FATHER," Li-shan said two hours later as he came into the private apartment at the rear of the palace that had been provided for Chang-mei. The latter was standing by a door that led out to a charming walled rock garden replete with ponds and a miniature pagoda. Chang-mei was being dressed by two of the Chung Wang's ladies in a beautiful plum-colored silk overgarment reaching to her knees, tight at the neck and waist, with loose sleeves and a large skirt slit at the sides. Beneath this she wore the usual loose black pantaloons. Though she generally wore little makeup on the junk, now she had painted her lips crimson with an alluring little cherry droplet depending below the middle of her lower lip. On each cheek was painted a soft round mark of cherry-red. Now she looked at Li-shan.

"How have I displeased your father?" she asked.

He came farther into the room, marveling at the beauty of the "Queen of the Pirates" and the effect it had on his heartbeat.

"He said you were cold to him, and that your enthusiasm for the Heavenly Kingdom was lukewarm."

"Leave us," Chang-mei said to the servants, who hurriedly backed out of the room, their slippers shuffling on the mat floor. When they were gone, Chang-mei said, "I haven't kept my feelings about the Heavenly Kingdom secret from you, why should I keep them secret from your father?"

"Because the Heavenly Kingdom is my father's life, and it would be sensible to ingratiate yourself with your future father-in-law."

"Perhaps I'm not sensible."

"That becomes increasingly apparent each day. Why are you being so stubborn? When everything could be so pleasant for us if you'd just go along, why are you upsetting everything?"

A tear formed in the corner of each of her eyes.

"What difference does it make?" she said quietly. "My life is over."

Li-shan came to her and took her hands. "What do you mean?"

"You wouldn't understand now. Perhaps later. I came into this world a rebel, and I will leave it the same way. Death holds no terror for me."

"What in Jesus' name are you talking about?"

She looked at him sadly. "It doesn't matter. But promise me one thing, Li-shan."

"Yes, of course. What?"

"You say you have become a Christian. Then swear on the Christian god, Shang-ti, that you will take care of Julie if something happens to me."

"This is madness—what's going to happen to you?"

"Swear!"

He hesitated, a look of confusion on his handsome face. Finally, he said, "All right, I swear. But I don't understand. . . ."

She placed her hand on his cheek. "You will someday. Now, go dress for the banquet. I have only seen you with everyday clothes on—or off, as the case may be. I want to see how you look dressed as a prince of the Heavenly Kingdom. No matter how many fights we've had, you still excite me, Li-shan."

"We have spoken much of this mysterious thing called 'love.' Do you perhaps love me?"

She hesitated. "I don't know . . . perhaps I do. Yes, maybe I do."

He took her hands and kissed her on her painted lips.

"Whether the feeling I have for you is the barbarian love, I have no idea," he said. "But what I feel for you I will feel till the end of time."

"The end of time may be sooner than you think," she said. Then she gently pushed him away. "My rouge. It took me an hour to paint my face. I must look beautiful for the Heavenly King."

"Tonight," he whispered, his sinewy body hard with desire. "Tonight, after the banquet, we will have clouds and rain."

She smiled. "Perhaps we will have a thunderstorm."

He laughed and left the room.

Promptly at eight that evening, Li-shan returned to Chang-mei's apartment to escort her to the summer banquet hall.

"You look very handsome," she said as she admired his yellow silk long-gown, yellow being a color only the Heavenly King and his four *wangs* or "kings" were allowed to wear. On Li-shan's feet were yellow pointed slippers embroidered with seed pearls. And a yellow silk scarf had been wrapped around his head like a cone-shaped turban. In the center of it was pinned a large tiger-eye ruby.

"If I look handsome," Li-shan said in a courtly fashion, "it is only because I reflect your beauty."

He led her through the palace to the summer banquet hall, which was a large outdoor rectangular colonnade surrounded on all four sides by a miniature moat in which goldfish swam. The hall was covered by a splendid silver dome from which one hundred yellow lanterns hung, glowing in the evening light. A long banquet table had been set up at one side of the rectangle with great silver trays holding mountains of fresh fruit, and numerous waiters in colorful robes stood outside the moat waiting to bring in dozens of dishes. Once again Chang-mei was reminded of the disparity between the palaces of the rulers of the Heavenly Kingdom and the horrible poverty of the peasants in the countryside whose farms and villages had been pillaged by the Taiping rebels. She told herself yet again that she had done the right thing.

Li-shan led Chang-mei across a small bridge into the hall where he introduced her to his two younger sisters: their mother had sent her apologies, but she was not feeling well and would not attend the banquet.

"Now," Li-shan said, "we must wait until my father brings in the Heavenly King."

They didn't have to wait long, for in a few minutes the sound of the great drums outside the Hall of Justice boomed and the Chung Wang's orchestra began playing. Chang-mei heard a chorus of boys' voices beginning to sing a hymn that was as peculiar to her Chinese ears as the cymbal-clashing, haut-boy-whining Chinese musical instruments would have been to western ears:

"We praise Thee, O God, our Heavenly Father,
We praise Jesus, the Savior of the world;
We praise the Holy Spirit, the sacred intelligence;
We praise the three persons, united as the True Spirit."

Chang-mei had no way of knowing it, but it was a Chinese version of the Christian doxology.

Shortly after, a strange procession appeared in the garden surrounding the summer banquet hall. First, the Chung Wang's musicians with their drums, flutes, cymbals, and lutes. Then the boys' choir, still singing. Then a half-dozen Taiping soldiers carrying colorful silk banners proclaiming the glory of the Heavenly Kingdom. Then a dozen members of the Heavenly King's harem, lissome ladies in revealing costumes—for Chang-mei had learned that although prostitution, opium smoking, gambling, and copulation between husbands and wives except at certain stated times were crimes punishable by death in the Heavenly Kingdom, the Heavenly King himself and his top-ranking "kings" were above the law and could do what they wished.

After the ladies of the harem came the Chung Wang with his honored guest, the Heavenly King himself.

The forty-four-year-old Hung Hsiu-ch'üan who had started the greatest civil war in the history of the world, which would before its end claim the lives of between twenty and forty million people, was not especially impressive in person. He was shorter than the Chung Wang, nor was he as handsome. He wore yellow "imperial" robes—for the Heavenly King had adopted most of the trappings of the Manchu Emperor in Peking—which were embroidered with imperial dragons. On his head he wore a strange cone-shaped crown that was festooned with pearls and large jewels. His eyes darted nervously to the right and left as if he were watching for a lurking assassin. What Chang-mei did not know was that the Heavenly King, who had prohibited opium smoking on pain of death, was himself an addict.

The orchestra, soldiers, choir, and ladies of the harem positioned themselves around the pavilion while the Chung Wang led the Heavenly King across the moat into the summer banquet hall. Leading him to Li-shan and Chang-mei, the Chung Wang said, "Great Lord, allow me to present my humble son, Li-shan, who has persuaded the lady Chang-mei to join our rebellion."

The Heavenly King nodded to Li-shan, saying, "Your son We know, of course, and he is anything but humble, being one of Our bravest warriors." Then he turned to Chang-mei, who bowed. "We had no idea," the Heavenly King said, having adopted the Manchu Emperor's royal "We," "that the Queen of the Pirates, whose exploits ring throughout China, was such a pearl. We welcome you to the Heavenly Kingdom, Chang-mei. Are you a Christian?"

Li-shan rather nervously broke in. "I have begun a course of instruction with her, Your Majesty."

Chang-mei looked at him coolly, but the Heavenly King smiled. "Excellent!" he said. "As Our rebellion sweeps through China like a wildfire, cleansing Our beloved country of the abominable Manchu dogs and their corrupt perversions, behind Us will come the Heavenly Wind which will announce the reign of Our Father, the Shang-ti. Meanwhile, Our esteemed Chung Wang, shall We feast before We receive the treasure?"

"Of course, Great Lord," the Chung Wang said, gesturing toward the banquet table. "I have ordered one of Your Majesty's favorite delicacies: Ningpo oysters."

Alcohol having been banned in the Heavenly Kingdom, the banquet's only drink was tea, and twenty courses were downed with gallons of the steaming beverage. Finally, when the last ginger cookies were eaten and the plates removed by the waiters, the Chung Wang gave a signal. As the orchestra played soft music, soldiers began carrying in the heavy chests that Chang-mei had brought from the vaults of her bank in Macao.

The Heavenly King watched with hungry eyes as the chests were set down in a row in front of the banquet table. Finally, when the twentieth chest had been deposited, two rows of ten chests each, Chang-mei got up from her seat, walked around the table, and came to its center, standing in front of the Heavenly King.

"I am told," she said, and Li-shan thought she had never looked more beautiful or alluring, "that you are the son of Shang-ti, the Christian god. I am told that you have founded the Heavenly Kingdom here on earth, a place where all are equal, both men and women, and all goods are owned by everyone. Is that true?"

The Heavenly King drummed his fingers impatiently. "Yes, that is true," he said. "Everyone knows that. Open the chests, woman. We are eager to see the treasure."

"And whose treasure is it?" Chang-mei asked in a rising voice. "Yours? Mine? Ours? Everyone's? I have brought all of my wealth a long way from Macao. I think I have a right to know where it's going to end up."

"It belongs to the Heavenly Kingdom, of course," he said, with mounting annoyance. "We will use it to chase the Manchu dogs out of China."

"That is good to hear, Great Lord, because I, too, have had a vision. In it, Shang-ti came to me. He is a man with a golden beard carrying a golden sword. And he said to me: 'Chang-mei, it is of the greatest importance that this treasure you bring to my son be used only for China, and not for the building of great palaces.' " Both the Heavenly King and the Chung Wang became stony-faced. Li-shan turned pale. Chang-mei continued: "The Shang-ti said to me, 'I must test the purity of my son's heart. If, when you deliver your treasure to him, the Heavenly King is true to his ideals, all will be well. But if, as I suspect, the Heavenly King has begun to waver in his goal to save China, then I will show a sign of my displeasure.' " Chang-mei stopped a moment. "Can you interpret this vision, Your Majesty?" she asked.

The Heavenly King was icy with rage. "Yes," he said. "You have either eaten too many Ningpo oysters and have indigestion. Or you are guilty of blasphemy!" He rose to his feet and shouted: "Guards! Seize this insolent woman and hold her for blasphemy and abominable crimes against Our person!"

As guards ran across the moat into the banquet hall, Chang-mei cried, "Are you the only person in China allowed to have visions? Or is the truth that you have fooled millions of people with your so-called 'visions' that are really nothing but pipe dreams!"

"Silence!" roared the Heavenly King, a manic look coming into his eyes. "Take her away—wait! First, the keys to the treasure chests!"

As guards grabbed her, Chang-mei threw a heavy brass key on the table. "Here's the key, Heavenly King!" she cried as all gaped at what was happening. "But remember: if your heart is not pure, Shang-ti will show a sign of his displeasure!"

"Silence, slut!" roared the Heavenly King. "Take her away! Hold her under house arrest until We decide a proper punishment for this insolent sea witch!"

The guards dragged Chang-mei over the moat as she continued to cry: "Watch for the sign! Shang-ti will send a sign! Watch for the miracle!"

"SILENCE!" screamed the Heavenly King, who was beginning to drool. Li-shan, staring at him, wondered if he were indeed going mad. The Chung Wang turned to his son and whispered, "Who is this meddling woman you brought here? Is she mad? She has dared to insult the Heavenly King!" Li-shan, being in a state of shock from what Chang-mei did, had no answer.

The Heavenly King, muttering to himself, had taken the key and hurried around the banquet table to unlock the first of the treasure chests. Now, he stuck the key in the lock, fiddled with it, finally turned it and opened the lid. What he saw made him gasp. The chest was filled with stones.

Silence. The Heavenly King stared at the rocks. Then, muttering to himself, he started taking the stones out one by one and throwing them on the floor. Rock after rock after rock.

The court, the soldiers, the harem girls, the musicians—all started mumbling, "The miracle! The miracle!"

"Where's the silver?" howled the Heavenly King, hurrying to the second chest. He opened it.

More rocks.

"The miracle!" chanted the court. "Shang-ti has sent a miracle! The silver has turned to stone!"

"Do something!" the Chung Wang said to his son. "Before there's a rebellion against the rebellion! Before the Heavenly King blames *us* for this fiasco!"

Li-shan hurried around the table to join the Heavenly King, who was opening the third chest. "Great Lord!" he yelled, raising his hands for silence. "This is no miracle! This is a swindle! One of the crew on our junk must have stolen the treasure and replaced it with these rocks!"

The Heavenly King, realizing rather dazedly that he was being saved by Li-shan, straightened and looked at the young warrior. "Yes," he finally said, "that must be what happened. There is no miracle. Only *I* receive visions. Only *I* know of miracles. Only *I* communicate with Shang-ti." He paused a moment, thinking. Then he said to Li-shan, "The woman must have known. This Chang-mei. And she must know where the treasure is hidden. Guards!" he turned and yelled. "Bring Chang-mei back!"

Two guards ran into the palace as the Heavenly King picked one of the rocks out of the third chest and held it up. "She's clever," he said to Li-shan. "She knew there was no silver in the chests, so she tried to turn my people against me by inventing this so-called 'miracle.' She will learn I can be clever too."

Li-shan realized, with a sinking heart, that Chang-mei had probably signed her own death warrant. And that she had known it. He remembered the odd scene with her before the banquet, when she had made him swear to take care of Julie. She must have known then that the moment the "treasure" chests were opened, she would be doomed.

His mind raced to find a way to save her. For a brief, intoxicating second, he even thought of stabbing the Heavenly King—who was only inches away from him—and proclaiming his father, the Chung Wang, the new Heavenly King.

But like a Chinese Hamlet, he hesitated.

When the guards brought Chang-mei back to the summer banquet hall, she looked marvelously composed.

"You! Wretch!" howled the Heavenly King, pointing an outstretched finger at her. "Are you some demon sent by Satan to destroy the Heavenly Kingdom? Are you a witch, speaking of false miracles? There is no miracle! Someone on your ship took the silver out of these chests and replaced it with rocks!"

"Yes," Chang-mei said quietly. "I did. At least, I ordered it done last night, before we arrived in Nanking."

"Why?"

She looked at Li-shan. "Because I had been betrayed. I was told the Heavenly Kingdom was paradise, which was why I was willing to bring my treasure here. But I found out it isn't paradise. It's just"—she shrugged—"like everywhere else. Oh, yes, the streets are cleaner, and things seem to be run better here than in China. But you live in a palace—"

"Silence!"

"If my lord wishes to learn where the treasure is, he must hear me out."

The Heavenly King fumed for a moment. Then he said, "Very well, speak."

"You and the other great lords live in palaces, you have a harem . . . yes, this is paradise—for *you*. It's not a paradise for me or anyone else. I decided I did not wish to give my wealth to a man who is more interested in being Emperor than the brother of Jesus Christ." She turned to the court and cried, "Your Heavenly King is a fake! He no more speaks to Shang-ti than you or I or anyone else!"

There was a murmur from the crowd at this blasphemy.

"You have one more chance to save your miserable life," the Heavenly King said. "And that is to tell me where the treasure lies."

"Then I am doomed," Chang-mei said without a trace of fear in her voice. "Because the treasure lies at the bottom of the Yangtze River."

A groan rose from the crowd. Li-shan closed his eyes.

"Take her to the Field of Executions," said the Heavenly King. "She will die at dawn."

"Great Lord," Li-shan said, opening his eyes. "If I may be so bold as to make a suggestion?"

The Heavenly King turned to him. "Yes? What is it, Li-shan?"

"Since the woman has been so foolish as to squander a great fortune by throwing it into the river, at least we could make *some* money off her if you allowed me to take her with a company of soldiers to the nearest encampment of the demon imps. I could hand her over to them and collect the reward of fifty thousand taels, which would be *something.*"

The Heavenly King looked impressed.

"Excellent thinking, Li-shan. Your son does you credit, Chung Wang. And this will help drain the treasure of the accursed Manchus. You have my permission to do that, Li-shan. Take her to the demon imps and collect the ransom." He smiled cruelly as he looked at Chang-mei. "The Manchus will make her death much more interesting than I could. I hear the Emperor has condemned her to the Death of a Thousand Cuts."

So saying, the Heavenly King left the summer banquet hall, followed by his court. When they had gone, Chang-mei turned to Li-shan and said, "May I see my daughter one more time?"

"I will bring her to you at the double hour of the ox."

22   AT TWO O'CLOCK IN THE morning, Li-shan went to Chang-mei's apartment, which was now guarded by two of the Heavenly King's soldiers. Li-shan was accompanied by Ah Ling, who was holding a sleeping Julie.

"I have brought the condemned woman's baby," Li-shan told the guards. "The Heavenly King, in his magnanimity, has allowed the accursed woman one final moment with her child."

"You may pass in, Prince," the first guard said as the second opened the door. Li-shan went inside, followed by the baby amah.

Inside, an oil lamp burned as Chang-mei lay on a bed. When she saw them enter, she sat up. Her makeup had been removed, and her fine clothes had been replaced by a long, ragged gray robe, known as the "robe of penitence." She wore sandals on her feet. As Li-shan closed the door, Ah Ling carried the baby across the room to her. Chang-mei got off the bed and took Julie in her arms.

"What a terrible mother I've been," she sighed as she rocked the baby. "I should never have had a child. And yet, I love this little thing. Will you forgive me, Julie? Will you forgive me for not staying home and being a loving, obedient momma instead of a pirate and a rebel and a troublemaker?"

Julie woke up and began crying. Chang-mei handed her back to Ah Ling.

"Tell her I loved her, Ah Ling," Chang-mei said. "Try to give her a good memory of her mother. There's no point in making her ashamed of me."

There were tears in the amah's eyes. "I will tell her her mother was a great lady," Ah Ling said. "I will tell her you died for the truth."

"Thank you, Ah Ling. I would like her to think I was some sort of heroine, even if . . ." She looked across the room at Li-shan, who was standing in the shadows by the door. "Even if I didn't have much of a hero." Her voice became heavy with sarcasm. "How much I owe you, Li-shan. First you lure me to a false paradise. Then you hand me over to the Manchus so I can have a proper death by torture. Will they hang my head on the walls of Peking, as they do in Canton, to warn us poor Chinese to obey the dynasty? Will flies buzz around my rotting skull and maggots crawl in and out of my eye sockets? How proud you must be, Li-shan. And to think I once trusted you. I deserve to die for being such a fool."

"Ah Ling, take the baby back to her room," Li-shan ordered.

"Wait," Chang-mei said. "You swore to me you would protect her, Li-shan. At least tell me you'll keep your word about that. Let me die knowing my baby has a home."

"I will raise Julie and love her as if she were my own. Have no fear about that, Chang-mei. I swore an oath and I will live up to it. Now leave us, Ah Ling. I want a final word with your *tai-tai.*"

"Yes, master."

When Ah Ling had left the room, Li-shan closed the door, then hurried to Chang-mei. "Listen to me," he whispered. "I haven't much time. I suggested to the Heavenly King that I take you to the Manchus to get you out of the city. Once we're in the countryside, I'll arrange your escape. Ride to Soochow." He pulled a folded note from his shirt and gave it to her. "I have an aunt there— her name is on this note. Give this to her. She will keep you hidden until I can make further arrangements."

Chang-mei looked confused. "But I thought . . ."

"You thought I lied to you. I did about everything but my love for you." He took her in his arms. "I never dreamed you would throw away the treasure. . . ."

"I couldn't give it to the Heavenly King after what I saw his armies have done."

"I know. I can see that now. You've taken the blinders from my eyes, Chang-mei. I can see that the Heavenly King has become a tyrant as bad as the Emperor. Tang Shumei told me he's going mad, and I can believe that too after what I saw tonight. Can you forgive me for what I've done to you?"

"Does it matter now?"

"Of course it matters."

"Then I forgive you. But what are you going to do?"

"It depends on my father. Before I came to you, he had told me he was beginning to have doubts about the Heavenly King. Perhaps I can persuade him to turn against him. My father controls the army. . . ."

"But what if you can't persuade him?"

A cold look came into his eyes, and Chang-mei sensed the great power that was bottled up in this warrior she loved. "Then I'll turn against my father," he whispered. "The rebellion is dying of corruption—you're right about that. It has to be purged to succeed. Perhaps destiny has chosen me to purge it. At any rate, whatever happens, I will come to you as soon as it's safe. But we must be careful—that's why I sent Ah Ling out of the room. If anyone suspects, we're *both* dead."

"Then I should pretend to hate you?"

"Loathe me!" He grinned. "Spit at me. Curse me. They all think you're a witch: act like one. Now: one final kiss."

He pulled her to him and kissed her. She dug her nails into his shoulders. There were tears in her eyes as her body burned with desire. "Li-shan," she whispered. "I'll admit I was afraid . . . forgive me for what I said a few moments before. Oh, God, I love you, my darling."

"Curse me. Yell at me as I leave. We have to fool the guards."

"You son of a snake!" she screamed, pushing him away. "Get out of here! I hate you, you son of a sea snake! Go away!"

She picked up a bowl and threw it at him. He ducked as it banged against the door. Grinning, he blew her a kiss.

"You whore!" he yelled. "I hope the Manchus slice your tits off!"

He opened the door and ran out of the room as she threw a stool at him. It hit the wall and crashed to the floor.

Word had swept Nanking, the Heavenly Capital, that the Queen of the Pirates had attacked the Heavenly King. The son of Shang-ti and Jesus Christ's younger brother might have encouraged his armies to pillage the countryside (in fairness to him, pillaging armies were a Chinese tradition), but the Heavenly King had been smart enough to keep the citizens of his capital well fed and reasonably content. Thus, when news of Chang-mei's "abominable" crime went around the city, the citizens were outraged. And the next morning, when a procession formed outside the gates of the Chung Wang's palace to escort Chang-mei out of the city, a great crowd gathered, and its mood was ugly.

"There may be trouble," the Chung Wang said to his son as they looked out a window. "Do you think you have enough men?"

"Yes," Li-shan said. "Tang Shumei has his Bamboo Company and he's added fifty men to it. We'll be all right."

"My spies tell me the nearest encampment of devil imps is on the western shore of Lake Tai. Proceed there directly, unless you encounter something unexpected. But of course I don't have to tell you that." The great General smiled and put his hand on Li-shan's shoulder. "My valued son has studied *The Art of War* and learned its lessons well. Someday you will take my place and lead our troops to glory."

Li-shan hesitated. "Father," he said carefully, "did you notice last night that the Heavenly King was actually *drooling?"*

The Chung Wang frowned. "Yes, I did."

"And he acted so . . . so strange."

"Well, it was a strange situation."

"Yes, but . . . Tang Shumei tells me there are increasing signs of the Heavenly King's mental instability. What if he goes mad? What will happen to all of us? What will happen to the rebellion?"

His father looked troubled. "I don't know," he said. "Or more to the point, I don't like to think about it." He hesitated. "I will not conceal from you that there is trouble with the other great lords. The Eastern King, for instance, is growing restive. There are rumors that he may turn against the Heavenly King. Who knows whether the rumors are true, but we must be clear-eyed. We live in a time of instability and tension. . . ." He added dryly, "Like the rest of Chinese history."

The crowd below the window broke into a roar. They looked out to see that Chang-mei was being led out of the palace to a horse-drawn wagon. Since the Heavenly King had aped the Manchus' handling of prisoners as well as their imperial trappings, Chang-mei wore a heavy wooden *cangue* around her neck in which her hands were locked. She wore her "robe of penitence" and on her back was a placard describing her "abominable" crime of blasphemy and rebellion against the Heavenly King. The crowd hurled insults and curses at her as she climbed in the wagon.

"Do you still have any feelings about this wretched woman?" the Chung Wang asked his son as they watched the scene below.

"Yes, Father," Li-shan said. "I have come to feel for her what the barbarians call 'love.' She is the most magnificent and brave woman I have ever known."

His father looked at him with surprise. "Surely you're joking," he said. "Particularly after what she said about the Heavenly King last night? Accusing him of being a fraud?"

"What if," Li-shan said, "she's right?"

The Chung Wang looked startled. He started to say something when a shot rang out below.

"Oh, Jesus—!" Li-shan cried out. "Chang-mei! Some fool shot her!"

Chang-mei had been hit in the chest and had fallen back on the floor of the wagon. Soldiers were beating a man with a pistol as the crowd screamed and surged in panic. Li-shan ran out of the room and down a stone stairs to the ground floor, out the main entrance of the palace and made his way through the crowd to the wagon, shouting at Tang Shumei to get a doctor. Jumping on the wagon, he climbed over the side and came to Chang-mei, kneeling beside her.

"Remove the *cangue!*" he yelled at the guard in the wagon. As the soldier fumbled with the lock, Li-shan saw the blood expanding on the robe of penitence over Chang-mei's heart. Her eyes were half-open. She smiled weakly as she saw his face looking down at hers.

"Li-shan," she whispered. "Who shot me?"

"Some idiot . . . hurry!" he hissed at the guard. They removed the *cangue,* freeing her hands. Li-shan took one of them in his own.

"The note," she whispered. "Take the note . . . it's in my pocket . . . they mustn't know. . . ."

"Don't worry about the note. A doctor's coming."

"Julie," she whispered. "I was such a bad mother to her. . . . I didn't want her because she was a half-breed girl. Do you mind that she's a half-breed?"

"No, of course not."

"You probably lie," she sighed. "It's odd how I've come to love her, funny little thing that she is . . ." She winced with pain. Her hand squeezed his. "Take care of her, Li-shan. . . . You swore. . . ."

Tears were in his eyes. "I will, my love. I swear."

"You called me your 'love.' Do you think we finally found the barbarians' love?"

He kissed her hand. "Yes," he whispered. "We found it. We now know what love is."

"Then I'm happy. . . . Kiss me, Li-shan. One last time. I always loved your kisses. . . ."

He leaned over and put his lips on hers. He heard a soft rattling sound as the breath left her body.

And then she was dead.

PART THREE

THE BALL OF THE ENCHANTED ROSE

23   JUSTIN SAVAGE STARED IN AWE at the forty-nine-year-old revolutionary who was the most famous man in the world. He remembered when Giuseppe Garibaldi had come to New York nine years before. Like most New Yorkers, Justin, who was then ten, had read the newspaper accounts of the world-famous general who had, the year before, defended Rome against the French, been defeated, escaped with his famous South American wife, Anita, and finally, after a thrilling chase through Romagna and Tuscany, been arrested in Genoa and sent into exile for the second time. Garibaldi had become a hero to Justin, who had hoped the city would honor the great man with a parade so he could see the person whose exploits in South America alone would have filled an exciting biography. But Garibaldi, with his usual modesty, had declined the honor of a parade and had gone to work for a candle manufacturer in Staten Island named Antonio Meucci. Thus Justin had never seen him in person. But he had seen hundreds of illustrations of him, as well as countless busts, medallions, and china figurines that were on tables and mantels all over the civilized world. Certainly his memory of the great man had never faded, so that when Sandhurst was ruled out by Sylvaner's sudden appearance in England, Justin had remembered the idol of his childhood. If any man in the world could teach him military tactics and the most up-to-date state of weaponry, it was Garibaldi.

The fifty pounds he had taken from Sylvaner financed his trip from London to the Continent and hence to Nice on the Mediterranean coast, where Garibaldi had been born. At this point Justin took a job as an ordinary seaman on a freighter and then jumped ship as it docked at the island of La Maddalena off the northwest corner of Sardinia. Leaving the port city of Maddalena, which faced the Strait of Bonifacio between Sardinia and Corsica, he walked east across the island. Reaching the coast, he saw the even smaller rocky island of Caprera, the north side of which he knew Garibaldi had bought the year before. Justin had paid a fisherman to take him across to the little island, which was only four miles by three. It was a wild and rugged place, covered with rock rose, tamarisk, lentisk, juniper, asphodel, and myrtle as well as stunted wild olive trees. Wild goats, which had given their name to the island, roamed the place, their voracious appetites leading them to eat everything in sight. A few goatherds lived on the island.

As Justin climbed out of the dinghy, the fisherman pointed to a wooden shack on top of the rocky hill before them and said, "Garibaldi."

"Grazie," Justin said, starting up the narrow path. Fifteen minutes later when he reached the top, he looked around. Certainly Caprera was no place of lush beauty, but the views of the sea were inspiring.

Hearing dogs barking, he turned to see several mastiffs coming around the wooden cabin heading for him. Justin picked up a wooden stick to ward them off, but they didn't attack him. Going to the house, he knocked on the door. After a moment, the great man himself opened it. Being only five feet seven inches tall, Garibaldi had to look up to see Justin, who by now had grown to his full height of over six feet. Garibaldi, whose heredity included Teutonic ancestors, had the same red hair as the young American.

"General," Justin said, "my name is Justin Savage. I'm an American from New York, and I want to serve with you and learn how to be a soldier."

Garibaldi's many admirers had idealized him into a handsome man, befitting the accepted image of a hero. In fact, he was somewhat bowlegged and had an enormous nose with a bridge so high that it made his cornflower-blue eyes seem to squint. Nevertheless, it was a pleasant face adorned with a world-famous graying red beard. Thousands of women all over the world dreamed of him and had read over and over the account of his famous love-at-first-sight romance with the sulfurous Anita da Silva, whom he had first spotted through a telescope off the coast of Uruguay, who had fought with him in South America and Italy, and who, unhappily, had died some years ago.

"I like Americans," he said in his heavily accented English. "I lived in New York once, for a year. Do you like shrimp?"

"Yes, sir."

"Come in. I'm about to have lunch." He hesitated. "But perhaps you're not hungry?"

"I could eat a horse. Two, in fact."

"We don't have horses, but we have some goat stew on the fire. I see you're a sailor, like me?"

In Nice, Justin had bought a horizontally striped black and white shirt, a pair of black trousers, and canvas shoes. "Yes, sir," he said, coming in to the main room of the house. It was a raw day in early March, and a fire burned in the hearth. He saw a young and rather swarthy peasant woman squatting by the fire stirring a pot of goat stew. She looked at the young American suspiciously.

"Battistina," Garibaldi said in Italian, "this young man has come from America to see me. What did you say your name was?" he turned to Justin, switching back to English.

"Justin Savage, sir."

"Savage? I remember there was a shipping company in New York named that. Any relation?"

"Yes, sir. It's my family."

Garibaldi looked impressed. "Beautiful ships you had, as I recall. At any rate, this is my . . . ah . . . cook, Battistina Ravello. Battistina, Justin Savage."

Battistina gave him a surly nod, but said nothing. The room was barely furnished with a few wooden chairs and a wooden table covered by newspapers on which were several dozen raw shrimp.

"Sit down, young Savage," Garibaldi said, indicating a chair by the table. "And help yourself to the shrimp. They're fresh and raw, the best way to eat them." He lit a cigar as a ravenous Justin pounced on the shrimp. After Garibaldi had taken a seat opposite him, he asked, "Now, Mr. Savage, what makes you think I can teach you how to be a soldier? I'm a retired general with no more armies. For years we've been trying to unite Italy into one great country instead of a patchwork of kingdoms and duchies run by rascals—the worst rascal of all being the current Pope—but frankly, right now it looks as if we've been wasting our time. The French control Rome, the Austrians control Milan and Venice, and the Bourbons control Naples and Sicily. The only Italian controlling anything in Italy besides the Pope is King Victor Emmanuel up in Piedmont. Now, I know the King and he's a fine fellow, but all he's really interested in is hunting and women. You know what he said in Paris?"

"No, sir."

"He said, *'Il y a une bonne chose que j'ai découverte à Paris. Les Parisiennes ne portent pas de caleçons. C'est un ciel d'azur qui s'est ouvert à mes yeux.'* Do you speak French?"

"Not enough to understand that."

"He said, 'I've discovered a wonderful thing in Paris. The Paris women don't wear underpants. It's a paradise that's opened up to my eyes.' "

Justin almost choked on a shrimp laughing. Garibaldi smiled and shrugged. "So you can see we've got our work cut out for us trying to unite Italy. But stick around if you like, son. I'll tell you everything I know, and you never know what'll happen. I always say, *'Bisogna approfittare dell'aura.'* 'Make the most of the breeze.' The winds of war may spring up again and then you might get some practical experience fighting. And meanwhile, my friends are helping me build a stone house, something more permanent than this. We could use a strong back and two young American hands."

This from the man whose name adorned streets and squares in a hundred towns in England and America. Millions of postcards depicting his face were sold all over the world. You could wear a Garibaldi blouse, drink Garibaldi wine, see a Garibaldi musical play, and eat a Garibaldi biscuit. The man was a myth in his own lifetime. Justin could already see that the reality was different from the myth, as was usually the case, and helping build a stone house in the middle of nowhere was not exactly what he had had in mind when he came to Caprera.

But something about Garibaldi intrigued him, and the man had achieved in a few short years more than most men achieve in a lifetime.

Two weeks later on a fine early spring day, Garibaldi set sail in his small boat for the island of Mondragone, four miles down the coast of Sardinia, where he was to meet with one of his several mistresses, Fiammetta, the Contessa di Mondragone. With a brisk northerly breeze, he made the journey in an hour, as always enjoying being at sea, for Garibaldi had started his adult career as a sailor, following in the footsteps of his father, who had owned a small ship and made his living transporting wine and olive oil up and down the coast of Italy.

If the island of Caprera was stonily forbidding, the island of Mondragone was downright sinister. In the sixteenth century, the then Count Sigismondo di Mondragone had built a stone castle on the highest point of the rocky island to try to bring under control the piracy that was rampant at the time. He had succeeded, mainly because he was a man of extreme ruthlessness and cruelty, and the stories of the tortures he subjected the captured pirates to in the bowels of the castle still curled hair three centuries after his death. Even on a sunny spring morning like this, Castle Mondragone looked eerily evil, like some monstrous stone toad squatting on a rock in the sea. It was a square, crenellated building two stories high with a square tower at each corner where once cannon had been in place. Garibaldi knew that the castle contained many rooms dug into the rock by convict labor, including the infamous torture chamber. Before the castle had been built, the island had been the home of hundreds of large lizards, hence the name *Monte di dragone,* "mount of the dragons." But the lizards had all been killed off, and the name over the years had been contracted to Mondragone.

Garibaldi docked his boat at the island's pier with the help of a *mousse,* or cabin boy, from the Countess's yacht, which was docked on the other side. This was a hundred-foot steam yacht that could ferry her across the Tyrrhenian Sea to the mainland of Italy, where she had a palazzo in Rome and a *castello* in Tuscany. Or, for that matter, the yacht could take her to France, Spain, Greece,

Africa, England, or wherever. Fiammetta di Mondragone was one of the richest women in Europe, and she liked her pleasures.

As Garibaldi started up the stone steps to the castle's entrance, anticipation of lunch and a dalliance with the Countess surged through his body with the vigor of a teenager. Garibaldi was a highly sexed man, attractive to women; and his views on marriage and sex, as well as politics and economics, were amazingly modern, as different from those of his Victorian contemporaries as the views of the Heavenly King were different from those of his Ch'ing Dynasty contemporaries.

Some twenty-five years before, when Garibaldi was a very young man, he had shipped as second mate on a vessel sailing from Nice to Constantinople. Aboard the ship were a group of followers of a strange and brilliant French aristocrat, who had fought in the American Revolution, named the Comte de Saint-Simon. Garibaldi became friendly with the leader of the Saint-Simonians, as they were called, a gifted orator named Emile Barrault. Night after night as the ship sailed east on the Mediterranean, the two men walked the deck, Barrault expounding to an eager Garibaldi the theories of Saint-Simon, who had died in 1825. To Garibaldi, Saint-Simon's ideas were as mind-opening as the Heavenly King's dream of Shang-ti had been to him. And in some ways, both the Frenchman and the Chinese came to similar conclusions.

Both propounded that women were the equal of men, although Saint-Simon, unlike the Heavenly King, believed that the body was to be enjoyed, especially in its sexual functions, so that he was a proponent of free love. His opinion on marriage was that it should be entered into for mutual enjoyment, but if the enjoyment soured, then both husband and wife should be free to go elsewhere. Saint-Simon believed that everything in the state should be run for the benefit of the people, which was an early version of socialism; but having little faith in democracy, which he believed invariably led to the election of the crowd-pleaser, he wrote that the state should be run by a strong, if benevolent, leader, or *duce,* which could be interpreted as an early version of fascism.

These ideas were considered wildly dangerous by the rulers of Europe at the time, most of whom, jolted by the terrors and excesses of the French Revolution and the carnage of the Napoleonic Wars, were doing everything in their power to turn the clock back to the eighteenth century. The Austrian Emperor, for example, snarled "Don't speak to me of citizens. I have only subjects."

Among the worst were a series of arch-reactionary popes who ruled the Papal States in central Italy. To protect their temporal power, they turned viciously against all liberal ideas, forced the Jews back into the ghettos and forbade them to have any relations with Gentiles on pain of death. They proscribed the railroad and telegraph in their domains as inventions of the Devil; they banned the waltz, tore down streetlights, outlawed vaccination against smallpox, reopened the medieval sewers that had been closed over for health reasons, and chained anyone suspected of liberal sympathies up in the papal prisons without trial, leaving them to starve to death and rot in their excreta.

But Garibaldi, listening to Barrault, became a convert to these "wild" ideas, in spite of the danger. He in turn had converted Fiammetta di Mondragone, who had become a rabid Saint-Simonian. Garibaldi especially believed in the idea of a strong leader, although he agreed with Saint-Simon that the leader must not set himself above the people like a king, but rather live with them. It was this idealistic state that he was trying to set up in a crude way on the island of Caprera.

Garibaldi's critics were to say he had dictatorship in his blood.

Reaching the heavy wooden doors of the Castle of Mondragone, he pulled the bell chain. In a few moments the doors were opened by a footman, who led Garibaldi through the entrance hall into the drawing room. And there, sitting at a writing desk overlooking the sea, was Fiammetta di Mondragone. When she saw her lover, Fiammetta put down her pen, stood up, opened her arms, and cried, "Giuseppe, my love! Thank God you've come! I haven't made love in ten days."

Smiling, Garibaldi came to her, took her in his arms, and kissed her.

"Shall we do it right here?" he whispered. "On the floor?"

"Cretino!" She shoved him away. "Do you think I'm a dog? No, we'll do it in my bedroom. Then we'll have lunch and talk. I have much to tell you from Rome."

He pointed to the stack of paper on her desk. "Are you still working on that wretched novel?" he asked.

"That 'wretched' novel is my soul," she said, putting her beautiful hands on her expansive breasts. "It will tell the world the story of my desires, my loves— you appear in it, under another name, of course. All women will read my novel and they will weep and sigh, because my novel will tell all the pain and joy and ecstasy of being a woman!"

"You are magnificent," Garibaldi said. "I worship you."

"But you sleep with that slut of a peasant girl, Battistina. And you smell like one of your goats. Come: I will bathe you, we will make love, then lunch. It will be a perfect day."

She took his hand and led him out of the drawing room into the entrance hall and up the great stone stairs. Fiammetta, who was somewhere in her twenties, was a big woman, taller than Garibaldi, with a voluptuous figure that her tight-fitting green velvet dress showed to advantage. She had beautiful skin, big green eyes, and blond hair that she wore pulled back into a cascade of curls. She loved jewelry and had a big oval-shaped opal ring on one hand and a cameo brooch over her breasts.

"I have an American on the island," Garibaldi said as he accompanied her up the stair. "A fine young man named Justin Savage."

"What in the world would an American be doing on that godforsaken island of yours?"

"I'm teaching him military tactics and he's helping me build my house. He's very bright. I'm becoming quite fond of him. He's learning Italian too, picks it up quite rapidly. But then, he speaks Chinese, so he must have an ear for languages."

"Why does he speak Chinese?"

"He's lived there for a number of years. He has a Chinese wife. He's led a rather extraordinary life for one so young. He's the bastard son of a rich New York shipping family."

"He sounds fascinating. You must bring him to dinner. I'd love to meet him."

"I think not."

"Why?"

He smiled as they reached the top of the stairs. "You'd devour him."

She looked at him, her big eyes becoming interested. "I take it he's attractive?"

"A young god."

Her lips crept into a smile. "Then I *insist* you bring him to dinner. Tomorrow night. You both can spend the night. Now: the bathtub. And I have good news for you. The Pope has a terrible cold."

"Excellent! Maybe it will turn into flu."

They both laughed as they walked down the upstairs hall.

"The Countess has an excellent library," Garibaldi told Justin the next day as the two men sailed from Caprera to Mondragone. "She told me you should feel free to borrow any books you want."

Justin, who was standing in the bow of the boat watching the forbidding Castle Mondragone loom up out of the sea, said, "Does she have *The Art of War?*"

Garibaldi had told Justin about the book written in China around 500 B.C. by a brilliant Chinese named Sun Tzu. Garibaldi had studied the book and found it fascinating because of the clarity of Sun Tzu's thought. It was Garibaldi's opinion that if Napoleon had studied *The Art of War,* he would never have been defeated.

"I know she's read it," Garibaldi said. "She's literate and well read. She also has a lot of history books—you said you were interested in the history of Italy."

"I want to learn everything I can," Justin said. "I want to do as you did and read everything I can get my hands on. I'm tired of being ignorant."

In his few weeks on the island of Caprera, Justin had come to admire Garibaldi to the point of near hero worship.

"You're not ignorant," Garibaldi said. "You're just young. If I could exchange all my knowledge to be young again, I'd do it in a second."

Justin considered this. The thought of wanting to be young had never occurred to him, because he never thought of growing old. He decided to change the subject. "Is the Countess married?"

"She's a widow. Fiammetta is from the north, which is why she is blond—although I think she helps God out with a bit of hair coloring. She comes from a very old titled family who didn't have much money. She married Count Mondragone, who had all the money in the world, but he died a few years ago in a hunting accident. I think I should warn you, Justin: she will undoubtedly try to seduce you."

The young American looked back at Garibaldi, who was sitting at the helm.

"Seriously," Garibaldi went on, "I told you how the ideas of Saint-Simon changed my life, and how I converted Fiammetta. Her opinion now is that since women are the equal of men, then a woman has as much right to try to seduce a man as vice versa. It's a revolutionary concept, but it's a fascinating one. And Fiammetta is very original. She's read *The Art of War* too, and one of the things Sun Tzu says is that 'the supreme art of war is to subdue the enemy without fighting.' Now, *that's* a piece of wisdom. At any rate, Fiammetta said to me once that the concept could also be applied to the art of seduction. I'm not sure what she means, but perhaps you will find out."

"Maybe I can learn military tactics from her," Justin said with a grin.

"I'm sure she can help. Fiammetta is a most interesting woman, and she's smart as a whip. I'm sure *The Art of War* has practical application to the war between the sexes, which is eternal. At any rate, Fiammetta believes with all her heart in the unification of Italy, and she's been very generous with me, financially. During the Roman campaign, she bought me a thousand fifty-two-caliber Sharps repeating carbines, which I think is the best rifle in the world. I'm not interested in riches for myself, which you can see by the way I live. But revolutions require money. I hope to get her to buy me more rifles soon. She's quite a woman."

"Are you in love with her?"

A sad look came over Garibaldi's face. "I'm still in love with my poor

Anita," he sighed. "I suppose I'll get over it someday, but my heart still aches for her. But in the meantime"—his face brightened—"Fiammetta is fun. And she has a most extraordinary wine cellar."

"How old is the Countess?"

"Ah, that's a military secret. The best spy in the world couldn't find that out, but I'd guess she'll never see twenty-five again. Still, women are like wine: they improve with age. Up to a point."

"Tell me about your wife," Fiammetta said to Justin that night as she cut into her pheasant. She, Garibaldi, and Justin were seated at a small round table at one end of the castle's big dining room, the walls of which were covered with a wine-colored brocade and huge fifteenth- and sixteenth-century paintings of gamboling nymphs and satyrs. Castle Mondragone reminded Justin somewhat of Saxmundham Castle, but the latter was a fake, while this was the real thing. Despite its lavish decoration, the castle had a dank air that was vaguely oppressive—or at least it seemed that way to Justin. However, the Countess was anything but oppressive. On the contrary, she seemed a jolly, generous woman whom Justin liked immediately. "Why did you leave her in China?"

"She didn't want to leave," Justin lied, having no intention of letting either Garibaldi or Fiammetta know the truth about his piratical past. Nor did he of course have any idea that Chang-mei was sailing up the Yangtze to her death.

"Does she have bound feet?" Fiammetta went on. "That strikes me as the most peculiar perversion, but I've read that Chinese men go mad with desire over the deformities."

Fiammetta, who had been sent to England to school as a child, spoke excellent English with an upper-class accent. But Justin's mind had wandered. Or rather, his eyes had sneaked a little detour to ogle her remarkable breasts that the décolletage of her low-cut celadon dress displayed perilously near the point of indecency. She wore a necklace of enormous rubies and diamonds, with matching earrings that blazed in the candlelight when she moved her head. In her blond hair she wore a diamond and ruby tiara, and her fingers and wrists were weighted with rings and bracelets. She smelled subtly of jasmine. Compared to Justin's ratty suit and Garibaldi's tan trousers and red shirt, she looked like something from another planet. Justin thought she was ravishing, which was exactly what she wanted him to think.

"I said," Fiammetta repeated, "does your wife have bound feet?"

"Oh . . . ah, excuse me." Justin wrenched his eyes away from her cleavage. Garibaldi bit his lip so as not to smile. "No, my wife is a peasant girl. Only the upper-class Chinese bind the feet of their daughters."

"And how did the son of a rich New York shipper marry a Chinese peasant girl?"

"Well, I . . ." Justin turned red. "We had a daughter, and I didn't want her to be illegitimate."

"Giuseppe, he's blushing," Fiammetta cooed. "How absolutely delicious Americans are! Justin, after dinner I must show you my torture chamber," she added matter-of-factly.

"I'd rather see your library," Justin said.

"You'll see both, dear boy. In fact, anything you want to see, just ask and it will be"—she smiled, showing her perfect teeth—"revealed to you."

"These dungeons were built by my late husband's ancestor, Count Sigismondo di Mondragone, during the papacy of the Borgia Pope, Alexander VI, in 1501," Fiammetta said an hour later as she led Justin and Garibaldi down a stone stairs. She held a four-branched silver candelabra in her right hand, and the flickering light of the candles pierced the stygian gloom. The stone walls were slimy.

"Why are the walls wet?" Justin asked.

"It's seawater," she replied. "We're below sea level now. During bad storms the whole island shakes slightly when the waves crash against it. It's wonderfully morbid. Do be careful: there may be rats. They tend to be friendly unless you're dead."

"Then they become unfriendly?" Justin ventured.

"Well, they eat you. The little creatures have big appetites, you know. Now, wait while I light one of the torches. Hold this for me, will you?"

They had reached the bottom of the steps. Fiammetta handed Justin the candelabra, then she took a wooden torch from an iron wall bracket and lit the end of it with one of the candles. After it sputtered to life, she put it back on the wall. Justin saw that they were in a vast stone chamber with an arched ceiling. Around the room were a series of barred cells.

"Sigismondo was like the unfortunate Marquis de Sade," Fiammetta went on. "He enjoyed inflicting pain. Of course, it's easy to say that our ancestors were crude and we today are much more civilized, but the modern popes are just as bad as Sigismondo. Giuseppe can tell you how they chain political prisoners in their cells and starve them to death. It's shocking. Now, here are some of our torture devices. Pardon me for sounding like a tour guide."

She walked to the center of the chamber. Justin, who as a child had devoured the stories of Edgar Allan Poe, in particular "The Pit and the Pendulum," followed her, fascinated by seeing in actuality what he had read about in gory fiction.

"This charming device, which was invented by the Inquisition—the Inquisitors were so terribly clever about torture—is called the strappado," Fiammetta said, pointing to the ceiling where a heavy pulley was embedded in the stone. A thick rope went through it, dangling to the floor. "Sigismondo was especially fond of it. The prisoner's hands were tied behind his back, then the torturers pulled the rope, hauling him up to the ceiling. By pulling his arms up behind him, the pain must have been excruciating. They would hang him up in the air until he either confessed or passed out. Then they would drop him, stopping him a few feet before he hit the floor. Of course, the jerking effect often pulled the victim's arms out of their sockets."

"I should have warned you," Garibaldi said to Justin with a smile. "Fiammetta's a ghoul."

"Well, you must admit it's fascinating," she said. "Sigismondo was a horror, but what he did, he did with passion, which is a lesson we all could learn. If anything is to be achieved in this world, it must be done with passion. That's why one day our dear Giuseppe will succeed in uniting Italy: because he is passionate about it. Which is why we are all so passionate about him. Now, here's an interesting device. It's called the aselli. The prisoner was placed in this wooden trough you see here and strapped in. Then water was forced down his throat while the guards turned these screws, tightening the sides of the trough. In the old records I have upstairs, it says that very often the prisoners burst open."

Interested as he was, Justin felt his stomach becoming a bit queasy.

"This was Sigismondo's own invention, the clever man," Fiammetta went on, picking up a long iron pole. "It's a branding iron, like the ones the American cowboys use in your West, Justin dear. It's the initial *M* for Mondragone in a circle. Sigismondo would heat the iron in that fire"—she indicated a circular fire pit in the center of the floor—"then brand his prisoners on the buttocks."

"I can think of several Italian politicians I'd like to brand," Garibaldi said.

"Yes, I can too. And a number of priests. What a thrill it would be! Sigismondo certainly enjoyed himself. I have one of his letters upstairs that he wrote to the woman he married—if you can imagine it! In it he says, 'I can assure you, my love, there is no greater pleasure than the inflicting of pain.' " She put the branding iron back in the fire pit, then smiled at her guests. "Well. Shall we all go back upstairs for a cognac and coffee? Then I'll show you my library."

As he followed her to the stone steps, Justin thought he could hear the screams of agony that must once have echoed through this chamber of horrors. Had he imagined it, or had there been a hint in Fiammetta's voice, speaking with that patrician English accent, that she might have enjoyed the inflicting of pain as much as her husband's cruel ancestor, Sigismondo?

"No, I don't have a copy of *The Art of War*," Fiammetta said a while later as she showed Justin around her capacious library. "Not here, at any rate. I have one in Rome. I'll send for it, if you'd like."

"That would be very kind of you," Justin said, his eyes devouring the titles of the hundreds of books behind the brass protective grills. "I couldn't pay you for a while. . . . I mean, right now I'm flat broke. But I have money in China. . . ."

"Please: let's not talk about money," she interrupted. "The book will be a gift from me. Giuseppe, aren't you paying this young man?"

Garibaldi, who was smoking a cigar in a red leather armchair by the fireplace, said, "What with? I haven't any money to speak of, as you well know. We're leading an idealistic, communistic existence on Caprera. Justin works on my house during the day, and I feed him and teach him what I know in return."

"Did you make him this perfectly ghastly suit?"

"No, I loaned him some money to buy it in Maddalena. He came to me with nothing but his sailor clothes."

She ran her finger over the lapel of Justin's brown suit, which was ill-fitting and shoddy. "It's junk," she said. "I wouldn't allow my servants to wear something this cheap. Well, I suppose it can't be helped. How old are you, Justin?"

"Nineteen."

"Mmm. Giuseppe tells me you want an education and to learn how to be a soldier. Why?"

"I am pledged to return to China after my education to help my benefactor, Prince I."

"You'd help the Manchus? They're worse than the Austrians and the Pope!"

"Perhaps, but I gave my word."

"The boy's irresistible! He's honest! Giuseppe, you've brought me a miracle." She turned to Justin. "But how can you get a proper education with Giuseppe? He has no library. You must stay here and use mine. And I'll get you a tutor . . . there's a young professor I know at the University of Bologna. He wants to take a year off to write a book about the decline of the Medici, who took a devilishly long time to collapse into total perversion. . . . I could hire him to come here and tutor you."

Justin looked at her with surprise. "That's very kind of you, Countess, but I couldn't accept your charity. . . ."

"It's not charity, you can pay me back later on. A young man has to have an education. And Giuseppe can come here every week to amuse me and teach you how to become a soldier. It will be perfect."

Garibaldi was puffing on his cigar, eyeing Fiammetta. Now he said, "Justin, it's late. We have to leave early in the morning. Perhaps you'd better go up to bed. We'll talk about this some other time."

Justin looked rather uncertainly at Garibaldi, then nodded. "You're right, General." He turned to Fiammetta. "You're very kind, Countess, and I appreciate your offer. But I couldn't allow myself to become a burden on you. Good night."

"Good night."

He crossed the room to the door, adding, "I really would appreciate it if you could get me *The Art of War.*"

"But of course, dear boy. I give you my word. I'm like you: I never go back on my word."

After Justin left the room, Garibaldi got out of his chair, lowering his voice: "Now listen, you *puttana:* lay off the kid! Don't you think I see what you're up to?"

"Giuseppe, you were right! I want to devour him! He's . . ." She put her fists to her breasts and closed her eyes in ecstasy. "He tears my insides with desire!" She opened her eyes, and they burned with excitement. "I must have him! I *will* have him! Nothing can stop me!"

"Except *me.* I've come to think of him as a sort of son . . . at least, I feel responsible for him. And I'm not going to have him corrupted by you."

" 'Corrupted'? Why, you old *cacapensieri,* what do you think I'm going to do to him, turn him into a *pappatore?* I'll give him an education, show him the world, make a gentleman out of him!"

"He's already a gentleman—you just want to get him in bed!"

She shrugged. "That will be part of his education. After all, it's in accordance with the teachings of Saint-Simon—as you've so often said to me."

"Saint-Simon never approved the corrupting of youth!"

"Youth? He's nineteen! And God knows what tricks he learned in China with those concubines. I'll probably be learning from *him!* But he's so fresh, so different, so American—! I have no children, he could be my son, my lover . . . I'm mad with excitement!"

"Well, you can forget it. I won't allow it."

"You old goat: as if *you* are in a position to preach morality! But, Giuseppe dear . . ." She smiled. "You've hinted to me often that you'd like me to buy you a thousand more rifles so you can start raising a new army. I mean, after all, nothing is more important to any of us than driving the foreigners out of Italy—am I right?"

A thoughtful look came over Garibaldi's face. He looked around the library a moment. "I'll admit you have advantages I can't give him," he said. "But . . ." He frowned. "No, I can't allow it."

"Maybe Justin will have something to say about it," she snapped irritably. "And, Giuseppe, you've been sulking on that dreary island of yours long enough. The Young Italy movement is dying! Give me a laundry list of what you need to revive your old army. I'll raise the money for you. The reactionaries are winning because we've stopped fighting them! Italy is suffering! Every right-minded Italian is crying out, 'Where is our leader? Where is Garibaldi?' It's time for you to act!"

"But we could never get the French out of Rome. . . ."

"Pooh, Napoleon the Third is full of hot air, a pompous little balloon of a man. You're ten times the general he is! It's only because he's Napoleon's nephew that anyone respects him at all. No, it's time for you to galvanize Italy, and I'll raise your money. But of course"—she smiled as she patted his cheek— "I know you won't stand in my way with my little romantic fling. I've never had an American as a lover."

He laughed. "I won't stand in your way. It's his decision."

2 4   JUSTIN HAD DREAMS THAT NIGHT, terrifying dreams of torture. He dreamed he was chained in the chamber of horrors below the Castle Mondragone while a person in a black cloak and mask heated Sigismondo's branding iron in the circular fire pit. Then, when the brand glowed a smoking red, the torturer came toward him, removing the mask.

It was Fiammetta, a look of fiendish glee in her green eyes. As Justin writhed in terror, she came to him, pulled down his pants, and pressed the branding iron against his left buttock as he screamed. . . .

He woke up, bolting upright in his bed, his face drenched with sweat. He put his hand under his nightshirt to feel his left buttock and sighed with relief when he felt nothing. Then he lit one of the oil bed lamps with a lucifer.

The bedchamber was a handsome room overlooking the sea, the furniture elaborately carved mahogany. The walls above a wooden dado were painted a pale yellow with stenciled red flowers, but there were so many pictures hanging, the stencils got lost. There could be no doubt that the castle, while perhaps oppressive and ominous, was the last word in luxury. The bedsheets were linen and the pillows goose down. The big four-poster was certainly a far cry from the thin straw mattresses he had been sleeping on in Caprera. When Justin thought back on the house in Pink Jade Lane in Canton, and his hammock on the *Sea Witch,* he reflected that he hadn't been so physically comfortable since his days in the mansion on Washington Square.

He was about to turn out the light and try to get back to sleep when he saw a light spilling underneath a door in the center of the wall opposite his bed. It was not the door from the upstairs hall. Then there was a soft rap on the door.

"Justin?" he heard Fiammetta's voice. "Are you all right? I heard you cry out, dear boy. May I come in?"

Without waiting for an answer, she opened the door and came in. She was holding a round-globed oil lamp. She was dressed in a flounced pink negligee, and she had tied a pink ribbon in her hair.

Justin, who was wearing the coarse flannel nightgown Garibaldi had bought him in Maddalena, said, "I guess I must have cried out in my sleep. I was having a nightmare."

She crossed the room to his bed. "I hope it wasn't caused by something you ate," she said. "Do you like your room? It used to be my husband's."

"Oh? Well, um, yes, it's very comfortable."

"That's why there's a door there, connecting to my room. Cesare would use it when he came to me to make love."

"Cesare was—?"

"My husband. A man of violent passion." She sighed. "Some times I miss him."

"I'm sure you miss him all the time."

"Oh, no. No, Cesare and I didn't see eye to eye politically. He was an arch-reactionary—he actually sided with the popes, if you can imagine. If he knew now how I am on the side of Garibaldi, he would come out of his grave and kill me." She set the lamp on a table. "But when he made love to me, I forgot his failings. He was quite good-looking—curly black hair, blue eyes, and the most dashing mustaches. He had many mistresses, but I forgave him. He was a devil of a husband, but I was an angel of a wife. He had wonderful taste in clothes. Did you look in the guardaroba?" She indicated a door by the bed. "I left many of his things in there. He was about your size: feel free to try anything on."

"I don't think . . ."

"Oh, Cesare was very clean. Like Garibaldi, he loved to take baths and he was always cleaning his fingernails. Come. . . ." Picking up her lamp, she moved around the bed, extending her free hand. "Let me show you."

Justin hesitated, then got out of bed. He took her hand. She led him to the door.

"Open it," she said. He obeyed. She led him in to a closet the size of a small room. There were racks of handmade shoes and boots, all with wooden trees. Above them hung rows of suits, uniforms, hunting outfits, tailcoats.

"Look," she said, opening a drawer. "His undergarments, all handmade by the nuns. And here, his shirts . . . aren't they beautiful? Cesare was very vain. And this crimson silk robe with the gold 'M' embroidered on the pocket . . . ah"—she smiled—"he wore that when he came to me to make love. Here, hold the lamp." She handed him the lamp and went farther back into the *guardaroba* where a leather box was resting on a shelf. "Here are his collection of cuff links," she said, opening the lid. Justin stared at dozens of cuff links, set in red velvet, many of them gold but others with sapphires and precious jewels surrounded by diamonds that glittered in the lamplight. She smiled at him. "Isn't it fabulous? Like a treasure from the *Arabian Nights.*"

"But one wonders with so much poverty . . ."

She dismissed him with a wave of her hand. "Cesare couldn't have cared less about the poor. He was a totally selfish man. He made selfishness an art." She lifted a pair of diamond cuff links from the box and handed them to Justin. "Here: a present from me."

"I couldn't accept them. . . ."

"Then sell them and give the money to the poor, if you're so concerned about them. Or give it to Garibaldi. He sucks up money like a priest, not for himself, but for his cause."

"I really can't," he said, giving them back.

She shrugged and put the links back in the box, closing the lid. "You don't like money?" she asked.

"Of course. But I like to earn it."

She smiled. "Well then, we'll have to find a way for you to earn it. Did the General tell you about the Comte de Saint-Simon?"

"Yes."

"Do you agree that women are the equal of men?"

"Absolutely. My wife convinced me of that."

"Had she read Saint-Simon?"

"No. She figured it out for herself. She's very smart."

"Do you love her?"

"Very much. And I don't intend to be unfaithful to her."

Fiammetta's smile froze. "I see. Well, then, we must do everything we can to safeguard your sturdy American virtue. And the first thing we'll do is tuck you safely back in your bed. Come."

She took the lamp from him and started out of the *guardaroba,* Justin behind her. Back in the bedroom, he closed the door and went to his bed. She watched him. After a moment, she laughed.

"Did I say something funny?" he asked.

"Oh, yes, several things. But I was thinking of the last time I saw Cesare in this room. It was the night before he was killed. He had just taken a bath and was strutting around the room singing some off-color Neapolitan street song. And he had nothing on at all. Cesare loved to be naked. He was very proud of his *cazzo.*"

"His what?"

She went to the door to her room and opened it, turning to smile at him. "Guess," she said sweetly. "I'll lock this door from my side. That way, we'll both be safe. Good night."

She went into her bedroom, closing the door. He heard the click of a lock.

He climbed back in his bed, turned off the lamp, and stared at the dark ceiling. He remembered Chang-mei's *cri de coeur:* "Don't forget me, Justin." He had almost betrayed her with Samantha, for which he had agonized. He would not betray her with the Countess, tempting as she was.

But he was awfully tempted.

The next morning Garibaldi came downstairs to the dining room where Fiammetta's servants had set out an English-style breakfast on the Renaissance credenza that an antiquarian would have murdered for. Antique silver chafing dishes held rashers of bacon, fresh-laid eggs with blooded yolks, kippers, toast, a carousel of jellies, cheeses. . . . Garibaldi loaded his plate, for he had a hearty appetite, then went to the small table at the end of the room where they had eaten dinner the night before. A servant poured him Turkish coffee as he took a seat. Through the windows, the sea shimmered in the morning sun of what promised to be a spectacular day.

He was buttering his second piece of toast when Fiammetta came downstairs. A servant poured her coffee as she sat next to Garibaldi. "Well, it seems Justin wishes to remain faithful to his wife," she said in French so the servants wouldn't understand. French was Garibaldi's first language, as he came from Nice. "An interesting turn of events. He's the first faithful husband I think I've ever met. Just my luck."

Garibaldi reached over and squeezed her hand. "It's better this way," he said. "Believe me."

"If you think I'm giving up, you don't know me very well. *Now* my appetite is really whetted. I'm going to Rome tomorrow, but I'll be back in a week. Bring Justin for dinner a week from tomorrow night. This campaign is just beginning." She sipped her coffee. She looked up. "Ah, but here he comes." She smiled. "Good morning, Justin. Did you sleep well?"

Look at him, she thought, her heart pounding. He's irresistible! I *will* have him, dammit. I *will!*

A week later Garibaldi sailed from Caprera in his boat alone. After docking at the island of Mondragone, he climbed the steps to the door of the castle and rang. As usual, he was dressed casually in baggy trousers and one of his red shirts, which had become a symbol of revolution by accident. He had originally bought them in South America because they were cheap, having been made for slaughterhouse workers, the red being protection against splattered blood from the animals. But the world had changed the symbol into the spilled blood of revolutionaries. After a servant admitted him to the castle, he was taken to the drawing room where Fiammetta was working on her novel. When she saw him, she said, "Where's Justin?"

"He wouldn't come. The poor boy's in terrible shape."

"Why? What happened?"

The General sank into a chair and lit one of his beloved cigars. "A letter came to him from a mandarin he knows in China. A certain Prince I, who is the Viceroy of Canton and apparently a cousin of the Emperor."

"How in the world would Justin know him?"

Garibaldi exhaled a cloud of smoke. "He was vague about that. I think our young American hasn't told us *all* the truth about his past. Anyway, this Prince I informed him that his wife has been killed and his baby daughter has vanished—it's presumed that she's dead also."

Fiammetta frowned. "How terrible. I feel a bit guilty, though I'm sure I'll get over it. What happened to his wife?"

"She ran away to join the great rebellion against the Manchus. Justin is devastated. He tells me he doesn't know what to do now, where to turn. . . . For some reason, he can't go back to America. I have the feeling he may be wanted for some crime. . . ."

Fiammetta stood up. "How very intriguing," she said. "A criminal past! He becomes more interesting by the day." She drummed her fingers on the top of a chair, thinking. "Perhaps now my offer of educating him may be more attractive to him. It would give him a direction, a goal. . . ." She looked at the manuscript of her novel. "I'll write him a letter," she said. "Put my offer down on paper . . . he could hardly not respond. . . ."

Garibaldi took his cigar from his mouth. "You're a determined woman, Fiammetta."

Garibaldi chuckled as she sat down at her desk, took out a sheet of her lavender, coronet-embossed stationery, dipped her pen in the crystal inkwell, and began writing:

> *My dear Justin:*
>
> *The General has told me the news about your wife and daughter. I am so very sorry. Please accept my condolences.*
>
> *Although this may be an awkward time to press you to make a decision about your future, let me tell you the arrangements I made last week in Rome. I spoke to Professor Tommaso Seghizzi of the University of Bologna about tutoring you. He is a charming young man of good family who can instruct you in Latin, Greek, history, mathematics, and biology. He is also an expert linguist who can help your Italian.*
>
> *I have also spoken to Signor Eduardo Tassoni, one of Italy's best fencers, who was the teacher of my late husband. He has agreed to come to Castle Mondragone for a few months, or however long it would take to make you proficient in that sport. Cesare also kept fit by regular workouts with the well-known gymnast Baldassare Russo, and there is a fully equipped gymnasium on the second floor of the castle. Signor Russo, who lives in Maddalena, has agreed to come to the island three times a week to train you in that sport, if you should so desire. Whatever other instruction you might be interested in—horsemanship, for example—could be arranged at a later date. Knowing your love of the sea, my yacht, the Aurora, would be available at all times for both our pleasure.*
>
> *Thus, the education you told me you want is available to you, dear Justin. The future can be as exciting for you as your past has been tragic. I lay at your feet the finest fruits of our ancient civilization. All you have to do is say "yes."*
>
> *You may well ask why I am doing this for you: I will not dissemble. I am a passionate woman, Justin. From the moment I first saw you, I was struck by what the French call a "coup de foudre." It was love at first sight; but every moment I have*

passed with you since that precious instant has only enriched my love for you. You have a sweetness that inspires me with the tenderest emotions, and your manly grace enflames me with desire. My greatest wish is to join my body and soul with yours; together, we can rise to the very heights of passion. Ah, my love, do not disappoint me. I offer you my fortune and my fate. But most important, I offer you my heart.

Believe me, with my sincerest expressions of love,
I am

Your Fiammetta.

Justin's grief over the news of Chang-mei's death and the probable death of Julie had ultimately turned to rage. He was beginning to feel like Job. His birthright had been stolen from him by Sylvaner, and even though he had extracted a confession from him in London, he wasn't sure it would hold up in court. It had been the best he could do, but it probably wasn't good enough, and he was afraid to return to New York to test it. Sylvaner had all the trumps: wealth, power, and legitimacy. Justin had nothing. And now, even his wife and daughter had been taken from him. It was devastating.

This had been his black mood when Garibaldi returned to Caprera with Fiammetta's letter, which he handed Justin to read as Battistina ironed in the back of the room. Justin went to the table and sat down. When he finished reading the letter, he looked up at the General.

"Can she be serious?" he asked.

"Fiammetta doesn't play games. She's deadly serious. She's fallen for you, as they used to say in New York, like a ton of bricks. I've tried to discourage her because, among other things, she's a bit older than you. Besides, after the tragedy of your wife and daughter I doubt that you're much in the mood for romance. Do you have any feeling for her?"

"The Countess? I hardly know her. I mean I think she's beautiful and exciting . . ." He hesitated, frowning.

Justin looked at the General a long time. Then: "Why would I say 'no'?" he asked quietly. "I, who have had everything taken from me? My mother, my father, my home, my fortune—and now my wife and child? Fiammetta is offering me an education. So she's a bit older than I—what do I care? She's a beautiful woman who loves me—why shouldn't I love her back? I say 'yes.' "

That night, as a rising wind moaned around Castle Mondragone, the three of them dined on suckling pig stuffed with wild rice. Fiammetta had been so ecstatic at Justin's acceptance of her "arrangement," as she tactfully referred to the deal, that she drank a bit too much of the excellent Barolo and got giggly, to Garibaldi's amusement. But the coffee sobered her up. And she started to climb the stairs to her bedroom, telling Justin she would await "her lover."

Justin watched her from the door to the drawing room. Then he came back inside and joined Garibaldi before the fire. "Do you think she means what she promised?" he asked. "Or do you think this is just a rich woman's fling?"

"Ah well, my boy, who can tell with women? As Maestro Verdi says, 'La donna è mobile'—women are fickle. But go upstairs and do your best to please her. Then we will see." He clapped him on the back. "Good luck."

When he reached Cesare's bedroom, Justin went into the large guardaroba, undressed, and put on the former husband's crimson silk robe Fiammetta had said Cesare wore when he came to make love. Putting on a dead man's clothes was an odd sensation for the young American, but the picture Fiammetta had painted of her vain husband who enjoyed strutting about in the nude rushed into his memory as he felt the silk on his skin. He knew that Italy, despite the presence of the Vatican on its soil, was still in its soul like pagan Rome, a country of hot passions and sensuality. Certainly Fiammetta was pagan, even to her name, which meant "little flame." Now, as he tied the black sash round his waist, with the robe's cool silk kissing his flesh, he began to feel pagan himself. It had been over half a year since he had made love to poor Chang-mei, and he hadn't had a woman since. Now the thought of Fiammetta's voluptuous breasts sent freshets of lust coursing through his loins. He felt like Priapus.

Coming out of the guardaroba, he crossed the room to the door and opened it without knocking. He went into Fiammetta's bedroom, which was the biggest in the castle, a very feminine room with dusty rose wallpaper and white and rose silk curtains swagging over the sea-viewing windows. A fire snapped in the hearth; above the marble mantel was a life-size portrait of Fiammetta standing in a garden wearing a bell-skirted white dress, her blond hair in a great chignon swooping almost to her shoulders.

"Do you like it?" Fiammetta said from the bed. "It was painted by Herr Winterhalter, who gets all the royal commissions because he flatters his sitters. I hope you won't say he flattered me?"

Justin looked to his left where the four-poster bed faced the fireplace. It had a canopy of the same silk material as the curtains gathered into big bows at each corner. Fiammetta was sitting up in the middle of the bed wearing a white bed jacket. She had unpinned her golden hair, which flowed around her head on the pillows like an aureole. She looked like an angel except for her green eyes, which burned with devilish lust.

"He didn't flatter you," Justin said.

She smiled. "You wore Cesare's robe. Good. You look much more hand-some than he did in it, and Cesare was a good-looking man. Oh, Justin, my darling"—she opened her arms to him—"tonight I am the happiest woman in the world. Let this be the first of ten thousand nights of love! Come here, my darling Justin. I want to feel your hands on my breasts, your lips on my mouth. Ravish me, my darling Justin. Make me feel incandescent. More to the point, take off that robe. I want to *see* you!"

Justin untied the sash, took off the robe, and dropped it on the floor. She clasped her hands, her green eyes drinking in his nudity. *"Che bello!"* she gasped. *"Dio mio! E che gran cazzo! Stravagante!* Turn around, my darling. I want to see your *culo."*

"My what?" Justin asked, turning.

"Your ass. I'm mad for men's asses. They make me lose what little control I have. Ah, and yours is so beautiful, so firm!"

"I'm glad you like it, because I had a dream you branded it with Sigismondo's branding iron."

"What a lovely idea! Then you'd be mine forever. Perhaps I shall. Climb in bed, *anima mia.* Teach me all the delightful perversions you learned in China. Transport me to the Matterhorn of rapture."

She took off her bed jacket and threw back the duvet, revealing her lush fig-ure in all its splendid nudity. Like Goya's *Maja Desnuda,* she was all curves, her pink flesh verging on the voluptuous, her breasts large and ripe, great mel-ons of desire. He climbed on the bed, kneeling over her until his genitals dan-gled on her toes. "Your skin is so smooth," he whispered.

"Cesare made me wax my legs. He said only peasant girls have hairy legs." She gently goosed him with her big toe. Justin, surprised, jerked upright. She giggled. "I didn't hurt you, did I?"

"You surprised me."

"Just getting to know you. Think of all the games we can play."

He put his mouth on her right thigh and began kissing, moving slowly up-ward. "The Chinese," he said, "have a game called 'The Rabbit Eats the Hair.' "

"That sounds fun. Show me."

He did. Fiammetta began moaning with pleasure. *"Divino! Dio mio, che ès-tasi!"*

The rabbit then began to lick his way up her body, sucking her nipples, lick-ing her cleavage, kissing her bosom, her neck, her chin, her cheeks, her eyes, her nose, and finally her mouth. He was straddling her now, and her hands rubbed his smooth back, then roamed lovingly over his buttocks.

"Your skin is like cream," she whispered. "Ah, you are perfection, the lover of my dreams. . . . Take me, *amore* . . . my sweet Americano. . . ."

He did. A half hour later she wanted it again. The third time, he collapsed in her arms, panting. "My God," he said, "are you sure Cesare died in a hunting accident? Or was it physical exhaustion?"

She screamed with laughter.

25 SYLVANER SAVAGE OPENED THE LETTER from Paris that had arrived in the morning mail at the offices of the Savage Shipping Company on John Street in Lower Manhattan. Sylvaner had changed the name of the company shortly after his father's death, dropping the "N" for "Nathaniel." He was also planning to build a new and much bigger building on a lot he had bought on Broadway across from the Trinity Church at the corner of Wall Street. Despite the uncertainty in the country about the slavery issue and a bad business recession that was hurting small businesses everywhere, the shipping business was booming. The fabric mills of England couldn't get enough of the South's cotton. The fact that the working conditions in the English mills were deplorable and that the cotton was grown by slaves bothered few of the businessmen reaping fortunes off the trade on both sides of the Atlantic. Certainly none of the misery on the Southern plantations bothered Sylvaner. He couldn't understand why the Abolitionists were making such a fuss about slavery in the first place, and he often said to his business associates at his club that he wished the Abolitionists would all "shut up." Of course, Sylvaner was making money off slavery in another, more devious way. He had leased several of his older ships to slave traders, although he had kept this lucrative little side deal to himself. The slave trade was illegal (though it still went on, earning huge profits); being involved with it was not something one mentioned at one's club.

Otherwise, the only regret Sylvaner had in terms of business was that he had been forced to issue Savage Shipping Company stock to the public to raise money to offset the enormous losses caused by Justin's pirating attacks on the clipper ships in the China Sea. The sale of the Savage stock had been successful, and Sylvaner was still the majority stockholder, maintaining eleven percent of the stock. But it wasn't the same as owning the company privately as he had before; and the fault was all Justin's. The terror Sylvaner had experienced in the house in London as he waited to be blown up by gunpowder had not only turned his hair and beard prematurely white, but had made him manic on the subject of his half brother.

Now, with this letter from Paris, perhaps there would be news that would enable him to achieve what had become an obsession: the destruction of Justin.

The letter was from the private detective he had hired in Paris. Of course, since Adelaide's change of heart about her nephew, he had told her nothing of what he was doing: he really didn't quite trust her anymore.

The letter read:

Paris. 10 March, 1857

My dear M. Savage:

I am pleased to report that I have traced the whereabouts of Justin Savage. I assumed that because of his nautical background he would try to leave France on a commercial ship. By checking the shipping lists of the principal ports of the country, I discovered that a young American fitting your half brother's description had shipped out on a freighter from Nice, bound for Algiers. He jumped the ship on a small island off the coast of Sardinia called Maddalena. I traveled to Maddalena and, by asking the local police, found that a young American named Savage has been working for the revolutionary Garibaldi.

"Garibaldi?" Sylvaner muttered to himself. "Extraordinary!" Then he continued reading:

General Garibaldi is a close friend—some say lover—of an extremely wealthy noblewoman named the Countess of Mondragone. The Countess is a dedicated Saint-Simonist and has advanced views on a number of subjects that have made her somewhat controversial in more conservative circles in Europe. She is known to be an advocate of free love. According to gossip on the island, Justin has become her lover and spends most of his time with her at her castle on another island off Sardinia, the Castle Mondragone.

"The swine!" Sylvaner mumbled. "He's become a gigolo and a Socialist!" He read on:

Regarding your instructions concerning how to "dispose" of your half brother if I could locate him: I have close connections with the Camorra in Naples, which, as you may know, is the Neapolitan branch of the Sicilian Mafia. For a price, they can be hired to do any job, and I have found them dependable and their fees quite reasonable. I would highly recommend them. And, thanks to the general corruption in the Kingdom of Naples, there

would be absolutely no problems with the police. A suggestion:
the Castle of Mondragone has a well-known torture chamber
which might be useful for your half brother's "disposition."

I enclose my bill for current expenses, and await your further
instructions, which will of course be treated with the strictest
confidence.

Believe me, sir, I am your most obedient servant,
Gaspard Benoit, Detective.

A slow smile came over Sylvaner's face as he folded the letter. "A torture chamber?" he whispered to himself. "How absolutely lovely."

"What a mess everything in Italy is," Fiammetta said as she filed her nails in bed. It was six weeks after Sylvaner had received the letter from the detective. Justin was lying next to her in the bed, staring at the ceiling. Outside the windows of the Castle Mondragone, the sea seemed sullen under leaden skies. "The Bourbon King in Naples doesn't want anything to change at all, the Pope wants to turn the clock back, and King Victor Emmanuel up in Torino wants to go to bed with me."

"Really? Did he proposition you?"

"Of course. He propositions every reasonably attractive woman, so it's hardly a compliment. Do you find me reasonably attractive, darling?"

"You know you're gorgeous. But you're putting on weight."

"You awful man!" She sighed. "Oh, I know it's the truth. I have to go on a diet again, or I'll have to buy some new clothes." She sighed and put the nail file on the bed table. Then she smiled and snuggled into his arms, kissing him. "But I'm so happy with you, my darling, and when I'm happy, I eat. Pasta, pasta, pasta! Isn't it wonderful to be in love? You *do* love me, don't you?"

He smiled and kissed her. "You know I do. By the way, when's your birthday?"

She frowned and sat up again. "Why do you want to know?"

"That's simple. You've never told me, and I'd want to get you a present. Not that I could afford an expensive one. . . ."

"You want to know how old I am! Admit it! That's what you're after! You think I'm growing old. . . ."

"Fiammetta," Justin sighed. "Here we go again. I don't want to know how old you are. I don't care."

"That's easy for you to say because you're so young! You're growing tired of me. You're going to leave me!"

"I'm not going to leave you. This is like the most wonderful university in the world! I'm getting an education from Professor Seghizzi, I'm learning how to fence, General Garibaldi's teaching me about soldiering, and I've got you. Why in the world would I leave?"

Fiammetta calmed down. "Oh, I'm so insecure," she sighed, going back into his arms. "I love you so much, *anima mia,* and I'm terrified I'll lose you because I *am* older. Perhaps I should be truthful with you. Perhaps I should tell you how old I am. Yes, that's better! And I'll tell you my birthday."

"When's your birthday?"

"September eighth. I'm a Virgo, very dull."

"You're anything but dull. And how old are you?"

"Twenty-five."

Justin smiled, "Oh."

"You don't believe me!"

"I didn't say that."

"All right, I'm twenty-six."

"Okay."

"You still don't believe me."

"Fiammetta, I don't *care!* Honestly! Now talk about something else."

"Tell me you love me."

"I already did."

"Tell me in Chinese."

"They don't have a word for 'love.' "

"They don't?"

"No. Not the way we mean it, romantic love. Women are different in China."

"How so?"

"They're considered inferior to men."

"That's not different."

"I mean, a poor woman is just a machine to have sons. And a rich woman is, well, a machine to have sons."

"How sad. And peculiar. Do you love me more than you loved Chang-mei?"

He looked sad. She squeezed his hand. "I shouldn't have asked that," she said. "I'm a wicked woman, I suppose, so hungry for your love I want you to think of no one but me. I'm a vampire feasting on you, my darling Justin, but I can't help myself. But it's foolish of me to be jealous of a dead woman."

"You have only one woman to be jealous of," he said.

She frowned. "Oh, yes: Samantha, the American girl. Well, I hope she gets a bad case of the pox or some other horrible disease."

"You mustn't say that!"

She bolted out of his arms and slapped his face. "You brute!" she cried. "I give you the world, and you still secretly love that missionary's daughter! How could she possibly compare with me? Is she as beautiful? As smart? As good in bed? She's younger! That's it—you love her because she's younger!"

He got out of bed and threw on his bathrobe. "Fiammetta, I'm not going to get into another fight with you," he said. "Every time I mention Samantha, you go into a screaming fit. I wish I'd never told you about her, but I was only trying to be honest with you. Obviously, honesty gets you nothing but trouble."

She burst into tears. "I can't help being jealous," she sobbed. "I adore you so, *anima mia.* Don't be cruel to your Fiammetta. Don't leave me."

"I'm not leaving you. I'm going down to the kitchen to get some breakfast. I have my lesson in an hour."

"We women are supposed to be the two-faced ones, but it's you men who are the hypocrites!" she cried. "Oh, you kiss us, you sing us serenades—if we're lucky—you pledge eternal love, but all the time you're thinking of someone else!"

"Chang-mei used to say the same thing to me. Maybe women in China aren't so different after all."

"All women are victims! The philosophers babble on about the equality of the sexes, but nothing ever changes, and we're fools to think anything ever will! You men are nothing but dogs in heat. Ah, what misery we women endure, and for what? A few brief moments of ecstasy! *È pazzo*—crazy!"

He came back to the bed. "You're having a wonderful time making this scene, aren't you?"

"It's not a 'scene.' I'm expressing the agony of my existence."

"And it's all going into your novel."

"Of course." He laughed and kissed her. She threw her arms around him and pulled him down on top of her.

"You really are crazy," he said, kissing her. "But I'll say one thing: they don't have many like you back in New York."

"You must take me to New York one day."

His smile faded. "I think not," he said.

"Why? What is it? Why won't you tell me why you're afraid to go back to New York? Was it a crime you committed? Tell me, darling Justin. Perhaps I can help you."

Justin was silent for a moment. He had not told her about Sylvaner and his past for fear that she might react badly to the fact that he was a wanted criminal. But now they had become so close, he saw no reason not to tell her everything. So he did. When he finished, there were tears in her big green eyes.

"My poor Justin," she said, taking him in her arms. "What a terrible injustice has been done to you! And this Sylvaner . . . he's a monster."

"My amah told me she once saw him stick pins in a cat."

"No! *Dio!*"

"And I heard that when he was a kid he used to love to catch pigeons in Washington Square and wring their necks."

"*Al nome d'Iddio!* But why does he hate you so?"

Justin sat up. "Because my father loved me, the bastard, more than he loved Sylvaner, the legitimate heir. As long as I can remember, Sylvaner has hated me. He tried to murder me, he tried to have me hanged . . . who knows what he might try next?"

"How you must hate him!"

Justin frowned. "Yes, I used to. I had fantasies of killing him, and I even came close to doing it in London. I could have killed him there in that old house, but I couldn't bring myself to do it. I mean, we share the same blood, and his wife is my aunt. Professor Seghizzi has been giving me various philosophers to read, and I'm beginning to see that hate and revenge are destructive forces, while love is a force that can build and heal."

"You are becoming wise. But could you ever love Sylvaner?"

He smiled. "No, I couldn't go that far. I'm no saint. But killing him would be as wrong as his killing me, and what would it accomplish?"

"A lot."

"But it would make me no better than he. He's ruined the good name of my father's company by trafficking in opium. Somehow I have to get Sylvaner out of the business and take it over myself—for the memory of my father, if nothing else." He sighed. "Of course, that's easy to say and hard to do. Especially for someone like me, who has nothing."

She put her hand on his arm. "Ah, but you have so much, my darling! You have courage and a good heart. You're young and strong: you'll prevail someday over this monster, Sylvaner. And last but hardly least," she said with a smile, "you have me."

He looked into her eyes. "Yes," he said, "I have you."

He took her in his arms and kissed her. She ran her fingers through his hair and purred, "Together, darling Justin, we will slay the dragon named Sylvaner."

26

"I'VE HAD AN IDEA!" FIAMMETTA exclaimed the next day at lunch as Justin came into the castle's dining room. He had just finished an hour and a half workout with Signor Russo, the gymnast, and another hour with his fencing master, Signor Tassini. That afternoon, he would spend three hours with Professor Seghizzi.

"What is it?" he asked, kissing her before sitting down opposite her at the round table at the end of the room. Outside, the sun glittered on a golden sea.

"I'm bored," she said, "and I want to do some shopping—and it's *not* because my dresses are too tight. I've actually lost some weight."

"Good." He didn't believe her.

A servant poured some Frascati from an etched crystal decanter.

"And you need a rest—I know, you don't want to leave the General, but he's going with us."

"To where?"

"Paris. And then to my château on the Loire. I've decided to give a ball and raise some money for Garibaldi. It will make the French Emperor furious, but he won't do anything because Giuseppe is so popular in France. The Church supports Napoleon III because he sent French troops into Rome to save the neck of the Pope, but to the people, darling Giuseppe is the hero. Ah, we'll have so much fun, *anima mia!*"

"But my studies—?"

She waved her hand in that dismissive gesture he had become so used to. Fiammetta had an imperious nature to begin with. Backed by her immense wealth, she dismissed problems with a wave of her hand, and magically they disappeared. Justin was learning a lesson in power.

"We'll bring Professor Seghizzi with us, and the others too. Cesare installed a small training room on the yacht, so you can continue with your fencing and gymnastics. You can work in the morning and we'll play in the afternoon. Paris! You'll love it as I do, my darling. Of course, they're tearing everything down, but there's still so much to see. And the food! Well, it's not as good as Italian cuisine, of course, but the French know how to cook."

"And your diet?"

She frowned. "Anyone who goes to France to diet is crazy. We'll leave on the yacht the day after tomorrow. This bouillabaisse is made with chicken instead of fish, infused with onions, garlic, tomatoes, fennel, and saffron. It's *divino.*"

"No."

She looked up from her stew. "Now what?"

"No, I'm not going to go. Listen, Fiammetta, it's one thing for us to be here, in the middle of nowhere. But if I go to Paris with you, everyone's going to laugh at us. . . ."

"Laugh? Why?"

"They'll say I'm your lover."

"Well? You are. What's so funny about that? I think it's wonderful!"

"Yes, so do I. But I'm a nobody. Everything I have—my clothes, my food, my tooth powder—you buy. You know what they're going to say about me—and you. So you go to Paris. I'll stay here and work."

She threw down her napkin. *"Cretino!"* she cried. "How can you be so stupid? What do I care what people say? I love you! That's the important thing! So what if they say you're younger than I? *Je m'en fiche!* I don't give a damn! Are we supposed to hide here the rest of our lives, as if we're criminals?"

"I *am* a criminal."

She stared at him. Then the anger faded from her face. "Of course, that's it. You're afraid of the police. I forgot. How stupid of me." She thought a moment. "Very well," she said, picking up her spoon again and dipping into the bouillabaisse, "we'll make a detour to Torino first."

"Why Turin?" he asked.

She smiled suggestively. "So I can see the King."

A week later, Justin, Fiammetta and her maid, and Garibaldi sat in a coach as it rumbled down the long drive of the *palazzina di caccia,* or hunting lodge, of Stupinigi a few miles outside Turin. The King of Piedmont, Victor Emmanuel II, had invited them to his hunting lodge for lunch. Fiammetta had spent a great deal of money shopping in Turin, and Louise, her French maid, had spent an hour that morning in their hotel doing Fiammetta's hair. The blond beauty looked radiant in a purple velvet dress with a sable-lined cape and tilted hat. Justin had asked her several times what she was up to, but she had remained unusually silent. The young American suspected that she was up to no good with the notoriously randy King, which irritated him. However, he knew by now that Fiammetta's code of morals was, to put the best light on it, adaptable. She did not play by the rules of the game that they at least paid lip service to in New York. She played by her own rules.

"Stupinigi is one of the most beautiful baroque palaces in Europe," she said as she pulled a gold mirror from her bag to inspect her reflection. "It was built in the last century and took years to finish. Napoleon used it as his hunting lodge several times, and his *puttana* of a sister, Pauline, lived in it for a while. But now it belongs to Victor Emmanuel's family again. How do I look, gentlemen?"

"Gorgeous," Garibaldi said. He was sitting opposite her next to the maid. Now he smiled. "Are you intending to seduce His Majesty?"

"That wouldn't be hard."

They all laughed except Justin, whose facial expression turned sour. "I don't think it's funny," he snapped.

Fiammetta put the mirror back in her purse, then leaned over to kiss his cheek. "Don't sulk, dear. This is strictly business and has nothing to do with love or romance. Do you like my perfume? It's called 'Passion,' which I think gets right to the point."

"I think it's too strong," Justin growled.

"Isn't he delicious?" She laughed. "He's jealous! I couldn't be more pleased. But wait till you see the King, darling. You won't be jealous anymore. He looks like a walrus."

"Then why would you flirt with him?"

"To get something I want, of course."

"But *what?*"

"You'll see. Now stop asking silly questions and look out the window. It's a sight worth seeing."

Justin did so, albeit grouchily. Not for the first time, he wondered about his dicey position vis-à-vis Fiammetta. Yes, he had gotten into this initially to help finance Garibaldi and to get an education, which he badly wanted. But his relationship with Fiammetta had rapidly blossomed into an *affaire de coeur,* and where did that leave him now? He certainly had no rights as a husband, and a good case could be made that he was just a gigolo, an idea that made him squirm. But if Fiammetta went to bed with the King, what could he do? It was maddening and he was jealous, but there was nothing he could do but accept it.

On the other hand, he had never met a king; and the sight certainly was worth seeing. The drive went through a formal French garden. Leaning out the window, he saw the palace of Stupinigi ahead of them, a handsome, vaguely classical building constructed in a V shape in front, with colonnaded outbuildings on either side. In the center of the building rose a big green dome surmounted by a statue of a stag. Beyond the palace stretched beautiful deer parks for as far as the eye could see on this beautiful early spring day.

The coach pulled into the hexagonal court of honor and grooms opened the doors. They climbed down to the gravel drive and entered the palace, which was guarded by soldiers in splendid uniforms. A chamberlain led them to the *salone centrale,* or the ballroom, which was the most spectacular room Justin had ever seen. It was a long oval that soared upward to the vast dome he had seen outside. Four enormous pillars rose to an elegant gallery supported by scrolled corbels and surmounted by statues of gods and goddesses. On the ceiling was painted a fresco of the goddess Diana leaving for the hunt. In the ripe baroque style, hardly a square inch was not ornamented with busts, sconces, pilasters, or elaborate gilt carvings.

Fiammetta and Garibaldi seemed completely at home in these sumptuous surroundings, for both of them had been there before. Now a footman hurried up and mumbled something to the chamberlain, who addressed Fiammetta in French, the language of the court. Fiammetta turned to Justin and said, "His Majesty had to cancel lunch, but he wants to see Giuseppe and me privately. Why don't you go back to the hotel? You can meet His Majesty tomorrow when he's rescheduled lunch. Take the carriage: His Majesty will loan us one of his."

Justin went back outside the palace and climbed in the coach, telling the driver to take him back into Turin. The coach rattled down the gravel drive as Justin sat alone inside, wondering what Fiammetta was up to with the King. He was burning with jealousy, a fact that surprised him. Had he fallen in love with Fiammetta without realizing it? He had been physically attracted to her from the very beginning, and their lovemaking had been spectacular for both. But beyond that, he had come to realize that Fiammetta, despite her imperiousness, was a good-hearted, generous woman who had nothing but the welfare of the human race in her mind. And she adored him with a passion that had kindled his own passion for her. Yes, he did love her. Again, as with Chang-mei, perhaps it was not the same love he felt for Samantha. But as time was the healer of all wounds, it was also the assassin of passion. Samantha was in his dreams; Fiammetta was in his arms. But what could his future possibly be with her? It was difficult for him to envision himself as her husband, which she probably wouldn't want anyway. And how long could he be her young lover without ridicule swamping them both?

These thoughts were in his head when the coach finally arrived at the hotel. Justin got out and started in the door, when a *ragazzo* ran up to him. "Signore," the boy said, tugging at his coat, "are you the American named Savage?"

Justin looked at the boy with surprise.

"Yes," he said.

"This is for you."

The ragged boy stuck an envelope in Justin's hand, then ran away down the street just as the hotel doorman started to chase him away. "I am sorry, Signore Savage," the doorman said, "but these boys . . ." He shrugged as if to say "they're hopeless."

"That's all right," Justin said, looking at the envelope. It was marked "Justin Savage." Tearing it open, he pulled out a piece of notepaper. On it was written:

Sir:

Enemies of Garibaldi are plotting to assassinate him and your friend, the Countess Mondragone. If you wish to learn more, come to No. 24 Via Vittorio Amadeo II. Time is of the essence. You must come alone.

A friend of liberty and Garibaldi

Justin's first thought was that it might be some sort of trap. But he quickly dismissed this as absurd: who in Turin, Italy, would be interested in him? He was a nobody, his only importance—if it could be so deemed—was his accessibility to Garibaldi, a man who was hated and reviled by some of the most important people in Europe, for Garibaldi had thousands of enemies. No, this was a legitimate warning; and he owed it to Fiammetta and Garibaldi to do everything he could to protect them.

"Where is Via Vittorio Amadeo Secondo?" he asked the doorman, who pointed down the street.

"It's the fifth street to the right," the man said.

Thanking him, Justin set off on foot down the cobblestone street that teemed with shoppers, businessmen, and strollers. Ten minutes later he turned into the Via Vittorio Amadeo II, which was a pleasant, tree-lined residential street lined with handsome town houses. Several blocks farther he came to Number 24, which was a stone house of no particular architectural distinction. Justin climbed the steps to the front door and rang the bell. While he waited, he looked up and down the street. A few carriages were passing by, servants were walking dogs, several ladies were walking down the opposite side of the street, chatting the latest gossip. Nothing seemed more normal or further removed from the setting of an assassination plot against Garibaldi.

"Yes?"

He turned back to see that the door had been opened by a pretty young girl in a pink dress. She had blond hair and was smiling at him. Justin thought she was perhaps ten years old. "Are you Signor Savage?" the girl said.

"That's right."

"Please come in."

The girl stepped back and Justin hurried inside a rather small entrance hall. The girl closed the door.

"Come this way," she said. "My father's expecting you."

She started down the hall. Justin followed her.

"Who's your father?" he asked.

"Professor Barberini."

"And what is your father a professor of?"

"He teaches political science at the university. Isn't it a pretty day? I think summer's coming early this year."

She had come to a door, which she now opened.

"Go in, please."

Justin went into a small library overlooking a rear garden. A man in a black frock coat was standing in front of one of the bookshelves. Now he turned to look at Justin. He had a full black beard that struck Justin, for some reason, as not looking quite real.

"Signor Savage?" the man said. "I am Professor Barberini. You are in grave danger."

"Me? The note said Garibaldi was . . ."

He was struck on the back of the head by something sharp and heavy. He fell to the floor as "Professor Barberini" took off his fake beard, revealing the scarred face of a young man. Two other men had come in the room behind Justin, one of them hitting him on the head with the butt of a pistol.

"Get him out back into the carriage," the fake professor said in a Neapolitan accent. "Then let's get out of here."

"Our young American friend seemed out of sorts," Garibaldi said three hours later as he and Fiammetta returned to Turin from the King's palace.

"Yes, he's moody, but he's had so much tragedy in his life. Besides, he'll cheer up when I tell him what I got out of the King."

Garibaldi shot her an amused look. "Aha. So that's what went on when His Majesty asked you into his *salottino.*"

"We had coffee."

Garibaldi snorted with laughter. "Fiammetta, *cara,* it's *me,* your old friend. But you were only in there a half hour!"

"His Majesty is very quick and to the point. Afterward, he was all business."

"You astound me. So, what did you get out of him?"

Her eyes lit up. "Oh, Giuseppe, it's going to work out splendidly! Did you know that Justin was a pirate in China?"

"A *pirate?* Are you serious?"

"Absolutely. He told me all about it. But because piracy is an international crime, he's wanted everywhere in the civilized world, poor man, so his hands are tied. You see, he has this monstrous half brother, Sylvaner Savage, who will do anything to kill him or get him hanged. So I got the King to agree that if I marry Justin, he will make him a citizen of the Kingdom of Piedmont, give him the title of Count of Mondragone, and make him a diplomat at the court. That way, he'll have diplomatic immunity anywhere he goes, and he'll be free! Isn't that wonderful?"

Garibaldi looked impressed. "Yes, it's clever. And the King agreed to this merely for a cup of coffee?"

She laughed. "You old goat, you know very well what the King wanted, and he got it. It was little enough price for Justin's freedom."

"But are you sure you want to *marry* him?" Garibaldi said. "I mean, he's so much younger. . . ."

"I won't hear a word said about my age!" she exclaimed angrily. Then she simmered down. "I know I'm older, but I love him so! I adore him! Every moment I'm not with him is agony to me. Ah, Giuseppe, this is the great romance I've dreamed of all my life. And I'll make our marriage work! Besides, I'm not *that* much older."

Garibaldi gave her a skeptical look. "He's nineteen now, and you're twenty-something. When he's twenty-something, you'll be thirty-something. When he's middle-aged . . ."

"Stop it!" she cried, her magnificent green eyes blazing. "It will work! I'll *make* it work! Don't say a word more."

He shrugged. "I'll shut up. But there's one little problem."

"What?"

"What if he doesn't want to marry you?"

She preened herself. "How could he say no? He's mad about me. His ardor never wanes. And now that he's been working out with the gymnast, his muscles are like steel and he has the strength of a bull. Ah, he adores me! Why shouldn't he?" She leaned back in her leather seat and smiled. "I'm adorable."

"The Americans have a saying: there's many a slip twixt the cup and the lip."

"Oh, shut up."

When they got to their hotel, Fiammetta went to the desk for her room key. "Is Signor Savage upstairs?" she asked the concierge.

"No, *Contessa*. He arrived at the hotel several hours ago, but never came inside. The doorman told me he was delivered a note."

"From whom?"

The concierge shrugged. "I have no idea. But he asked the doorman where the Via Vittorio Amadeo II was, then started walking toward it. He hasn't come back."

Fiammetta turned to Garibaldi.

"How very peculiar," she said. "Well, I suppose he'll be back soon."

She went upstairs to her suite.

But by eight o'clock, when there was still no sign of Justin, she began to panic.

"Something's happened to him," she said to Garibaldi as she paced around the drawing room of her second-floor suite. "I know it in my bones."

Garibaldi also looked concerned.

"I think we should notify the police," he said, going to the door.

"Yes, yes, the police. . . . *Al nome d'Iddio,* if he has been hurt . . ."

Garibaldi said nothing, leaving the room. He would notify the police, but he had little confidence in them. He was also going to contact some of his own intelligence sources, in whom he had more confidence.

Justin couldn't understand much of what his captors were saying because their Italian was so heavily accented. But he understood enough to realize that he was going to an unusually gruesome death, which was hardly calculated to raise his spirits. When he had regained consciousness, he found himself blindfolded and gagged, as well as bound at the ankles and wrists. He was in a coach that was traveling fast over a bumpy road. As his head throbbed with pain from the blow, he tried to reconstruct what had happened: the note delivered at the hotel, the pretty girl at the house on the Via Vittorio Amadeo II, the mysterious Professor Barberini . . . It had been a trap after all, an elaborate trap at that, but why? What was the point of it? What did they want out of him? Justin, the nobody?

Then one of his captors saw that he was awake. He poked him in the stomach and laughed. "Hey, the lover boy is awake!" he said in English that was so mangled by a Neapolitan accent that it was barely understandable. "Listen, lover boy," the man went on, digging his finger into Justin's chest. "We have a message from your half brother, Sylvaner: and the message is, you're gonna die."

Sylvaner! How in the world did Sylvaner . . . ? Then he began to understand. Sylvaner must have hired Italian criminals to do his dirty work for him, just as once he had hired Captain Whale and First Mate Horn. . . . Judging from the Neopolitan accents, these men were members of the dreaded Camorra, the Neapolitan version of the Sicilian Mafia. The Camorra would do anything, if paid enough.

With sinking heart, Justin wondered what new nightmare his half brother had concocted for him.

"He's been kidnapped by the Camorra," Garibaldi said as he came into Fiammetta's suite at four in the morning.

"The Camorra? Who told you, the police?" Fiammetta said, who had not yet undressed. She had been up all night worrying about Justin.

"The police are useless, although I notified them. If you want to find out what's going on in Italy, you have to go to paid informers, which I did. You owe me some money, by the way."

"I'll pay you back, you know that . . . But why the Camorra? What would they want with Justin?"

"It's his half brother . . . the man with the odd name?"

"Sylvaner?"

"That's it. He hired them to take Justin to the Castello Mondragone and torture him to death."

"The fiend!" Fiammetta cried. "Oh, my God . . . we must stop them. . . ."

"I have a carriage downstairs to take us to the sea. They have a big head start: we must hurry."

Justin had no idea where his captors were taking him, but at some point he had been carried out of the coach and put into a boat. Again, his Italian wasn't good enough to understand what they were saying, but it was obvious from their frequent laughter that they considered the expedition wonderful fun. And then he heard the words "Isola di Mondragone." At first he thought it was just a reference. But when he heard it several times again, he began to understand that they were taking him to the castle. But why? Obviously to kill him, but why there? Why not just shoot him in a wood, or dump him overboard?

And then he began to understand what a truly diabolical fate his half brother had devised for him: a sadistic death by torture. He told himself not to show his fear, but he was terrified.

Power! he thought, not for the first time. If only I had power! If I had a way to fight back, this wouldn't be happening to me. Am I a fool not to have learned by now that the world belongs to the ruthless? Sylvaner had pursued him halfway around the world yet again. Hatred surged in his veins. Ah Pin had been right: he should have killed him in London when he had the chance, but he had been too decent. They could put that on his tombstone:

JUSTIN SAVAGE. 1837–1857. HE WAS DECENT.

The boat ride took hours, perhaps a day, he had no idea. The passage was relatively smooth. His captors were eating and drinking, but they offered him nothing. He was ravenous.

Then they landed. He was grabbed by both arms and taken off the boat onto a dock. Someone cut the rope on his ankles and he was led up a series of stairs. Yes, it was the island of Mondragone. Sylvaner, that latter-day Sigismondo di Mondragone, had been inventive.

He heard them banging on the gates of the castle. He knew that when they left the castle, Fiammetta had given the servants a vacation and there was no one left but the aged caretaker, Tommasso. Now the gates were opened. Tommasso cried out. There was a shot. Tommasso grunted and fell to the floor. Justin was pushed into the entrance hall. His captors were babbling with excitement. They dragged him down a corridor. How did they know their way around the castle? Had one of the servants been bribed? Of course, there were a number of books about the infamous Castello Mondragone, one of the wonders of the world for three and a half centuries. . . .

They stopped. He heard the scrape of metal. The squeaking of ancient hinges. Then he was dragged forward onto the first of the two hundred stone steps leading down to the torture chamber of Sigismondo di Mondragone. Down, down, down. The damp chill of the crypt, the musty smell of slimy walls. He remembered Fiammetta's description of the "friendly" rats. Were they waiting for supper? "The Pit and the Pendulum." The Inquisition. If only he could see, if only he could speak . . .

They were at the bottom of the steps. He could hear the crackling of torches being lit. He was pushed across the room to the center. Much talk from his captors, talk mixed with laughter. He heard a fire being lighted, he smelled smoke. Then someone grabbed his wrists, which were behind him, and tied a thicker rope around them.

The strappado! As panic gripped him, he began kicking. He heard yells and curses. Two men grabbed his legs and his ankles were retied. Then he heard the creaking of a wheel.

The rope slowly started pulling his arms up behind his back. Then, just as his feet lifted off the stone floor, the wheel stopped. The pain was horrible.

Someone untied and removed his blindfold. He saw a fat, bearded man who had removed his mask. He was grinning.

"Hey, lover boy," he said in his mangled English. "Welcome to the funhouse. Your half brother, Sylvaner, he tell us to give you a good time, eh? You havin' fun, eh? Is that why you big blue eyes look so frighten? Hey, *la Contessa,* she love those eyes, I bet—*si?* Why you face all sweaty, huh? Hey, la Contessa, she buy her lover boy fine clothes! Looka this jacket! Real nice, custom-made

I bet. And this shirt! Pure silk, eh? Pretty nice job, bein' a lover boy, no?" He grabbed Justin's shirt, which Fiammetta had bought him in Turin, and tore it open. Then he spat out a stream of rapid-fire Italian. Justin saw that a fire had been lit in the circular stone pit. One of the men had been heating the branding iron.

Now he lifted it out of the fire. The **M** was smoking and red hot.

As Justin twitched with terror, the man slowly carried it toward him.

This is a dream, he thought. I had this dream before. It's just a bad dream, and I'll wake up soon. . . .

27   LIGHTNING FLASHED IN THE DARK sky, thunder rumbled, and the wind howled as the yacht *Aurora* made its way through a fierce storm toward the island of Mondragone. Fiammetta, who was standing on the bridge wearing a yellow rain slicker, yelled over the wind to her captain, Orlando Sfuggi, "Did you arm the crew? There may be trouble if they're still on the island."

"I did, Signora, but I'm telling you: I may not be able to dock in this storm!"

"*Sciocca,* you'll dock or you're fired!"

Captain Sfuggi, a big, burly man with a black beard, rolled his eyes and muttered to himself. The yacht, which had been built five years before in a Belfast shipyard, was, like Commodore Vanderbilt's steam yacht the *North Star,* state of the art and powered by steam that propelled two paddlewheels on each side. The ship also carried sail in case of engine breakdown, which was not unusual in these early days of steam. On this stormy afternoon, the engine was fortunately functioning well, but Captain Sfuggi knew that the ship maneuvered awkwardly in rough seas, and the thought of docking the hundred-foot vessel made him break into a sweat. But Fiammetta was hell-bent on reaching her island, and the Captain had had enough experience with his employer to know that one didn't cross her lightly.

Another jagged fork of lightning illuminated the great stone castle that was now less than a quarter mile away. It loomed dark and, as far as Sfuggi knew, empty except for the caretaker, for when Fiammetta wasn't in residence she sent the servants home. Fiammetta had told him the Camorra had taken her young American lover to the castle. Sfuggi thought she was mad, even though the presence of Garibaldi on the ship lent credence to her story. But mad or no, Fiammetta was the boss. One didn't argue with her: one obeyed. Also on the bridge were Garibaldi and Dr. Armando degli Angeli, whom Fiammetta had brought from Genoa in case Justin was still alive. The Doctor, who was a slight young man with a black beard, had brought medical supplies and blankets. Now, as he looked at the ugly stone castle on the island, he muttered to Garibaldi, "It's as frightening as I've read. Have you been in it?"

"Oh, yes, many times."

"And there really is a torture chamber?"

"Absolutely."

"Bizarre."

Fortunately, the dock was on the lee side of the island, where the seas were somewhat calmer. With much yelling and cursing at the crew, Captain Sfuggi managed to dock the ship with a minimum of damage. Fiammetta hurried from the bridge to go ashore, followed by Garibaldi, Dr. degli Angeli, and ten members of the crew, who were armed with .52-caliber Sharps repeating carbines. Both Fiammetta and Garibaldi carried .36 Old Model Navy pistols. Her heart pounding with fear, Fiammetta started up the steps to the castle as the rain poured relentlessly and lightning continued to skewer the sky.

Whatever doubts she might have had about the informer's story were dispelled when she reached the doors of the castle. The big doors were wide open, banging in the wind. She ran inside the dark entrance hall, telling one of the crew to light a bull's-eye lantern. When he obeyed, she saw the body of her aged caretaker on the stone floor, a bullet hole through his left temple.

"The murderers!" she said to Garibaldi and Dr. degli Angeli. "*Assassini!* God knows what they've done to my Justin. Follow me . . . ," she cried to the crew. She ran across the hall to the corridor that led to the kitchens. Halfway down, she stopped in front of a door made of solid iron and painted black. This door, three and a half centuries old, led down to the crypts and the torture chamber.

"Give me the lantern," she said to the crewman as another lifted the heavy iron crossbar from its flanges. He pulled the door open. It squeaked eerily on its ancient hinges. Below, there yawned a black hole.

Fiammetta, a believing Catholic, crossed herself and muttered a brief prayer. Then she took the lantern and started down the stone steps. Behind her came Garibaldi, Dr. degli Angeli carrying his black bag and a blanket, and the crewmen. The light from Fiammetta's lantern cast flickering shadows on the slimy stone walls as the eerie procession descended into the blackness.

Less than twenty years before, Garibaldi had been tortured in Uruguay by a military despot, and he had never forgotten the experience. To climb down these steep steps, as he had done weeks before with Fiammetta and Justin, to view the crypt as some sort of museum of torture was one thing. But to climb down these steps with the possibility that torture had been committed on Justin was something else entirely, and his skin felt clammy. He dreaded what he was about to see, as fond of Justin as he had become. It was a scene from Dante.

Halfway down the long stairs Fiammetta called, "Justin! We're coming, my darling!"

Silence.

"*Dio,* he's dead," she muttered, continuing down the steps. When she finally reached the bottom, she ordered the crewmen to light the flambeaux on the walls.

And then, as the light filled the stone chamber, she saw him and screamed.

He was hanging by his arms from the strappado, his arms raised behind him almost to the level of his neck and tied to the rope at the wrists, his feet dangling a few feet above the floor. He had been raised to the ceiling, then dropped and jerked to a halt. Most of his clothes had been torn off him, and on his left buttock was branded the **M** of the Mondragones.

Fiammetta, Garibaldi, and Dr. degli Angeli hurried to the center of the chamber.

"Is he dead?" she asked, tears in her eyes.

The Doctor, who looked horrified, reached up and felt his chest.

"By some miracle, he's still alive," he said. "You!" he yelled at one of the crew, pointing at the steel winch that operated the infernal machine. "Get him down, but slowly. Please help me, Signor Garibaldi."

As Fiammetta watched, tears in her eyes, the two men held the blanket into which Justin was slowly lowered. Then, gently, they untied his wrists and laid him on the blanket on the floor. Justin's face was filthy and had several days' growth of beard on it. The doctor knelt beside him and raised one of his eyelids.

"He's in a coma," he said. "From the shock and the pain." Then he felt his shoulders, which were swollen and purplish. "I fear his arms have been pulled from their sockets," he said to Fiammetta. "His back may also have been broken, and God knows how many torn ligaments and muscles there are. Do you have any idea how long he's been hanging here?"

"Perhaps two days," Fiammetta said, her face pale. "They must have left him to starve to death, the *cacastecchi!*"

The young Doctor looked rather startled to hear such vulgarity coming out of the mouth of the beautiful Countess.

"Perhaps you could go upstairs and make some broth while I examine him. I don't want to move him until I know what's broken, but when they dropped him from the ceiling and then stopped him"—he shook his head—"it was devastating to his upper body. While he's still in a coma, I'll try and put his arms back in their sockets. If anything saved him, it's that his shoulder muscles are extremely well developed."

"He's been training as a gymnast. . . . I'll go up to the kitchen . . . these monsters! But at least he's alive, thank God."

She hurried past the crewmen and started up the stairs. A half hour later, when she returned with a bowl of soup, she found they had wrapped Justin in the blanket. He was still unconscious. The doctor was standing beside him.

"He's a very lucky young man," he said. "His spine seems to have survived the fall. However, both his arms are broken and there are several cracked ribs. I managed to get his shoulders back in their sockets. Fortunately, gangrene has not set in, but there will be terrible swelling—it's already starting—and he's going to be in excruciating pain for weeks."

"Should I try to get some soup down him?"

"No, he's still unconscious. He might choke on it. Do you have some place we can take him?"

"Yes, upstairs. Is he going to recover?"

"Yes, eventually. But he's going to go through hell first. I'll have to tie him to boards so that he remains completely immobile."

"He'll never recover mentally," Garibaldi said. "I was tortured in Uruguay by a sadistic general when I was a young man, and I've never forgotten it. Sometimes I still wake up in the middle of the night screaming."

"Sylvaner Savage," Fiammetta said, "will have much to answer for when he meets God."

"This bottle contains laudanum," Dr. degli Angeli told Fiammetta a few hours later as they stood beside the bed in Cesare's room on the second floor of the castle. The sun was trying to pierce the remaining clouds of the dying storm. "It's tincture of opium and a very strong painkiller. But it's dangerous because it's addictive, like opium. You mustn't give him more than four doses every twenty-four hours, one tablespoon every six hours. No matter how great the pain he has, no more than that. Do you understand, Contessa?"

"Yes, Doctor," Fiammetta said, taking the brown glass bottle. "I sent my yacht to the mainland to buy supplies and get my servants. Could you find me some nurses? There's a convent . . ."

She was interrupted by a moan from the bed. They turned to look at Justin. The Doctor had strapped his upper body to wooden planks so that he could not move, and his chest had been tightly bandaged. Now his eyes opened and his moans escalated into a howl of pain. The Doctor took the bottle back and hurried to the bed, picking up a spoon from the bed table.

"Justin," he said, "take some of this. It will help the pain. . . ."

"My arms . . ." He started struggling against the ropes.

"You mustn't move! I've tied you to these planks to keep you immobile. Both your shoulders were dislocated and your arms broken. Take this."

He filled the spoon and put it in Justin's mouth. Justin swallowed the liquid, then looked at Fiammetta.

"How did you . . ." he began, then winced. "Jesus . . . how did you know where I was?"

"An informer," Fiammetta said, coming to him and leaning over to kiss his forehead. "But you're safe now, my darling. Thank God you're safe."

"I had a vision," Justin said three days later. He was in his bed, still strapped to the planks, but he had been washed and shaved and was beginning to look stronger, although he was still in great pain. Fiammetta was sitting in a chair beside the bed. One of the nuns Dr. degli Angeli had hired on the mainland was sitting in the corner.

"Tell me your vision," Fiammetta said.

"It was after they had left me alone, in the dark. I knew I was going to die, that Sylvaner had sent them to kill me."

"You said there were six of them, and they were from Naples?"

"That's what I assumed from listening to them. I couldn't understand much of what they said, and I was blindfolded the whole time. Anyway, when I heard them slam the iron door at the top of the stairs, I knew that was the last link I would have with the living. It was terrifying. And the pain was so horrible. . . ." He closed his eyes a moment. "Like now," he whispered. "Oh, God . . . could I have more of the medicine?"

"No, darling. Your next dose isn't for two more hours."

Justin sighed. "I'm now beginning to see why opium is so popular. Anyway, I don't know how long I was down there in that damned place. . . . I lost all track of time. I heard the rats. . . ."

"Nostro signore!"

"Scurrying around waiting for me to die. I remembered what you had said, that they were friendly until you died. . . ."

"Poor darling."

"And I saw a light, a bright light . . . it filled the room and was very beautiful, and I thought, I'm dead. This is what death is, and it's really not so bad at all, it's even sort of beautiful. . . ."

"Straordinario!"

"And then I heard a voice saying, 'Justin.' It was the voice of my father, and

I was so happy. I think I said something like, 'Father, is it you?' And he answered, 'Yes, my dear son. It is I and I am reunited with your sweet angel of a mother and we are very happy in Heaven.' "

There were tears in Fiammetta's eyes. *"Bello,"* she whispered. *"Bellissimo."*

"And then my father said, 'Justin, my son, you must not kill Sylvaner, for you will never come to Heaven if you do that. You must *ruin* him.' And that's all I remember until I woke up in this bed."

"A message from beyond the grave," Fiammetta said in awed tones. She crossed herself. "It's another miracle. The first miracle is that you are alive, and now *this*. . . . Oh, my darling, it means God is on our side! That all of your trials and troubles are God's way of making you stronger and better. And He will help us ruin that monster, Sylvaner. Yes, that's much better than killing him: we'll *ruin* him!" She stood up, her eyes filled with excitement. "There is nothing that makes an Italian feel better than revenge!" she exclaimed. She leaned over and kissed Justin. "And now, my sweet love, I must go downstairs and talk to Cook about dinner. Is there anything you'd especially like?"

"Yes: a slug of the laudanum."

"You'll just have to wait."

"But my shoulders are killing me. . . ."

"No. I love you too much to allow you to become an addict."

"I think you're being *slightly* overcareful. . . ."

"Dr. degli Angeli said one tablespoon every six hours: period. He was very particular about that, and we won't say anything more on the subject. I know: we'll have osso buco tonight. And with it, a nice Villa Antinori Chianti Classico Riserva. That will help your pain."

"What a wonderful choice," Justin said sourly. "I'll either be an addict or a drunk."

"You'll be neither, and you're getting better every day. I can see it in your sweet face." She started toward the door, saying to the aged nun, "Sister Maria Felice, you might open one of the windows. It's a little stuffy in here."

"Sì, Contessa."

As Fiammetta left the room, the Dominican went to one of the windows overlooking the sea and opened it. It was a bright, beautiful morning. The nun returned to her seat, smiling at Justin, for whom she had taken a liking. "It's a beautiful day, signore," she said, sitting down again. "And *la Contessa* is right: you're looking much better."

"But I'm not feeling better. My shoulders really ache something terrible. . . ."
He lowered his voice. "Sister, *la Contessa* won't mind if you give me just a little sip now."

"Oh, no, signore. She was very specific about your doses. You heard her."

"But she'll never know. Please: I'm in such pain. . . ."

Sister Maria Felice hesitated.

"Please: just a sip. It makes me feel so much better. It lets me sort of float out of my body. Please."

Sister Maria Felice stood up and sighed. "Very well, but just this once. We're not going to make a habit of this."

She brought the brown glass bottle and the spoon to his bed. Justin's eyes riveted on the bottle.

"Sister," he said, "you're a kind and wonderful person."

"Sister Maria Felice," Justin said a week later, "you know that I'm in absolute torture, and my shoulders and back ache all the time. . . ."

"I know," the aged nun interrupted from her chair in the corner of the room. "You want me to give you more of the laudanum. You're a naughty boy. You work on my sympathies because you know I'm fond of you and hate to see you in pain."

"Please, Sister."

"You know that the bottle's almost empty because I've been giving you the extra doses. There's going to be all sorts of trouble. . . ."

"I don't care. Give me the stuff. I have to have it."

Sister Maria Felice sighed, stood up, and brought the brown glass bottle to his bed. She filled the tablespoon with the liquid and held it to his mouth. He hungrily sucked the spoon's contents.

After a few moments, the laudanum began to take its effect. The pain in his upper torso, especially in his shoulders where the drop of the strappado had taken its most devastating toll, eased.

"You know how to wheedle me," the nun was saying, "but it is *I* who will pay. When *la Contessa* finds out"—she shook her head—"she loves you too much to yell at you, but she'll surely yell at me. *Dio,* what a vale of tears this life is!"

But Justin wasn't listening to her. He knew he was becoming addicted, but he didn't care. The constant pain in his shoulders and back was like rats chewing at him night and day, and the only escape was through the drug. He had maneuvered Sister Maria Felice into giving him more and more of the laudanum. Now the bottle was empty, but he could get more, and he could deal with the addiction later. The thing now was to avoid the pain while his body slowly healed.

His brain felt slightly giddy, and then he was out of his body. It was odd, because he was aware of where he was—lying in his bed in the room over-looking the sea—but at the same time, he was somewhere else, floating near the ceiling of the room. The horrible pain drifted away and he was filled with sweetness instead as the room seemed to shift slowly, taking on wondrous new dimensions and shapes and a kaleidoscope of marvelous colors: blues, pinks, heliotropes, oranges, reds, indigos, violets: his mind became a rainbow. In his ears strange harmonies sang.

Then he drifted out of the castle, up into the air until he was moving through a cloud. In the distance he saw a woman coming toward him, seeming to float. She was wearing a white gown of some filmy substance, which swirled about her like an aureole. When she was close enough, he realized it was Fiammetta. A feeling of joy surged through him, and he opened his arms to embrace her.

But when she was almost in his arms, Fiammetta turned into Samantha.

"Samantha!" he cried. "I love you! God, I love you so. . . ."

But just as he was about to touch her, she vanished.

28

"YOU FOOLISH OLD WOMAN!" FIAMMETTA cried that afternoon as Sister Maria Felice trembled. "You've addicted him!"

She had discovered the empty bottle of laudanum.

"*Contessa,* he begged me," the old nun said. "I didn't have the heart to say no. . . ."

"It's poison!" Fiammetta screamed. "Get out! If you weren't a nun, I'd . . ."

"Fiammetta," Justin said from his bed, "it's my fault. Don't blame her. I wanted relief from the pain."

Fiammetta came to the bed, her eyes flashing green fire. "Yes, I blame you too," she said. "How Sylvaner would be laughing if he knew you'd become an opium addict! Oh, it's a lovely irony, a wonderful joke! The Savage Shipping Line makes a fortune out of opium, and Justin Savage becomes one of its best customers."

Justin winced, this time not from pain.

"I'll admit I was wrong, but if you knew the pain . . ."

"Justin, in the past I joked about hurting you. I even joked about branding you. Well, the horrible joke is that it's been done to you by your half brother. If I had a wish, it would be that this terrible experience you've gone through would not have happened. But that can't be. So now I *am* going to inflict pain on you, and it's because I love you as no woman has ever loved a man. I'm not going to let you have any more laudanum."

His face showed panic. "You can't. . . ."

"Oh, but I can. From now on, your only nurse is going to be me. The door to my room will always be open. I'll do everything for you the nurses have done. I'll feed you, I'll wash you, I'll clean your bedpan. But there will be *no more opium.*"

He was sweating with fear. "I'll go crazy!" he said. "I can't take the pain! Please don't do this to me!"

"I'm doing it because I love you. You!" She turned to the nun. "I told you to go! I'll have my yacht take you and the other one back to the mainland."

Sister Maria Felice hurried out of the room. Fiammetta slammed the door after her, then went to the door to her room and opened it. She turned to look at Justin, who was trembling.

"The nuns tell me you cry out for Samantha in your sleep," she said. "Maybe I'm a fool to love you as I do. Maybe I'm obsessed by you, I don't know. Maybe you'll never love me the way you love Samantha. But I'm not going to let you destroy yourself with opium."

She left the room, leaving him alone with the pain that was beginning to gnaw at him as the last of the laudanum passed out of his system.

"Fiammetta!" he cried that night. "I can't take it! Please, in the name of God, give me something. Please!"

He saw the light in her room turn on. She appeared in the doorway holding a lamp. She looked beautiful in a nightgown of pale gauze.

"There's no laudanum left," she said, "and even if there were, I wouldn't give it to you."

His face was covered with sweat. "Then let me get drunk!" he cried. "I can't sleep, these damned bandages make my skin itch . . . give me something, some wine. . . ."

"You may have wine."

She set the lamp on a table and went back into her room. A few minutes later she returned with a bottle of Chianti and a glass. She poured some wine, then held the glass to his lips. He swallowed the rich red wine, then leaned his head back on his pillow. She wiped the sweat from his face with a cloth.

"My poor darling," she said softly. "I know you suffer, and it breaks my heart to have to deny you relief. But I know I'm doing the right thing. Someday you'll thank me."

He looked at her a moment. Then he said, "I don't have to wait for some-day. I'll thank you now. This is hell, but I'll live through it. And in my heart, I know you're right about the opium. One day, when I'm well, I'll take you in my arms again and there won't be any pain. I love you, Fiammetta. I may dream about Samantha, but it's only because my mind is confused. God knows, after what I've been through it's a wonder it's not more confused—or even crazy. But it's you I love. If I had the nerve, I'd ask you to be my wife."

"The nerve? What do you mean?"

"You couldn't possibly want me for a husband. I'm a nobody. A woman like you, who has everything . . . you could marry a great nobleman, a prince or something. . . ."

She was smiling. "I'd settle for the Count of Mondragone."

"What do you mean?"

She sat on the edge of the bed and took his hands in hers.

"I didn't have a chance to tell you, because the day I met with the King was the day you were kidnapped. But I told His Majesty about you, how your half brother had tried to murder you, and he agreed that if we were married, he'd make you a citizen of Piedmont, give you the title of Count of Mondragone, and make you a diplomat, which would give you diplomatic immunity. We could go anywhere in the world and no one could try you for piracy. You'd be free, Justin. Sylvaner could never hurt you again. And we could begin to plot his ruin."

He looked amazed. "The Count of Mondragone?" he said slowly. "Me? Justin, the bastard son?"

She smiled. "You've already got the brand on a very important part of your anatomy."

For the first time in days, he laughed. "My God, to hell with the pain!" he exclaimed. "Hey, my beautiful bride: let's start planning our wedding!"

She leaned forward and kissed his lips, and now they were both laughing and crying.

Through the castle windows, the first light of dawn appeared over the shimmering sea.

Six weeks later Dr. degli Angeli untied him from the wooden planks and for the first time Justin was able to move his arms and get out of bed. By now, the torn ligaments and muscles had begun to heal, and the pain had considerably subsided. Fiammetta hired a masseur to give him daily massages; and such was the resiliency of his young body that within another month he was feeling almost as good as new.

Physically. Mentally, though, Garibaldi had been right: he would never forget the torture, and his determination to square accounts with Sylvaner was now an obsession. But now he was no longer powerless. Now he would be the Count of Mondragone.

He told Fiammetta he had to get away from the castle. The place had such horrible memories for him that he wasn't sure he could ever come back to it. Fiammetta agreed, and she made plans to leave as soon as possible for Nice, thence to her small château on the Loire where now she could put into operation her original plan of raising money for Garibaldi by giving a ball. "I've been thinking about it," she said to Justin. "I'm going to call it the 'Ball of the Enchanted Rose.' "

"Mmm, I like that. It's very beautiful. What does it mean?"

"Many years ago, a beautiful girl lived in the château. And she fell in love with a handsome young prince. Unfortunately, the prince was in love with someone else, which drove the poor girl to distraction. And every night, she prayed to the angels for the love of the prince. Well, one night a good fairy came to her and told her that there was a rosebush in the garden of the château that she was going to enchant. And if the girl could get the prince to smell one of its roses, he would forget the other woman he loved and love only the girl.

"Well, you can imagine how pleased the girl was about that. So she sent a message to the prince, begging him to come to the Château de la Rose—that's the name of my château—and she would give him the most beautiful flower in the world. So the prince arrived on his horse the next day, and the girl led him into her garden and picked one of the roses from the enchanted bush. She gave it to the prince, who thanked her very politely. And the girl said, my lord, you must smell the rose, because its fragrance is so lovely. The prince put the rose up to his nose, took a sniff of the perfume, forgot immediately all about the other woman in his life, and proposed to the girl. And they lived happily ever after." She smiled at Justin. "Isn't that a lovely story?"

"I'm not so sure the other woman thought it was so lovely."

Fiammetta laughed as she ran her hands through his hair. "The other woman married a cranky businessman and gave him seven children, all of whom were brats. Now, my darling groom-to-be: we'll leave tomorrow for Nice and go by coach to Paris, where I'm going to buy the most beautiful wedding dress in the world. Then we'll get married in Paris and go to the Château de la Rose for our honeymoon. I may even get you to smell one of those enchanted roses."

Justin smiled and put his arm around her waist. They had been walking on the battlements of the castle. "Just to make sure about Samantha?" he said.

"Just to make sure."

Paris was in the process of being transformed into the beautiful city we know today by the combined efforts of the Emperor, Napoleon III, and his prefect of the Seine, Baron Georges Haussmann. Over the howls and protests of many

Parisians, the old medieval quarters of the city were being torn down with their pestilential sanitary conditions, and great new boulevards, beautiful bridges, and fine parks were being constructed in their stead, with a wonderful new sewer system that was the marvel of the age. Cynics said the wide boulevards were planned to give the police and the army a straight line of fire against revolutionaries; but whether that was true or not, Justin, as he and Fiammetta drove around the city in an open carriage, thought Paris, even in its state of ongoing construction, was about as beautiful a city as there could be.

They were married in a small church and then repaired for their wedding night to the Grand Hôtel du Louvre, the city's biggest and most spectacular hotel, where they had rented the bridal suite.

"Any regrets?" Fiammetta asked, taking off her white lace bridal veil and tossing it on a gilt sofa as Justin locked the double doors and took her in his arms.

"Only that I hadn't met you years before," he said, kissing her passionately.

"Ah yes, before you knew Samantha. I regret that too."

"I'm going to make you forget Samantha," he said, picking her up in his arms and carrying her across the overly ornate living room of the suite to the bedroom.

She put her arms around his neck and kissed him.

"Oh, no," she purred. "I'm going to make *you* forget her."

He pushed open the double doors with one of his feet and carried her over to the huge bed with its vulgar headboard of swirling gilt cupids and entwined hearts. Fiammetta giggled. "It's all rather horrid, like a fancy bordello, isn't it?"

"Yes, but I like it."

"Oh, dear, is it going to turn out you have terrible taste?" She nibbled his ear. "But you don't taste terrible, that I can *certainly* vouch for. Wasn't it a lovely ceremony? So simple."

"Only fifty of your closest friends."

"I want to save the *grand spectacle* for the ball. Then you can meet *all* my friends who are all so interesting and liberal. I thought it was sweet of the King to send his ambassador to Paris. And now you have the scroll officially making you the Count of Mondragone. Isn't it exciting?"

"Yes, it is. But not as exciting as you."

He placed her gently on the bed.

"Oh, Justin," she sighed, "we're going to have such a wonderful marriage— I feel it in my heart and soul! Together, we will know nothing but rapture. . . ."

He leaned down to kiss her. "Save it," he whispered, "for your novel."

"I gave up my novel. Since I met you, I've been *living* it."

A week later as they were sipping their café au lait on a balcony overlooking the rooftops of the city, there was a knock on the door.

"I'll get it," Justin said, wiping his mouth and getting up to go inside. It was a lovely, warm spring morning. He was wearing a silk bathrobe. He went to open the door. Outside was a bellboy with a large envelope on a silk tray.

"This was just sent over from the British Embassy, milord." All Englishmen—and the boy assumed Justin was English—were called by the French "milord" for the purpose of getting tips. Justin tipped him, then took the letter out to the terrace. The envelope was addressed in English, but Justin recognized the red wax seal.

"It's from Prince I," he said, sitting down again.

"The Viceroy of Canton?"

"Yes." He opened the envelope and looked at the date inside.

"But how in the world would he know you're in Paris?"

"He doesn't. This was written five months ago and sent to the Foreign Office in London to be forwarded to me. The Chinese have no embassies in Europe—that's part of the problem the Emperor has with the French and English, who want embassies in Peking. But it's the old thing, the Emperor regards us all as barbarians beneath his dignity, and he refuses to open up China to us, or have any official dealings with western governments. It's all a matter of 'face.' If any Chinese wants to contact foreigners, he's forced to do it through English merchants or English representatives protecting English interests in China. The Foreign Office in London read about our getting married and forwarded this here to me."

"Can you read Chinese? All those strange wiggly things?"

"No. That takes years. The Prince hires a translator to do his letters in English." He paused, frowning as he read. "Oh, my God . . ." he muttered.

Fiammetta looked alarmed at his tone. "What's wrong?"

"My daughter, Julie . . . she's alive!"

Fiammetta looked amazed. "How could that be?"

"Her amah escaped from Nanking and went back to our old house on Pink Jade Road. When she went to the Viceroy to find out what had happened to me, she told him Julie is being raised by the son of one of the Taiping generals, a warrior named Li-shan. Prince I wants me to come back to China, help him train his troops so we can capture Nanking, and I can get back Julie. My God, this changes everything . . . !"

Fiammetta looked alarmed. "But surely you wouldn't consider doing it . . . ?"

"I have no choice! I want my daughter back. She's in danger in Nanking, but the whole countryside is boiling with rebellion! Besides, I don't know anything about this Li-shan, and he sure as hell is not going to keep my daughter!"

"But aside from everything else, what about our plans with Sylvaner? And your commitments to Garibaldi?"

"Garibaldi doesn't need me as much as I need Julie. Oh, Fiammetta, you're going to love her! She was the cutest little baby, and now she'll be over two. . . ."

Fiammetta stood up, threw her napkin down on the table, and stormed into the hotel. Justin looked confused. He got up and ran inside the living room.

"What's wrong?" he exclaimed.

She turned on him. "Everything!" she shouted. "Are you going to run off and leave me a week after we're married?"

"Of course not, you'll come with me! We'll go together! You'll love China—it's a fantastic part of the world." She simmered down. He came to her and took her in his arms to kiss her. "Believe me, darling, it will be a great experience."

"But how in the world are you going to get into Nanking to get Julie out?"

"I'll figure that out when we get there. But, darling, this is the most wonderful thing—my daughter is alive!" He picked her up around the waist and twirled her around the room. "I have the most beautiful wife in the world, and now I'm going to get back my darling daughter! You know, I really am a lucky man after all!" Sharp pains bit his shoulders. He winced and set her down.

"Are you all right?" she asked.

"Just Sylvaner's calling cards," he said. "I suppose I'll have those the rest of my life."

"Should we invite Sylvaner to our ball? We could poison his punch."

"No, it's too easy. Sylvaner has earned a most glorious ruination. I don't know what it will be yet, but when it happens, it's going to retire the cup for vengeance."

29

"I'M SURE YOU AND SYLVANER must be thrilled about the news of the wedding?" said Florence Rhinelander. The "Cash Flo" twins were having tea with Sylvaner and Adelaide in the drawing room of the latters' Washington Square mansion.

"What wedding?" Adelaide asked as one of her footmen passed the cucumber sandwiches. Adelaide had just finished redecorating the double drawing rooms for the second time in as many years, and she was especially proud of the pair of new crystal chandeliers that hung, one to a parlor, their double tiers of gaslights protected by smoked glass bowls with glittering crystal pendants hanging in profusion. The walls had been painted a pale "Chinese" yellow that was all the rage, and vermillion pseudo-Gothic arches and trefoils had been stenciled below the heavily carved wooden coving as well as above the wooden dado. Over the tall windows fronting on Washington Square, great galleons of sea-green watered silk curtains swirled and swagged, while beneath them pale ivory silk "underdrapes" filtered the spring sunshine.

"What wedding?" Florence asked, giving her sister a very smug look of gossipy satisfaction. Both the Cash Flos knew that Sylvaner and Adelaide had not yet heard the news, since it was hot off the London mail that morning. "Well, my dear, it was *the* wedding of the year. Naturally, we assumed you knew since the groom is your dear half brother, Justin, who for so many years we feared had been lost at sea. Justin married the Countess di Mondragone last month in Paris. You mean, you weren't invited?"

Sylvaner, who was standing by the fireplace, teacup and saucer in hand, now gagged on his tea.

"Justin?" he sputtered. "You mean, he's not dead?"

"Oh, no, dear Sylvaner," Florence cooed. "He's very much alive. But it's a most sensational story, which we assumed you knew."

"He was kidnapped by hooligans," said Floribel.

"Not hooligans," snapped her sister. "You never get it right, Floribel. He was kidnapped by the Camorra, the Mafia of Naples, and taken to Mondragone Castle. . . ."

"Where he was *tortured!*" Floribel chirped merrily. "Can you imagine?"

"But didn't they kill him?" Sylvaner exploded. "I mean," he added, remembering he wasn't supposed to know, "how did he get out?"

"He was saved by Garibaldi and the Countess of Mondragone, who is *madly* in love with him!" Florence said, clasping her hands, a rhapsodic look on her beak-nosed face. "I mean, my dear, it is one of the *great* love stories of our time! But I still can't believe Justin wouldn't have invited you to his wedding? You, his dear half brother?"

Adelaide was as rocked by the news as her husband, but she managed to keep her control. "Florence, you of all people know it is no secret that Sylvaner and Justin were never close in their affections."

"Of course I had heard that, dear Adelaide, but one discounts so much that one hears as the invention of idle tongues and vicious minds. However, it is a pity you weren't invited, since people were fighting to get invitations. Only the very crème de la crème of European society were the lucky few. It is said the Empress Eugénie is furious because she wasn't invited."

Adelaide, who was a world-class snob and title-worshiper, dug her nails into her palms to prevent herself from screaming with envy. "I'm sure it was all very elegant," she said sweetly, "although the match could hardly be considered *comme il faut*. From what I've read of the Countess, she must be much older than Justin, who only just turned twenty. One could hardly call it a proper match."

"Oh, but, my dear, they don't care in Europe," Florence said. "And the Countess is only in her twenties."

"I fear we Americans are somewhat provincial in that regard," Floribel said.

"And she's so rich!" Florence went on. "The richest woman in Europe, they say. Castles, palazzi, a yacht, a gorgeous château on the Loire . . ."

"Where she's giving a ball for Garibaldi that *everyone*'s coming to, dukes and duchesses—"

She was interrupted by the sound of crashing china. Sylvaner had crushed his teacup with his fist, then dropped it on the floor.

"Dear Sylvaner, you're bleeding!" exclaimed Florence.

"It's nothing . . . excuse me. . . . Clean up the mess!" he roared at the footman as he rushed out of the room, sucking the blood from the cut on his hand. The footman hurried out to get a dust broom.

"Sylvaner seems overwrought," Florence said with a smirk. "The news of his half brother's great triumph has obviously overwhelmed him."

"It's hardly a 'great triumph' for a good-looking young man to marry a rich widow!" Adelaide snapped, her blood seething. "Whose morals," she added, "must be nonexistent!"

"As to her morals, well . . ." She looked at Adelaide and smiled slightly. "How is Tony Bruce these days, my dear?" Adelaide went white. "I hear his investment pool is doing quite nicely, which is pleasant news. Poor Tony had such bad luck in the past until you and Sylvaner decided to back him. How pleased you must be. Come, Floribel: we must be on our way. Mrs. Astor's thé dansant must have begun by now."

The two sisters stood up. Adelaide, rocked by the mention of Tony Bruce, saw them out, then hurried back to Sylvaner's study where her husband, a handkerchief tied around his cut hand, was seated at his desk, sobbing, pounding his other fist over and over again on the desktop. Adelaide closed the door.

"Did you do this?" she asked. "Did you hire the Camorra to kidnap him?"

"Yes," Sylvaner sobbed. "And they cheated me, the incompetent bastards! He's alive and rich. . . ."

"And social!" agonized Adelaide.

"I can't stand it!" Sylvaner gagged, banging the desk. "I can't! The little worm, the toad, the . . . the SHIT!"

"Sylvaner!" gasped his wife, placing her hand on her breast.

"I don't care!" he screamed. "He can't do this to me! He keeps escaping me, the little bastard. . . ."

"Keep your voice down! The servants! And your language—for shame! It's indecent! Shocking!"

Her husband slowly rose to his feet, tears running out of his bloodshot eyes, coursing down his reddened cheeks to dribble into his white beard. He wiped his runny nose with the back of his bandaged hand.

"As God is my witness," he said in a hoarse voice, "I will someday destroy the little bastard! I'll DESTROY him!"

"Sylvaner," Adelaide said nervously, "he may destroy *us.*"

They exchanged looks, fear in their eyes.

The Château de la Rose, which many people called one of the most beautiful small châteaux in France, was a fairy tale in stone. Built in the fifteenth century on a hill overlooking the Loire River, it was dominated by one round tower three stories high with a witch's-hat slate roof rising to a point. The building was an L with the tower as fulcrum. From it, a short kitchen wing jutted south, while the main part of the building, a long two-story wing with eight sets of shuttered French doors, stretched west. The entire building was surrounded by a small moat. There was an apple orchard, a walled kitchen garden, and a small but exquisite formal garden, in the center of which was the fabled rosebush where legend had it that the girl had won the heart of the prince by giving him the enchanted rose to smell.

On a warm June evening, elegant carriages began pulling up to this quintessentially romantic château, which was illuminated by dozens of Bengal lights strung from the branches of trees. It was the night of the Ball of the Enchanted Rose, and the Cash Flo twins had not been entirely correct in saying that all of European society was gathering. The more reactionary of Fiammetta's titled friends were rabid Garibaldi-haters and would have much preferred to hang him rather than honor him at a ball. But still, almost a hundred guests had accepted invitations, and many of them represented the progressive elements of English, French, and Italian society. A small platoon of grooms opened the doors of the carriages, and the beautifully dressed guests stepped out to cross the short bridge over the moat and enter the château, where they were greeted by Fiammetta and Justin, the latter looking dashing in his tailcoat and white cravat, the former breathtaking in a low-cut evening gown of pale lemon *peau de soie* swathed in festoons of organdy. She was wearing her famous suite of rubies and diamonds, and she glittered in the candlelight like a

Christmas tree. Most of the guests had indulged in orgies of gossip and speculation about the young American Fiammetta had lost her heart to and married, but even the most cynical had to admit they made a remarkably handsome couple and both looked radiantly happy—which was what life was supposed to be all about.

Precisely at eight-thirty, a gong was struck and the guests moved into the dining hall of the château where they seated themselves at ten round tables of ten each and were served by liveried footmen an eight-course banquet featuring belon oysters from Brittany, *quenelles de brochet, poulets de Bresse,* a magnificent *gigot d'agneau,* and, in honor of Garibaldi and Italy, a huge *torta rustica* was rolled in on a table, a six-foot-high cake stuffed with Parma ham, *funghi porcini,* truffles, and cheese. With this flowed a river of wine: Corton-Charlemagne with the fish, pouilly fumé with the chicken, a stunning Romanée-Conti with the lamb, and a suave Barolo with the *torta rustica.* A dozen footmen lighted sparklers to announce the arrival of the ten Grand Marnier soufflés that were washed down by Dom Perignon.

Then Fiammetta rose to propose a toast to the guest of honor.

"Dear friends," she said, "there is a spirit haunting Europe today: the spirit of liberty and progressiveness. And no man of our time personifies this spirit more nobly than our honored guest and my beloved friend, the great General Garibaldi. Let us all drink to him and the success of his noble cause: a united Italy."

A half hour later Garibaldi waltzed with Fiammetta in the crowded ballroom where a ten-man orchestra was playing Weber's "Invitation to the Dance."

"How can I thank you?" he said. "This wonderful evening, all the money you raised . . . you are magnificent, my Fiammetta. How much you have given me and Italy."

"How much you have given *me,* Giuseppe. You gave me Justin."

"I *brought* you Justin. You took him—I might say you grabbed him. Is it true you're going with him to China?"

Her smile faded. "Yes. I don't much want to. China sounds horrid to me, and dangerous. But his mind is set, and I can't blame him. He wants his daughter." She sighed. "But I'm not looking forward to it."

"Justin is your destiny, as Italy is mine. You can't escape your destiny."

"Nor do I want to," she said, smiling. "But Justin's making my destiny a bumpy ride. And if he should be hurt again . . ." She frowned. "Well, I won't think about that. And he tells me that all you have taught him about warfare will make him the best-informed soldier in China, so I'm sure he'll be all right. He does love China so. Who knows? Maybe I'll love it too. But there are so many 'if's. . . ."

"Justin's a very resourceful young man. By the way, how's his bottom where they branded him?"

She smiled. *"Bellissimo."*

"What a night," Justin said four hours later. The last of the guests had just left, and he and Fiammetta were strolling hand in hand through the formal garden, which was bathed with soft light by a full moon. "I'm half-drunk."

"With love, I hope?"

He smiled. "Of course. Love and champagne, a potent combination. What a wonderful thing you did for the General."

"Yes, he thanked me from his heart, and he has a great heart. As do you, my sweet love. Look: here's the enchanted rosebush from the legend. And there is the first rose of summer. How wonderful! It's God's gift to our love. Isn't it a beautiful color?"

One rose had blossomed into a passionate bloodred.

"So this is the bush that made the prince forget his other love?" Justin asked.

"Yes. He took one sniff and forgot her forever."

Justin smiled at her. "Well, I'm no prince. But I believe in legends."

He leaned down and inhaled deeply of the rose's perfume. Then he straightened, a look of surprise on his face. "I think it worked," he said. "I can barely remember Samantha."

"Ah, if I could only believe you," sighed Fiammetta.

He took her in his arms. "Believe," he said, kissing her in the moonlight. And the enchanted rose trembled in the soft breeze.

Part Four

THE FORBIDDEN CITY

30

THE FORBIDDEN CITY, THE HEART of the vast Celestial Empire, was a box within a larger box, the Imperial City, within an even larger box, the Tartar City, all of which was bordered to the south by the rectangular Chinese City. Each of these cities was surrounded by high walls pierced by a number of gates that were closed at night for protection; the Forbidden City was also surrounded by a moat. Every building in Peking faced south; out of respect for the Emperor, no building could rise higher than the walls of the Forbidden City, for to have been able to peer into the sacred grounds of the Emperor's home would have been an abomination. Indeed, one of the Hsien-feng Emperor's severest objections to allowing the foreign devils to establish embassies in Peking was his fear that they would put up high buildings, as he had been informed they did in Shanghai, from which they could view his comings and goings through their devils' lenses, as binoculars were known in China.

On an autumn day in 1858, the procession of Prince I entered the southern Chinese City through the south gate. The Prince sat in his silver palanquin borne by eight bearers who grunted under his ever-increasing weight. The Prince was proceeded by fifty of his Bannermen and followed by a train of attendants in wagons that held his personal possessions, five palanquins carrying a selection of his concubines borne by eunuchs, and ten million taels in silver, his annual tribute to his cousin, the Emperor. The tribute was guarded by fifty more Bannermen, who brought up the rear of the impressive procession. The Viceroy of the Two Provinces liked to travel in style.

It was a clear day, free of the fierce winds that so frequently swept down from the great Gobi Desert bringing stinging sandstorms to the city, which had a wretched climate of fiercely hot summers and icy winters. The intermediate seasons, though, could be pleasant and the fat Prince was in a beamish mood anticipating the many pleasures of the capital. The raised causeway the procession was traveling on was flanked by woods filled with cawing crows and muddy, swampy land over which wandered a few thin sheep plucking at scanty tufts of rank grass. Ironically, beyond this dismal scene on either side stretched the vast grounds of the Temple of Agriculture, 320 acres, and the Temple of Heaven, 640 acres, where at the summer and winter solstice, the Emperor came to pray to his ancestors. Otherwise, the Chinese City, as its name implied, was essentially a slum: to the Manchu rulers of the Celestial Empire, the Chinese were second-class citizens with few rights. However, over the years, the Chinese culture and language had, with insidious stealth, enslaved its masters. Few Manchus bothered to speak the Manchu language anymore, even though it was the official language of the court. And Yehenala, the mother of the little Heir Presumptive, prided herself on the purity of her Mandarin, the language of the northern Chinese.

When Prince I's procession reached the massive Ch'ien Men, the central gate of the Tartar City with the brilliant yellow glazed eaves of its gatehouses towering above them, they passed into the bustling world of the capital. The great avenue, sixty feet wide, then led straight north to the Wu Men, the Gate of the Zenith in the wall surrounding the Imperial City, the second box within the box. Along the way teemed the life of China: mat-shed booths and shops, three deep on either side, sold the thousand necessities of life, each booth advertising its wares by a flag. Organized bands of beggars preyed on the unwary, soothsayers sold almanacs of lucky days and for a price threw the *I Ching* to tell fortunes. Acrobats, jugglers, and rope dancers provided entertainment, along with decapitated heads of criminals hanging in wire baskets from tall poles as cautions to would-be thieves and murderers. Barbers shaved heads in the open air, while sloe-eyed camel caravans from the steppes of Asia swayed lazily by. Peddlers pulled their carts and banged drums to announce what they were selling, be it sweetmeats or rice cakes or doughnuts, carrying their wares to high-born ladies who could barely walk on their bound feet, hobbling in the "lily walk" that so enflamed the male Chinese. Nightsoil merchants collected human and animal manure in jars and carried it off to the country to sell as fertilizer: most houses in the hundreds of *hutungs* of the city built their privies against the back wall with a small door, or pass through, which facilitated the collecting of the family fecal matter. Craftsmen, dentists, storytellers, scribes, quacks, and puppeteers all jostled in the vast sea of humanity in this capital of the most populous nation in the world. The Prince wrinkled his patrician nose at the many smells of the city—garlic, cloves, tobacco, human sweat, camel dung—but he was snooting the smells of life.

The avenue was muddy and the crowds were ragged and diseased: the Prince's snobbery was not without some foundation in fact. Nor was the city particularly beautiful; in fact, to an outsider, the many houses with their tiled, upturned roofs appeared dilapidated, if not squalid. Even the houses of the rich seemed unpretentious from the outside: Chinese architecture preserved its serene beauties for the inside. Only from the top of Prospect Hill, an artificial mountain put up to protect the capital from the evil spirits of the north, could this secret Peking be revealed.

But elsewhere, all was dirt. The population teemed with lice: the highest officials of state didn't hesitate to inspect their attendants' necks for the troublesome bugs, which they would often pop between their teeth. The city guards, who patrolled the streets at night after the gates were closed, carrying rattles to frighten off evil spirits, were in rags. Only a century before, China had been the richest nation on earth. But the corruption and arrogance of the dynasty were rapidly turning it into one of the poorest nations on earth as the barbarians from the west with their steam engines and greed for gold more and more challenged the ancient ways of the Celestial Empire.

Finally, the Prince's procession reached the great Tien An Men, or Gate of Heavenly Peace. Then it passed through the great gate, then a second gate, the Wu Men. At last, they crossed the greasy green waters of the moat and entered the purple walls of the Forbidden City.

That night, the kitchen eunuchs worked feverishly to prepare a princely feast for the Emperor's cousin, yelling curses at the eunuch scullery boys, who were known for their laziness. Eunuchs, who chose their career-determining operation at the age of twelve, burying themselves waist-deep in sand for three days after the chop, lost much of their vitality by their mutilation, but seemed to gain in venality: they were well known to be deceitful and mendacious, and were roundly despised by the general population. Still, the profession attracted hundreds of boys yearly because it was the path to riches; over and over again in Chinese history, eunuchs had gained control of the court, gathering great power. In one sixteenth-century reign, the eunuch Liu Chin amassed in a few years a fortune of one quarter billion taels. The eunuchs often kept their severed members in jars to be buried with them after death, so that their spirit would be a "whole man."

Promptly at eight, a procession of eunuchs headed for the Pavilion of Feminine Tranquility bearing dozens of blue and white Ming dishes containing such delicacies as simmered bear's paws, honey-fried hummingbirds, Tientsin prawns, *tsung-tze,* sticky rice in lotus leaves, and that favorite of the capital, *chiao-tze,* steamed or crunch-fried dumplings. The pavilion was one of a number of minor buildings at the north end of the Forbidden City, beyond the principal pavilions of the compound, the Palaces of the Emperor and the Empress and the Throne Hall of Supreme Harmony. All the buildings of the imperial compound with their roofs of imperial yellow tiles had been constructed during the Ming Dynasty, and it was a credit to the Ming architects that these many halls were juxtaposed with elegance and harmony.

Inside the Pavilion of Feminine Tranquility, inaccurately named considering the amount of intrigue that went on among the Emperor's many concubines, his favored concubine, Yehenala, was pouring Hsien-feng another cup of rice wine as two of her *shih-tzu kou* lion dogs frolicked behind her seat. Yehenala was now twenty-three and at the height of her cold beauty. Her face was painted pinkish-white, her eyes outlined with kohl, her lids painted sapphire, and on her lower lip was painted a small red dewdrop pendulum, a hallmark of Manchu makeup guaranteed to make warriors writhe. She wore an elaborate dragon robe embroidered in seed pearls and coral with the purple dye she loved in the diagonal stripes at the hem. Included in the design were the characters for "double joy" or "wedded bliss"; bats, the symbol of happiness; and the Eight Felicitous Buddhist Emblems. On the fourth and fifth fingers of each of her hands were three-inch gold filigree nail guards. In her ears were white jade pendants in the shape of a hare with a mortar and pestle, the hare being a denizen of the moon and the maker of the Chinese elixir of life. On her head was an elaborate Manchu headdress extending over each ear by half a foot, ending in foot-long tassels. Prince I, who was wisely wary of this tigress, had to grudgingly admit she was a thing of beauty. Even his jaded loins tingled slightly beneath their layers of waxy fat.

"We are badly served," moaned the Emperor, who never tired of complaining. "Our generals are lazy and stupid, Our eunuchs are thieves, Our mandarins lie and cheat . . . is it any wonder this *Kua* turns to the delights of the wine cup to escape His many tribulations? It is not easy to be the Lord of Ten Thousand Years. We have absolute power, and yet when We tell Our generals to rid Our empire of the cursed foreign devils and slay the verminous Taiping rebels, nothing happens. Nothing!" He sobbed drunkenly. "We'd be better off a poor peasant. At least when We planted a cabbage, something would sprout."

"Divinity," said Yehenala, signaling the eunuchs to put the dishes on the table and remove the lids, "this slave's heart weeps to even consider the Son of Heaven demeaning Himself by soiling His celestial fingers with common dirt."

Yehenala had mastered the tortured prose of the Court and could lay it on thick. "It was merely a metaphor, Nala, a device to express the extreme sorrow and desperation of Our soul. You, Cousin." He turned to Prince I, who was sitting next to him at the banquet table. The pavilion was illuminated by dozens of octagonal lanterns hanging from the gilt and scarlet roof beams.

"You bring Us Our yearly tribute, for which We are grateful. And not a moment too soon, for Our treasury is bare. This cursed rebellion in the south is draining Our wealth as well as Our strength. The verminous rebels should be easy to exterminate! Have not they turned on each other? Has not that upstart who has the nerve to call himself the 'Heavenly King' turned on one of his best generals, the so-called 'King of the East,' and ordered his so-called 'King of the North' to butcher him and all his family and followers? It was a bloodbath! Hundreds died! Then, drunk with power, the King of the North turned on the 'Assistant King'—where, We ask, do they come up with all these absurd titles?—and promptly butchered him and all his followers. At which point, the Heavenly King had the King of the North murdered! He has gone mad, and Nanking is awash with blood! It should be easy to take the Southern Capital. But when We order Our generals to do so, nothing happens!" Again, he sobbed and held out his peony cup to Yehenala to refill. "Alas, is it any wonder We drink?"

"Majesty," Yehenala purred, lifting the cloisonné ewer to pour him more wine, "this slave weeps at Your sorrow. And yet, Divine One, Your courage and wisdom will one day prevail, and these long-haired devils will die a hundred deaths. You will soak the fields of China with their blood, and their severed heads will draw flies till they rot."

The Emperor made a face. "Please, Nala, my stomach is queasy enough."

"Sorry, Divinity. This slave is a fool."

"Oh, no, Yehenala," said Prince I with a smile. "You are anything but a fool." She shot him a venomous glare.

"But I bring interesting news from the south," the Prince went on, turning back to his imperial cousin whose eyes were beginning to cross slightly from drink. "A red-haired barbarian has arrived in Canton, an American named Justin Savage."

Yehenala pricked up her ears. The Emperor, his energy sapped by drugs, alcohol, and general dissipation, had, at Yehenala's suggestion, given her "access to the Memorials," thereby plugging her into the nerve center of the Celestial Empire. Yehenala, who lusted for power and whose energy was boundless, thus began to read every "Memorial," as official reports were called, of the far-flung empire. In this way, she knew everything that was going on in China—or at least everything that was reported to Peking—and with this knowledge, she of course began to acquire power.

"Justin Savage?" she said. "The name is familiar. Was not he the husband of that she-devil, the pirate Chang-mei?"

"Yes."

"Then why have you not arrested him? Chang-mei blew up one of His

Majesty's war junks! She would have died the Death of a Thousand Cuts had she not been shot instead, depriving His Majesty of the divine pleasure of watching her writhe in pain. Her husband's neck should be kissed by the executioner's sword! Why have you not done something?"

"Yes, why?" repeated Hsien-feng, turning his bloodshot eyes on his adipose cousin, who was gorging on his second helping of honey-fried hummingbird, a delicacy he had a passion for.

"For the simple reason that he has remarried an Italian countess. . . ."

"Italian?" snapped Yehenala. "What's that?"

"She comes from Italy, which is a boot-shaped country that sticks out from the bottom of Europe into the Mediterranean."

"What's the Mediterranean?" asked the Emperor, who looked totally confused.

"It's a large inland sea, Divinity, that separates Europe from Africa. Perhaps the Lord of Ten Thousand Years would be better served if one of his advisers purchased him an up-to-date map of the world."

This barb was thrown at Yehenala, whose sapphire-lidded eyes narrowed. "Why should the Lord of Ten Thousand Years know what lies beyond the borders of His Celestial Empire?" she asked imperiously. "The barbarians and their puny kingdoms are of no interest to us."

"I beg to differ with you, *Yi Kuei,*" the Prince said and Yehenala stiffened at the insult. *Yi Kuei* meant "Virtuous Concubine" and was her formal title, bestowed on her by the Emperor after she delivered him a son and he raised her from *Yi Ping,* Concubine of the Third Rank, to *Yi Fei,* Concubine of the Second Rank. But as mother of the Heir Presumptive, Yehenala considered herself more a wife than a concubine. To be reminded of her actual status by the Prince was a bona fide insult that she would not forget. "We must interest ourselves in the barbarians because they are our enemies," the Prince went on. "The great Sun Tzu says over and over that the primary target must be the mind of the enemy, you must know everything you can about the enemy, you must use spies and gatherers of intelligence: then and only then can you defeat him—and if you are clever enough, you can defeat him without even fighting. We know little about the barbarians, and it is making us weak. For this reason, I sent the young American to England to study at that country's military academy, a place called Sandhurst. . . ."

"You sent the barbarian out of the country knowing he was a pirate?" Yehenala interrupted, poised for the kill. "Knowing he was a criminal?"

Prince I moved on from the fried hummingbirds to the Tientsin prawns, another of his favorites. "Yes, I did," he said calmly. "He is a young man of great qualities and keen intelligence, and he loves China. He agreed to learn the ways of the west and return to help us. He was a spy sent to learn about the enemy, just as Sun Tzu recommends. To have cut off his head at the Field of Executions would have been a waste. The Celestial Kingdom needs his head."

Yehenala pointed a long-nailed finger at him. "Might I suggest, Prince, that you protected him because his wife, the she-pirate, was paying you squeeze?"

"Enough!" snapped the Emperor. "You presume, Nala. The Prince is Our cousin, a member of the Imperial Clan. Besides, what he's saying makes sense. Perhaps we *should* know the enemy."

Yehenala bit her lip and swiftly backed down. "Divinity, this slave is impetuous. But in her all-consuming love for the Lord of Ten Thousand Years, she only wishes to protect His sacred person."

"Mmm. Then give Us some more wine. Go on, Cousin. Tell Us more of this American." He stuck out his peony cup.

"As I said, he has remarried an Italian woman of great beauty and wealth, the Countess of Mondragone."

"Why would a rich countess marry a poor pirate?" Yehenala snapped, refilling Hsien-feng's cup.

"For reasons you might understand, *Yi Kuei,*" the Prince said. "He is young and handsome and she fell in love with him. These things happen, even in China."

Again, the sapphire lids narrowed. She knew what he was insinuating: her love affair with the man she had known all her life, the young and handsome warrior, Jung-lu. She panicked as she realized Prince I knew. As careful as she had been, somehow news of her liaison must have seeped out of the Forbidden City. Again, she backed down, appearing as cool as possible. If the Emperor found out about her dalliance, it would be *her* neck that kissed the executioner's sword.

"I know nothing of such things," she said primly. The Prince gave her a knowing look, then turned to the Emperor.

"The young American has been ennobled by the King of Piedmont," he said, "which is a small kingdom in the northwest corner of the Italian peninsula. . . ."

"That sticks into the Mediterranean!" chirped the Emperor, pleased to show off how fast he could learn. "You speak wisely, Cousin. Buy Us a map."

"It will be delivered tomorrow, Divinity. The King has ennobled him and given him diplomatic status, so there is nothing we could do to him even if we wanted to. But he has studied with a great general in the west and knows the barbarian ways. He is offering to raise a private army at his own expense— or rather his wife's—and lead it against the Taiping rebels at Soochow. He believes he can take Soochow for us, which would be the beginning of the end for the Heavenly King."

The Emperor looked stunned, as did Yehenala. "Why would he do this?" asked Hsien-feng. "Is he mad?"

"Far from it, Divinity. He is quite sane. But I will admit there is a personal motive to his offer. The General commanding the rebel forces at Soochow . . ."

"Is Li-shan," Yehenala interrupted. "The son of the Chung Wang. He is one of their best generals."

Prince I nodded at her. "You have studied the Memorials well, *Yi Kuei.*"

"My name is Yehenala!" she snapped.

"But your title is Virtuous Concubine, something you seem to forget at times. At any rate, as I was saying, the American, Savage, had a daughter by Chang-mei. The daughter has been raised by Li-shan and is with him in Soochow. Part of the American's purpose is to get his daughter back and kill Li-shan for stealing her. So you can see, Divinity, the red-haired barbarian is well motivated and could be a great asset to us. Of course, I would never authorize his expedition without the permission of the Lord of Ten Thousand Years."

The Emperor burped and beamed.

"Why not?" he exclaimed. "We have everything to gain and nothing to lose. Of course you have Our permission, and We will send prayers to Our ancestors that the red-haired barbarian succeeds!" He raised his wine cup and added, "Let us all drink to that!"

He drained his cup, then his face fell forward into his bowl of crunch-fried dumplings and he passed out.

The population might have despised the eunuchs, but Yehenala had grown fond of them almost out of necessity, because there were over three thousand of them in the Forbidden City. The real men she came in contact with, aside from the slobby Emperor, were few: aged statesmen and ministers, Mandarins, guards and soldiers whose entry into the private quarters of the concubines was strictly prohibited. Of course, the very idea of eunuchs was to ensure that the charms of the Emperor's harem would be reserved for him alone; the "Forbidden" part of the city's title was taken literally.

So she had little choice but to befriend the eunuchs in this orchidaceous world. Moreover, there was something in the eunuch's lack of virility that appealed to the masculine streak in Yehenala's complex character. Which was not to say that she didn't have a very feminine streak that was wildly attracted to dashing men, warriors in particular. Needless to say, the drunken, pudgy, dissolute Hsien-feng did not exactly bank the fires of her desire.

But a young Manchu officer named Jung-lu did.

After Yehenala gave birth to the Heir Presumptive, whom the Emperor named Tsai Chün (*Tsai* meaning "to promulgate" and *Chün* meaning "pure" and "majestic"), her prestige soared in the court. The Dynastic Laws did not include primogeniture, so it was possible the Emperor could have another son who might become Emperor; thus little Tsai Chün was designated Heir Presumptive rather than Crown Prince. Still, for the time being she was the mother of the Emperor's only son, which made her a rising star. The eunuchs were swift to sniff a winner, and they began to fawn on her. Yehenala was intelligent enough to know what they were up to, but she was human enough to love the attention and flattery. After all, before she gave birth to the Heir Presumptive, she had been roundly snubbed, if not ignored.

Yehenala's favorite eunuch was a tall, handsome, and exceedingly greedy eighteen-year-old named An Te-hai who had hitched his wagon to her star. He had already made a good deal of money thanks to Yehenala, and he dreamed of making much, much more, enough one day to buy an imposing mansion for his numerous family, for he was one of nine siblings of a wretchedly poor farming couple. That night, after the Emperor had been carried to his bed, Yehenala retired to her apartment in the Pavilion of Feminine Tranquility and summoned An who, like all eunuchs, wore an orange and green robe embroidered with the five-clawed imperial dragons.

He entered Yehenala's bedroom, which gave off onto a charming, small walled garden. The room was lit by a single candle, and Yehenala, who had changed from the elaborate dragon robe she had worn at dinner into a simple blue silk shift, was looking out at the night sky. When she heard the eunuch enter, she turned, came to him, and slapped his face.

"My lady, what have I done to deserve this?" asked An in a shocked tone. "Have I displeased you?"

"He knows," she whispered.

"Who?"

"The fat one, Prince I. Have you betrayed me?"

"No, I swear! Do you think me mad? If I betray you, who do you think will go to the Field of Executions first? Me—and I've already had enough of me cut off."

She glanced scornfully at his midsection. He had once shown her his scar, as she was curious to see what it looked like. It was difficult for her to imagine how a man could abandon all hope of sexual pleasure for money. Now, she rubbed her forehead. She had a terrible headache from the wine and the worry.

"Then how does he know?" she said. "We've been so careful. . . ."

"Peking is full of rumors. Perhaps the Prince has heard one about you, and is using it to frighten you. Did he mention anyone by name?"

"No, but the look he gave me . . ." She gestured angrily. "How I wish he were dead!" she spat out. "He has enriched himself at My Lord's expense, he's as twisted as a waterspout . . . damn him! I'd like to get my hands around his fat throat. . . ."

An Te-hai gulped nervously. Yehenala was well known for her temper, and he had seen her throw things when she lost all control, including chamber pots, one of which had hit his head.

But tonight, she managed to keep some control. "Go to him," she said. "Tell him to meet me at the Hall of Flowering Literature at the hour of the cock."

"My lady, it is dangerous. . . ."

"You fool, don't you think I know that? Here. . . ." She took a purse, opened it, and pulled out ten silver taels. "Bribe the guard at the east end of the hall. Tell him to leave his post for fifteen minutes. Five taels for him, five for you. And don't cheat me! Now go!"

The eunuch hurried out of the room as Yehenala lit a joss stick to Kwan Yin, the goddess of mercy. To even *think* of betraying the Son of Heaven was one of the Ten Abominations punishable by prolonged torture followed by decapitation.

And Yehenala had gone much further than mere thinking.

At five A.M. she slipped out of the Pavilion of Feminine Tranquility and hurried through the darkness to the Hall of Flowering Literature, the Forbidden City's library, which held thousands of scrolls dating as far back as two thousand years. The city was quiet—it was an hour before dawn—although in the distance beyond the Sea Palaces situated on three artificial lakes to the west of the Forbidden City, she could hear the faint rattles of the night watchmen warding off evil spirits. Shivering as much from fright as from cold, she gathered her hooded cloak around her and waited in the shadows at the east end of the graceful hall. An Te-hai had done his work well: there was no guard in sight.

She jumped as she felt a hand on her shoulder. Turning, she sighed with relief.

"Yehenala," whispered Jung-lu. "My love."

He took her in his arms and they kissed, a long, passionate kiss, the kind of kiss she hungered for, not the half-drunken, slobbering kisses of the Emperor. She thrilled as she felt the strength of his body, hardened by exercise and hunting, so different from the soft, flabby body of Hsien-feng. Her body ached for his love, but her brain told her that to do it here, up against the cold wall of the Hall of Flowering Literature, was beneath her dignity. Besides, she didn't have much time. Jung-lu was a lieutenant colonel in the Imperial Guard, a highly visible warrior in the court, known for his friendship with Yehenala—they had known each other as children—as well as for his extreme good looks—a cultivated Englishman who had seen him dubbed him the "Alcibiades of China." Her trysts with this dashing Manchu had to be carefully planned and carried out with extreme discretion. Of course, the danger inherent in this romance only served to make it that much more intense.

"My sweet," she finally whispered, tearing her mouth from him, "I must be brief. If we are caught . . ."

"I know. We die. But I would die happy to be your slave."

"True, but I'm not happy about either of us dying. Prince I suspects us. Is there any way you could kill him?"

Jung-lu considered this.

"No," he finally said. "He's too well guarded. It would be impossible."

"Damn. But you are right to be cautious, my love. Oh, how I wish we could be together always!" She hugged him again, and again they kissed. "But we must somehow discredit the fat one. He told us tonight of an American named Savage whom he is sponsoring. The American wants to organize a private army and capture Soochow from the Long Hairs."

"Soochow is heavily defended, and Li-shan is a great warrior."

"Not as great as you, my love. If I got the Emperor to give you an army, could you capture Soochow?"

"I'd certainly love to try, but I'd need many men. . . ."

"How many?"

"Our spies say Li-shan has two thousand troops in Soochow. But our spies are notoriously inaccurate, so I'd want at least double that."

"Four thousand? I can get it for you. What about equipment?"

"I would need at least ten cannons to breach the walls of the city. And of course rifles for the men. Modern rifles, not the junk the army has."

"I'll see what I can do. The Emperor is hard to move, but I have my tricks. And if you could capture Soochow and bring Li-shan back to Peking in chains, it would be a great victory for the Emperor, and you will become our foremost general—I'll see to that. But most important, we can discredit Prince I, so that if he accuses us of anything he will be humiliated, his accusations merely the smoke of jealousy. You will become China's greatest hero, and the Emperor would not dare harm you!"

"Your resourcefulness and cleverness dazzle me, flower of my passion. You should be Empress: then China would again be great!"

She smiled. "Perhaps one day that can be arranged, and then you will be at my side, making love to me day and night."

"The thought inspires me, though I might wear out."

"You? Never. There's one thing. Li-shan has a baby girl—she's really the daughter of the barbarian American and he wants her back. If you can capture Li-shan, bring the girl with him."

"Why?"

"She's worth money! The American is rich: we'll make him pay till his soul shrivels and shrieks. Besides, his first wife sank one of our war junks: for that, he must pay."

"You are inspired."

"Now kiss me once more. I will send An Te-hai to you when I know more. Next time, we can arrange a proper tryst."

"My soul aches for your love."

"My body aches for yours."

Again, they kissed. She saw a man coming across the courtyard toward them. She pushed Jung-lu away.

"The guard's returning," she whispered. "I must hurry. Good night, my love."

She vanished into the shadows.

31   THE JADE PHOENIX SALOON IN the Chinese City of Shanghai was owned by an American from Chicago named Chester Speakes. Along with thousands of others, Chester had gone to California during the Gold Rush; along with thousands of others, he found no gold. Broke in San Francisco at the age of thirty, he shipped out on a clipper for China, and in Shanghai he found the gold he had missed in California: prostitution. Chester became a pimp for the hundreds of European and American sailors crowding the seedier sections of the fast-growing boom town that reminded him of San Francisco at the height of the Gold Rush. He matched up pretty Chinese girls with love-hungry sailors and in so doing made himself rich enough to realize his dream of opening a western-style saloon in Shanghai, like the ones he had frequented on San Francisco's notorious Barbary Coast.

The Jade Phoenix had saloon-style swinging doors, a long wooden bar replete with the requisite female nude on the wall, round tables where men played poker all through the night, and even a small stage where a Chinese singsong girl named Shanghai Sally warbled off-color songs in execrable English.

Seated at one of the tables playing poker was a small man in a rather threadbare black suit. His name was Ben Lieberman, but because he was only five feet four, he was nicknamed "Bantam" Ben. He was thirty-four, a Jew from, of all places, Alabama. Now he pushed a pile of chips into the middle of the table.

"I'll open for five dollars," he said, chewing his unlit cigar as he eyed the four other men at the table.

A fat Dutchman to his right threw in his hand, muttered a curse, and weaved to the bar to get another beer, even though French champagne was the favored drink in Shanghai. However, the Dutchman had lost his shirt to Bantam Ben and couldn't afford champagne.

"I'm in," said a third man, shoving chips into the center of the table.

Bantam Ben jotted some figures down on a pad.

"Lieberman," huffed the fourth man at the table, a fat man with a black beard. His name was Mahoney, and he hailed from the Ozarks of Arkansas. Because of his size and huge belly, he was known as Man Mountain Mahoney. He was, like most of the men in the Jade Phoenix, drunk. "I want to know why the hell you keep writin' on that damned fool pad."

Bantam Ben smiled. He had beautiful teeth, a fine-featured face, and big brown eyes that snapped with intelligence. He spoke with a magnolia-scented Alabama drawl. "It's my system," he said.

"Well, it annoys me. Stop scribblin' and play poker."

"I'm not gonna stop, Man Mountain. That's why I win: I've got my system. I'm not gonna play without my system, and it ain't botherin' you none."

"Uh-huh. Well, let me tell you something, you damned little Jew boy: I think your system is a pile of shit. I think the reason you're cleanin' us all out is that you cheat!" He stood up, pulling a gun from his holster and pointing it at Bantam Ben. Suddenly the smoke-filled saloon fell silent as everyone turned to watch the action. "Stand up, Jew boy," said Man Mountain, "and take off your coat. I wanna see what you got up your sleeve."

He was so drunk, he was weaving; but he meant what he said literally. The hundreds of professional gamblers who swarmed all over America had a myriad of mechanical devices they strapped on their arms that could surreptitiously slide aces into the palms of their hands. Bantam Ben stood up, looking a little nervous.

"Man Mountain," he said, removing his coat, "you're just a little bit overly suspicious. I don't have to use mechanical devices to win. I have my system, which works because I got a terrific head for figures. Why, when I was in high school back in Birmingham, Alabama, I won every prize there was in 'rithmetic."

"Uh-huh. They say you Jews is good with numbers. But I've taken a real intense dislike of you, boy. And I want to see you dance. Go on: get out there and dance for me." He fired at Ben's feet. Ben jumped. "Go on, dance, dammit!" He fired again.

Ben started hopping around in a circle as Man Mountain kept firing at his feet.

Justin, in a white suit with a white planter's hat on his head, came through the swinging doors of the Jade Phoenix Saloon, saw what was happening, pulled a gun from his jacket, and fired at Man Mountain Mahoney, hitting him in his gun hand. Man Mountain howled and dropped his gun on the floor.

"Goddam you!" he bellowed, tearing off a piece of his sleeve to wind around his wound. Bantam Ben pounced on the gun, grabbed it, and pointed it at Man Mountain. It was all too much for Man Mountain, who ran out of the saloon. The customers burst into applause.

Bantam Ben put down the gun and stuck out his hand. "I don't know who you are, mister," he panted, "but I sure as hell like the way you shoot. Thanks a heap."

"I don't like bullies," Justin said, returning his gun to his armpit holster, then shaking Ben's hand. Then he turned to the others in the saloon and announced in a voice that rang around the room, "Gentlemen, my name is Justin Savage, I'm from New York City, and I'm recruiting a private army to take on the Taiping rebels. The pay is three dollars a day with food and shelter provided, plus a uniform and rifles with ammunition. If any of you are interested, I'll be interviewing recruits tomorrow morning at my house at Number Ten Bubbling Well Road. I promise you a rousing adventure, lots of fresh air and exercise, and a chance to improve your characters."

There was a round of boos and hisses. Justin laughed. "All right, forget the last," he said. "Still, I hope to see some of you tomorrow."

Tipping his hat, he left the saloon. Bantam Ben, who though small was perfectly proportioned, looked impressed.

"Hot damn," he muttered to himself. "That sounds interesting. Hell, it even sounds fun."

The small green lizard on the white ceiling was immobile, but Fiammetta, who was watching it, knew that when it moved, it darted quickly. They were amazing creatures, called *tjik-tjaks,* and when she had first seen them she had frozen in horror, thinking they were dangerous. But when Justin assured her they were not only harmless but beneficial, since they ate mosquitoes, she had calmed down a bit, though she knew now that their droppings fell randomly on furniture and bedsheets.

She went to a window to get a breath of air, wiping her forehead with a handkerchief. The window had a quasi-curtain of glass beads to keep out flies. The heat was appalling, a steamy, tropical heat much worse than anything she had ever encountered in Italy. Even though Justin had told her the heat would break in a few weeks, this wasn't much consolation now. She hated being hot and sticky.

They had been in Shanghai a week. The western-style house they had rented on Bubbling Well Road, across from the Shanghai Country Club, was pleasant enough and one of the biggest in the city, belonging to a rich British merchant. It came furnished and with a staff of servants: she lacked none of the creature comforts except relief from the heat. The house was surrounded by a Chinese-style wall, and there was a lovely garden with bamboo trees and a carp pond.

She was wearing a loose-fitting white negligee, the coolest thing she could think of besides total nudity. A mosquito buzzed by her ear. She waved it away and went into the living room, which was filled with rattan furniture. Two large wicker fans hung from the ceiling; they could be operated by coolies, but now they were untended. She moved around the room listlessly.

She wished she could love China the way Justin did, but she couldn't. Canton with its stinky streets she had hated, and Shanghai wasn't much better. But she knew how important it was to Justin to get back his daughter, and because she loved him to distraction she would try not to complain about the heat and the boredom. Not that the ladies of the various Foreign Concessions had been unfriendly. On the contrary, she and Justin had been swamped with invitations to dinners, dances, and the racetrack. After all, the Count and Countess of Mondragone were a glamorous couple, and Justin had been running ads in the *North China Herald,* the local English-language newspaper, for recruits. The ads had sparked a lackluster response so far. Justin assumed it was because his potential recruits didn't read newspapers, which was why he was out today, touring the various gin joints in the Chinese City to drum up some business.

But it was certainly no secret why they were in Shanghai. In fact, the town was buzzing with what Justin was up to. They had agreed to go to one dinner party in the French Consulate on the Quai de France, facing the Huangpu River. The people, a mixture of French, British, and Americans, had been friendly, but she found them boring. The longer she was away from Europe, the more she wanted to return. She missed her homes, her friends. She longed to gossip, to read the latest novels, to shop.

And there was the baby. She put her hand on her stomach. She imagined she could feel the life in there. She was in her second month, and she had been as thrilled as Justin at the news. She had had two miscarriages with her first husband, Cesare, and she desperately wanted a child.

But did she want it in China? China with its superstitions and lack of what she considered proper medical facilities? She had already been sick once from the food, and although Justin had assured her that was perfectly normal for foreigners, she certainly might get sick again, and how might that affect her baby? True, there was a British doctor in Shanghai as well as a French one; she had no reason to believe they were incompetent, and it was patently obvious the Chinese had no problem having children—Shanghai teemed with humans. But still, there was all the uncertainty of being in a foreign place halfway around the world from home, and there surely was no place more foreign on the planet than China.

She had a dozen reasons to leave China, ranging from the trivial to the convincing. She had only one reason to stay, and that was her passion for Justin. She knew the conventional wisdom was that the most exciting moment of a romance was climbing the stairs to the bedroom; her passion for him should long ago have dimmed. And yet she still listened for him when he was away, still thrilled when he touched her. His sweetness still enchanted her, as his growing maturity fascinated her. Since returning to China, he had seemed more a man than an adolescent. No other man interested her at all: her heart belonged to Justin. She knew full well the European tradition that marriage was an institution more than a romance.

But her marriage was a romance, so in the last analysis the heat, the boredom, the uncertainty, all faded away. She was happy with him, and miserable without. She still believed in the theories of the Comte de Saint-Simon; she wholeheartedly believed that men and women were equal.

But in one fundamental way, they were different, and *vive la différence.*

She heard the clatter of the rickshaw wheels on the pavement outside the moon gate, and her heart quickened. She hurried into the garden, staying in the shade of the bamboo trees to protect her skin from the burning sun. The gate opened, and there he was. Forgetting her skin and the heat, she ran into his arms and they kissed.

A half hour later he came out of the bathroom drying himself with a towel. Then he came to their European-style bed where she waited for him, naked, arms outstretched. He climbed in bed as she patted the **M** brand on his buttock, a little marital ritual she was convinced brought good luck. Then they made love that, in the steamy heat, left them both drenched with sweat again.

"I think I may have got some men interested," he said, turning over on his back and putting his hands behind his head, staring at the green *tjik-tjak* on the ceiling whose tongue flickered out and grabbed a mosquito. "Although you'd think when I'm offering three bucks a day I'd be swamped with recruits. Anyway, I went to some real dives in the Chinese City today. By the way, I shot a man."

He said it casually. "You *what?*" Fiammetta exclaimed.

"Some big slob of a man was shooting at a very small man, bullying him, so I shot the big man's gun hand. It worked. He stopped bullying him."

She ran her hand over his chest, which had a faint line of red-gold hair down the middle. "You're turning into a real desperado," she said.

"Do you mind?"

"Oh, no, I think it's terribly exciting—as long as you don't shoot me."

"That's not very likely."

"But tell me, darling: how many men are you trying to recruit?"

"Fifty."

"How can you capture Soochow with fifty men?"

"I can't."

"But that's what you told Prince I you wanted to do."

"I lied. Obviously, I can't hope to outnumber Li-shan's forces. But if I can train a small group of men—what Garibaldi called 'guerrillas'—we could possibly trick or lure Li-shan to come out of Soochow and we could capture him. Then I could swap him for Julie and we could go home."

"But that isn't what Prince I wants. He wants you to capture the city."

"Then let him or the Emperor give me two thousand troops. Meanwhile, I'm going after Julie. Look: you once said to me that helping the Manchus was worse than fighting for the reactionary popes, and you were right. Since we've come back to China, I've seen that the corruption is worse, the people are hungrier and more ground down by the public officials . . . the Emperor's degenerate and his court is a sinkhole. Why should I fight for them? It was a crazy dream in the first place, and to hell with it. Besides, we've got Junior to think about now"—he leaned over and kissed her belly—"and I can see you don't like China. So we'll get Julie and go home."

She smiled as she put her hand on his cheek. "You've just made me very happy."

"Good. I like that." He kissed her mouth, then lay back down again. "We'll know more in the morning. But I can tell you one thing: my army may be made up of the scum of the earth. Most of the men I saw today looked like river rats, and that's being complimentary."

"But they'll be my darling Justin's river rats. Will you hire Chinese?"

"I'll hire whatever I can get."

32   SHANGHAI MEANT "ABOVE THE SEA" in old Chinese, even though it wasn't actually on the sea at all. Rather, it was at a conjunction of the broad Huangpu River and the much smaller Soochow Creek. Before the Opium Wars, there had been no westerners at all in Shanghai. It was only when the victorious English forced the Manchu authorities to grant them concessions along the Huangpu that the influx of westerners began. Before then, Shanghai had been considered a backwater, certainly not as important as Soochow, a beautiful city of lakes and canals, or Canton. But after the incursion of the British, Shanghai began to change.

Although the Chinese had never really thought about it, Shanghai was ideally situated for trade, being almost exactly in the middle of the great China coast and near the mouth of the Yangtze River, which led far into the interior. Thus, while the Manchu Mandarins, in their usual myopic way, looked elsewhere, the Europeans poured in and westerners began making fortunes, importing opium and exporting tea and silk. Later the French, and then the Americans, came in. By the time Justin and Fiammetta arrived, Shanghai was a bona fide boom town.

But as was usual, the westerners came to exploit the Chinese, who were crammed into the walled Chinese City. And two worlds existed: the world of the west, privileged by concessions wrung out of the Manchus; and the world of the Chinese. The western world was increasingly pleasant, though sophisticates like Fiammetta found it provincial and boring. But there grew many of the amenities of western civilization: a library, scientific societies, amateur theatricals, teas and balls, and, most important to the horse-mad British, racing.

But the Chinese world became worse as the Chinese from the hinterlands began pouring into Shanghai, fleeing the dreaded Taipings, who had been menacing Shanghai for years. These refugees, desperately poor, crowded into the already overcrowded Chinese City, worsening the poverty and disease.

But also pouring into Shanghai were the freebooting soldiers and sailors from all over the world—the port of Shanghai could handle as many as two hundred ships a day. And it was from this ragtag pool of humanity that Justin hoped to draw his little army.

However, the next morning, as he waited impatiently at a table in the garden of his house on Bubbling Well Road, nobody came until ten o'clock. And then it was the diminutive Bantam Ben Lieberman, the young man from Alabama.

"You!" Justin exclaimed as his houseboy led Ben into the garden. "I remember you—yesterday at the Jade Phoenix!"

"That's right, Mr. Savage," Ben said in his drawl. "You saved my life, and that's why I'm here."

"I saved your life?"

"Sure. Man Mountain Mahoney hates my guts, and he was drunk enough to start shooting higher than my boots if you hadn't come along. So I owe you a big favor. And I thought I'd drop by and tell you why you ain't gonna get no recruits for your army."

"So there's a reason no one's showing up?"

"Yep."

"Come over here in the shade and tell me. By the way, what's your name?"

"Ben Lieberman. For obvious reasons, they call me Bantam Ben."

"Pleased to meet you, Ben."

Justin shook his hand, then led him to a corner of the walled garden where a clump of bamboo trees shaded a white wrought-iron table and two matching chairs. After they sat down, Bantam Ben said, "Did you ever hear of the Triads?"

"Of course. They're secret societies organized to fight the Manchus and try to throw them out of China. You could say, I suppose, that the Taipings are a Triad grown enormous."

"That's right, Mr. Savage. . . ."

"Justin."

"Okay, Justin. That's the way the Triads started out. They have a lot of secret rituals and all sort of funny stuff goes on—some say they drink each other's blood." He grinned. "Sorta like the Masons back home."

"I don't think George Washington ever drank blood."

"Well, you never know. Anyway, the Triads started out as patriots, but in the last few years a lot of secret societies has sprung up and they call themselves Triads, but what they really are is gangs. One gang calls itself the White Lotus Triad, and they're really nothing but crooks for hire. Well, last night, these leaflets started appearing all over the Chinese City where you went yesterday. They were printed in Chinese, English, French, Dutch, and Malay. This one's Chinese." He pulled a piece of paper from his pocket and handed it to Justin, who examined the Chinese ideograms.

"What does it say?" Justin asked.

"I thought you spoke Chinese?"

"I do—or at least Cantonese—but I can't read it."

"I can't either, but I was told it says, 'Whoever goes to Bubbling Well Road to work for the red-haired barbarian will face the wrath of the White Lotus.' " He grinned. "Sounds real mean, don't it? But it looks as if it worked."

Justin scowled. "Yes, it does." He crushed the paper into a ball. "But who the hell would want to stop me?"

"There's all sorts of rumors. Some say it's the Taipings . . . you know, General Li-shan has a lot of Taiping spies in Shanghai and you haven't been exactly secretive about what you're up to. So some say Li-shan hired the Triad to scare away recruits. Then there's another rumor."

"Which is?"

"That someone high up in the Forbidden City wants to keep you from getting an army."

"But that's crazy! The Emperor himself has authorized me to do what I want."

"Looks to me like you don't know how things work here in China. You never know who's for you or agin you. Presto, chango! Those who were for you are agin you and vice versa. Wonderful place, China. You wouldn't have a beer, by any chance? In Shanghai it's mighty hard to stay stone cold sober."

Justin, who had been trying to figure out this new wrinkle, snapped out of his reverie. He clapped his hands, and one of his houseboys appeared. "Two beer chop chop," he ordered in pidgin. "I don't understand Shanghaiese very well," he explained to Ben, referring to the local dialect.

"I don't understand *any* dialect very well, but I'm beginning to catch on to some of the basics. Chinese is sorta hard for a Southern boy."

"Excuse me for asking this, but I've never heard of any Jews in the South."

"Oh, there's some of us down there," Ben said, "but not many. Them slave-owners don't much cotton to my people, and the feeling is mutual. You see, my father left Germany twenty years ago to escape being conscripted into the army, and I say 'mazel tov' to him for doing it."

" 'Mazel tov'?" Justin looked confused.

"You know, cheers to him for getting out. That's Yiddish. So he ended up with me in New Orleans—my maw died on the trip over."

"I'm sorry."

"I hardly remember her. I was only two or three. Anyway, my pa started peddling. He had a real good head for it. We wandered all over the South buying and selling. . . ."

"What?"

"Pots, pans, cloth, sewing stuff . . . you name it. He did real well, and we settled down in Birmingham, where he opened a junkyard. And then, three years ago"—his normally cheerful expression clouded over—"he dropped dead, just like that." He snapped his fingers and paused a moment. It was obvious the memory of his father's death still hurt. Then he forced a smile and shrugged. "So I sold the junkyard and decided to see the world before I figure out what to do with myself. And here I am."

"How long have you been in Shanghai?"

"Almost four months. I didn't think I'd stay that long, but I'm making so damned much money at poker, I can't pull myself away. You see, I've told all these rubes I have a so-called 'system.' I have this little pad on the poker table and I write down figures in it all the time. It drives the other players so crazy, they make damned fool mistakes, and I win."

Justin laughed. "So your system is to *pretend* you have a system, which rattles them? That's damned clever!"

Ben grinned and touched his head. *"Yiddischer kopf,"* he said.

"What's that?"

"Smart."

"Mm, I see what you mean." The houseboy came into the garden with two beers on a tray, which he served. Justin raised his glass. "Well, here's to you, Ben. And I sure appreciate your coming over to tell me what's going on about the White Lotus Triad. *Mazel tov*—did I get it right?"

"Absolutely—*mazel tov.*" He drank. "I hear this General Li-shan has your daughter—is that true?"

"Yes."

"Listen: we'll figure out some way to get her."

"Did you say 'we'?"

"Sure. You saved my life, so I owe you. I'll work for you, and you don't even have to pay me. This way, maybe I can get my ass out of Shanghai. Ah: love this beer! Guess there's more German in me than I like to think."

He wiped his chin and leaned back in the chair. Justin eyed him, thinking he liked this diminutive man who had dreamed up a nonexistent poker system that worked. And something told him Ben Lieberman was a fighting Bantam.

"Maybe," he said, "I could use a *Yiddischer kopf*—did I say it right?"

"Sure. You catch on quick. I think you may have one yourself."

They both laughed.

That morning, at the double hour of the monkey, Justin felt something sharp at his throat. He swam up out of a dreamless sleep to realize it was a knife.

"Don't move, barbarian," a soft voice said in Cantonese, "or you're a dead man."

A tall young man was leaning over him, holding the dagger at his throat. Someone had lit one of the lamps in the bedroom, and Justin saw through sleep-sticky eyes that the man had long black hair and thus was a *chang-mao,* or long-haired Taiping rebel. His eyeballs moving rapidly, he saw that there were two other *chang-maos* in the bedroom, both holding old-fashioned rifles aimed at him. They might have been old-fashioned, but Justin knew that their firepower could blow his head off. His eyeballs rolled to the left, where he saw Fiammetta sitting up, holding the sheet up before her nakedness, fear in her beautiful eyes.

"Who are you?" Justin whispered.

"I am General Li-shan," the warrior said. "I became Chang-mei's lover after you abandoned her."

"I didn't abandon her, I went to England. . . ."

The knife bit deeper. "Chang-mei said you abandoned her. Bitterly, she turned her love from you to me. I was the lover of her dreams, I brought her to the heights of ecstasy. And before she died, she entrusted Julie to me. Julie is mine. *I* am her father, not you. Therefore, barbarian, I have come to warn you to leave China tomorrow. If you do not swear to do so, I will kill you and this blond-haired barbarian strumpet, your wife."

Justin was sweating heavily. He heard Fiammetta whimpering with fear.

"I don't believe you," he said. "Chang-mei loved me. And I am the father of Julie. She's mine."

The blade bit deeper. A thin line of blood began to seep from Justin's throat, oozing over the blade.

"You are trying to recruit an army to attack Soochow and take Julie from me. You fool. Before I would give Julie up to you, I would kill her and myself."

"Then you love her?"

"Of course. She is Chang-mei's daughter, and I loved Chang-mei and swore to her I would protect Julie. But enough of this talk: will you give me your word you will abandon this foolish quest of yours? The only reason I am giving you this chance instead of killing you outright is that your blood flows in Julie's veins."

"Justin," Fiammetta said in a fear-choked voice, "who are they? What do they want?" She of course didn't understand the Chinese.

"It's Li-shan. He wants me to swear to leave China, or he'll kill me."

"Then for God's sake, swear it!"

"What is she saying?" Li-shan asked.

"She's telling me to agree."

"She's a smart barbarian. Give me your word. I will trust you because Chang-mei told me that except for betraying her, you were a man of honor."

"I didn't betray her . . ."

Two shots rang out in rapid succession. The two Taiping guards grunted and fell to the floor, dead. Ben appeared in the bedroom door aiming his gun at Li-shan. "Tell him to take his knife from your throat or I'll blow his brains out," he said to Justin.

Li-shan didn't need a translation. He stood up, removing the dagger and raising his hands.

"Who is this?" he said to Justin, who jumped out of bed and ran to one of the guards, picking up his rifle. Like Fiammetta, he was naked. He aimed the rifle at Li-shan.

"My bodyguard," Justin said. "I hired him this afternoon. Ben, you just earned a raise."

"You're not paying me anything."

"I am now. Take his dagger. I'll cover him."

Ben obeyed, coming to Li-shan and taking the dagger from his hand.

"Fiammetta, darling," Justin said, "go wake the cook. Tell him to make some tea. We're going to have a little chat with General Li-shan, who has just saved me a lot of trouble."

33   "I'LL SAY ONE THING: LIFE with you is never boring," Fiammetta said five minutes later, returning from the kitchen. She had put on a robe. Justin was dressing, having dragged the bodies of the two Taipings out of the bedroom into the garden.

"I guess you're right," he said, pulling on his boots. "I'm sorry you were frightened."

"It gave my blood a good tingle. And so did Li-shan."

"What do you mean?"

"I can see why Chang-mei ran off with him. He's terribly dashing."

Justin stood up to stick his shirttail in his pants. He frowned. "More dashing than me?"

She smiled, putting her hand on his cheek. "Never. But it's fun to see you jealous." She kissed him. "It doesn't say much for the security in Shanghai, when Li-shan can stroll into our bedroom and put a knife to your throat. Does it hurt?"

She ran her finger lightly over the thin line of blood, which had clotted to black.

"No, but I'll admit I was a little uncomfortable. Come on: let's have a talk with Li-shan. And don't you think about running off with him."

"You never know: it sounds terribly romantic."

They went into the living room where Ben, an unlit cigar in his mouth, was sitting in a chair aiming his gun at Li-shan, who was standing by a window looking out at the moonlit garden. A terrified houseboy brought in a pot of tea and some cups, setting them down on a table. He was trembling so, eyeing Li-shan, that he almost dropped a cup. Then he scurried out of the room.

"Some tea?" Justin offered politely.

Li-shan turned to look at him. "I don't drink with my enemy," he said.

"Perhaps we're not enemies. We have several things in common. For instance, we both loved Chang-mei." He poured Fiammetta a cup of tea. "And we both love Julie. It seems to me there's a more intelligent way for us to work out our differences than threatening to kill each other."

"If you trust me enough to talk," Li-shan said, "tell your man to put down his gun."

"I never said I trust you."

"Then kill me. We have no room for negotiation. I will not give up Julie. I swore to Chang-mei I would raise her and protect her. You mean nothing to Julie. She doesn't even know you exist."

"But I *do* exist, and I'm her father. Did you hire the White Lotus Triad to frighten off my recruits?"

Li-shan's hawk face looked confused. "No. Why would I do that? I am a prince, the son of Chung Wang, the Faithful King. I wouldn't stoop to hire thieves to do my work."

Then it must be someone from the Forbidden City, Justin thought, someone less finicky than Li-shan. But who?

"Then you are a brave man," he said aloud, "to come into Shanghai with only two guards. If the Manchus caught you . . ."

"Yes, I know. The Death of a Thousand Cuts. I don't fear the Manchus. My father and I have beaten them dozens of times. Their soldiers are cowards and their generals corrupt. I came to Shanghai because I wanted to see what Julie's father looked like. Now I see you are as ugly as all the foreign devils. Fortunately she had a beautiful mother."

Justin, who was not used to being called ugly, found his nose a bit out of joint.

"What color is her hair?" he asked. "The last time I saw her, it was just fuzz."

"Her hair is a rich dark brown."

"I remember that her eyes were an unusual color: amber."

"Their color is not Chinese, and her eyes are almost round, like yours. She is a half-breed. Normally I would detest her. But"—he sighed, and for a moment Justin saw that this warrior, the famed Li-shan, had a soft side—"the child has wormed her way into my heart." His coldness returned. "You will not have her, barbarian. You have no claim on her. You abandoned her."

"That's not true, but I can see I can't convince you. So I'll make a deal with you, Li-shan. If you arrange to have Julie brought to me, I'll release you and you'll be free to return to Soochow."

"And if I don't agree?"

"I turn you over to the Manchus."

Li-shan spat on the matted floor. "I laugh at you, roundeye," he said. "Send for the Manchus."

"Li-shan, be reasonable!" Justin shouted, anger overwhelming him. "Julie's my daughter—you have no claim on her except that you raised her! Yours is the claim of an amah!"

"And what's your claim?" Li-shan shouted back. "You, who don't even know the color of her hair! All you did was makee jig-jig with her mother and then run off to England! Yours is the claim of a dog in heat!"

" 'Makee jig-jig'?" said Ben, surprised to hear the pidgin words for making love.

"Justin, what is going on?" Fiammetta asked impatiently.

"We're getting nowhere," he said in English. "The man's as stubborn as a mule."

"I will fight you," Li-shan said softly, a smile on his face. "And the survivor takes Julie."

Justin turned back to him. "The 'survivor'?"

Li-shan spread his hands. "The loser dies."

"What weapons are you talking about?"

"No weapons. Just my feet and my hands. I am a master in kung fu."

"But I'm not."

"Then you can choose any weapon you want except a gun. I'll still beat you. And then, with one blow of my hand, I'll break your miserable neck. And it will give me great pleasure to do so, round-eyed foreign devil."

"You're pretty sure of yourself, Li-shan. But on the outside chance that I won, how would I get Julie out of Soochow? No thanks, your deal stinks. You're my prisoner, and I'm going to swap you for my daughter. Your father the Chung Wang will give up Julie to get back his number-one son."

A look of fury came over Li-shan's face. He let out a banshee howl and leapt across the room at Ben, his right leg hitting him in the chest, knocking him and his chair over backward. At the same time, Ben fired, hitting Li-shan in the stomach as he fell over backward. Li-shan groaned as he rolled on the floor, holding his stomach. Ben scrambled to his feet, aiming the gun at Li-shan, but Justin grabbed his arm. "Don't kill him!" he said. "Dead, he's useless."

Li-shan was lying on his back, blood spreading on his shirt and starting to trickle out of his mouth.

"If you want him alive," Ben said, "you'd better get a doctor, fast."

Justin was already halfway to the door.

The eunuch An Te-hai carried a long, exquisitely carved walnut box through the halls of the Pavilion of Permanent Satisfaction in the Forbidden City. He was accompanied by Yehenala, who had a look of intense excitement in her kohl-rimmed eyes. When they reached the door to the Emperor's bedroom, which was guarded by two more eunuchs, Yehenala took the walnut box from An Te-hai. The eunuchs opened the door, and she went inside where the Hsien-feng Emperor was lolling on his bed in an alcoholic haze.

"This slave brings interesting news from the south," Yehenala said, crossing the room to the bed. "It was just delivered by courier from Shanghai." She placed the walnut box on a low table beside the Emperor's bed. Also on the table was a small silver oil lamp burning with a low flame. She knelt beside the table and opened the box, revealing a long ivory pipe and six opium pellets, which looked like molasses.

"What news?" asked the Emperor, his bloodshot eyes fixing on the opium.

"The red-haired barbarian has captured Li-shan in Shanghai."

A glimmer of interest came into the Emperor's eyes.

"How?"

"Li-shan had sneaked into the city with two guards to warn the barbarian away. But the barbarian had hired a bodyguard who had moved into his house. The bodyguard killed Li-shan's men and shot Li-shan in the stomach. The cursed rebel hovers between life and death in the barbarian's house."

She had turned up the flame of the oil lamp. Now she inserted one of the opium pellets onto a long iron needle and placed the pellet above the flame.

"This is great news indeed," said the Emperor, "and justifies Our faith in

Prince I's plan to send the barbarian against the rebels. We will bring the long-haired son of the Chung Wang to Peking in a cage and display him to Our public as Our torturers make him scream with pain."

"If this slave may be so bold as to make a suggestion?"

"Of course, Nala. We always welcome your views."

"My Lord may recall that Savage, the red-haired barbarian, did not go out to capture Li-shan. In fact, the reports coming from Shanghai indicate that he has not been able to raise one recruit for his so-called army. The truth is that Li-shan came to him."

"We fail to see the difference? Li-shan is captured just the same."

"It is only because the difference is obvious, and My Lord, whose mind pierces the secrets of the Universe, looks for the subtle."

"This is true," said the Emperor, more than a little confused by Yehenala's circuitous way of calling him a ninny.

"The point, Divinity, is that for all Prince I's talk of helping the Dragon Throne with this American, rumor has reached these lowly ears that Prince I's true objective is to use the American to help him usurp the Dragon Throne."

The room was filling with the sickly sweet smell of the heating opium. Unlike tobacco, opium could not burn.

"Beware, Nala," said the Emperor. "You speak of Our cousin."

"The Lord of Ten Thousand Years may beat this slave, but she feels compelled to tell Him what she hears for His own divine safety." She placed the heated pellet in the bowl of the ivory pipe and passed it to the Emperor with both hands. Hsien-feng took the pipe and put it to his mouth, taking three deep inhales on the smoke.

"Go on, speak," he said. "We listen."

"Instead of immediately handing Li-shan over to our authorities, as any righteously faithful ally of the Dragon Throne should have, the red-haired barbarian instead asked the American Consul in Shanghai to issue a demand to the Heavenly King in Nanking for the trade of the barbarian's daughter for Li-shan. Furthermore, the head of the British armed forces in China, General Sir John Michel, has stationed a dozen of his own British troops around the barbarian's house on Bubbling Well Road to protect him and his wife from any prospective raids from the Chung Wang to rescue his son."

The Emperor frowned. "It is complicated, Nala. Our poor brain is weary from the many duties of Our office. Do not go too fast."

"This slave would rather suffer the Death of a Thousand Cuts than confuse My Lord. Yet events are happening at a rapid rate and this slave feels it her duty, low as she is, to reveal all to Your Majesty."

Hsien-feng sighed and took another puff on the pipe. How he hated listening to all these tedious details! If he could only be alone with his opium pipe and his wine bowl to enjoy the delights of oblivion . . . "You are right," he mumbled. "Go on."

"This slave's point, stupid and obvious as it is, is that the loyalty of the barbarian as well as the loyalty of Prince I is placed in a dubious light by these actions. Furthermore, the actions of the American Consul, by appealing to the Heavenly King to trade the barbarian's daughter for Li-shan, strike these lowly ears as an unforgivable interference in the domestic affairs and tranquility of the Celestial Empire."

"There is truth in what you say, but what can We do? We are weak, Nala—so weak! And the foreign devils in Shanghai have all along trod a treacherous path with relation to the Taipings. Neither We nor Our ministers of state know which side they are truly on, the Taipings' or Ours. One moment they side with the cursed rebels because the Taipings claim to be Christians, though the real reason is that the Heavenly King has promised not to interfere with their devilish foreign trade. The next moment they side with Us because We are, after all, the legitimate government of China. The white devils are two-faced."

"How beautifully and concisely Your divine wisdom sums up this complex issue, Lord of Ten Thousand Years! How can You speak of Your wits being tired?"

"Ah, but they are, Nala, they are. But how do the foreign devils side in this instance?"

"Alas, they are siding with the barbarian, because the westerners have a strange affection for girl children, and they wish Savage to be reunited with his daughter."

"We will never understand the barbarian mind. All this fuss over a girl."

"They are indeed curious creatures, Lord of Ten Thousand Years. However, it is this slave's thought—which is probably unworthy of mention—that perhaps right now it would seem to be a propitious moment to show a sign of strength."

"You mean to demand that Li-shan be turned over to Us?"

"No, Master, though that is of course the subtle thing to do, a thought worthy of Your divine wisdom. My poor intelligence, chained to the obvious course, is that now we should allow Jung-lu to attack Soochow. With Li-shan gone, the morale of the Taipings must be low. Jung-lu could take the city and drive a stake into the very heart of the odious rebellion."

"But where is the Chung Wang?" the Emperor asked, taking another languid puff of the pipe. "And why has he not replied to the American Consul's demand? It would seem to Us that the Chung Wang would gladly trade the girl child for his number-one son."

"Alas, there is another tedious complication to weary the mind of the Lord of Ten Thousand Years. The Heavenly King is jealous of his great general, the Chung Wang. Our spies in Nanking tell us that the Heavenly King, who, as You know, has drenched himself in the blood of his generals in his insane lust to maintain control of his abominable rebellion, now thinks that the Chung Wang plots against him. And indeed, the reports of our spies suggest there may be some truth to this. Of all the Taiping dogs, the Chung Wang is not only the best general but the only general who has so far refrained from looting and pillaging the countryside. Thus, he is the only Taiping who retains the affections of the peasants. It is not out of the question that Chung Wang could turn against the Heavenly King and take over the rebellion.

"For this reason, tiresome as these explanations must be to My Lord . . . the Heavenly King has refused the Chung Wang to answer the demand of the American Consul. We can only assume that this has further embittered the Chung Wang, who is presently fighting our armies north of Nanking. Thus, if Jung-lu could take Soochow, the Chung Wang would have every reason to turn against the Heavenly King, and the odious rebellion could eat itself."

"Ah, if only you were right, Nala! Then peace and unity could return to China, and We could confront the foreign devils without this cancer eating at Our guts."

"My Lord, Jung-lu is strong, thanks to Your wisdom and foresightedness. Jung-lu could be our greatest general! This slave beseeches You to give him a chance! Let him march against Soochow!"

It had taken her days of cajoling, suggesting, and innumerable Jade Girl Playing the Flutes to get the vacillating Emperor to agree to setting up a task force equipped with modern rifles under the command of Jung-lu. Now her heart pounded as she waited for the words that could send her lover with his army south to Soochow and, if he were victorious, further strengthen her grip on the Dragon Throne.

"Let it be done," the Emperor finally said.

The red dewdrop on Yehenala's lower lip curved into a smile.

34 LI-SHAN SAT UP IN his bed in Justin's house, a bandage over his stomach where Ben had shot him five days before. Fiammetta had just brought him a cup of hot tea. The Taiping warrior had never seen a roundeye woman up close before, and he had certainly never seen a blonde. As he watched the curvaceous Italian, whose ripe beauty was so different from that of Chinese women, the lust within him almost, but not quite, made him forget the pain in his stomach where the English doctor had removed the bullet.

Fiammetta, who was wearing a white cotton dress tight-fitting from the waist up, as was the fashion, eyed Li-shan as she stood beside his bed. "I have an idea what you're thinking," she said softly, in English, knowing he didn't understand her. Her eyes traveled over his broad naked shoulders and muscled chest. She had to admit that if she weren't so blissfully happy with Justin, she would be . . . interested.

"Tha . . . thank you," he said, taking the teacup from her. She had been trying to teach him a few English phrases. The small bedroom that gave out onto the walled garden was hot, even though it was late November. The cool weather was slow arriving this year. In the garden, two of the twelve British soldiers assigned to guard the house against any possible attempt on the Taipings' part to rescue Li-shan were standing, smoking Manila cheroots, talking to Ben, whose bedroom was next to Li-shan's. The house was certainly well protected from attack from the outside.

But what was troubling Fiammetta was the danger inside her brain. She loved Justin, she was carrying his child . . . and yet why, in a house full of servants, had she insisted on bringing the tea to Li-shan's bedroom herself?

She knew the answer, which deeply troubled her. The Chinese warrior with his un-Chinese hawk nose, his fierce eyes, and his sculpted body was as exotic to her as Justin, the young American, had once been. And she knew from the way his eyes feasted on her that the attraction was mutual.

"You are nothing but trouble to me," she said in English, a note of annoyance in her voice. "I'm in love with my husband." He didn't understand the words, but she thought he could read her mind. He smiled as he sipped the tea, watching her. After a moment, he set the teacup down on his bed table and reached out a hand to take hers. She tried to withdraw it, but he held on to her, not too tightly, but firmly.

"Makee jig-jig?" he whispered.

Fiammetta had learned enough pidgin to know what that meant. She jerked her hand from his and slapped his face. Then she hurried out of the room. As she closed the door, she looked back at his bed.

He was smiling at her.

She turned and went into the garden just as Justin and Lieutenant Barclay Strand came through the moon gate that led to Bubbly Wells Road. Lieutenant Strand, a sandy-haired native of Devon, was in charge of the detachment sent to protect the house by Sir John Michel. When Justin spotted Fiammetta, he and Barclay Strand came over to her. Justin was holding a copy of the *North China Herald.*

"Darling," he said, "the Emperor has sent an army to attack Soochow."

"It's under the command of Colonel Jung-lu," Barclay Strand added.

Fiammetta's eyes brightened. "Isn't he the one they say is Yehenala's lover?"

Young Barclay Strand looked properly embarrassed. "Well, um, yes, they *do* say that. Shocking, these Chinese. Can you imagine Queen Victoria taking one of her Coldstream Guards as a lover? Unthinkable, actually. But this whole thing is a rum business, Chinese attacking Chinese, can't tell which side anyone's on."

"Well, *I'm* on my daughter's side," Justin said firmly. "And this news has thrown everything into a cocked hat. If the Manchus conquer Soochow, God knows what they'll do to Julie."

"They wouldn't harm a child," Fiammetta said.

"Wouldn't bank on that, ma'am," Barclay Strand said, his white pith helmet protecting his ruddy face with its swooping mustaches from the sun. "These Manchus are beasts. They'll loot, pillage, and torture and think it's a bloody picnic—begging your pardon, ma'am, for my language. A man forgets his manners in this beastly climate."

Ben joined them from the other side of the garden. "Did you hear about Jung-lu?" he asked.

"I was just telling Fiammetta," Justin said. "You all wait out here. I'm going to tell Li-shan. It should be interesting to hear his reaction."

"Justin . . ." Fiammetta said, intending to tell him about Li-shan's insufferable behavior to her a few minutes before.

"Yes?"

She changed her mind. This was no time to be bringing up such matters. "Nothing, darling. Go on."

Justin looked at his wife a moment, then went into the small bedroom where Li-shan was still sipping his tea. The Taiping warrior turned hostile eyes on the American. Justin came to the foot of his bed.

"The Emperor has sent an army to attack Soochow," he said. "Under the command of Colonel Jung-lu."

Li-shan set down his teacup, waving a fly from his nose.

"He will never succeed," he said calmly. "Jung-lu is a warrior of the bedroom."

Justin held up the newspaper. "The *Herald* says he has four thousand troops and ten cannons. Some bedroom."

Li-shan's defiant expression softened slightly.

"My father will never allow Soochow to fall," he said.

"Your father is fighting in the north. And why hasn't he responded to my offer? Because your leader, the Heavenly King, has forbidden him to."

"That's guesswork on your part."

"Perhaps, but it's what everyone in Shanghai is saying. Do you deny that the Heavenly King fears your father? He's killed off every one of his other top generals—don't you think he would kill your father if he dared? Or do you deny that the Heavenly King is mad?"

Li-shan frowned. "No, I can't deny that. The power and debauchery have twisted his mind. But why would he aggravate my father needlessly . . . ?"

"Perhaps he is forcing him to do something he doesn't want to do by using you as bait?"

"Yes, that's possible. . . . So they say the Heavenly King is forbidding my father to trade Julie for me?"

Justin noted with some satisfaction that Li-shan's previous blanket refusal to agree to such a deal now seemed to soften somewhat.

"That's what they say. Li-shan, you may hate my guts, which is your privilege, but you'll have to agree that under the circumstances I've treated you decently. Most important, I haven't turned you over to the Manchus, which would have meant certain death for you. You may sneer at death, but the Manchus know how to do it in the grand manner. You also may sneer at my offer to swap you for Julie, but it's not a bad deal for you even if it means your losing Julie. The point is, if Jung-lu takes Soochow, there won't be any Julie for either of us."

"What do you mean?"

"You know damned well they'll kill her."

Li-shan said nothing, but the look on his face told what he was thinking. He was seeing in his mind's eye the adorable child he had come to love.

Justin saw that he was making some headway. "Can't we forget our differences for a moment? We both love Julie. Isn't there some way you could help me get her out of Soochow? Then we can make some sort of agreement about who's to have her. Maybe we'll even fight for her, as you suggested. But we *have* to save her."

Li-shan eyed his adversary. As hurtful as it was for him to admit it, the barbarian spoke the truth. Julie had to be saved, and he was powerless, his wound still so painful he could not leave his bed. He closed his eyes a moment, thinking. Then he began softly speaking. At first, Justin didn't follow his thread.

"Two centuries ago," Li-shan spoke, "before the Manchu hordes invaded

China and destroyed our own Ming Dynasty, there ruled one of the last Ming, or Chinese, Emperors, the Wan-li Emperor. When as a young man he ascended the Dragon Throne, he decided he would build for himself a great tomb that would be a monument to his reign. The tomb took six years to build and cost eight million ounces of silver. When it was finished, Wan-li, still a young man, gave himself a great party in his own tomb. Thirty years later, when he actually died, he was buried there with his two empresses and a great treasure. The tomb was called *Ting Ling,* the Royal Tomb of Security. No one today knows where the tomb is." He opened his eyes. "It has been one of the goals of my life not only to throw the cursed Manchus out of China, but one day to find the tomb of Wan-li, which the scrolls say is sealed forever by an ingenious device that prevents it from being opened from the outside, and recover the treasure. It is morbidly fascinating, don't you think, to give a party in one's own tomb? Imagine the thoughts that must have gone through Wan-li's young mind as he consorted with his concubines in the very place where now his bones have lain for two centuries. Is it not a strange world we live in where the river of time can turn young men into skeletons?"

"Yes it is," Justin said, rather confused. "But we'll both be skeletons before you tell me what this has to do with Julie."

"Patience, barbarian. China's culture is many thousands of years old. You Americans are barely a century old. You must learn that there are many paths to enlightenment. While he was still a young man, Wan-li came to Soochow, a city he loved because of its beautiful canals. They say there is a city in the west built on canals . . . ?"

"Yes, Venice. In Italy."

"Ah, Italy." He paused. "Where's Italy?"

Justin gestured with impatience. "In Europe. Go on!"

"As he traveled to Soochow in his palanquin, Wan-li spotted a beautiful girl working in a rice paddy. Even though she was a peasant, her face shone with the beauty of the moon. The Emperor was smitten, and he sent the captain of his guard to bring the girl to his palace in Soochow.

"That night, she was smuggled into the Emperor's bedchamber and they made love. He called her the Moon Concubine. But because the Emperor's mother would have been outraged if she had found out her son was making love to a low-born peasant girl, Wan-li could not bring her into his harem and was forced to keep her a secret. He instructed his guards to dig a secret gate or tunnel, through the city wall of Soochow so that the Moon Concubine could come to him each night without his mother, the Dowager Empress, finding out.

The gate was built, with a secret door on the outside of the city wall. It was known as the Gate of the Secret Concubine. It still exists." He paused. "I know where it is."

He looked meaningfully at Justin, who began to understand.

35   "HE'S EVEN DRAWN ME A map of Soochow's wall," Justin said an hour later as he unrolled a scroll of paper on the dining-room table, "showing where the Gate of the Secret Concubine is. Look."

Standing beside him at the table were Fiammetta, Ben, and Barclay Strand. They stared at the crude map Li-shan had painted for Justin with brush and ink.

"Soochow is situated on the Tai Hu, or Great Lake, and the Grand Canal, which connects Hongchow to the northern provinces," Justin went on. "The town, like most Chinese towns, is surrounded by thick walls that zigzag to follow the interior canals. Cargo isn't off-loaded outside Soochow, as it is in most cities. Rather, the boats go through the great Water Gate, and then into the city to off-load.

"Most of the city is surrounded by a wide moat, but at one place, here"—he pointed to a place Li-shan had marked with a cross—"the moat is narrow, and it's here, hidden by a clump of bamboo trees, where the Gate of the Secret Concubine is found. Li-shan told me that it had been bricked up after the Wan-li Emperor died two hundred years ago. But recently, his father had it reopened."

"Why?" asked Barclay.

"The Chung Wang is smart. In case Soochow ever fell to the Manchus, he and Li-shan have a way to sneak out of the city."

"Clever," said Ben.

"Li-shan says that once I'm through the gate into the city, his father's palace is ten minutes away in what is called the Garden of the Humble Administrator."

"Why can't the Chinese give a place a plain old name, instead of making it so darned flowery?" grumbled Ben.

"Because the Chinese are very poetic. The interior of the town isn't guarded at night since they rely on the city walls to protect them," Justin went on. "Li-shan says I can easily get into the palace, which isn't guarded either, go to the nursery, overpower Julie's amah, and take Julie away with me."

"But, Justin," Fiammetta said, "how can you possibly trust this Li-shan, who'd love nothing better than to see you dead?"

"I trust him because he knows what I know: that Julie's in danger from the Manchus. He wants her out of there as much as I do."

"Then why doesn't he simply give you a letter to whoever's in charge of the place, telling him to give Julie to you?"

"Because he doesn't trust him. Soochow is as filled with traitors and spies as every other city in China. He tells me he thinks his second in command is disloyal to his father, the Chung Wang—which may be the reason the Heavenly King is preventing the Chung Wang from answering the American Consul's request for the swap with Julie. As it is now, the Heavenly King has one of his men in charge of Soochow, while he could never completely trust Li-shan, who is the Chung Wang's son. No, I realize I may be a fool to trust Li-shan, and there's obviously some risk involved, but I can't think of any way to get my daughter out of Soochow other than to go in and get her. Which is what I'm going to do."

"What we're gonna do," Ben said.

"No, Ben, I can't ask you to take the risk. . . ."

"Hey, Justin, you're not askin'! It's my job to protect you. Besides, this sounds too good to miss—the Gate of the Secret Concubine? Wow! Now there's where I say the Chinese are right to think up flowery names."

Fiammetta burst into tears and ran out of the room into the garden. Justin hurried after her.

"Darling, what's wrong?" he asked, coming to her under the bamboo trees and taking her in his arms.

"I'm frightened for you, that's what's wrong!" she sobbed. "Justin, this sounds so . . . crazy! Surely there must be a safer way to get Julie out! And you haven't given the Chung Wang enough time to respond to the Consul. Wait a few more days, at least. You're only assuming the Heavenly King is preventing him from answering—how can you be sure? You owe it to me and our baby to be more careful."

A look of guilt came over his face. He kissed her, passionately. "You're right, my darling," he said. "I have to be careful. I'll wait."

"How long?"

"A week. But then, if there's no answer, I'll have to do it. Because by another week, Jung-lu's Peking army will be close to Soochow."

She hugged him tightly, kissing him as passionately as he had kissed her, her passion tinged with guilt over her attraction to Li-shan.

"I love you," she said. "If I lost you, I'd die."

"You're not going to lose me, and neither of us is going to die. We're both going to live to be cranky old people and have dozens of grandchildren."

Despite his bravado, he thought of the Wan-li Emperor throwing the lavish party in his own tomb, and the Angel of Death flew low to brush him with its icy wings.

"There it is: Soochow!" Justin said to Ben eight nights later. They were on horseback atop Tiger Hill, looking down at the ancient city with its huge crenellated Water Gate and its curious walls. Only a few lights shone in the city, for it was the Hour of the Monkey, a cold, clear night with a half moon that made the moat outside the walls and the canals inside shimmer like silver snakes. Justin was wearing a fur-lined parka he had bought at Jardine-Matheson, the great English-owned emporium in Shanghai. Both men carried in holsters .36-caliber Colt Old Model Navy revolvers weighing two pounds ten ounces each, manufactured by the famous American Samuel Colt. Colt's guns were the most popular guns in the world because of their deadly accuracy. Justin hoped he wouldn't have to use his gun, but it was comforting to know he had the best.

Since no reply had come from the Chung Wang about the American Consul's offer, Justin and Ben had set out the previous morning from Shanghai, riding along the Wushan River that led directly west fifty miles to Soochow through countryside rich with rice paddies and orchards. This was the lushest part of China, often called the "breadbasket" of the Celestial Empire. Indeed, the gigantic Grand Canal had been dug in the sixth and seventh centuries, at a cost of untold thousands of lives, just so the rich bounty of the south could be brought to the north. Justin and Ben could see the Grand Canal below, coming from Wu-chiang to the south, then turning to the northwest as it left Soochow on its way to the Yangtze. They could also see the thousand-year-old White Pagoda that stood above the underwater grotto that supposedly held the tomb of Soochow's founder, the King of Wu. In the moonlight, the fabled city, the most beautiful in China, was magical.

"Shall we?" asked Ben. "I'm rarin' to go! Gate of the Secret Concubine—hot damn!"

Justin suppressed a laugh as he spurred his horse. He had become fond of Ben, whose "good ole boy" Southern humor and sense of adventure were comforting. He was glad Ben had insisted on coming with him. Under the circumstances, his extra gun and sharp head were useful.

The two horses rode down Tiger Hill and stopped under a grove of trees not far from the moat. Even though it had turned unusually cold for the semitropical climate of Kiangsu Province, the trees still had their leaves, so they were out of the moonlight. The moat was perhaps twenty feet wide. On the other side loomed the dark walls of the city. All seemed quiet as Soochow slept.

"Li-shan said there's a small stone shrine opposite the secret gate," Justin said in a soft voice. "Let's ride north till we find it and stay in the shade of the trees as much as we can. I don't see any guards on the wall, but I assume they're there."

They proceeded beneath the trees along the side of the moat, which varied in width and changed direction as the great wall zigged to the east and zagged to the west. Finally, they saw a stone shrine, about six feet high.

"That's it," Justin said. "Let's tie up our horses. Can you swim?"

"Yeah, but that water looks mighty chilly. Shit, Justin, we're gonna freeze our asses."

They dismounted, tied their horses to trees, then took off their clothes. Justin left his parka with his horse, trying to reduce his weight load as much as possible. Shivering in the cold, they tied their clothes in a bundle, putting their guns in the middle, then strapping their bundles with their belts.

"How deep is the moat?" Ben asked.

"Li-shan told me I could wade it with my head above water."

"Which means I'll have to dog-paddle. Which means you're gonna have to carry both bundles. Price of bein' tall, my friend."

They hurried through the moonlight to the edge of the moat, where Justin took both bundles and held them on his head with both hands. He stepped into the moat, grimacing at the cold water, and immediately sank to his waist.

"Be careful," he whispered to Ben. "It'll almost be over your head here."

"Yeah, I see. Here goes." He sat on the edge, then let himself into the water. "Shit," he whispered, "I'm gonna freeze my pecker off."

"Ssh."

Moving slowly, Justin proceeded into the moat, the water rapidly coming up to his chin. Ben began dog-paddling. They moved across the moat, which was narrower than usual here, toward a small islet that jutted from the base of the wall. Whether it was natural or artificial, Justin didn't know; but it was covered with bushes, as Li-shan had described to him, and from the bushes jutted a clump of bamboo trees. Reaching it, Justin put the bundles under a bush, then hoisted himself out of the water. Turning, he reached a hand down to Ben, helping him out. Fortunately, the high wall blocked the moon, so they were in the dark. Quickly they dried themselves off with their shirts, wrung them out, then got dressed. "So far, so good," Justin whispered, buckling his holster on. "Now let's find the Gate of the Secret Concubine."

"She must have been a secret *wet* concubine."

"I'm sure the Emperor was a sport and bought her a boat."

"Justin, not to get personal, but what's that weird-lookin' thing on your ass? That M with a circle around it?"

"It's a birthmark. Isn't it pretty? Come on."

He made his way through the bushes to the wall, which loomed fifty feet above them. The wall, which was made of big, handhewn stones, was studded with rows of thick, upturned iron spikes a foot apart, each row alternated with the next above so that it would be impossible to avoid stepping on one if someone were foolish enough to try to crawl down.

"Why the hell are the spikes turned up?" Ben whispered.

"Li-shan told me it was to prevent anyone from the city escaping."

"Nice friendly place."

"One of the spikes opens the secret door."

Justin grabbed one and tried to turn it to the right. "One of them will turn to the right," he whispered to Ben. "One on the third row up."

They both started testing the spikes. The fourth one that Ben tried actually did turn.

"Jesus. . . ."

A section of the wall the size of a door moved silently out, pushing him back into a bush, then slid to the right, revealing a dark tunnel.

"You did it!" Justin whispered, hurrying up beside him. "Good work."

"You're goin' in there? It looks spooky."

"Yeah, I know."

Justin went inside the narrow stone tunnel. The air was musty. Ben came in behind him. The massive stone door slid silently shut. Total blackness.

"Shit. Justin?"

"I'm here. Come on, there's nothing to worry about."

"Then why am I worried? Do you know how to open that door?"

"No, but we'll figure it out."

"Why did I ever leave Alabama?"

The two walked through the blackness, Justin's hands outstretched to avoid bumping into anything. However, the tunnel was straight. After five minutes, his hands touched cold, clammy stone.

"This is the other end," he said to Ben, who bumped into him.

"Thank God. How do you open it?"

"I don't know. Li-shan didn't tell me."

"He's a big help."

Justin's hands roamed over the stone until his left hand bumped into an iron ring. "This must be it," he whispered. "It's a ring. I'll turn it to the right. . . ."

He did so. A door, much like the other, moved silently outward, then slid to the left.

Twenty *chang-mao* Taiping warriors, five of them holding torches, were standing outside, aiming their rifles at Justin and Ben.

"Raise your hands," said their leader, a tall man in a yellow silk robe with a curious, turbanlike yellow cone on his head.

"This wasn't part of the plan," Ben gulped as he followed Justin's lead and raised his hands. He didn't understand the Cantonese, but the guns did the translating.

"Welcome to Soochow, Mr. Savage," said the leader. "We've been expecting you. I am Li-shan's father, the Chung Wang."

36

"HEY, JUSTIN, ARE THEY GONNA kill us?"

Ben asked the question as he stood on a stone trying to peer out of the barred window of the cell the Chung Wang and his Taiping guards had locked them in three hours before. The sun was just rising, and Ben was trying to get a look outside. But he was so short he couldn't quite see over the stone sill. Now he grabbed two of the window bars and hoisted himself up by muscle power. Peering through the window, he saw that outside was a stone courtyard where two prisoners stood in wooden cages, their hands locked at neck level in *cangues.*

"Of course they're not going to kill us," Justin said. He was sitting on the other stone, the two stones being the only seats in the cell. Presumably, he and Ben would have to sleep on the straw-strewn stone floor. Now that the sun was coming up, they were getting a first look at their new surroundings, and the view was not exactly cheering. "But I'm kicking myself for walking into a trap."

Ben dropped to the floor. "So you think Li-shan suckered us?"

"What else?"

They heard the rattling of a lock, and the thick wooden door opened inward. Two Taipings came in. One barked, "Make the obeisance!" as he pushed Justin off the stone onto the floor.

"What's he want?" Ben asked.

"We're supposed to bow to them." He got to his feet, saying to the guard in Cantonese, "Why should I bow to you? Go to hell."

The guard raised a thick wooden stick and crashed it down on his left shoulder. "Dog of a foreign devil!" he screamed. "Make obeisance to the Chung Wang!"

The gentleman in question appeared in the cell door. His face was cool, and he looked regal in his yellow robe and strange, cone-shaped turban.

"Bow to him," Justin mumbled to Ben, and the two prisoners bowed. The Chung Wang came into the cell. He ignored Ben as he spoke to Justin in Cantonese.

"So you are the famous barbarian who is holding my son for ransom."

"Yes, I'm Justin Savage. But I'm not holding your son for ransom. Why haven't you agreed to my offer to trade Li-shan for Julie?"

The Chung Wang smiled and spread his hands. "Why should I? Now you are *my* prisoner. I can trade you for my son and still keep Julie. You!" He pointed at one of the guards, who pulled a knife from his belt and grabbed a handful of Justin's hair, which had grown to shoulder length since leaving Italy.

"What the hell—?" Justin yelped.

"You will not be harmed," soothed the Chung Wang. "I need a lock of your hair to send your wife to prove to her you are my prisoner."

The guard sliced off some of Justin's hair, then released him.

"How did Li-shan get word to you that I was coming through the Gate of the Secret Concubine?" Justin asked.

"Mr. Savage, you must underestimate my intelligence. I would never have allowed my son to come to your house in Shanghai if I didn't know that most of your servants are Taiping spies. I might add that if you had killed my son, your servants would have killed you and your wife. As it is, they kept me informed of everything that was said in your house. When I heard you were coming to Soochow to kidnap Julie, I returned to the city to greet you. I even know how many times you and your wife make love."

Justin's face turned red. It had never occurred to him that his house servants, who seemed so anonymous and friendly, were actually Taiping spies.

"I also know," the Chung Wang went on, "that you have treated my son well and obtained for him the best medical treatment available. For that I am not ungrateful. Until we can make the arrangements to exchange my son for you and your friend, I will endeavor to make your stay with us as pleasant as possible—under the circumstances. In the meanwhile, welcome to Soochow."

Smiling slightly, he nodded his head and turned to leave.

"Wait!" Justin exclaimed.

The Chung Wang, a man of immense personal dignity, turned back. "Yes?"

"Your Majesty, may I at least *see* Julie? You're a father—surely you can understand how I feel?"

The Chung Wang stared at him a moment, then said, "Very well, you may see her for a few minutes on the condition that you don't tell her who you are. She believes that Li-shan is her father and I am her grandfather. Of course, the child is no blood relation to us. But she is important to Li-shan, who has come to love her—as have I. I do not wish for her to be confused. Do you agree to the condition?"

Justin hesitated. It was so bizarre to be reunited with his own flesh and blood and then to have to deny it . . . and yet, he desperately wanted to see Julie.

"Very well," he said. "I agree."

"Then follow me."

The Chung Wang left the cell with Justin behind him. He in turn was followed by the two guards, who closed and locked the cell door, leaving Ben alone. They were in a stone corridor that led past five other cell doors to a stone stairs. When Justin had been brought to the palace that was the Chung Wang's home in Soochow, he had been unable to get anything more than a fleeting impression of the palace. But he knew it was big: the Chung Wang, like all of the Taiping *wangs,* or kings, built to impress, and he remembered that the roof of the two-story building was made of black tiles with spikes and that it undulated weirdly, giving the impression that the palace of the Chung Wang was a great, brooding dragon.

After climbing the stone stairs, which were guarded at the top by two Taipings, they went through a metal door into a pleasant columned loggia that surrounded a small garden in the center of which tinkled a round fountain. It was a bright chilly day, and Justin wished he had his fur-lined parka that he had left with his horse before wading across the moat outside Soochow's walls the night before.

The procession passed into yet another small garden. The Chung Wang stopped before a door and said, "This is Julie's nursery. Remember, Mr. Savage, you must not let her know who you are. If you do, I will be forced to kill your friend, the small barbarian you call Ben."

It was the first time the Chung Wang had threatened him. Justin said, "I understand."

The Chung Wang opened the door and went into a cheerful, sunlit room filled with dolls and toys. A plump amah was sitting by a window doing some needlework. Seeing her visitor, she rose to her feet and bowed.

"Grandpa!"

Justin saw a little girl run from the corner of the room with her arms outstretched. She looked like a Chinese doll: she wore a gaily embroidered red and gold vest, lightly padded to protect against the chill. The vest had long ivory sleeves. Below the vest she wore a lovely ivory skirt with a rich silver trim. The Chung Wang bent down to pick her up, kissing her as she hugged him. Justin felt a pang of jealousy: it was obvious the girl adored her grandfather and that the adoration was mutual. He now began to understand Li-shan's stubbornness in refusing to give Julie up.

"Grandpa, Shu-mei is making me a beautiful new dress for Te-ling," Julie chirped happily.

"Who is Te-ling?"

"One of my dolls. Now Te-ling will have ten dresses. Isn't that wonderful?"

The Chung Wang gave her another kiss. "You may have all the doll dresses you want," he said, smiling at her. "Now, I have someone who wants to meet you."

He carried her over to Justin, who stared at the most incredibly beautiful child he had ever seen. The admixture of Chang-mei's Chinese blood and his "barbarian" blood had produced an exotic flower that was awesome to behold. Most riveting were her amber eyes, just slightly slanted to produce a haunting loveliness. "Julie," said the Chung Wang, "this is Mr. Savage from America." The Chinese word he used for "mister" was *shansheng*.

Julie stared at her father. "He's funny-looking," she said to the Chung Wang. "Why does he have red hair?"

"In America," Justin said, "there are a lot of people with red hair."

"Where's America?"

"On the other side of the world. It's a very beautiful country. Perhaps someday you'll come visit it." The Chung Wang shot him a threatening look. "Might I hold her for a moment?"

The Chung Wang hesitated. Then he handed Julie to her father, who smiled as he hugged her. "You're a very pretty girl, Julie," he said. "I love your eyes."

"Thank you, Shansheng Savage. Your eyes are very pretty too, even if they're funny-looking. Your eyes look like the sky. Do people in America all have blue eyes?"

"Some do. Others have brown eyes and green eyes."

"Who is the Emperor of America?"

"We don't have an emperor. We have a president. His name is Shansheng Buchanan. Can you say that? Buchanan?"

"Bew-ca-nun." She laughed. "What a funny name! America must be a very funny place."

"We must let Julie play with her dolls now," the Chung Wang said, holding out his arms to take her back.

"Please . . . just one more moment. . . ." Justin hugged her even more tightly. "I love you, Julie," he said softly, putting his cheek on hers.

"You do? Why so, Shansheng Savage?"

"I just do. May I kiss you?"

Without waiting for an answer, he kissed her forehead. Then, tears in his funny blue eyes, he handed her back to the Chung Wang.

I'll get you back someday, Julie, he thought. I don't know how, but one day I'll get you back.

Lieutenant Barclay Strand of the British Armed Forces in China handed Fiammetta a folded piece of paper. "Here is the English translation of the letter left under your garden door this morning," he said. "It reads pretty much as I expected."

They were in the living room of the house in Shanghai. Fiammetta, who was wearing a cinnamon silk dress, took the paper and unfolded it, a worried look on her face.

"Madame," it began, "your husband and his American friend are my prisoners. I enclose a lock of your husband's hair to prove I do not lie. When my son is able to travel, you will send him to the great Water Gate of Soochow. Then I will release your husband and his friend. Do not try to trick me if you value your husband's life. [Signed,] The Loyal King."

"The 'Loyal King' is the Chung Wang?" Fiammetta asked, her hands trembling. She had already seen the lock of Justin's hair in the Chinese letter so mysteriously placed under the moon gate to her garden the night before. She had guessed he had been taken prisoner.

"That's right," said Barclay Strand.

"At least I know he's alive."

"Yes, that's good news. Justin's plan must have gotten mucked up somehow. I've talked to my commander, General Michel. He is shocked and instructed me to deliver to you his heartfelt sympathy, but . . ." He shrugged.

"I know. There's nothing he can do."

"Actually, all of us westerners here in Shanghai are in a bit of a fix. After all, it's not our country and we don't have much business interfering in the internal affairs of China. We don't much like the Manchus—they're bloody awful people, absolute barbarians. But while we'd like to see the Taipings run them out of the country back to Manchuria, there's not *too* much we can do to help them without making the Manchus squeal like pigs and cause all sorts of difficulties. So while General Michel is willing to send soldiers here to protect this house, he can't very well send an expedition to Soochow to try to liberate your husband. It would cause a frightful row, and besides, we're outnumbered. I *do* hope you understand?"

Fiammetta forced a sad little smile. "Yes, I do. You've been very kind, and I appreciate your help. But of course, none of this gets me back my husband." She sighed. "I suppose we'll have to go along with the Chung Wang. Do you speak any Chinese?"

"Yes, some. I'm not fluent by any means, but I can communicate with the beggars."

"Then would you mind talking to Li-shan? He might as well know about his father's letter, and the only conversation I can carry out with him is unprintable."

The Englishman looked shocked. "I say, he hasn't—?"

"The only thing he says to me is 'Makee jig-jig?' "

"The swine!"

Fiammetta, with her strong streak of Italian earthiness, was amused by Strand's properly Victorian stuffiness. "Shall we go to his bedroom?" she said. "He's much improved physically, and yesterday was up and about for a while. I see no reason why he couldn't travel to Soochow in a few days so we could get Justin back as soon as possible."

"Yes, of course. Except there *is* one small problem. I didn't want to upset you further, but . . ."

"But what?"

The ruddy-faced Englishman with the swooping mustaches nervously cleared his throat. "General Michel just received word an hour ago. The Peking Army of Jung-lu has arrived at Soochow. A great battle has broken out. I don't think it would be wise—or, for that matter, possible—to send Li-shan to Soochow until the battle is over. And naturally, it would be extremely unwise to try and get Justin and Ben out."

A new fear bloomed in Fiammetta's breast. "But if the Chung Wang wins . . . ?"

"Then there will be no danger. And all our information indicates that the Chung Wang will defeat the devil imps. After all, the Chung Wang is a great general, to give the beggar his due. From what we hear, all Jung-lu has going for him are his good looks. Of course"—he grinned, showing the gap between his two front teeth—"apparently with Yehenala, good looks are all one needs."

37 BECAUSE YEHENALA HAD A SALLOW complexion, which was not admired in China, she had learned to spray her face with a mixture of glycerine and honeysuckle, which she believed kept her skin soft, and then painted it with a pinkish powder, rouging her cheeks and lips. On this chilly evening, she was joining the Emperor at one of the pavilions of the Sea Palaces, a collection of lovely buildings on three artificial lakes to the west of the Forbidden City. Since she needed the full force of her powers of seduction and persuasion, she scented herself liberally with musk and sweetened her breath with betel nuts that she carried in a small purse. Then, as the eunuch An Tehai made a few final touches to her elaborate Manchu hairdo, one of her hand-maidens slipped a pair of intricately beaded Manchu slippers with the raised central heels onto her small feet. Yehenala adored shoes, and as her power over the Emperor had increased, she employed a dozen old women in a corner of the Summer Palace to design and sew hundreds of pairs for her round the clock: rank definitely had its privileges.

Finally, sumptuously adorned in one of her hundreds of dresses, each inch of which was woven with the finest of threads, she left her apartment in the Pavilion of Feminine Tranquility, climbed into her sedan chair that was picked up by eight of her personal eunuchs and carried to one of the western gates of the Forbidden City. She was taken across the moat to the Bridge of the Golden Sea Monster and the Jade Rainbow that led from the Middle Sea to the North Sea and the Green Mountain. This was an islet in the North Sea that was crowned by the curious White Dagoba, a grotesque, bottle-shaped, Tibetan-style temple built by the first Ch'ing Emperor in 1652 to honor the Dalai Lama. As Yehenala's sedan chair slowly moved up the mountain toward the Dagoba, it passed graceful pavilions of ebony, scarlet, and gold named after passages from the Chinese classics. A fan-shaped house was named the Delay of Southern Fragrance, another on the shore of the lake was the Pavilion of Distant Sails. Placed among berry-laden jujube trees, cypresses, Peking pines, willows, and magnolia trees in a seemingly hazardous pattern as if they had been strewn by the hand of a god were the Hall of Sweet Dew, the Building of Felicitous Skies, the Hall of Sparkling Brightness, the Peak with the Wonderful Cloud Wreath . . . the pavilions were as exotically lovely as their fragile names. Long colonnades of elaborately carved filigree wood afforded restful views of the artificial seas and the Forbidden City. The names of other pavilions reflected the classic Chinese pursuit of inner peace: the Study of Reflection on Remote Matters, the Cultivate Elegance Hall, the Study of Single-ness of Heart. Yehenala's restless and power-hungry personality had another side that sought repose in the Chinese classics and brush painting in the Chinese style of landscapes, often idealized, which were poetry in paint.

Arriving at the Hall of Sweet Dew, her eunuchs lowered her sedan chair and she stepped out to enter the enclosed pavilion that was heated by a fat Chinese stove and guarded by ten imperial eunuchs. The Emperor was seated in a wooden chair sipping kumiss from a porcelain bowl.

"*Huang-shang wan sui!*" exclaimed Yehenala, making the kowtow. "*Wan wan sui!*" "Majesty, ten thousand years! Ten thousand times ten thousand years!" She rose to her feet. "This slave brings glorious news, Divinity. May she sit at Your feet to report the events from the south?"

"Of course, Nala. Has Jung-lu engaged the armies of the Chung Wang?"

Yehenala knelt on a stool by Hsien-feng's feet, running her hand with its long filigreed nail guards over his plump thigh. "He not only engaged the Chung Wang's army, he has routed it!" she said, triumph flashing in her kohl-rimmed, turquoise-lidded eyes. "Soochow is taken, Majesty! Soochow is ours! *Ai-kuo!*" which meant "Love your country!"

The Emperor's flaccid face lit up. "This is glorious news indeed, Nala! Was the Chung Wang taken captive?"

"Alas no, Divinity. He escaped through a secret passage in the city wall built by your glorious predecessor, the Wan-li Emperor. He barely escaped, I might add. Jung-lu's troops had encircled his palace in the city, but they had no way of knowing about the secret passage, which is called the Gate of the Secret Concubine."

"We have read about it in the Ming scrolls. But We thought it had been bricked up centuries ago?"

"The dog, Chung Wang, had it unsealed to facilitate his escape in an emergency, which in fact happened. Our spies report he has returned to Nanking where he faces the wrath of his master, the so-called Heavenly King. If this slave might be so presumptuous as to suggest, might not this crowning moment of My Lord's glorious reign be memorialized by a few moments of clouds and rain? This slave is ever ready to please her master."

"Alas, Nala, it is a felicitous thought on your part, but We are too weary for such ardor. On the other hand, since We are in the Hall of Sweet Dew, perhaps the jade girl could play the flute while We savor this victory."

"This slave's heart overflows with joy to be able to honor her Lord with her humble talents."

"Your talent is hardly humble, Nala. You're the best flute player in the Forbidden City."

"You honor me, My Lord," she said, removing her nail guards so as not to accidentally prick the Divine Worm, a social gaffe that could earn her a quick trip to the Field of Executions. But Yehenala had learned well from her studies of the ancient *Manuals of Erotic Art:* she was excellent at her job.

When she was finished, leaving the Emperor limp with pleasure, she popped two betel nuts into her mouth to sweeten her breath. Then she went on: "There is more news, Divinity. At risk of boring You, may I proceed?"

"Speak, Nala. Tonight there is nothing but pleasure in your felicitous mouth."

"To hear these words makes my lowly life worth living, My Lord. Jung-lu's troops found in the basement dungeons of the Chung Wang's palace two American barbarians."

"Americans? We are stunned, Nala. How could there be American barbarians in Soochow?"

"One was the red-haired barbarian from Shanghai."

"The foreign devil named Savage?"

"My Lord's grasp of the facts leaves this slave speechless with admiration."

"But how did Savage end up in the dungeons of the Chung Wang? We had authorized Prince I to allow him to raise a private army to attack Soochow! We are confused, Nala."

"I have suggested to My Lord in the past that Prince I's motives are clouded, that in fact he weaves a web of deceit. At risk of displeasing My Lord, I now have proof that he has betrayed the Dragon Throne."

"Take care, Nala! You speak of Our cousin!"

"That knowledge weighs all too heavily on my humble heart, Divinity." She pulled a scroll from the long sleeve of her robe and handed it to Hsien-feng. "This, Lord, is a letter written by Prince I to the head of the abominable White Lotus Triad in Shanghai. As You will see, in it Prince I hires the White Lotus thugs to prevent any man from joining the American Savage's army by threats of retaliation."

"Yes, We see," said the Emperor, studying the scroll. "But why would Our cousin do that? It makes no sense! He petitioned Us for permission to do what he now pays the Triads to prevent?"

"Read on, Divinity, and you will see how cunning this asp, Prince I, is as he reveals his odious schemes. He instructs the White Lotus thugs to abduct the American, Savage, and then demand ransom from his Italian wife, who is worth millions. Prince I intends to use the ransom money to buy modern weapons for his Bannermen so that he can march to Peking and capture the Dragon Throne for himself! Oh, My Lord, how this slave wept when I read this! That any subject of the greatest Emperor that ever reigned in the Celestial Empire could concoct such venomous, traitorous plots. . . ."

The Emperor's face had turned red with rage as he finished reading the scroll. "How did you get this?" he barked.

Yehenala wiped the crocodile tears from her eyes. "I paid an informer, one of my spies who had infiltrated the Triad. He stole it and brought it to Peking." Which was a total lie. She had had the document forged. She herself had hired the White Lotus Triad to frighten away recruits from Justin's army, all with the intention of frustrating and eventually entrapping her enemy, Prince I. Now was her moment of triumph, having wisely softened the Emperor up with her expert flute playing.

"We can hardly believe such rank treachery!" gasped the Emperor. "But how did the American end up in Soochow?"

"Before the Triad could carry out its vile scheme, Savage had gone on his own to Soochow to try and capture his daughter. But he was foiled in his attempt by the Chung Wang, who had learned of his attempt and arrested him and his companion, another American of diminutive stature. Thus, Prince I's nefarious plot was foiled. But, Divinity, You now have proof that this humble slave's warnings about Prince I have not been misguided."

"Yes, Nala, you have earned Our eternal gratitude. We will send for Prince I and bring him to Peking in chains to face trial by the Imperial Clan Council. If his guilt is proved, Our fat cousin will be sent to the Empty Chamber to meet his ancestors. But where are the Americans now?"

"They are being brought to Peking by Jung-lu. Savage will prove a useful pawn, as the Chung Wang's son, Li-shan, is still a prisoner in the American's house in Shanghai. We can arrange a trade, and when Li-shan is our prisoner here in Peking, we can flush out the Chung Wang. And thus, O Lord of Ten Thousand Years, this odious rebellion that has disturbed the tranquility of Your reign can perhaps be finally crushed."

"You bring Us such happiness, Nala, that Our loins are filling with renewed lust! On this glorious night, perhaps We should try for clouds and rain a second time!"

"It is this slave's joyful destiny to bring pleasure to the Son of Heaven." She started removing her nail guards again. "Might this slave test the bounds of audacity by suggesting that in light of Jung-lu's glorious victory for the Dragon Throne, might the Lord of Ten Thousand Years consider rewarding him with a promotion? He could become a popular hero for the masses and strengthen their ties of love to their Emperor."

"An excellent idea, Nala. We will make Jung-lu a general. You are inspired. And to have uncovered the snakelike plot of Prince I! How can We reward you?"

"This slave's reward is simply to allow her to remain at Your side. No greater happiness could be given me."

In fact, the Emperor had already rewarded her. With Jung-lu a general and Prince I on his way to the Empty Chamber, Yehenala's hold on the Dragon Throne had become a grip. As she lowered her mouth on the Divine Worm, her brain reeled with excitement.

Ultimate power was inches away.

38   THE HORSES OF THE IMPERIAL Peking Expeditionary Force, as Jung-lu's army had been officially named, galloped across the Shantung Peninsula toward Peking as a cold wind swept out of Mongolia to the north. The troops Jung-lu had been allowed to pick and train, thanks to Yehenala's influence over the Emperor, were some of the finest in China, the flower of the Manchus—for Jung-lu had chosen only warriors from the ruling Manchu class on the theory they would be most loyal to the throne. Both Justin and Ben had been impressed by these soldiers, who had recaptured the bravery and dash of their ancestors who had invaded China two centuries earlier and ousted the Mings. They had surprised the Chung Wang by routing his army. From what Justin had learned from one of the soldiers who spoke Cantonese, the troops were fiercely loyal to Jung-lu, whom they revered. For once, it seemed, the dissolute court in Peking had picked a winner: Jung-lu not only looked like a hero, he acted like one. He had trained his men in a Spartan regimen: they were tough, resourceful, and fanatically loyal to the Dragon Throne. Unlike most Manchu generals, who lived luxuriously even when in the field, Jung-lu lived no better than his men, sharing their diet and hardships, leading them with incredible fearlessness into battle. Like most great generals, he seemed totally unconcerned about his personal safety. Even though he was a strict disciplinarian who was known personally to decapitate any of his men who breached his rules of conduct or showed cowardice in the face of the enemy, his men loved him. Justin thought that if there were more like Jung-lu in China, the tottering Ch'ing Dynasty might have a new lease on life.

Jung-lu had personally freed Justin and Ben from the Chung Wang's prison. Even though Justin could barely communicate in Mandarin, he got the impression that Jung-lu knew exactly who he was, even though he was a bit confused by Ben. Jung-lu treated them both with respect and courtesy, and when it came time to leave Soochow and return to Peking, he furnished them with horses. Although their hands were not tied, there was no possibility of escape: Jung-lu was traveling north with four hundred of his troops, the remainder of his army having been left in Soochow to guard it against a return of the Taipings.

Besides, Justin had no desire to escape. He had learned from the Cantonese-speaking soldier that Julie and her amah, Shu-mei, had been sent ahead of the army to the Forbidden City. He had no idea what interest the court could have in his daughter, but this new situation offered new opportunities.

Perhaps with the Chung Wang out of the picture, Justin could bring his daughter back where she belonged: with him. He had come halfway around the world to find Julie. He wasn't about to give up.

Prince I had lost fifteen pounds in the three weeks since he was arrested at his palace in Canton by the Emperor's younger half brother, Prince Kung, and brought to the Forbidden City in chains. His entry into Peking this time was a

far cry from his triumphal entry the previous fall when he had brought his annual tribute to the court. Then he had traveled in a silver palanquin. Now he
rode in an open wagon under oyster skies as the populace, always thrilled to
see one of their masters brought low, jeered and hooted at him, throwing rotten eggs and vegetables. It was a supreme humiliation for the proud Manchu
prince, and he knew why it was happening to him. His enemy was Yehenala.
He had attended enough trials at the Imperial Clan Court in the Hall of Earnest
Diligence to know that the so-called "trials" were a farce, where often the accused was not even allowed to speak, much less be represented by legal coun-
sel. If he could not find an ally or do something in the few days left before his
trial, he was a dead man. He had argued and pleaded with Prince Kung, trying
to convince him that Yehenala's growing ascendancy over the Emperor was a
danger to *all* the princes, himself included. But Prince Kung—short, wiry, a
mighty hunter and a man of sharp intelligence who would have made a much
better Emperor than Hsien-feng—turned a deaf ear to his cousin.

A rotten egg smashed against Prince I's cheek, and its smelly yolk dribbled
down his double chin. He who had had everything but was about to lose everything, and all because of Yehenala. His mind raced, searching for a way to strike
back at her, searching for an ally. . . .

Suddenly an idea struck him. Was there a glimmer of hope? Perhaps he *did*
have an ally, and Prince Kung had told him he was being brought to Peking.
Perhaps the red-haired barbarian could help him. At least he could tell Justin
Savage the truth, how Yehenala had rigged this false charge of treason against
him. . . . At least Justin would *listen* to him. . . .

Two days later, a far different reception was given to Jung-lu as he and his
troops entered the Tartar City of Peking. Yehenala, who was not unaware of
the uses of propaganda, had made sure the capture of Soochow by her lover
was trumpeted throughout the Celestial Empire, and great cheering crowds
jostled to catch a glimpse of the slim hero on his horse at the head of his cav-
alcade. Mounted drummers banged their kettledrums as the ancient Manchu
instruments of conch shells and long brass horns made martial music, stirring
the crowds to even more excitement, for the Chinese loved nothing better than
a show, even if it was put on by the hated Manchus.

But something else was attracting the attention of the Pekingese on this bright
winter day besides the Manchu warriors with their scarlet helmets and their
yung ideograms on their tunics—*yung* meaning "brave." It was the two foreign
devils riding behind Jung-lu. In particular, the red-haired foreign devil. The vast
majority of Pekingese had never seen a westerner, for unlike Shanghai, Can-

ton, and other treaty ports, the capital did not attract westerners who had business to perform. Now the populace gawked and pointed at Justin and Ben.

"Hey, we're freaks!" Ben laughed, pointing back at the crowd. "What do you think of that, Justin?"

"Maybe we should put together a vaudeville act."

But something else was on his mind besides starring in a freak show: Julie. Now that he was in the capital, would he be able to free her—for he had reasoned that somehow his daughter was being used as a pawn in this complicated chess game, though exactly how, he wasn't sure.

Finally, the procession reached the Tien An Men, the great Gate of Heavenly Peace, the south entrance to the Forbidden City. Here, the Emperor, at Yehenala's suggestion, had erected a huge striped tent beneath which a hundred cooks were preparing roast pigs that were to be distributed to the populace free in celebration of the great victory.

As Jung-lu waved to the jubilant throng, the gates of the Forbidden City swung slowly open and the procession entered the home of the Emperor. Justin drank in the awesome architecture of the place, the vermillion walls of the first courtyard soaring some fifty feet surmounted by a columned loggia with a roof of golden tiles. In front of him rose the Wumen, or second gate of the Forbidden City. Seated on a throne in the center of the parapet over this gate was a pudgy man in a yellow dragon robe and crown, surrounded by mandarins and officials of the court.

"I think," Justin said to Ben, "that's the Emperor."

In fact, Jung-lu and his warriors raised their arms and shouted, *"Huang-shang wan sui! Wan wan sui!"* over and over.

Hsien-feng, who looked singularly unprepossessing despite the splendor of his robes and crown, gestured condescendingly to his troops. Justin thought he looked a little woozy; in fact, Hsien-feng was drunk.

Justin felt something tugging at his right leg. He looked down to see a tall young man in an orange and green gown standing by his horse. The man shouted in Cantonese over the noise of the soldiers, "Follow me, please."

Justin said to Ben, "See you later."

"Who's this guy?"

"Haven't the faintest notion."

Justin dismounted and followed the man through the soldiers to a small door in the wall.

"In here," said the man, opening the door.

"Who are you?" Justin asked.

"I am An Te-hai, eunuch to the Virtuous Concubine. She has sent me to take you to Prince I."

"He's here, in Peking?"

"Yes. He wants to speak to you. Please: inside."

Justin, who had never seen a eunuch before, stared at An Te-hai a moment. Then he ducked through the door. An Te-hai followed him, closing the door.

"Follow me, Mr. Savage."

They were in a long corridor. Now An Te-hai led him down the stone hall. "How did you know my name?" Justin asked.

"There are very few red-haired Americans in the Forbidden City."

"Yes, but still . . ."

"The Virtuous Concubine knew you would be with Jung-lu. In fact, she instructed him to bring you to Peking."

"Is the Virtuous Concubine the woman known as Yehenala?"

"That is correct. She also brought your daughter to Peking."

Justin's heart skipped a beat. "Julie? Where is she?"

"With the Virtuous Concubine."

"Is she safe?"

"Of course, Mr. Savage. Why would the Virtuous Concubine wish to harm your daughter?"

"I don't know . . . may I see her?"

"All in good time, Mr. Savage. The Virtuous Concubine sent me to find you because I am from the south and, as you can see, speak Cantonese. The Virtuous Concubine is the mother of the Heir Presumptive, the ever-glorious Prince Tsai Chün." He led Justin into a lovely garden. "The Virtuous Concubine," he went on, "is forced by custom and court etiquette to call herself a 'slave' before the Emperor. But such are the powers of my august mistress that in fact she has turned the Emperor into her slave. This building before us is the Hall of Earnest Diligence. It is where the Imperial Clan Court meets to judge those members of the Imperial Clan who have committed abominations against the Dragon Throne. It is where Prince I awaits you."

Justin looked at the tall eunuch. "Has Prince I committed an abomination?"

"Yes. He was tried yesterday and found guilty."

"But what did he do?"

"He hired the White Lotus Triad in Shanghai to prevent you from recruiting your army by threats of retaliation."

"But that doesn't make any sense!"

"Mr. Savage, you will find that things that do not make sense still can be true in China. My august mistress, the Virtuous Concubine, had a document that the accursed Prince I sent to the head of the White Lotus Triad in which he clearly stated his abomination of treason against the Dragon Throne. It is fortunate he did not implicate you in his odious plot, or you, too, would be in the Empty Chamber."

"The what?"

"The Empty Chamber. This room, in fact."

They had reached a door at one side of the graceful Hall of Earnest Diligence. The eunuch opened the door. "Prince I awaits you, Mr. Savage."

He stepped aside. Justin hesitated. The eunuch smiled and gestured for him to enter.

He did. It was a small room with vermillion-painted wooden beams supporting the ceiling. There were large iron hooks in the beams. Hanging from one of them, a red silk noose around his fat neck, was Prince I. He had been dead for twenty-four hours. He wore a plain white tunic that hung to his ankles. His bare feet were swollen by the settling of his bodily fluids. Beneath them, a stool lay on its side where he had evidently kicked it.

Justin winced. "I can't believe he was plotting against the Emperor," he said. "He sent me to England so I could come back to China and help the Emperor."

"The Prince was duplicitous. He used you for his own purposes. Because of his high rank, he was granted the privilege of committing suicide. My august mistress, the Virtuous Concubine, wished you to see what happens to traitors in the Celestial Empire."

Justin took one last look at the sagging flesh. Then he turned to the eunuch.

"He's beginning to stink," he said. "Don't you think it would be decent to cut him down and bury him?"

"His cursed body will be burned and his ashes scattered over the Field of Traitors. But my august mistress wanted to be sure you saw him. Now, Mr. Savage, I will prepare you to meet the Virtuous Concubine. You smell almost as bad as Prince I. You will need a bath, a shave, and new clothes to meet the most powerful . . ." he corrected himself, "the second most powerful person in China."

39 IT HAD BEEN TWENTY-THREE days since Justin and Ben had left for Soochow, and Fiammetta, who knew nothing of their fate, was in an agony of anxiety. "Where *is* he?" she said one night to Barclay as they dined. She had come to ask him to dine with her often, not only because she liked him, but because she was so miserably lonely and she could at least communicate with him.

"I told you we have reason to believe they took him and Ben to Peking," the Englishman said, cutting into the Australian lamb Fiammetta had ordered from Jardine-Matheson. Barclay was in mufti, wearing a well-cut frock coat and neat white cravat. He had never grown fond of Chinese food, so he was attacking the lamb with gusto. Although he hated to admit it to himself because it was so thoroughly caddish a thing to do, he was more than a little in love with another man's wife, namely Fiammetta.

"Yes, but you're only guessing," she went on miserably. "He could be in Timbuctu, as far as that goes. Or dead. It's the not knowing that's so ghastly."

"Yes, I realize that, and I certainly sympathize with you. But you've been in China long enough to know this is not a civilized country in the way *we* think of civilization. I mean, the beggars have no postal system so that Justin can hardly drop you a note. I think we can safely fall back on the hoary bromide that no news is good news."

He indicated his wineglass, and the Chinese houseboy in the white jacket picked up the crystal decanter and refilled the goblet with a robust Château Calon-Ségur '31. Fiammetta had not abandoned her love of fine wine, and fortunately for the bibulous Europeans in Shanghai, Jardine-Matheson imported the best from Europe. In fact, the level of luxury in the house was as high as was to be found in Shanghai, a state of affairs that had not been overlooked by Barclay Strand. He liked the crystal and china, the napery and silver hurricane lamps, as much as he liked Fiammetta's alabaster décolletage gleaming in the candlelight. Tonight, despite her anxiety, she looked especially lovely in a low-cut pale blue evening dress. What a swine I am, he thought, even to *think* of making love to her. But I can't help it. I do think about it.

"Well, I assume you're right," she sighed. "I'll just have to assume my darling is safe, since there's nothing else I can do except worry myself into a state. As if I didn't have enough to worry about with Li-shan lurking about the house."

"Has he given you any more trouble?"

She hesitated. "No, actually. But he's almost well now, and he's very restless. I have a feeling he's going to try to escape."

"He'll have twelve of England's finest to contend with if he does, and I have a man posted outside his bedroom door, as you know. The fellow's no fool. He knows he can't get out of this house."

"But I don't exactly relish the role of jailor. Isn't there some way he could be transferred to your prison?"

"If we do, the Manchus will start clamoring for us to release him to them, and it will become an international incident. I need hardly tell you how hungry they are to get their hands on him. As it is, Sir John can hide behind the useful fiction that he is merely protecting you, a private citizen, from the Tai-pings. Of course, it's a bit Jesuitical, but that's how things are done out here. This claret is jolly good, by the way."

"Help yourself. There's plenty more." She was well aware that Barclay had a very English love of French wine.

"Yes, I think I will." Again he indicated his wine goblet to the houseboy, who looked perhaps fifteen. "We must also bear in mind," he went on, "that if Justin has been taken by the Manchus, as we believe, then it is of the utmost importance that we retain Li-shan. Li-shan is the greatest guarantor of Justin's safety, because the Manchus want Li-shan and they have no possible use for Justin. So they'll swap. I can assure you that's what's going to happen. It's just a matter of time."

"I suppose you're right. But the waiting is still nerve-wracking."

"Can't be helped, I fear. This lamb is jolly good and done to a turn. I don't suppose—?"

"Of course." She signaled the houseboy to serve him more.

Outside, in the garden, a man crouched in the bushes watching them through the window.

It was Li-shan. In his right hand he held a knife slipped to him that morning by the same houseboy who was serving Barclay his second helping of lamb. The knife was bloody. Li-shan had just slit the throat of the guard outside his room. Now he looked at the soldier smoking a cigarette ten feet away from him in the garden. The other ten English soldiers were stationed outside the house.

Moving like a cat, Li-shan crept along the side of the house toward the smoking soldier. Crickets chirped sleepily as a cloud sailed slowly across a gibbous moon. Li-shan crept up behind the soldier, who put his cigarette out on the ground. Li-shan grabbed the man's mouth with his left hand while his right hand gashed the soldier's throat open.

The soldier grunted slightly. Li-shan released him. He dropped to the ground, dead.

Li-shan ran across the garden to one of the bamboo trees that he shimmied up with the agility of a monkey. Reaching the tile roof, he jumped onto it and made his way across a mango tree to the rear of the house, stooping low so as not to be silhouetted against the moon.

Reaching the mango tree, he swiftly climbed down and jumped on a horse that was held by Fiammetta's cook. The Taiping cook grinned and saluted Li-shan as the latter galloped away in the night toward Soochow Creek. Then the cook hurried back into the kitchen.

"A lovely dinner," Barclay Strand said a half hour later as he kissed Fi-ammetta's hand. They were standing in the door leading to the garden. "I really . . ." he burped. "Pardon me . . . I really enjoyed the wine, though I may not enjoy it so much in the morning . . . I say, what's that?"

He had spotted something lying on the ground.

"Excuse me. . . ."

Releasing Fiammetta's hand, he hurried across the garden to the body of the soldier Li-shan had murdered. It was lying facedown. Barclay stooped beside it and turned it over. He winced as he saw the sliced throat, a mass of clotted blood.

"Bloody hell—!" He stood up, yelling, "Guards."

"What is it?" Fiammetta called.

"Someone's killed one of my men. . . ." He was running back into the house as the soldiers poured through the Moon Gate. He ran to Li-shan's room where the other soldier was lying on his back, his throat also neatly slashed.

"Oh, my God!" Fiammetta cried as she hurried up beside him, putting her hand over her mouth.

"Bloody Li-shan has bloody well ESCAPED!" Barclay roared, furious at having been tricked.

Justin was taken by An Te-hai to a small house just outside the east wall of the Forbidden City. An explained to him that this was one of the guest houses used by the Emperor. As Justin came through the front door, he was surprised to see Ben wearing a dark silk long robe with a black Manchu cap on his head.

"Ben!" he exclaimed. "Where'd you get that robe?"

"They brought me here and two good-lookin' gals gave me a bath and a shave and this robe, and here I am, Chinese Ben!"

They laughed and slapped each other's backs as they shook hands.

"What's going on?" Ben asked, looking curiously at An Te-hai. "And who's this guy?"

"Well, he's not exactly a 'guy,' " Justin explained. "He's a eunuch."

Ben gaped. "He's a eunuch? You mean, he ain't got no pecker?"

"He ain't got no nothing."

"How does he pee?"

"Look, Ben, I'm not going to ask. I don't think it would be polite."

"Please," An spoke in Cantonese, "come this way. The handmaidens will clean you and prepare you to meet the Virtuous Concubine."

"What is our status?" Justin asked. "Are we prisoners?"

"Oh, no, Mr. Savage. You and your friend are honored guests of the Virtuous Concubine. Please come this way for your bath."

"We're honored guests of Yehenala," Justin said to Ben in English. "And I'm going to get cleaned by the handmaidens. See you later."

"You know something?" Ben said. "This isn't half-bad. I could get used to this real quick."

"Maybe you should sign up as a eunuch."

Ben gulped. "No thanks. Circumcision's about as far as I'm going in *that* department."

An hour later Justin, bathed and shaven and wearing a black silk long-gown, rejoined Ben in the living room of the guest house.

"You look great, Justin, like a proper Chinese," said Ben. "But now what?"

"I don't know."

"The eunuch guy took off. . . ."

He was interrupted by the door being opened. An Te-hai came back in. "I trust you both are comfortable?" he said to Justin.

"Very comfortable."

"Your long-gown fits well?"

"Very well, thank you."

"Concubines are not permitted to leave the Forbidden City," An went on, "as eunuchs are not permitted to leave Peking. On the other hand, whole men are of course forbidden to enter the Forbidden City. Since the handmaidens have ascertained that you are both whole men, my august mistress has been forced to get special permission from the Emperor to allow you to enter the Forbidden City. This permission has been granted on the grounds that you are both barbarians and therefore no concubine could possibly be tempted by you because of your extreme and hairy ugliness."

"What's he saying?" Ben asked.

"He said we're both so repulsively ugly, we're being allowed into the Forbidden City."

"Oh. Well, I'm a sucker for flattery."

"Follow me, please," An said. "The Virtuous Concubine awaits you with the midday meal."

"We're going to lunch," Justin explained to Ben as they followed An Te-hai out of the guest house.

Ten minutes later they were led into the banquet hall of the Pavilion of Feminine Tranquility where An told them to wait, then vanished behind a large, twelve-panel Coromandel screen depicting silver birds and trees on a black background. Ben looked around the room, which was lavishly decorated.

"I shouldn't be nervous, should I?" he said to Justin.

"No."

"Then why am I? I have this feeling lunch is going to be *us.* "

"Look, Ben: think of it this way. We're probably the first westerners who've been in the Forbidden City since Marco Polo seven hundred years ago. And we're certainly the first Americans. We're making history."

"Huh. What happened to Marco Polo?"

"He went home and wrote a book about his adventure, which made him a fortune."

Ben brightened. "Hey, I like that! Maybe I'll go home, write a book, and get rich!" A distant gong sounded. "Oh-oh: I'm nervous again."

An Te-hai appeared from behind the Coromandel screen.

"Make the obeisance to the august and revered Virtuous Concubine!" he announced solemnly.

"Bow," said Justin.

They bowed as Yehenala came out from behind the screen. She had on her usual garish makeup, her eyes lined with kohl and her eyelids painted turquoise. She had on one of her tasseled Manchu headdresses, a vermillion dragon robe, and her platform-heeled beaded shoes. As she came toward them, Ben's eyes widened. "She's never gonna make it in vaudeville with that makeup," he whispered. "And those crazy shoes!"

"Ssh."

"I wonder if she can get us some singsong girls?"

"What is the small barbarian saying?" Yehenala said in Mandarin.

An Te-hai translated into Cantonese.

"My friend," Justin said, "tells me he is dazzled by the beauty of the Virtuous Concubine."

Yehenala's lids narrowed as she listened to the translation. Then she came to Justin, reached out her right hand, lowering her two filigreed gold nail guards so as not to put out his eyes, and touched his hair.

"Tell the barbarian I find his hair surprisingly soft. I thought it would feel like copper. Was he born this way?"

"Yes," Justin said after listening to the translation.

"They say the barbarians have hair on their chests," Yehenala went on. "Tell him to unbutton his long-gown. I want to see."

An Te-hai translated.

"She wants to see if I have hair on my chest," Justin muttered to Ben as he unbuttoned his long-gown and bared his chest. Yehenala stared at the thin line of red hair, then reached out and yanked some out. Justin yipped "Ouch!" as

Yehenala examined the hairs close to her eyes. Then she grinned slightly. "This barbarian is like one of my lapdogs," she said to An Te-hai. "How interesting. Tell the eunuchs to bring in the food. Seat the barbarians on either side of me."

An Te-hai raised his right hand and the gong rang again as Yehenala seated herself at the head of the long table where, a few months before, she had dined with the Emperor and Prince I. An Te-hai indicated to Justin and Ben to sit on either side of her as a procession of kitchen eunuchs began to file into the room, each carrying a dish.

"So," Yehenala said to Justin after he had taken his seat to her left, "did you have a pleasant conversation with Prince I?"

"It was rather one-sided," Justin said, speaking through the translator.

Yehenala laughed. "Yes, I can imagine. The point is, my young barbarian friend, Prince I had become my enemy. I wanted you to see how I deal with my enemies."

"I know very little about the case, but I find it hard to believe Prince I was ever disloyal to the Dragon Throne."

"Nevertheless, he was, and he paid the price for his treachery. Some bird's nest soup? It's one of my chef's specialties."

"Yes, thanks. I'm very fond of it." He leaned to Ben and said in English, "It's bird's nest soup. Very good, you'll like it."

"Ugh."

The eunuchs served the soup and poured rice wine.

"Tell me about America," Yehenala said. "I have seen it on the map. It looks very big, although of course not as big as China. Do you have concubines?"

"Uh, no," Justin said tactfully. "Well, some men have mistresses, but that's not quite the same thing."

"Do you have one of these mistresses?"

Justin looked rather embarrassed. "No, I love my wife very much and would not cheat on her."

" 'Cheat'? A curious concept. Is your wife beautiful?"

"Yes, very."

"Hmm. And Chang-mei? Was she beautiful?"

"Yes."

"Your daughter is very beautiful. When she grows up, she will make an excellent singsong girl. I will send her to the Flower and Willow lanes of the Tartar City to learn the secrets of the erotic arts." Justin almost gagged on his soup. But his years in China had taught him the necessity for face. He wiped his lips and drank some rice wine to stall for time while he thought how best to react.

"That's an interesting idea, but could a half-breed—who, after all, shares my lowly barbarian blood—could a half-breed be a successful singsong girl? Would she not contaminate her clients with her impurity?"

Yehenala picked up a chicken leg and bit into it, dexterously keeping her long nail guards away from her mouth. She shot Justin an admiring glance: she decided he was an adversary worthy of her sharp wit.

"That of course is true," she said, chewing the chicken, "but in some ways the Celestial Empire is perhaps behind the times. By the time Julie is ready to be trained in the glorious art of concubinage and taught how to please men, how to play the jade flute and so forth, the prejudice against half-breeds may have dissipated a bit. We must move forward with the times, to a certain degree."

"As Julie's father, it would of course be the highest honor for me to have my lowly daughter a concubine. But my admiration and love for the Celestial Empire forces me to reveal the sordid truth about Julie: she is a mongrel. You see, I am a bastard son. Therefore, my daughter is not only a half-breed, she is not even a legitimate half-breed."

Again, Yehenala shot him a look as she held out her hands for a kitchen eunuch to wash with a hot towel.

"You present difficulties, barbarian, and I appreciate your honesty. But even this is not an insuperable barrier. On the other hand, perhaps you're right: Julie probably isn't good enough for first-class concubinage."

Justin smiled inwardly with relief to see that his ploy was working. "You are wise, Gracious Lady. I was sure you would see the unacceptability of my lowly daughter."

"Perhaps, then, the Flower and Willow lanes are the answer after all."

In other words, become a prostitute. Again, Justin almost gagged, but he told himself: face! Play her game! Face! "Alas, then you condemn her to a life of poverty, for who would pay for a half-breed? I know you could never be so cruel."

Yehenala chuckled. "You are clever, barbarian," she said. "I rather admire your clumsy wits. Now: as to what to do with you and your friend. I have discussed the matter with the senior mandarins of the court. They tell me that as the husband of the odious Chang-mei who blew up the imperial war junk *Yellow Lotus* at great loss of life, you are guilty of the abomination of treason to the Dragon Throne, punishable by the same death as Prince I."

Justin stared at her. "But I wasn't even in China when that happened!"

"Nevertheless, the guilt lies on you because you are her husband. However"—she picked up a Peking duck pancake—"there are extenuating circumstances. You are a roundeye, and if we executed you, there would undoubtedly be a tedious uproar. More to the point, we want Li-shan. Therefore, tomorrow you and your friend will depart for Shanghai with an honor guard of General Jung-lu's troops. They will escort you to your house on Bubbling Well Road where, after Li-shan is placed under their guard, you and your friend will be released. Does that please you?"

"It's certainly an improvement over the alternative."

"I thought that would be your attitude. But you still owe me one million American dollars."

"I do? Why?"

"As compensation for the war junk your first wife blew up. When you pay me the money, your daughter will be returned to you."

The gong sounded. She rose to her feet as the kitchen eunuchs prostrated themselves on the floor in a low bow.

"My Lord summons me," she said. "I bid you a pleasant journey, barbarian. Do not fail to deliver me Li-shan, or your daughter dies."

"Gracious Lady," Justin blurted out, "I don't *have* a million dollars!"

"That's your problem, barbarian. However, I know you are resourceful. When you bring me the money, your daughter will be returned to you. Otherwise, she becomes either a concubine or a flower girl. Good-bye, barbarian. I like your hair."

40   BARCLAY STRAND HAD BEEN so enraged by Li-shan's escape, as well as by the murder of his two soldiers, that he became almost manic. Telling Fiammetta he was convinced the escape had been stage-managed by someone inside the house, he grilled every one of the six house servants with the aid of an interpreter. The servants all professed innocence, which was not unexpected, leaving Barclay nowhere. But he told Fiammetta he was still convinced some of the servants had been in on the escape, in particular Sammy, the fat cook, and he recommended to Fiammetta that she fire all of them so he could turn them over to the Manchus, who had less delicate means of extracting information from suspected Taipings. But at this, Fiammetta balked. She was nervous enough about the escape of Li-shan without getting the Manchus further involved. Besides, she liked her servants, and the thought of submitting them to torture was repulsive to her: she had seen the horrible results of torture firsthand when Justin had been almost killed in Castle Mondragone. Barclay backed down on that demand, at least for the time being, but insisted she keep a gun in her bedroom, to which she agreed.

But Fiammetta was far more worried about Justin's welfare than her own. The news of Li-shan's escape had swept Shanghai; and although General Sir John Michel had insisted that the publisher of the *North China Herald* keep the story out of his newspaper, it was only a matter of time before the news reached Peking. Without Li-shan as a bargaining pawn to free Justin, the latter's safety was seriously compromised. And Fiammetta, like every European in the Celestial Empire, had heard hair-raising stories of the cruelty of the Manchus.

Her nights were rendered sleepless by her anxiety about Justin. Nevertheless, Li-shan's escape gave her one cause for relief: with the Chung Wang's son no longer there, there was no longer any reason to guard him, so Sir John Michel ordered Barclay to return his soldiers to their barracks. Fiammetta, who had chafed at being jailor, was freed of at least one burden.

On the third night after Li-shan's escape, she lay in her bed, the gun under her pillow, staring at the inevitable *tjik-tjak* on the ceiling. Her mind went back over her tempestuous relationship with the young American whom she adored so much and whose child she was carrying. She marveled yet again at the intensity of her animal passion for him, even more so now that he had been gone twenty-six days. She itched and ached for him. Fiammetta was a passionate woman, so perhaps this was understandable. Yet she marveled that her passions could remain so focused on one man to the exclusion of all others.

With the exception of Li-shan. Once again, a wave of guilt swept over her as she remembered the Taiping's exotic face and chiseled torso. "Makee jig-jig?" he had whispered, and yes, she had been tempted. She sighed and turned on her side. Oh, well, she was far from perfect.

It was an unseasonably hot night for a week from Christmas. The glass bead screens in her open windows tinkled softly as a slight breeze shook them. A few mosquitoes buzzed around the netting over her bed. She figured it was close to midnight, and she wondered if she would ever fall asleep.

She heard her bedroom door creak slowly open and flickering candlelight spilled into the room.

"Missy Tai-tai, may I come in?"

She saw Sammy, the fat cook, in the door. She sat up, her right hand reaching under her pillow for the pistol.

"What is it, Sammy?" she asked.

"Missy Tai-tai, man here to see you chop chop."

"Who is it?"

To her amazement, Li-shan appeared beside Sammy. The light from the cook's candle illuminated his strange, hawklike face from below. He was wearing black trousers and a loose green shirt. He was staring at Fiammetta. Her fingers found the gun.

Li-shan whispered to Sammy, who smiled and said, "Missy Tai-tai, Li-shan say he wanna makee jig-jig with you. He come from far away cause he no can get you outta his head. He wanna make you his number one wife an' take you to Nanking, makee jig-jig all resta your life."

Li-shan pushed by Sammy, came into the bedroom. He took the candleholder from the cook and came to the foot of her bed. He spoke rapidly to Sammy, who said, "Missy Tai-tai, Li-shan say he feel very strong for you. He learn foreign devil word 'love.' He love you."

He giggled self-consciously, but Li-shan's face was deadly serious. He spoke to Sammy in Cantonese.

"Missy Tai-tai, Li-shan say will you let him to kiss you?"

Li-shan's free hand started to raise the mosquito netting. He handed the candle back to Sammy, then ducked under the netting and crawled onto the foot of the bed.

He's going to rape me, Fiammetta thought, panicking.

"Sammy, tell him to go away," she said aloud.

Sammy spoke in Cantonese. Li-shan answered back.

"Missy Taitai, Li-shan say if he no makee jig-jig with you, he go crazy. Very strong feeling for you. He no sleep three nights now. Go crazy with love."

I can't kill him! she thought. If I kill him, the Manchus will keep Justin.

Li-shan was beside her now. She could almost feel the intensity of his desire, which was kindling her own. Sammy giggled as Li-shan slowly put his left hand on Fiammetta's right arm, leaned down, and kissed her on the mouth. His kiss was hot with passion.

I can't kill him, she thought.

Slowly he pulled down his black pants till they were below his knees. Then, gently, his bare buttocks gleaming in the candlelight, he maneuvered his body on top of her, continuing to kiss her.

Sammy giggled.

Li-shan hissed at him in Cantonese.

Sammy put the candleholder on a table and hurried out of the room, closing the door.

Li-shan turned his face back to Fiammetta. "Makee jig-jig," he whispered tenderly. He stuck his tongue out like a *tjik-tjak* and licked her lips.

She pulled the gun out from under the pillow and placed it between his eyes.

"No makee jig-jig," she said. "Makee prisoner."

"I've got to get rich," Justin said to Ben. They were sitting around a fire on a hill north of Soochow. The weather had turned cool again. Their escort of eight of Jung-lu's soldiers were either sleeping on the ground or smoking. It was near midnight beneath a star-strewn sky, the twenty-second of December, 1858. They would reach Shanghai the next morning.

"You've been saying that over and over," Ben said, "and I understand you want to get a million bucks so you can buy your daughter back from the Old Bitch. By the way, she's holdin' you up. If you'd told me what she was sayin', I coulda got her price down. Can't tell me any war junk is worth a million bucks. Maybe fifty thousand, at most. Those tubs don't even have engines."

"You're probably right, but I have a hunch she doesn't give a damn about the war junk. That million is for *her,* Yehenala."

"Yeah, that could be. I still don't see why you can't borrow it from your wife."

"No, that's out. She'd have to sell everything. I'm not even going to tell her—and you're not going to either. Julie isn't her daughter. Besides, that's exactly how marriages get ruined, especially when the wife has a lot of money and the husband has nothing, like me. I went through this with my first wife, Chang-mei. I want my *own* money."

"From what you've told me, that no good half brother of yours, Sylvaner, owes you a lot. Didn't he steal your inheritance?"

"Yes, but it wasn't any million dollars. Besides, I have other plans for Sylvaner. I've been doing a lot of thinking. What do you know about banking, Ben?"

"Oh, hell, not much. People put money in 'em, the banker loans it out, and if the place don't get held up, everybody makes money. It's just like peddlin' pots and pans, except you're peddlin' money instead. Why?"

"I'm thinking of starting a bank on Wall Street. Banks seem to have a lot of power, and that's what I want: power. I've been kicked around enough in my life. I would ask Fiammetta for a loan to get started—that would be a business deal, and I could make some money for her. Anyway, would you be interested in working with me? I have a hunch your *yiddischer kopf* might come in real handy on Wall Street."

Ben laughed. "Sure, why not? With my looks and your brains, we'll wipe 'em out. What'll be my title? Vice President?"

"I don't know yet. We'll figure all that out later. But I saved your life once, and you saved mine with Li-shan, so I figure that's about as good a basis for two guys trusting each other as there can be. And my father once told me that the most important thing in business is trust."

Ben stuck out his hand. "Let's shake on it," he said. "We can call it the Lieberman-Savage Bank and Trust."

Justin laughed as he shook his hand. "I think," he said, "I like Savage-Lieberman better."

The next morning Justin, Ben, and the Manchu Bannermen entered Shanghai, going directly to the house on Bubbling Well Road where they were met by Fiammetta and Barclay Strand. Seeing his wife, Justin quickly dismounted and took her in his arms, kissing her.

"*Anima mia,* thank God you're safe!" Fiammetta exclaimed. "How I missed you! Did you miss me?"

"With all my heart." He kissed her again, hungrily. "There were times," he whispered, "when I wondered if I'd ever see you again."

"If that horrible woman had hurt you, I'd have gone to Peking and scratched her eyes out!"

"The prisoner!" the head Bannerman shouted, dismounting. "Where's the prisoner?"

Justin released Fiammetta to shake Barclay's hand.

"Welcome back, old chap," the Englishman said. "We had a bit of adventure here while you were away. Li-shan escaped . . ."

Justin looked amazed.

"You mean he's not here?"

"No, he came back and was captured by your wife. We've got him under guard again, this time locked up in your scullery."

Justin looked at Fiammetta.

"Why in the world did he come back once he'd escaped?"

Fiammetta smiled rather proudly.

"He's in love with me," she said. "He tried to play Romeo, Chinese style, but I had a gun under my pillow."

"Your *pillow?* You mean he was in your bedroom?"

"Where else? He couldn't resist me. I hope you're jealous?"

Justin stared at his wife in wonder.

"Fiammetta," he said, "you amaze me."

"Where is the prisoner?" yelled the chief Bannerman again. "The Virtuous Concubine awaits him in Peking. We have no time to waste!"

"What did the beggar say?" Barclay asked.

"They want Li-shan," Justin replied with a troubled look. "I know what they'll do to him. As much trouble as he's given me, I can't help but feel sorry for him. He's a brave warrior, the kind of man China needs. If *he* were Emperor . . ." He shook his head sadly. "But instead, they have that fat drunk,

Hsien-feng, and that greedy bitch Yehenala, who wants to suck China dry like
a vampire. The whole thing is a farce and a tragedy at the same time. I wonder if China will ever get the government its people deserve?" He turned to the
Bannermen. "I'll bring you Li-shan."

He went through the moon gate into the courtyard, accompanied by Fiammetta. Across the yard, four British soldiers were standing guard outside the
scullery. "Did Li-shan really try to seduce you?" Justin asked.

"Of course. But he wouldn't have hurt me. I tell you, he's really in love
with me."

"Would you have *let* him seduce you?"

She smiled sultrily, taking his arm with one hand as her other held a white
parasol to protect her skin from the sun. "Well, I was tempted, darling. He really is terribly attractive—not as attractive as you, of course."

"Huh."

"What will the Manchus do to him?"

"I don't want to describe it to you, it's too horrible."

"Really, darling, you forget that I adore tortures—except when it's you
that's being tortured, of course."

"It's called the Death of a Thousand Cuts. I'll let your imagination supply
the details."

Even the gore-loving Fiammetta looked shocked.

"Is there any way we can save him? Even though he tried to make love to
me, I hate to think . . ."

"Yes, I know. I hate to think too. But Yehenala holds the big trump: Julie.
If she doesn't get Li-shan, she'll kill my daughter. So my hands are tied." They
had come up to the English guards. "I've come for the prisoner," he said.

"Yes, sir, Mr. Savage."

One of them unlocked the padlock on the wooden door and opened it.

"He's tricky, sir, and dangerous. We've got his hands bound, but even so,
be careful."

"I understand."

Justin ducked through the low door into the small room used to store food.
It was dark inside, for there were no windows, and it was cool. It smelled faintly
of beer, which was stored in a big cask in one corner.

In another corner crouched Li-shan. Justin saw his eyes first. They almost
glowed in the darkness, like a wolf's.

"The Manchus have come for you," Justin said quietly. "They're going to
take you to Peking. I'm . . ." He spread his hands slightly. "I'm sorry, Li-shan.
I've come to respect you. I wish I could help you, but I can't."

Li-shan slowly rose to a standing position. His hands were tied behind his back. Now he crossed the small room until he was inches in front of Justin.

"Where is Julie?" he asked.

"In the Forbidden City. Yehenala says that if I don't send you to her, she'll kill Julie."

Li-shan's hawk face became stony.

"So the evil concubine has won," he said. "And the Manchus will win. The great rebellion that started out so full of promise will, like everything else in China, be destroyed by its own corruption. You are lucky to be a barbarian. But I will admit I have come to respect you too, red-haired roundeye. You are a brave man. What will happen to Julie?"

"Yehenala has put a price on her of one million dollars—a great fortune. Somehow, I have to try and get my hands on it."

"Chang-mei asked me to protect Julie just before she died. I came to love the little half-breed with the amber eyes. Now, before I die, I ask *you* to protect her."

"Don't worry: she's my daughter. I'll move heaven and earth to raise the ransom."

The two men looked into each other's eyes.

"It is strange, barbarian," Li-shan said. "We have both loved the same women. Chang-mei, little Julie, and the golden-haired woman from Italy. Chang-mei used to speak to me about barbarian love, and I never quite understood it. Now I understand. My father would tell me I'm a fool because I came back to make love to a woman. Perhaps I am a fool. Perhaps love makes men foolish."

"If you could do it over again—?"

Li-shan smiled slightly.

"I would probably do the same thing."

He started toward the door.

"You're a Christian," Justin said. "Are you afraid?"

The Taiping prince turned to look at him.

"No," he said.

"I believe you."

Li-shan stepped out into the sunlight.

Justin thought, There goes a man.

Five mornings later a golden palanquin emerged from the Emperor's Palace in the Forbidden City and made its way across the Dragon Pavement Terrace over a marble bridge crossing the Golden Water River toward the Tien An Men, or principal southern gate. The palanquin was borne by ten imperial eunuchs and was preceded, as well as followed, by a company of Bannermen led by General Jung-lu, Yehenala's protégé and lover. Inside the gently swaying palanquin sat the Virtuous Concubine, as usual elaborately made-up and wearing a golden dragon robe and platform shoes sewn with seed pearls. Though custom forbade concubines ever leaving the Forbidden City, it was a testament to Yehenala's power over the alcoholic Emperor that she had extracted permission from Hsien-feng to attend the execution of Li-shan. The capture of the son of the Chung Wang was Yehenala's greatest coup to date, and the crafty concubine wanted to exploit it by showing herself to the people of Peking in her new position of ascendancy.

She had also scheduled a post-execution tryst in Jung-lu's house.

Crowds lined the streets of the capital and cheered as Yehenala's procession headed for the Field of Executions where an even greater crowd had gathered to watch the son of the notorious—or beloved, according to one's politics—Chung Wang be subjected to the excruciating Death of a Thousand Cuts. A cold wind blew in from the Gobi Desert under leaden wintry skies, causing the wretchedly poor Pekingese to shiver in their rags.

But they at least had rags. Li-shan, crouching in a wooden cage hanging five feet in the air from a wooden beam supported by two huge wooden tripods, was naked except for a loincloth. A sign attached to the cage read:

HERE HANGS THE TRAITOROUS DOG, LI-SHAN, SON OF
THE TRAITOROUS DOG THE SO-CALLED CHUNG WANG,
CONVICTED OF ABOMINATIONS AGAINST THE SON OF
HEAVEN. DEATH TO ALL TAIPING DEVILS!

As Yehenala's procession approached the field, the crowd parted to allow her palanquin to be carried onto the killing ground. Two companies of the White Banner were stationed around the field to maintain order.

In his cage, Li-shan watched the procession with what might have been taken for patrician bemusement. He knew he was about to undergo a horrible death. But he also knew the execution was part circus, to feed the hungry masses of the city gory entertainment. The Chinese, like everyone else on the planet, loved blood.

He vowed to himself he would not give them the satisfaction of hearing his agony.

When the procession stopped, the golden palanquin was set on the ground and Yehenala waved a red silk scarf. It was the signal to begin.

The cage was lowered to the ground by a winch and two Bannermen opened it, pulling Li-shan out. The crowd fell silent as his wrists were tied to ropes hanging from the beam. He was winched up until his feet dangled off the ground. His ankles were tied.

Then a half-dozen Bannermen carrying swords surrounded him and began cutting strips of skin and sinew from his torso, pulling the flesh slowly off and throwing the strips on the ground. Blood gushed from his body as he was flayed alive.

But to Yehenala's annoyance, Li-shan, the Taiping prince, uttered no screams of agony.

He remained defiantly silent.

PART FIVE

THE COUNT OF MONDRAGONE

41   THE WHITE-GLOVED BUTLER CARRIED the envelope on a silver salver into the dining room of the Savage mansion on Washington Square. "This was just delivered by hand, madame," he said to Adelaide Savage, who was absorbed in the details of a "love-nest murder" as reported in James Gordon Bennett's hugely successful tabloid, the *New York Herald*. Adelaide put down the newspaper and took the envelope off the salver. The paper was heavy and creamy, the kind, she knew, that was sold only by the finest stationers. Across it was written in elegant penmanship:

> *Mr. and Mrs. Sylvaner Savage*
> *Number Four Washington Square North*

"Thank you, Sheffield," Adelaide said.

"More coffee, madame?"

"No thank you. My husband should be down in a few minutes. Tell Cook to put on his eggs."

"Very well, madame."

The butler went into the pantry, leaving Adelaide alone. She had just redecorated the house for the third time, and the dining room had fallen victim to the newest fad in New York decor, "period rooms." Adelaide had chosen a "period" and "place" for each of the main rooms of her house, and the dining room had become "Pompeian." The hand-blocked wallpaper depicted a panorama of life in Pompeii, without any references to the scandalous erotic diversions available in that ancient city before the volcanic eruption, and she had replaced the old chandeliers with a large Roman-style hemispherical hanging alabaster lamp, suitably piped with gas. The windows overlooking the rear garden were draped with gauzy curtains in Pompeian red, the color that was the rage that season, some demented draper's idea of window treatments in ancient Rome, which Adelaide had bought at Lord & Taylor, the fashionable department store at the corner of Grand and Chrystie streets.

Now, she turned the envelope over. The flap was blazoned with a coat of arms, under which one word was written on a lateral scroll: Mondragone.

Adelaide felt a chill of apprehension. Her hands trembling, she opened the envelope and pulled out a stiff engraved invitation that read:

The Count and Countess of Mondragone
Request the Pleasure of the Company of
Mr. and Mrs. Sylvaner Savage
at a Ball
Wednesday, October the Twenty-fourth, 1860
The Villa
Fifth Avenue and Thirty-seventh Street
Eight o'Clock
Supper Will Be Served at Midnight, précis.
Cravate Blanche   *R.S.V.P.*

Adelaide leaned back in her chair, which was upholstered in Pompeian red to match the curtains, closed her eyes, and put her hand to her breast to calm her palpitating heart. What she had been dreading for so long had finally happened: Justin was making a move. All New York had engaged in an orgy of gossip and speculation ever since the mysterious Count and Countess of Mondragone had sailed into New York harbor from Europe on their private yacht two months before. Not that his identity was a mystery: by now, everyone knew that the Count was Sylvaner Savage's bastard half brother, Justin, returning to New York after ten years, presumably to square accounts. The mystery was, how was he going to square them? Did he have some secret poison he had acquired in China? Was he going to climb down the chimney and give Sylvaner the Death of a Thousand Cuts? The popular imagination, whetted by thousands of lurid plots served up in the penny dreadfuls the public devoured, went on a revenge binge, dreaming up the goriest way Justin could Get Even.

He certainly had a lot going for him: the Mondragones were said to be the most beautiful couple in the world, as well as the richest. It was whispered that they indulged in bizarre sexual practices that Justin had learned in China, that the Countess's one-year-old son, Gianfranco, was really the bastard son of one of the Emperor of China's concubines, fathered by Justin and smuggled out of the Forbidden City by opium-smoking eunuchs. The little facts the public knew were magnified a hundred times into the most grotesque fantasies. The city's army of reporters had tried in vain to interview the Mondragones, but they had remained sequestered in their suite at the St. Nicholas Hotel, further banking the fires of speculation by staying out of sight and telling nothing. The Mondragones were an even hotter topic than the impending presidential election, although that was getting considerable attention as well. After all, it was said that if the gawky lawyer from Illinois won, the South might secede. In which case, the Mayor of New York, Fernando Wood, had suggested that New York might also secede. It was all very heady that autumn in New York. Certainly, no one was bored.

But with Justin in town, Adelaide was circling the wagons. Now she opened her eyes as her husband came into the Pompeian dining room. Sylvaner had put on weight in the past few years, and his hair and beard were snow-white. But he was still an imposing man whose well-cut suits and grave demeanor imparted a sense of authority and sincere solidity so admired by his contemporaries. But the rumors that had swirled around his head for so many years had given his eyes a furtive, nervous look. Furthermore, he had developed a tic douloureux in his right cheek that could attack at any time, causing him moments of excruciating pain. There was no known cure; but while it was not life-threatening, the very randomness of the attacks made it impossible for Sylvaner to have any real peace. Except in the bottle: the only known painkiller that worked for the disease, and one that had been prescribed by his doctor, was gin. On this morning, as most mornings, Sylvaner was looking a bit hungover. This eminent businessman, one of the pillars of New York Society, had definite feet of clay.

"Have the children gone to school?" he asked, seating himself at the opposite end of the table as Adelaide rang for the butler.

"Oh, yes."

"You look rather pale. Is something the matter?"

The butler had come in the room with the elaborate silver coffeepot. "Sheffield, give this to Mr. Savage," Adelaide said, handing him the invitation.

He took it to the other end of the table. Sylvaner read the invitation while Sheffield poured his coffee from the Regency pot. The coffee was a special blend of powerful mocha-java. Suddenly Sylvaner started gagging, bending over his plate and drooling into the China export. Sheffield, ever the perfect English butler, did not blink an eye at this extraordinary performance, assuming his employer was having another attack of his tic doulourex. But Adelaide knew it was something else: an explosion of the fear and dread that had assaulted her husband since Justin's return to New York. After all, the several murder plots Sylvaner had hatched against Justin had been predicated on the assumption that they would work. To have Justin back in New York alive and well, rich and famous, was worse than the ghost of Hamlet's father blowing the whistle on King Claudius. Sylvaner knew that he faced not only social ruin but possibly criminal prosecution as well. He was a wreck.

"You fool!" Adelaide shouted, jumping to her feet. "Don't just stand there—do something! Help him!"

"But, madame, it's merely one of his attacks. . . ."

"It's not, you idiot! Oh, my darling . . ."

She raced down the table and put her arms around Sylvaner as he continued to drool and gag. She took a glass of water from the table and held it to his mouth. "Drink!" she commanded. He obeyed.

After a moment he calmed down. Straightening, he wiped his mouth with his napkin. Summoning all of his self-control, he said, "Thank you, dear. I'll be all right, Sheffield. You may serve breakfast."

"Very good, sir."

After the butler had left the room, Sylvaner pointed to the invitation and whispered, "What does it mean?"

"How do I know?"

"It's a trap! I know in my bones it's some sort of trap!"

"It may well be, but dare we not go to the ball?"

He gave her an icy stare. "I wouldn't miss it," he said, "for the world."

But for all his bravado, Sylvaner was scared. He knew full well what he had done to Justin.

But he had no idea what Justin was going to do to him.

Fifteen years earlier, a rich merchant had built one of New York's most extraordinary private residences on Fifth Avenue between Thirty-seventh and Thirty-eighth streets, a section of Murray Hill that was becoming increasingly fashionable. The house, which ran the full length of the block on the west side of the avenue, was a brownstone Gothic Revival castle, replete with a five-story octagonal tower topped by a crenellated parapet, several bays and oriels with leaded windows, an arched front door—all surrounded by a lawn and a brownstone retaining wall along the sidewalks surmounted by an elaborate wrought-iron fence. The builder's brother sniffed that the towers, bays, and porches reminded him of a mustard pot, pepper bottle, and vinegar cruet, and that the whole thing was a pretentious monstrosity and waste of money. But the merchant was happy. He and his wife entertained lavishly until the Panic of 1857 brought him to his financial knees. He put the castle, which he modestly called the "Villa," on the market, but times were tough and there were few buyers for what was now deemed a first-class folly.

A month after landing in New York, Justin offered the owner thirty-five thousand dollars cash for the place. It represented a considerable loss, but the desperate owner was in no mood to quibble; he accepted. And on the eighteenth of September, in the middle of the night so as to avoid reporters, Justin, Fiammetta, and their son, Gianfranco, moved from the St. Nicholas Hotel to their new home.

On the night of October twenty-fourth, the carriages of the city's most powerful and richest citizens began rolling up in front of the Villa as police held back a crowd of gawking onlookers. New Yorkers might not know much about the mysterious Count of Mondragone, but they knew he was a "Magnificent" Savage and thus likely to put on a good show. The Gothic castle was ablaze with light. Readers who thrived on such things had read in the tabloids of the dozens of cases of French champagne and French and Italian wines the Mondragones had ordered for the gala, the jars of caviar, the hams, roasts, and ducks that would be served at the midnight supper. But what drew most people was the human interest angle of two half brothers at each other's throats. Over the years the New York rumor mills had churned out stories of Sylvaner's attempts to murder Justin and of Justin's career as a pirate. Nothing too specific had been said in the tabloids for fear of libel suits. But the hints were broad enough for a scandal-hungry public to infer the worst. Besides, Sylvaner was in no position to sue anyone for libel. Now Justin was back to settle the score. It was so good, the spectators on Fifth Avenue didn't mind the cold wind from Canada that was sweeping the city. They huddled in their coats watching the carriages of the mighty disgorge their occupants.

When Sylvaner and Adelaide climbed out, they were greeted by jeers and catcalls.

"Hey, Sylvaner!" yelled one teenager, who had devoured every speculative word in the tabloids about the Savage drama, "watch out Justin don't pee in your soup!"

Howls of laughter from the rowdier spectators, shocked gasps from the more genteel. Adelaide, who was wearing a hooded cape, squeezed her husband's arm. "Get inside!" she hissed, and they hurried up the sidewalk to the arched front door.

Inside a small foyer, two footmen took Adelaide's cloak and Sylvaner's top hat and fur-collared coat. Then the couple went into the three-story-high entrance hall that soared to a stained-glass dome where they joined a line of guests waiting to be received by their hosts, the Count and Countess of Mondragone. Dozens of candles illuminated the gilt Corinthian columns supporting the galleries that circled the hall on the second and third floors.

It was a scene of feudal magnificence, a far cry, Adelaide thought, from the quarters Justin slept in when he shipped out as a cabin boy on the *Sea Witch* so many years before. What will he look like now? she wondered nervously. How will he act? What will he say? Were we wrong to come here tonight? What will he do?

Adelaide, who looked sufficiently magnificent herself in an aubergine taffeta ball gown and wearing her best sapphires, was usually known for her coolness under fire. But tonight she was nervous.

"I think I'm going to be sick to my stomach," Sylvaner whispered.

"No you won't. Be strong!" she whispered back, flashing a smile at Mrs. Gilford Charterhouse, the wife of a prominent banker who was standing in line in front of her.

"Dear Adelaide," cooed Mrs. Charterhouse, smiling back as she extended her gloved hand. "How lovely you look tonight. And Sylvaner: how anxiously you must be looking forward to seeing your long-lost half brother. Although it is *rather* peculiar he hasn't called on you before, since he's been in town two months."

"My half brother is a very busy man," Sylvaner mumbled, unable to think of anything else to say. Go away, you old bitch! he thought. Turn around! Stop gloating at me!

Giving him a smile that dripped catty condescension, Mrs. Charterhouse answered his prayers by turning her back to him.

The line inched forward. This is agony! Sylvaner thought. Agony! What the hell can I say? Dear Justin, how good it is to see you? Thought you were dead? God, why did we come? And yet, we can't leave. . . . They're all watching, waiting, ready to laugh at me if I show what I'm thinking. . . . Agony! Damn him, why *isn't* he dead? The son of a bitch survived *everything!* And now it's too late to kill him. . . . Or is it?

And then, suddenly, there they were.

The room fell silent as the two Savages confronted each other. The blond Countess of Mondragone looked spectacular in a white velvet ball gown cut low to reveal a broad breastscape. She had on her magnificent suite of rubies and diamonds, including her tiara. In "democratic" New York, one saw few tiaras; but then, one saw few bona fide countesses, and not a little of the attraction of the evening was that Fiammetta was the real thing.

After a moment Fiammetta smiled and extended her gloved hands to Adelaide. "Dear sister," she said in a loud voice so no one could possibly fail to hear, "Justin's told me *so* much about you. How enchanting to meet you at last. May we kiss?"

It was the last thing Adelaide expected. Gulping, she forced a smile and leaned forward as Fiammetta kissed her cheek.

"Dear brother," Justin said with a smile as he opened his arms. "It's been ten long years. How I've missed you! May we embrace?"

Sylvaner stared at him, mouth agape. Justin, so much taller than he remembered, was remarkably handsome in his white tie and tailcoat, his beautiful hair hanging to his shoulders. He came to Sylvaner and hugged him.

"We have so much catching up to do," he whispered in Sylvaner's ear.

Then he released him and stepped back. Everyone in the room applauded. Smile! Sylvaner thought. Play his game! Shake his hand! Smile!

What is he up to? screamed through Adelaide's brain. What is happening? I expected thunder and lightning, and I'm getting kisses and smiles!

What is he up to?

"If this gorilla, Lincoln, wins the election, what the hell am I going to do?" asked Rowland Macy, the former Nantucket whaler whose department store was the hottest new emporium in town. "I think the slave states are serious about seceding if he wins, and that means all sorts of problems for business. I do a lot of business in the South. I buy their cotton and sell them clothes. If they become another country, they'll have a different currency, a different customs service . . . it could ruin me!"

"Don't you worry about it, Mr. Macy," said Ben Lieberman, who was standing next to the merchant at the edge of the ballroom watching the waltzers twirl by. "Lincoln don't stand a chance. Douglas is gonna be the next President of the United States, and there's not gonna be no secedin' from the Union. Now, sir, I submit that there are some mighty fine-lookin' women here tonight. Mighty fine."

The ballroom on the second floor overlooked Fifth Avenue and was illuminated by two enormous round-globed crystal chandeliers that hung from an ornate coffered ceiling. The curtains were heavy gold damask, and the walls were white and gold. The waltzers were dancing to a fifteen-man orchestra. Ben, a glass of champagne in his hand, was smiling happily as he tapped his patent leather dancing pumps in time to the music.

"Well, I certainly hope you're right, Mr. . . . ."

"Lieberman, Mr. Macy. Ben Lieberman."

"Ah, yes . . . Mr. Lieberman. You sound as if you're from the South, sir?"

"Yes, I am. Alabama."

"And you think Douglas will win?"

"Yes, sir. No problem at all. I'd even bet on it. Give you good odds too."

"I'm not a betting man. But I don't know . . . that gorilla, Lincoln . . . and the Democrats are divided. . . . It's very uncertain times we live in."

"If you want uncertainty, you ought to go to China."

"You've been to China?"

"Yep. With my pal, Justin. I might say my boss, Justin. He just bought a bank today."

Rowland Macy looked down at the young man in the brand-new tailcoat with surprise.

"He bought a bank?" Macy said. "Which one?"

"The Mercantile Trust Company at Broadway and Wall Street. He's re-naming it the Savage Bank and Trust. He's President and I'm Vice President. We're gonna make millions."

Rowland Macy chuckled.

"You certainly sound sure of yourself, young man."

"Yep." Ben smiled up at him and touched his head. *"Yiddischer kopf.* Can't beat it. Well, this is mighty good champagne, and it's on the house. Guess I'll go get some more."

He walked away. Rowland Macy might have been amused by Ben's cock-iness, but he did not discount his boast. Although only one percent of New York's population of 810,000, already the Jews were a vital part of the city's retail business. It would certainly be interesting to see what a Jew could ac-complish in that citadel of Gentile rascality, Wall Street.

"What a fabulous party!" Tony Bruce said to Adelaide as he held her chair for her. The midnight supper had just been announced, and the guests had moved from the ballroom to the picture gallery next to it where twenty round tables seating ten apiece had been set up with a large placement chart near the door indicating where the guests were to sit. The gallery was a long, rather narrow room with a few second- and third-rate paintings on the walls to give some cred-ibility to its name. "How my poor, dear late wife would have enjoyed it."

Francesca Stuyvesant Bruce had been killed in a traffic accident on Broad-way the year before. Adelaide had been sincerely bereaved by the death of her shopping partner.

"Yes, Francesca loved parties," she said, unfolding her napkin as Tony sat to her right. In the center of each table, a tall vermeil vase exploded with a mass of beautiful flowers, while six vermeil candlesticks held tall tapers.

"And you, Adelaide," Tony went on, "are you enjoying this party? Or is it something of a strain?"

Adelaide shot him a look. Tony was one of those unusual people whom time never seemed to touch. He looked as young that night as he had that day ten years before when he and Adelaide had gone on the picnic to discuss Manhattan real estate—and other matters. "You know very well it's a strain on both Sylvaner and me," she said. "As does everyone else here tonight. Neither Sylvaner nor I has ever pretended that all was sweetness and light between himself and Justin."

"No, no one believes it was 'sweetness and light.' On the other hand I'm sure no one believes *all* the rumors."

"What rumors?"

"You know: we've discussed them before. The alleged confession Sylvaner signed in London some years ago."

"That canard is so absurd, it doesn't even merit denial. And I assume you remember what happened the last time you brought that up?"

"Oh, yes, the St. Nicholas Hotel." Tony laughed. "Poor Geraldine. They deported her back to Ireland. How sad."

"I still have those sketches of you and her in bed."

"But you see, poor Fran is dead, so they're really useless to you now, aren't they? And everyone in town knows I'm not exactly a monk, so you might as well either throw them out or frame them and hang them in Sylvaner's study."

"I think I'll keep them."

One of the dozens of waiters in the conversation-ringing room poured Perrier-Jouët into the tall flute glasses.

"All things considered," Tony went on, sipping the champagne, "I think Justin and his wife behaved very generously to you and Sylvaner tonight. It would seem he wants to signal the world that he's letting bygones be bygones. That family solidarity is more important than revenge, which tends to get messy."

"Perhaps. I hope you're right. Whatever happened in the past, Justin is family."

"Oh, he's family all over the place. He's not only Sylvaner's half brother, he's your nephew."

Adelaide shot him another sharp look. "Where did you hear that?"

"He told me."

"When?"

"Oh, I've talked to him several times since he came to New York. He's really an extremely likable chap. Quite bright too. But perhaps *you* didn't know you're his aunt? I can remember everyone in town trying to figure out who was Justin's mother."

"Yes, I knew. But did Justin ask you to meet him?"

"Oh, no, I came here."

"Why?"

Tony smiled. "That's my business."

"I can see you're being tedious again. I really think I'd prefer talking politics."

"Why? There's nothing to talk about. Lincoln's going to win and there'll be a war. Wonderful opportunity for profiteers. Have you noticed how many bankers there are here tonight? I wonder why?"

The waiters began serving the first course, which was listed on the menu as:

Première Assiette
Le Jambon Persillé Dijonnaise
relevé de bonne Moutarde forte de Dijon
escorté d'un Bourgogne Aligoté frais et gouleyant
des Hautes Côtes de Nuits

"Justin has bought a bank," Sylvaner said an hour later as he and Adelaide returned downtown to Washington Square in their carriage. He was staring out the window at the passing gaslights. "That's why there were so many bankers there tonight. The little bastard's suddenly become the Golden Boy of Wall Street, and everyone wants to kowtow to him. They all think he has unlimited riches—or at least his wife has."

"Does she?"

"Well, she's certainly rich. They say she's loaned him a million dollars in gold to put in the bank's vault as a specie reserve. . . ."

"What's that?"

"Banks by law have to have a certain amount of gold on hand for payment on demand. When banknotes say 'redeemable in gold,' it means someone can come in with a fifty-dollar bill and turn it into gold. That doesn't happen too often, but banks have to keep enough gold on reserve to satisfy the normal demand. All the New York banks combined have only forty-three million dollars in gold in reserve, so that means Justin, that little brat, controls one forty-third of all the gold on Wall Street. It gives him a lot of power."

"He's not so little anymore."

"You're right. He's taller than I am."

There was bitterness in his voice. He winced and trembled as an attack of his painful tic hit his cheek. "Quick," he gasped, "the gin. . . ."

Adelaide took a silver flask from a pocket on the carriage door and handed it to him. He took a slug of the gin, then sank back in his seat.

"I'm convinced I got this damned tic from brooding about Justin," he said.

"In all fairness, he and his wife couldn't have been more friendly tonight."

"But do you believe it? I don't. It's an act. Everybody expected him to challenge me to a duel, at the very least, but instead he plays the friendship card. It's all a ploy to disguise what he's really up to."

"Which is?"

"God, I wish I knew."

Their carriage turned into Washington Square.

"Momma, you know what they say at school?" asked nine-year-old Francis Savage the next morning at breakfast in the Pompeian dining room. He was sitting opposite his four-year-old sister, Georgiana, while Sylvaner and Adelaide were at the head and foot of the table. The two Savage children were stunning.

"No, darling. What do they say?"

"They say the Count of Mondragone is related to me. Is that true?"

Adelaide looked down the table at her husband as Georgiana poured more cream on her oatmeal. Sylvaner put down his fork.

"Yes, it's true," he said, clearing his throat. "You might as well hear it from me, rather than other people outside the family. The Count of Mondragone is my younger half brother, Justin Savage. We both had the same father."

"Who was his mother?" Francis asked, intrigued by this family scandal.

"My sister," said Adelaide. "So Justin is really my nephew."

"Golly, so he's *my* cousin—and Georgiana's. Is that right?"

"That's right, dear. Finish your oatmeal."

"When do we get to meet him? He sounds really interesting! They say at school he was a Chinese pirate and he's been to the Forbidden City in Peking and fought with Garibaldi in Italy—I want to meet him!"

Sylvaner cleared his throat. "Perhaps someday you will, Francis. But not now."

"Why?"

"There are reasons. For one thing, he's not a nice man. He's really not what one could properly call a gentleman."

"But he's a count?"

"A title of nobility does not necessarily mean a person is noble. You see, this Justin was born out of wedlock."

Adelaide shot him a "don't say that" look, but it was too late.

"What's that mean?" Georgiana asked, licking her spoon.

"It means he's a bastard," her brother explained matter-of-factly.

"Francis!" gasped his mother. "Wherever did you learn that shocking word?"

"At school." Francis looked embarrassed.

Adelaide groaned. "What is the modern world coming to? We send our children to the finest, most expensive private schools in Manhattan, and they come home swearing like stevedores! If you ever say that word again, young man, I'll wash your mouth out with soap!"

"I'm sorry, Momma."

The butler came into the dining room. "Excuse me, sir," he said to Sylvaner. "There is a gentleman in the drawing room who wishes to see you."

"Tell him to wait till I've finished my breakfast," Sylvaner snapped, buttering his toast.

"Excuse me, sir. The gentleman is a marshal of the City of New York. He says this is an official matter."

A look of fear came over Sylvaner's face. He put down his toast and got to his feet. "Very well," he said. "I'll see the man. You might pour me some fresh coffee."

"Yes, sir."

He left the room. The moment he was gone, Francis turned to his mother and said, "Is the Count of Mondragone *really* a bad man? I mean, is he like a villain in a play?"

Adelaide stirred her tea, thinking of her sweet younger sister. The fact that she had conspired to murder Constance's son weighed on her like a ton of guilt. She raised her teacup to her mouth as a tear appeared in her eye.

"No," she finally said. "I don't think he is a bad person. It's just that families sometimes can develop strains and jealousies and . . . well, relatives sometimes never speak to each other."

"Does that mean we'll *never* get to meet him?" Francis sounded disappointed.

"Perhaps someday, as your father said. Now finish your breakfast. You mustn't be late for school."

"ADELAIDE!" The apoplectic roar came from the direction of the drawing room. "ADELAIDE, COME HERE AT ONCE!"

The children looked frightened as their mother got out of her chair.

"Poppa must have had another tic fit," Georgiana said.

"It's pronounced 'teek,' dear," Adelaide said, hurrying to the door. "It's French. 'Tick' is something found on dogs."

Even in a crisis, Adelaide was alert to the nuances of snobbery. In New York, the wrong accent could mean social ruin, and no matter what disaster might befall her, Adelaide would fight to the death to avoid social ruin.

When she arrived in the drawing room, Sylvaner was standing by the mantel leafing through what looked like a legal document. He looked up as she came in the room, closing the sliding doors behind her.

"Sylvaner, what is it?" she asked.

"Tony Bruce is suing me. He claims Francis and Georgiana are really *his* children, and he wants them. Is this true, woman?"

"Sylvaner, keep your voice down. . . ."

"Is it TRUE?" he roared.

"Of course not. There must be some mistake. . . ."

"You lie! He says in here he has the dates and times that you slept with him at the St. Nicholas Hotel, he has bank deposits of the sums you paid him. . . . It's all making sense now, the tens of thousands you euchred out of me during your pregnancies, and I was stupid enough to think you were redecorating the damned nurseries. They went to him, didn't they? You paid him to impregnate you, like a damned stud! Do you deny it?"

"NO!" she cried. "I wanted children, and you couldn't give them to me because you're infertile! I went to four doctors, and they all told me there was nothing wrong with me, so it had to be you!"

He looked so thunderous, she feared he might have a stroke. "Why did you pick Tony Bruce, of all the rotten, no-good . . ."

"Because he's from one of the best families in New York, and he's handsome! And look at our children: they're beautiful!"

"STRUMPET!" he roared, throwing the papers at her. "Whore! They're not *mine!* They're his! You've taken away the most precious thing in my life. . . ."

"Sylvaner!" she screamed.

He was lumbering toward her. Now he took her throat in his big hands and started to choke her.

"They're not mine," he kept repeating, sobbing with fury and despair. "Not mine. . . ."

"You're choking me!" she gasped, trying to pry loose his fingers. "I can't breathe. . . ."

"Poppa, stop!"

It was Francis and Georgiana, who had slid open the doors. They looked terrified. "Stop, *please—!*"

"Poppa—!"

He looked at them, wildness in his eyes. He hesitated a moment. Then he released Adelaide, slapping her so hard that she fell back against a table, knocking it over as she sprawled backward on the floor.

"You can reach me at my club," he panted, lumbering out of the room into the entrance hall. She heard the front door slam.

The children ran to Adelaide, who was sitting up. Blood was running down her chin where Sylvaner had slapped her. Georgiana was sobbing.

"What is it, Momma?" she cried, hugging her. "Why is Poppa so angry?"

It's Justin, she thought, painfully getting to her feet. Somehow Justin is behind this. This is how he's getting even. Tony doesn't give a damn about these kids, all he wants is money. Perhaps we deserve it for what we did to Justin, but dear God, I have to protect my children. . . .

Wiping the blood from her chin, she said, "Children, you're going to skip school today. I want you to go upstairs and put on your best clothes."

"Why, Momma?" Francis asked.

"We're going to meet your cousin Justin."

42   "ISN'T HE THE CUTEST BABY you've ever seen?" Justin said, holding up his son under his arms. Gianfranco, who had big blue eyes and curly blond hair, was giggling happily as his father dunked him into the water in his bathtub on the third floor of the Villa on Fifth Avenue. "And look how he loves water! He must be half fish."

"He's almost as cute as you were," said Ah Pin. When they sailed to New York from London, Justin had talked his old nanny into returning to America with them. She had moved into the Villa and was now nannying Gianfranco, who had been named after Fiammetta's father. Ah Pin stood next to the tub in the big marble bathroom, holding a towel with both hands as Justin sat in the tub playing with his son. "Isn't it amazing, Ah Pin?" he said, dunking a squealing Gianfranco into the water again. "When he was born, Gianfranco weighed seven pounds six ounces. And now, just in one year, he's more than tripled his weight. Isn't nature incredible?"

"Yes, and human nature's incredible too. Yours, in particular."

Justin looked up at the nanny, who continued to wear western clothes. "What do you mean?"

"How could you have been so nice to that snake, Sylvaner, last night? Have you forgotten he tried to have you murdered twice? Have you forgotten he tried to murder *me*? The man's a dangerous, cold-blooded killer, and yet you ask him and that vampire wife of his into your house and treat them both like . . . like family!"

"They *are* family," Justin said. "My family. It's important to me to keep up a certain show of solidarity in public. Everyone expected us to be at each other's throats, and I've learned that you never do what people expect. Okay, you cute kid: want to go dunk-dunk again?"

Gianfranco giggled as his father dipped him in the water. The baby splashed his hands, throwing water everywhere, including Ah Pin's bombazine skirt.

"He cheated you!" Ah Pin persisted. "He stole your inheritance, he trafficked in opium, he caused you to be tortured—the man's a monster! In China, you invite your enemy to your house, you feed him, then you *kill* him."

"But we're not in China. We're in New York, and the tabloids have already turned this into a circus. I'll deal with Sylvaner, but in my own way, in private."

"The only way you 'deal with' a killer is to kill him! Aiyee, you're too damned nice! You could have killed him in London, but you let him live. I must breathe the fire of the dragon into your veins! Remember: he wants you dead. He's tried twice, and don't think he won't try a third time! You should kill him before he kills you. Never be nice to your enemy."

"Ah Pin, you're never going to win the Christian Turn-the-Other-Cheek Award."

"Christianity is a foolish religion. I tried to read the Bible, but it doesn't make any sense. Who ever heard of the meek inheriting the earth? A ridiculous idea, contrary to all reality. But if you won't kill him, why not bring him to trial? We have his signed confession."

"I've talked to lawyers, and they say it won't hold up in court. Besides, I don't want to go to court. I'm trying to save what little dignity we Savages have because I think that's what my father would have wanted. A public trial would just become another tabloid circus, and there's been too much of that already."

"Aiyee, I'll never understand you Americans!" Gianfranco started to sneeze. "Here: give me the child. He may be part fish, but we don't want him catching cold."

She took the baby from Justin and wrapped him in the towel as Justin picked up a long-handled brush and started scrubbing his back.

"Come, Gianfranco," Ah Pin said, "it's time for your wet nurse."

She took the baby out and closed the door. Justin continued scrubbing his back in the tub, humming to himself the latest hit song that had swept the country, "Listen to the Mockingbird."

Five minutes later Fiammetta opened the door.

"It's your Aunt Adelaide," she said. "She's here with her children. She wants to see you. She looks terribly upset, and someone has hit her face—hard."

"What's this all about?"

"I have no idea."

Fifteen minutes later he came into the first-floor drawing room where Adelaide was standing with her two children. There was a large bruise on her face where Sylvaner had struck her. She had tried unsuccessfully to disguise it with powder.

"You wanted to see me?" Justin said in a coolly formal manner.

"I wanted to speak to you for a few minutes, if I may," Adelaide said. "And I wanted you to meet your cousins. This is my son, Francis, and my daughter, Georgiana. Children, go shake hands with Cousin Justin."

The children crossed the big room. Francis bowed and Georgiana curtsied, a grave look on her pretty face.

"How do you do, Cousin Justin?" they said in tandem.

Justin, who adored children, was enchanted. He leaned over to shake Francis's hand, who was eyeing him with awe. "How do you do, Francis?"

"Sir, is it true that you were a pirate?" he asked.

"My first wife was. I just steered the junk."

"The junk? How do you steer a piece of junk?"

"A junk is a Chinese boat."

"Oh. Is it true you know Garibaldi?"

"That's right. He's my son's godfather."

"Gosh. When he invaded Sicily last May, I thought that was really exciting."

"Yes, he's a great man."

"Is it true you—"

"Francis," interrupted his mother. "You're monopolizing the conversation."

"I'm sorry, Momma. But there's so many things I want to ask Cousin Justin. I mean, he's really led an exciting life, and all I get to do is go to school, which is boring."

"School may be boring, but it's important," Justin said, turning to Georgiana. "So you're Georgiana," he went on. "You're a very pretty little girl."

"Thank you, Cousin Justin," she said.

"May I kiss you?"

"Oh, that would be nice, I think."

He picked her up, cradled her in his arms, and kissed her, thinking of Julie in faraway Peking. His heart ached.

"May I whisper something in your ear?" Georgiana asked.

"Of course."

She cupped her hands around her mouth and whispered in his left ear. Justin's smile faded.

"I'll do what I can," he said, kissing her again, then putting her down to the floor.

"You two wait in the carriage while I talk to Justin," Adelaide said.

"Good-bye, Cousin Justin," Francis said, taking his sister's hand. "Some-day I want you to tell me all about being a pirate. Gosh, wait till I tell the guys in school I know a real pirate!"

When they were gone, Justin laughed. "I used to be ashamed of being a pirate," he said to Adelaide, "but maybe I should write a book about it. They're wonderful children."

"Thank you. What did Georgiana whisper in your ear?"

"That Sylvaner hit you. She doesn't know why, and she's afraid he'll never come home again. Why *did* he hit you?"

"You don't know?"

"No."

She hesitated, folding and unfolding her gloved hands nervously. "Justin," she finally said, "you must believe me when I tell you I had no idea your mother was my dear sister. That came to me as a total surprise. If I'd known . . . well, let me just say there are certain things I would never have agreed to."

"Like having me murdered on the *Sea Witch*?"

She looked at him, tears in her eyes.

"Oh, Justin, I know we've done you a terrible injustice! I can't expect you to ever forgive us or to forget what we've done. But *please:* don't take our children away from us! You've seen them now: you have to admit they're sweet and totally innocent of their parents' crimes! Don't punish them by taking them away from their home. Just knowing that they are not his has been a cruel punishment to Sylvaner. Perhaps it's not enough to make up to you for the terrible things he did in the past, but—"

"What *are* you talking about?" Justin interrupted.

She wiped her eyes. "You don't know?"

"Know what?"

Again, she hesitated.

"You mean, this wasn't your doing?"

"What?"

"Tony's lawsuit?"

"Tony Bruce? Whom is he suing?"

"He's suing Sylvaner for custody of Francis and Georgiana. He says he's really their . . . father. . . ." She stopped. "Have I made a mistake?"

"Adelaide, I don't know what this is all about, but I assure you I would never sink so low as to hurt your children. I intend to settle with Sylvaner my own way, but I would never hurt anyone's children."

"But then, why did . . ." She looked confused.

"Tony Bruce has come to me several times in the past few weeks telling me he has valuable information about you and Sylvaner that could ruin both of you. Naturally, I was curious to know what he was talking about, but he said he wanted me to invest in one of his stock schemes first. He was talking about quite a lot of money."

"Now I'm beginning to understand," Adelaide said.

"I asked some of my friends on Wall Street about him, and they said he was, to put it bluntly, a crook. When I told Tony I wasn't interested, he went into a rage and said that I was as cheap as all the other Savages and that he'd *force* us to pay him money. I didn't know what he was talking about, but now I'm beginning to see what he meant."

"Knowing that, why did you invite him to your party last night?"

"When I invited him, I didn't know. And I wanted to see what kind of relationship he had with you, which is why I seated him next to you."

"We've hardly been 'cheap' with him. He's been draining me for years. I talked Sylvaner into investing a large sum with Tony a few years ago, and he lost it all. So now he's upping the stakes with this lawsuit."

"Is it true?"

"That he's the father? Yes."

Justin let out a low whistle of surprise, thinking that Aunt Adelaide was not exactly what she appeared to be. "And Sylvaner didn't know?"

"He knows now. That's why he hit me. Oh, I know what you must think of me, and I'm hardly proud of what I did. But I wanted children so desperately, and Sylvaner's infertile. You see, I thought Constance had no children, and I didn't want to be the last Crowninshield. . . . If only I'd known about you, things might have been different. By the way, I brought you something." She opened her purse and pulled out a silver-framed picture. She came to Justin and gave it to him. "It's a daguerreotype of your mother," she said. "My dear, sweet sister. It was taken a year before she died. Wasn't she beautiful?"

Justin looked at the lovely girl seated in a chair, smiling at the camera.

"Yes," he said softly. "Yes, she was."

"It was one of the first daguerreotypes ever taken in New England. I remember the photographer came to Salem and took all our pictures. I thought you'd like to have it."

"Yes, thank you. It's very kind of you."

She put her hand on his arm. "Don't hate me, Nephew," she said quietly. "Hate Sylvaner if you must, but don't hate me."

She squeezed his arm slightly, then walked out of the room. Rather to his surprise, Justin realized that he didn't hate her at all.

Tony Bruce kissed the waitress good-bye, then let her out of his brownstone house on West Thirteenth Street in Greenwich Village. After he closed the door, he smiled, pulled a handkerchief from his pants pocket, and wiped her rouge off his lips. Then he went into his drawing room to pour himself a nightcap. He was glad his children were away at boarding school. It allowed him to do his romancing at home, which was so much cheaper than going to hotels.

As usual, Tony was up to his neck in unpaid bills, and his house was beginning to show it. The upholstery on his chairs and sofas was worn, and the house looked generally rundown and tatty. But, again as usual, Tony never let the precarious state of his finances spoil his fun. The whiskey he poured was top quality, and the waitress he had just bedded was certainly one of the prettiest teenage girls pouring beer at the Gaieties, a popular beer hall at 616 Broadway.

The grandfather clock in the hall struck three A.M. Tony knew the Gaieties would still be going full blast. If New York worked hard by day, it played hard by night. The theater was booming, although the *Herald* piously and hypocritically deplored the fact that too many plays glorified "murder, adultery, fornication, arson, lying, robbery and a few other choice crimes without name." That the *Herald*'s enormous popularity was due to the fact that it glorified in lip-smacking detail the exact same crimes was, needless to say, left unsaid.

Tony tossed off the whiskey neat, then put the glass down and yawned. "And so," he said to himself, "to bed. This time, alone."

He started to turn down the oil lamp when a voice behind him said, "Leave it on."

Tony literally jumped. He turned to see a man in a top hat and black, fur-collared coat standing in the door to the hall. The man was holding a gun. The man was Sylvaner Savage.

"How did you get in?" Tony said.

"Your kitchen window's unlocked," Sylvaner replied. "A little detail you overlooked as you romped with that girl in your overused bed. That's very careless of you, Tony. There's a lot of crime in this town."

His speech was slurred.

"You're drunk," Tony said.

"Very drunk."

"Get out of here, or I'll get the police."

"You're not going to get anything except what you deserve, you adulterous bastard. You're not going to take my children away from me. They're *mine*, not yours. I'm going to keep them."

Tony was beginning to sweat. He forced a smile.

"Look, Sylvaner, let's talk this over. How . . . how about a drink?"

"No. And there's nothing to talk over."

"Sure there is! Look, I'll be straight with you, Sylvaner. I'm terribly hard up. I've got bills up to my ears, the market's . . . well, I've had some bad luck. I don't want your kids. Hell, I can barely pay the tuitions for my own kids, I don't need to take on more. If you'll give me a break financially, I'll withdraw the lawsuit. . . ."

"No."

"Just fifty thousand. That's all I need, Sylvaner. Then I'll never bother you again. Trust me."

"That's what all blackmailers say, Tony, and I wouldn't trust you farther than I can spit. But that's not why I'm going to kill you. I'm going to kill you because *I'm* the father of Francis and Georgiana, *me,* not you. There's only room for one of us in this town."

He cocked the gun.

"You're mad . . ." Tony gasped.

"Possibly. I don't know what sanity is anymore."

He fired, hitting Tony in the chest. Tony sank to his knees, raising his hands in a futile gesture of self-protection.

Sylvaner fired a second time, again hitting him in the chest.

Tony slumped over, dead.

Sylvaner looked at him a moment. Then he swayed into the hall and started toward the kitchen.

How easy it was to kill, he reflected. What a nice feeling it gave you. A real thrill, a sense of satisfaction and finality.

What a nicer feeling it would give to kill Justin.

"Mr. Savage," said the young man in the hound's-tooth suit, "my name is Detective Barney O'Toole. I'm with the Metropolitan Police. May I speak with you for a few minutes?"

"Of course," Justin said, indicating a chair. The detective had been brought to his study by his butler. "Take a seat."

"You've read about the murder of Mr. Anthony Bruce in his house on West Thirteenth Street early this morning?" the detective asked, sitting down.

"Yes. Someone broke into his house and shot him."

"Twice, in the chest. Are you aware that yesterday morning Mr. Bruce sued Sylvaner Savage, claiming that he was actually the father of Sylvaner's children?"

Justin leaned back in his chair and smiled. "Yes," he said, "but that was something of a joke. I think if you ask around Wall Street, you'll discover that Tony Bruce's character was pretty shady, and that he was not above blackmail. In fact, he'd been trying to get me to loan him a considerable amount of money in return for this cock and bull story about Sylvaner's children."

"I'm surprised to hear you say that, Mr. Savage."

"Why? Because you've read in the tabloids that Sylvaner and I have had our problems? Well, you have to understand that the tabloids blow things out of proportion in order to sell papers. You surely don't suspect Sylvaner of murdering Tony Bruce?"

"Yes, frankly. He's high on our list of suspects, because he had a motive."

"Lots of people had a motive to kill Tony. You may know that he was a lady's man. There are dozens of husbands in this town who would love nothing better than to put a bullet or two through him. Besides, Sylvaner was here last night."

The detective looked surprised.

"Here? In this house?"

"That's right. He and I are in the process of mending fences, and I've been buying Savage Line stock so it was also a business meeting. We sat up most of the night, drinking and talking. I fear we both drank a little too much, but I can guarantee you he couldn't have shot Tony Bruce because he was here."

"Would you testify to that in court?"

"Gladly."

The detective stood up. "In that case, Mr. Savage, I won't take any more of your time. And I thank you for saving us a lot of time. I'll take Sylvaner's name off our list of suspects."

"*Cherchez le mari*," Justin said, escorting him to the door. "Look for the husband. Then you'll find your murderer."

"You may be right."

He shook Justin's hand and left. Alone, Justin went to another door and opened it. Fiammetta came in.

"Did you hear?" he asked.

"Yes, but I don't understand. Why would you, of all people, defend Sylvaner? Here was a perfect opportunity to have your dirty work done for you by the City of New York!"

"Yes, and have Francis and Georgiana grow up knowing their father was an executed murderer? No thanks. I don't want any murderers in the family."

"But you already have one: Sylvaner!"

"Nevertheless, I'll deal with him my own way: quietly and in private. I've got Gianfranco to think of too. No, the Savages are going to be paragons of

respectability. We're going to get out of the tabloids. We're going to stop entertaining the public like a bunch of buffoons. We're going to become stuffy
and dull. After all, I'm a banker now."

She smiled slightly as she coiled her arms around his neck. "I hope not *too*
stuffy and dull?"

He grinned. "Never with you," he said, kissing her.

After a moment she pushed him away.

"What's wrong?" he said.

"I forgot that I'm angry with you," she said, a pouty look on her face.

"Why? What have I done?"

"You talked me into coming to New York, but all the excitement's happening in Italy with my darling Giuseppe."

"We just had a murder, isn't that exciting enough?"

"You know what I mean. Giuseppe's conquering Italy, and all you want to
be is a stuffy, dull old banker. I miss Rome and Europe. New York's so dirty
and provincial. The shopping's not bad, but the food!" She made a face.

"Maybe this is a good time to lose some weight?"

She turned on him, her eyes blazing. "I've lost five pounds!" she exclaimed.
Fiammetta's weight problem had become linked in her mind with their disparity
in age, and she was touchy about her tendency to put on poundage—almost as
touchy as she was about her birthdays. She sighed. "Oh, all right: that's a lie.
But, Justin, I want to go home for a while."

He took her in his arms again. "Give me some time to get the bank on its
feet. Then we'll take a trip to London, Rome, or wherever you want to go. And
you can shop, shop, shop."

Her face lit up. "Oh, darling, that would be wonderful! When can we go?"

"Maybe for Christmas, after the election."

"Christmas in Rome," she sighed. "That sounds like Heaven."

"The only problem is, there just might be a little thing called a war."

"Oh, darling, who believes that? Everyone says it would ruin business. New
Yorkers don't want to fight wars: they want to shop."

That night, Justin took a taxi down Fifth Avenue to Washington Square. He
got out in front of Number Four. After the taxi left, he stood under a gaslight
for a while, looking at the house he had grown up in. A wave of memories broke
over his brain. His father, Nathaniel. He had always been so proud of him, proud
of the fact that he had been a sea captain. There was something so clean and
fine about being master of one of those beautiful clipper ships. Now the clipper ships of the Savage Line were gone, replaced by ugly, smoke-belching

steamships. Justin supposed it was progress of a sort, but the world had lost something beautiful.

Justin wondered what his father would have thought of what Sylvaner had done to the Savage Line. First there had been the opium. Justin had been able to put a stop to that, although at great cost in terms of lost crews and sunken ships. Now there were rumors that Sylvaner was leasing some of his ships to "blackbirders," as the slave traders were known. Although the slave trade had been illegal for years, Justin knew that it still went on, encouraged by the Southern slaveholders and the enormous profits in it. Justin had no proof the rumors about Sylvaner were true. But now he knew how to find out, and if they were true, once again he would stop it. The Savage Line must be a company that men could respect again, as it had been under his father. Justin was the man to do it.

He crossed the sidewalk and climbed the stairs to ring the doorbell. It was a cold, quiet evening. He remembered looking out the windows of the house as a boy, watching Washington Square undergo its seasonal changes. He was no longer a boy, but at least now he knew who his mother was and, thanks to Adelaide, what she looked like.

Sheffield opened the door.

"Yes?"

"Tell Mr. and Mrs. Savage that Justin Savage would like to see them."

Sheffield looked slightly startled, as if Justin were a bad ghost. "Please come in, sir. Mr. and Mrs. Savage are in the drawing room."

"I know the way."

He walked past the butler into the entrance hall. How familiar it all seemed, and yet how different. He remembered his excitement the day the *Sea Witch* was sighted off Sandy Hook, breaking the China Run record.

He walked into the double drawing room. How different it looked after Adelaide's latest reincarnation of its decor. What had once been a handsome Federal parlor was now a "period room," some decorator's Moorish fantasy, perhaps the harem of a sultan. Sylvaner and Adelaide were seated in front of the fire, reading. When he saw Justin, Sylvaner stood up.

"It's time we had a talk," Justin said, sliding the double doors behind him shut. He walked into the room as both Adelaide and Sylvaner watched him. "Have you ever been tortured, Sylvaner?" he asked in a pleasant tone.

Sylvaner, who looked as if the Devil had just walked in, said, "No."

"I have. I wouldn't recommend it for your health, but I suppose you could say it's an interesting experience. Those Camorra goons you hired took me into an actual torture chamber, tied my wrists behind me, branded me on the ass which hurt like hell, then hauled me up to the ceiling and let me drop almost, but not quite, to the floor. It tore both my arms out. The pain was so excruciating I almost became a drug addict, which was a bit ironic considering the profits you've made off the opium trade. I owe you for that, Sylvaner, as well as several other things."

"If you've come here to threaten me—"

"I've come here to punish you," Justin interrupted. "Or more exactly, to *start* to punish you. It's going to take a long time, Sylvaner, because you've done so many things to be punished. You're bad, Sylvaner. You could almost qualify as a monster. I think you're up there with Attila the Hun, Cesare Borgia, and Iago, although perhaps that's unfair to them. But the curious thing is, I saved your skin today with the police. They were going to arrest you for the murder of Tony Bruce. . . ."

"So it *was* you!" Adelaide interjected, turning to her husband.

"That's a lie!" Sylvaner shouted.

"Keep your voice down," Justin said. "One reason I gave you an alibi was so that Francis and Georgiana would be spared seeing their alleged father dangle from a hangman's noose, so don't wake them up now. I told the police you were with me last night, so you're no longer a suspect. But there's a price for my saving you, Sylvaner."

"I won't be blackmailed!"

"My God, you're really despicable. Does your mind ever climb out of the gutter? I don't want your damned money. But you're going to do what I say. I've been buying Savage Line shares on the market. Very quietly, a few thousand here, a few thousand there . . . but they all add up. I now own six percent of the stock, and I want a seat on the Board. Otherwise, I'll go to the police and tell them I lied about being with you last night."

There was a long silence. Finally, Sylvaner said, "Why do you want to be on the Board?"

"Because you've disgraced my father's name. You trafficked in opium, and now there are rumors you've leased Savage Line ships to slavers. If I find out that's true, it's going to be stopped. I'm going to force you to be honest, Sylvaner, which may be the worst punishment for you I could think of. I'll expect a formal invitation by noon tomorrow, or I go to the police. Good evening, Aunt Adelaide."

He walked out of the room, closing the doors behind him. Adelaide turned to her husband and said, "You'll do it, of course."

"I have no choice, damn him." He went to a sideboard and poured himself a glass of gin.

"So you murdered Tony Bruce?" she said quietly.

He drank the gin. "Once again, I had no choice, thanks to your treachery."
He refilled the glass. "There's an interesting thing about murder, Adelaide. It's
rather like making love. It makes you feel good." He drank more gin, looking
at his wife. "And it makes you want to do it again."

43 FIAMMETTA'S LACK OF INTEREST IN American politics was understandable: she was an Italian. But Justin, like most other Americans, was
being sucked inexorably into the vortex that was inching the country toward
the bloodiest conflict of its history. He had become interested in Lincoln when,
to most people's surprise, the former Illinois congressman had gotten the nomination of the Republican Party. When Lincoln came to New York to make a
speech to the Young Men's Republican Union at the Cooper Union, Justin
bought a ticket for twenty-five cents.

The low-profile way that Lincoln came to New York reflected the casual
politics of the day. No one was there to meet him when he stepped off the
Cortlandt Street ferry. He made his way to the Astor House Hotel, across from
City Hall, by himself, as if he were a tourist rather than a candidate for the
highest office in the land. The next day, Sunday, Lincoln took a two-cent ferry
ride to Brooklyn to hear the well-known antislavery preacher Henry Ward
Beecher at the Plymouth Church. Then one of the Young Republicans finally
arrived to show him some of the sights of the city, including the notorious
slum known as the Five Points where gangs like the Dead Rabbits terrorized
the neighborhood and indulged in every known vice. Lincoln was told that
so far in that year, 1860, seventy-one thousand crimes had been recorded in
the city.

Lincoln was shown Sweet's Restaurant on Fulton Street where illegal slave
traders, "blackbirders," liked to gather to exchange notes on their infamous,
lucrative profession. Even though slave trading was punishable by hanging, no
one had ever been hanged for it, few were even arrested, and no less a personage
than United States District Attorney James I. Roosevelt had said publicly that
President James Buchanan would "probably pardon" anyone convicted of slave
trading. So there was little incentive for Sylvaner *not* to lease his ships to the
traders, which was exactly what Justin found he had done after coming on to
the Board of the Savage Line. Now he had yet another weapon to use against
Sylvaner. But again, he didn't want the publicity. He forced Sylvaner to cancel the leases, which was done quietly. The Savage Line was again cleansed

by Justin. And Sylvaner's hatred of his half brother increased almost to the bursting point.

The popular view that the North was solidly antislavery was solidly wrong. Lincoln knew that most of the business interests in New York wanted to appease the slaveholders—Sylvaner was certainly not alone. Even the highly respected and devout New York branch of the American Tract Society had come out strongly for slavery. Thus, the speech that Lincoln delivered at the Cooper Union was anything but inflammatory: after all, he wanted to get elected. Still, Justin was enormously impressed by the tall, awkward midwesterner. Though he spoke with a twang, his delivery was firm and engaging. At one point, he electrified the audience by saying: "If slavery is right, all words, acts, laws, and constitutions against it are themselves wrong." Justin leapt to his feet, applauding and cheering. Technically he was a citizen of the Kingdom of Piedmont with diplomatic immunity, so he couldn't vote. But if he could, he would have voted for Lincoln with all his heart.

In the event, Lincoln lost the heavily Democratic New York City, but carried the state by a narrow margin and won the election. And the curtain started rising on what was already being called the "irrepressible conflict."

In some ways, it was not an auspicious time to buy a bank, which Justin was aware of. He could not see the future any more than anyone else, but even the cloudiest crystal ball showed the danger of war. And after South Carolina seceded from the Union, doomsayers wailed and the stock market got a bad case of the jitters. After the New Year, the market seemed to regain its nerve somewhat as the do-nothing, South-leaning Buchanan administration said it was planning to send warships south to Charleston. But the "warships" turned out to be the unarmed *Star of the West* sent to reinforce the besieged Major Anderson in charge of the federal Fort Sumter in Charleston Harbor. And when the South Carolinians fired on the ship, it turned tail and hurried back to New York. The market jitters returned with a vengeance. New York businessmen began receiving odd replies from their Southern customers when they demanded payment for overdue bills. Some Southerners said they would pay in Confederate currency. Others said they were investing the money owed in muskets "to shoot you damned Yankees." Needless to say, confidence in Southern customers began to erode.

But despite all this, the Savage Bank prospered. Early on, Justin displayed a flair for bringing business to the bank. He was, of course, a celebrity; and as the Count of Mondragone, he had considerable social clout in a city intoxicated by glamour. He and Fiammetta entertained lavishly at the Villa, and as his business contacts spread through the city it became smart business to open an account at the Savage Bank because this guaranteed an invitation to one of the Mondragones' many galas where one could connect with the city's elite and pick up useful contacts. At a time when the nation was chewing its collective nails in suspense, waiting for the inauguration of Lincoln on March fourth, Justin brought in over two million dollars in new business to the bank.

Even more important, he listened. As always, Wall Street operated on rumor, gossip, and inside tips—with the emphasis on the latter. And as Justin's personal account swelled, creeping nearer the magic number of one million, at which point he could buy back his daughter from Yehenala, he began to relish his role as the Golden Boy of Wall Street. Making money was fun. What's more, as the war hysteria heated up and the Federal Government began letting out contracts to equip its woefully inadequate army and navy, making money became patriotic.

On the evening of April twelfth, he and Fiammetta were dressing to go to the Academy of Music to hear Verdi's *Masked Ball*. Fiammetta, who was sitting at her dressing table putting some last-minute touches to the elaborate coiffure her hairdresser had concocted that afternoon, was in a peevish mood.

"When am I going to see my home?" she said.

"Aren't we home?" Justin was standing at a full-length mirror, adjusting his white tie.

"I seem to recall sometime in the dim, dark past that you promised to take me to Europe for Christmas? Now it's past Easter, and the closest I've gotten to Europe is my French hairdresser."

"I'm sorry, darling, but you know how busy we've been at the bank. And with all this war talk, it's not the best time to travel."

She threw down her comb. "This silly so-called 'war'!" she exclaimed, standing up. "I'm sick of hearing about it! At least Garibaldi is trying to put Italy together! This crazy country is tearing itself apart. I want to go home."

He turned from the mirror. "What's gotten into you?"

"All this war talk. I'm afraid."

"Afraid? You? You've never been afraid of anything in your life. Besides, Johnny Reb isn't going to take New York. He might take Washington, but New York? Those farm boys would get lost in the Bowery."

"I'm not afraid of that: I'm afraid of losing you." She came to him and took his hands. "Oh, Justin, promise me you're not going to do something foolish and get involved with this madness."

"Where in the world did you get the idea I'm thinking of joining the army? I'm not even a citizen of this country, and if I did volunteer to fight I'd lose my diplomatic immunity and could be hanged for piracy."

"Well, that's a relief."

"If there's a war, the only way I'll get involved is with the bank."

"How do you mean?"

"Ben and I have worked out a plan to help the North raise money, if there is a war. It's pretty simple, really. Ben said we could peddle government bonds all over the country the way his father used to sell pots and pans."

"You mean, door to door?"

"Well, not exactly. But we could advertise in local newspapers, which the Government wouldn't do because they think it's beneath the Government's dignity. The Treasury only likes doing business with the old, established bond houses on the Street—you know, keep it all within the club, so to speak. If there's a war, they're going to have to go outside the club because war these days is getting to be damned expensive—Garibaldi taught me that. It's going to take hundreds of millions, and the best way to raise that kind of money is to go to the people. If we can do that for the Government, we'll make a nice pile of money for ourselves too. Anyway, Ben and I are going down to Washington to pitch the idea to the Secretary of the Treasury."

"Washington's such a dreary town," Fiammetta said snootily.

"Yes, I know. By the way, Ben's got a new girlfriend."

"Really? Who?"

"August Belmont's niece from Germany, a girl named Hildegarde. She's very pretty. I think Ben's working up his nerve to ask her to marry him."

Fiammetta sat back down at her dressing table and went back to her hair.

"Good for Ben," she said. "I hope he'll be happy."

Justin came up behind her and put his arms around her shoulders, kissing the top of her head.

"As happy as we've been," he said. "And if you're really homesick, I'll take you to Europe—war or no war."

Her face bloomed into a smile as she looked at his reflection in the mirror.

"Oh, darling, *will* you?" she exclaimed.

"I was trying to keep it as a surprise, but since you're getting so sulky on me . . ."

"I've not been sulky."

"Oh, yes, you have. We'll go to Paris and Rome. And then I'm going on to China."

Her smile vanished.

"China?" She made it sound like a dirty word. "What in the world for?"

"I've arranged a big loan for myself," he said. "It's enough for me to pay the ransom on Julie. I'm going to Peking to get back my daughter."

"But they're having a war over there!" she exclaimed. "It will be dangerous!"

"That's why I'll leave you in Rome."

She turned to him and took his hands.

"*Anima mia,* you'll be careful?"

"I won't be much use to Julie dead. But I *have* to get her back before that bitch, Yehenala, makes her as corrupt as the rest of the Forbidden City. Eunuchs and concubines are not exactly my idea of a healthy environment for a young girl."

"You have a point."

44 A HALF A WORLD AWAY at the Imperial Hunting Lodge in Jehol, Manchuria, the Hsien-feng Emperor "mounted the fairy chariot and returned to the nine sources"—in other words, he died—of dropsy, debauchery, and alcoholism at the age of thirty. Fortunately for Yehenala, the last words of the dying Emperor were to proclaim her son the heir, thus officially ensuring the Dragon Throne for the young Prince Tsai Chün. Yehenala became one of two Dowager Empresses (Hsien-feng's other wife, Niuhara, was a meek, bovine woman who was never a threat to the strong-willed and murderous Yehenala). Both Dowager Empresses were proclaimed Regents to the child monarch and given the position of *"chiu-lien ting-cheng,"* "listening behind the screen and administering the state." Yehenala took the title of Tz'u-hsi, "Motherly and Auspicious." And after ruthlessly putting down a palace revolt of senior mandarins and princes, she became the most powerful, and richest, person in China.

Though she had achieved more than the wildest fantasies of her childhood, the twenty-six-year-old Tz'u-hsi had gained control of a tottering empire. China was already ravaged by ten years of the Taiping Rebellion. Moreover, in 1858, French and British troops had attacked the imperial forts at Taku on the Bay of Pechili that protected the approaches to Peking. With vastly superior weaponry, the Europeans overwhelmed the forts. There followed two years of intermittent warfare and negotiation, for the Europeans were determined to increase their trade privileges with the Chinese, legalize the opium trade, protect Christians and Christianity on Chinese soil, and establish diplomatic relations with the haughty Dragon Throne. The Manchus bobbed and weaved during the negotiations: one curious sticking point was the Europeans' insistence on being able to approach the Dragon Throne without the humiliating kowtow, a mark of respect the Son of Heaven refused to abrogate. To prod the Manchus out of the stalemate of the negotiations, the British Minister, Lord Elgin, issued a shocking order: he authorized the looting and destruction of the fabulous Park of Radiant Perfection, or the Summer Palace, outside Peking. This was tantamount to a Chinese army invading France and ordering the destruction of Versailles. It was this Lord Elgin's father who, a half century before, had taken the Elgin Marbles from the Parthenon to save them from the "barbarous" Turks.

The destruction of the Summer Palace, one of the most shameful acts of western imperialism, was carried out with barbaric efficiency. A terrified Hsien-feng fled with his court to Manchuria, where he died. The humiliated Manchus had no option but to submit to the European demands, one of which was that they could no longer be described as "barbarians" in official Manchu documents.

This was the situation when Tz'u-hsi, the former Yehenala, achieved supreme power over the Celestial Empire. In one sense, the triumph of the girl from Pewter Lane was one of the great success stories of all time. Though it could be argued that the key to her success was her ability as a flute player to make "clouds and rain" for the dissolute Emperor, her achievement was nonetheless remarkable.

But the empire she had won was dying.

"Bring Us the half-breed girl named Julie."

The order was given by the Dowager Empress Tz'u-hsi as she sat on the Dragon Throne in the Hall of Supreme Harmony in the Forbidden City. It was an icy December morning. The Chief Eunuch An Te-hai, whose fortunes had waxed in direct proportion to his mistress's, bowed to Tz'u-hsi and hurried out of the throne room. It was the double hour of the snake.

Coal-burning braziers struggled to heat the huge, drafty hall, but Tz'u-hsi didn't mind the cold. She was wearing one of her heavy yellow dragon robes that was padded to protect against the bracing Gobi winds. With her tasseled Manchu headdress, her long filigreed gold nail guards, her raised pearl-encrusted slippers, and her strange dewdrop cherry painted on her lower lip, she looked, as usual, somewhat lurid and vaguely sinister. Tz'u-hsi loved to sit on the Dragon Throne. Though technically she had no right to do so, for it was reserved for the sole use of her son, the Emperor, when she was alone or with An Te-hai she enjoyed climbing one of the three stairs that led to the elaborately carved dais on which stood the gilt throne, flanked by two life-size statues of pale blue cranes, symbols of longevity. Then she would sit on the throne and look out at the lacquered hall, which was 200 feet long and 110 feet wide, its roof rising 100 feet above the ground. Here she thought that she was at the very center of the universe. Understandably, it never failed to give her a thrill.

The Ming architects had designed most of the hall in faint colors, to focus and magnify the glory of the throne with its crimson, gilt, and cloisonné columns, urns, and screens. Now she heard the shuffling of shoes on the marble floor. Out of a dark corner reappeared the Chief Eunuch with the half-breed girl, Julie.

Julie, now eight, was wearing a white dress that was notably simple compared to Tz'u-hsi's elaborate outfit. But Tz'u-hsi's beauty was beginning to fade. Julie's was blooming. She might have been looked down upon by the court because she was half "barbarian," but she was a flower of rare gorgeousness. Her amber eyes alone were breathtaking.

An Te-hai gave her a nudge and whispered, "Kowtow."

Julie obeyed, throwing herself on her hands and knees before the throne's dais and banging her forehead three times on the floor. She was more than a little apprehensive. Over the years Yehenala had summoned her to her apartments from time to time to inquire about her health and the progress of her education. She had always treated her kindly, and Julie had been given instruction in the classics by the learned mandarins in the Forbidden City. But Yehenala was now the Dowager Empress Tz'u-hsi. And Julie had no idea what to expect from this awesome and august lady seated on the Dragon Throne.

"Rise," Tz'u-hsi said after Julie had finished the kowtow, the reverence that had caused such an uproar with the Europeans. Julie got to her feet. The dim December sunlight barely penetrated the huge hall; even though it was ten in the morning, the octagonal ceiling lanterns had been lit.

"We have received a letter from your father," Tz'u-hsi began. In her arrogance, she had assumed the royal "We." No one in the court dared correct her, which tickled Tz'u-hsi. After years of being forced to call herself "this slave," it felt good to be able to speak as Hsien-feng had spoken. Power tasted delicious. "Do you remember your father?"

"Yes," Julie said in a trembling tone.

"Speak up, girl. We cannot hear you."

"Yes."

"Yes what?" Tz'u-hsi bellowed.

An Te-hai whispered in Julie's ear, "Yes, *Your Majesty.*"

"Yes, Your Majesty," Julie called out, gulping.

"That is better. Remember who We are. We are the Dowager Empress Tz'u-hsi, mother of the Son of Heaven and Regent of the Celestial Empire. We are the all-powerful. You are the lowest of the low, daughter of a pirate mother who was a traitor to the Dragon Throne and a despised barbarian father with ugly round eyes and red hair. You are a half-breed and a freak. You should thank the Goddess of Mercy that We have allowed you to stay in the Forbidden City, where normally only the purest Manchu blood is allowed."

"But Your Majesty has been kind to me in the past."

"This is true. Because of the cosmic glory of Our magnificence, We can occasionally condescend to be kind, even to the lowliest."

"May I ask Your Majesty a question?" Julie said, still trembling despite Tz'u-hsi's "condescension."

"Proceed."

"You speak of my father as a barbarian with ugly round eyes and red hair. But I thought my father was Li-shan, who was so handsome and sweet to me?"

"Poor child, it is no wonder you are confused," Tz'u-hsi took on a kindlier tone. "Although Li-shan claimed to be your father, as the despised Chung Wang claimed to be your grandfather, this was not the truth. It is fortunate for you that this is so, for Li-shan was put to death by Us in the most horrible manner for his treachery."

"He's dead?" Julie exclaimed, bursting into tears.

"Stop blubbering!" Yehenala shouted. Julie was so afraid of the woman, she obeyed. "If these depraved monsters were truly related to you," Yehenala went on, "there would be no hope for you: We would be forced to execute you. It is written in the Great Scrolls that children of criminals who perpetrate one of the Ten Abominations are themselves liable to the same punishment."

Julie was on the verge of tears. She remembered the Chung Wang and Li-shan with great affection. "Then who *is* my father, Your Majesty?"

"It is a barbarian from a place called America."

Julie's amber eyes widened. "America?" she repeated, her memory flashing back a number of years. "I've heard about America! They don't have an emperor, they have something called a president, a Shensheng Bew-ca-nun."

Tz'u-hsi looked surprised. "It is now a bearded barbarian of repellent aspect called Leen-conn," she said. "But how did you know this, child?"

"There was a man who my grandfather brought into my playroom in Soochow a long time ago . . . a man with round blue eyes and red hair . . . and he said he was from America! He was very nice. I remember he picked me up and kissed me. Do you think *he* is my real father?"

"This is possible. The barbarian Savage was in Soochow."

"Savage? Is that his name, Your Majesty?"

"Yes. We deigned to meet him. He has red hair on his chest, like a lapdog. These barbarians are animals! However, We digress. This Justin Savage has sent Us a letter from New York, which is the largest city of America. We had the letter translated by Our court scribes. Apparently, this Savage creature has made a great fortune in a place called Wall Street. He also owns a shipping company that has eighteen smoke-belching sea dragons. He owes Us—I mean, he owes Our government—a considerable sum of money which he is now prepared to pay. He informs Us that he will arrive in Tientsin in three months."

"Will I be able to meet him, Your Majesty?"

"You will not only meet him, you will go back with him to America."

Again, Julie burst into tears. "But I don't want to go!" she sobbed. "I don't want to leave China! The barbarians will eat me, as they ate our Bannermen when they burned the Summer Palace! Please don't make me go, Your Highness."

Tz'u-hsi rose from the Dragon Throne. "We do not blame you for your fears, child. It is true the barbarians are despicable. They have dared to invade Our kingdom and burn and loot Our palaces. Someday, an accounting will be made. But you have no choice, Julie. We made the deal with the barbarian, and Our imperial honor demands that We carry it out." She came down the steps of the dais and took Julie's chin in her hand. "Poor Julie," she said. "We will remember you with affection, despite the crimes of your mother. And remember: your best protection against the barbarians is to hate them. Do you understand that?"

Julie sniffed, tears running down her cheeks. "Yes, Your Majesty."

"Good." She kissed Julie's forehead. Then she said to An Te-hai, "Return her to her quarters. We must prepare Our divine person for lunch with the Viceroy of Anhwei. He has news for Us of the dispersal of the remaining odious Taiping rebels, and the interesting new tortures he has devised for their punishment. It should be amusing as well as instructive."

45 HOW I HATE HIM! THOUGHT Sylvaner Savage as he sat in the boardroom of the new Savage Shipping Line Building on Broadway. Look at Justin! Twenty-three years old, indecently good-looking, and the world's at his damned feet! *He's* the magnificent Savage, not I. *He's* the head of the family, and he's not even legitimate—a damned bastard! Oh, how I loathe him! I wish I had been in that torture chamber at Castle Mondragone—I'd have done more than drop him from the strappado!

"Before I leave for the Orient," Justin was saying to the fourteen directors of the company, "it is my sad duty to announce the retirement of our president, Sylvaner Savage, for reasons of health. . . ."

"Reasons of health" hell! Sylvaner thought. "Retire" hell! You're pushing me out, you bastard—you and that Jew sidekick of yours, Ben Lieberman. You've bought up all the stock, and now you have the controlling shares! But what can I do? I can't stop him from buying stock, and he's made millions on the market—millions! He has nothing but money. I sometimes think he's sold his soul to the Devil—yes, that must be it! I'd gladly sell *my* soul to the Devil to destroy him . . . oh, God, my cheek! Another attack of the damned tic!

Wincing with pain, Sylvaner picked up the "water" glass in front of him and took a gulp of gin. The other directors, who were well aware of his condition, pretended not to notice. The dignity of the Savage Shipping Line had to be preserved. But because of Sylvaner's "problem"—and the rumors circulating around town that Sylvaner had been somehow involved with the murder of Tony Bruce—the directors were unanimous in wanting to get rid of him.

"Therefore, as Secretary of the Board," Justin went on, "I hereby declare this meeting open for nominations for the position of president of the Savage Shipping Company."

Ben Lieberman, who was seated three away from Justin at the long oval table, shot up his hand. "I nominate Justin Savage."

"Thank you, Ben. I'm flattered. Any seconds?"

What a farce! Sylvaner thought, refilling his glass with gin from the bottle. What a howling farce! He's packed the Board with his pals . . . I'm being railroaded. . . . Oh, how I hate him! He drank the gin, and his brain swirled.

"Are there any other nominations?" Justin went on after his nomination had been seconded by the Chairman of the Manhattan Insurance Company, which had switched its fifteen-million-dollar account recently to the Savage Bank and Trust across the street. The boardroom of the new, eight-story Savage Shipping Building, which had a sensational "vertical railroad," or elevator, was handsomely paneled. At one end of the room hung a life-size portrait of Nathaniel Savage, painted in his prime. Justin looked around the room. There were no more nominations.

"Then let's take a vote. All in favor of the nomination say 'aye.' "

Everyone at the table said "Aye" with the exception of Sylvaner, who poured himself another glass of gin.

"Then it seems," Justin said with a smile, "that I'm the new president."

The Board burst into applause. The suave, German-born August Belmont, who was the American representative of the Rothschilds and had married the beautiful daughter of the naval hero Commodore Perry, rose to his feet. "Gentlemen, as a relatively new member of this distinguished Board and as a friend of our new young president, I would like to take this opportunity not only to congratulate Justin, but to say a few words in praise of him. I can guarantee you that Justin is the first ex-pirate to head a shipping company and a bank—though he's not the only pirate on Wall Street." Laughter and applause.

I may vomit, Sylvaner thought as Belmont went on extolling Justin's virtues. He reached for more gin. Belmont's such an ass-kisser. Now that Justin's a big shot, he's kissing *his* ass! Damned hypocritical Jew . . . I hate them all! All! This is *my* company, *I'm* the legitimate Savage, and it's been taken away from me by that bastard, Justin . . . Oh, God, why can't I bring myself to murder him? Why did I do it secondhand and have it bungled? I murdered Tony Bruce, why can't I murder Justin? Is it because I'm afraid of him? Or is it . . . No! No, that's not true. And yet, yes, it *is* true. He's better than I am. Oh, God, it kills me to admit it, but it's true, true, true . . . he's better. He's outsmarted me all along. Damn him! More gin. . . .

"And in conclusion," August Belmont was saying as Sylvaner poured himself more gin, "I think we have chosen a fine and distinguished new president. . . ."

"BULLSHIT!" Sylvaner roared, lurching to his feet. The Board gaped and gasped. "He's a bastard who's stolen this company from the legitimate Savage—me! You kiss his ass, Belmont, because you're a professional ass-kisser who's been kissing the Rothschilds' Jewish asses for years! Why don't you tell the truth about the 'great' Justin Savage?"

"Sylvaner, you're drunk!" Belmont exclaimed angrily. "Sit down, sir!"

"No, let him talk," Justin said, turning to Sylvaner. "What is the 'truth' about me, dear brother? You tell us, then I'll tell the truth about you."

Sylvaner's face paled. "The truth is . . ." He started to weave slightly. "The truth is, if it weren't for your wife's money, you'd be a nothing. Worse than a nothing: you'd be dangling from a rope for piracy!"

"Yes, you're right," Justin said. "I admit that, and everyone here knows it. Am I right?"

He turned to the other directors. They all nodded "yes." Sylvaner looked manic.

"You fools!" he cried. "You all think it's amusing and glamorous that he was a pirate, but do you know how many of my cargoes were stolen by him in the China Sea? Do you know how much this company lost because of him? I had to issue public stock to save the company, and now he's bought a majority of that stock so he can push me out! He's evil! He's a bastard! I hate him! And you've elected him president of my company! You fools! You damned fools!"

He sank back into his chair and started sobbing drunkenly, leaning over the table and burying his face in his hands. Justin looked at him with an emotionless face.

"Justin," Ben said, "tell them the truth about Sylvaner. Tell them what he did to you." He turned to the other directors. "He tried to have Justin murdered—twice! He stole his inheritance and had him tortured. . . ."

"Ben, be quiet," Justin said. "There's no point in digging up the dirt from the past. I'm satisfied with the way things have turned out. I think my brother is paying for what he did to me. The rest, I'll leave to Heaven." He looked around the room. "Gentlemen, as you know, my wife and I will be leaving for Europe next week, then I'm going on to China. In my absence, both this company and the Savage Bank will be under the expert management of my friend, Ben Lieberman. I thank you again for your vote of confidence, and I now declare this meeting adjourned."

He walked out of the boardroom. The other directors rose and followed him, looking back at Sylvaner, who was still bent over the table, sobbing. When the doors were closed and Sylvaner was alone, he sat up and poured himself another glass of gin. Then he turned his eyes to the portrait of Nathaniel Savage. Slowly, he rose to his feet.

"You won," he said softly. "You loved him and hated me. And now *he's* the magnificent Savage!" He threw the glass. It hit the portrait, then smashed to the floor. "But I'm not through yet!" he yelled. "I'll destroy the Savage name! I can do it! I'll *destroy* it!"

He started laughing maniacally, running his fingers through his white hair. Then the laughter turned to strangled sobs. He picked up the bottle, put it to his mouth, and drank the rest of the gin.

As they emerged from the Savage Shipping Building onto Broadway, August Belmont took Ben aside. "What a grotesque performance," he said. "Sylvaner's definitely gone round the bend. I don't know whether it's the gin, or his tic, or plain jealousy—or perhaps all three. But his mind is going. I think the man's dangerous. And I certainly didn't appreciate his anti-Semitic remark to me."

"Do you think he's an anti-Semite?" Ben asked.

"They all are."

"Not Justin. I could swear to that."

"No, you're right there. I think because Justin was born an outsider, he can appreciate other outsiders. And we're outsiders here, Ben. Never fool yourself on that score." He checked his gold pocket watch. "By the way, we're expecting you tonight for dinner. And Hildegarde's going to play afterward."

"Oh, I'll be there, Mr. Belmont. Wild horses couldn't keep me away."

Belmont smiled at him. "I've told my niece you're a financial genius and a young man of fine character. So you can see I'm giving you what they call in the theater advance publicity. I hope you won't disappoint me."

He shook Ben's hand, then started down Broadway. Ben's heart was racing, wondering if tonight he might pop the Big Question. . . . That is, if he had the nerve.

What the hell, he told himself as he started across the street. If the Dowager Empress of China didn't scare me, why should Hildegarde Belmont?

"My uncle tells me you and Justin Savage have raised over one hundred million dollars for the Federal Treasury by selling government bonds," Hildegarde Belmont said that night to Ben, who was sitting opposite her in August Belmont's dining room.

"One hundred and six point four million," Ben said, immediately kicking himself mentally for bragging. He could barely take his eyes off Hildegarde, who was a raven-haired beauty of twenty with an oval face and violet eyes that could melt the hardest heart. She was wearing a flounced white dress with décolletage that sent Ben's pulse to the ornate ceiling. Belmont's house at Fifth Avenue and Eighteenth Street was decorated with heavy opulence. The dining room's walls were papered scarlet and hung with huge, gilt-framed pastoral scenes of what Hildegarde had flippantly called "Uncle August's Swiss cows."

"I wouldn't have thought there was that much money in the world," she said, sipping her lobster bisque. "Why would Mr. Lincoln need so much money?"

"Because his generals stink," Ben said.

August Belmont, sitting at the head of the table, laughed. "Well put, Ben. Perhaps not very elegant, but certainly to the point. But tell me: isn't Justin putting himself in considerable danger going to China now? From what I read, the Dowager Empress is not to be trusted, and she hates all foreigners."

"That's true, sir. But Justin can take care of himself."

"He must love his daughter very much to go to such extraordinary lengths to free her," Hildegarde said.

"Yes, he does love her very much," Ben replied.

As I love you.

Forty-five minutes later, Hildegarde sat down at the grand piano in the drawing room and began playing the *Appassionata*. Ben sat between Mr. and Mrs. Belmont, watching her. As the tempestuous music swirled in his eardrums, he told himself that if he could only win this German beauty he would be the happiest man in the world. But was he crazy to think she might possibly love him? She had everything: looks, class, she played like Chopin, she could speak three languages . . . What did he have to offer her? He was a pint-sized Southern boy with a redneck accent who still wasn't sure which fork was used for what. She couldn't *possibly* be attracted to him.

And yet, an hour later, when, in Mr. Belmont's observatory, Ben screwed up his courage and proposed, this paragon said "yes."

He was so overwhelmed that when he kissed her, he accidentally knocked over a potted palm.

Sylvaner silently opened the desk drawer and pulled out a pistol, which he slipped into his jacket pocket.

"I've been giving a great deal of thought to Justin," he said, reclosing the drawer, then crossing to his wife, who was sitting in front of the fire, doing petit point. It was a snowy November night, a week after Justin and Fiammetta had sailed for Europe.

"If you want my advice," said Adelaide, "you'll put Justin out of your mind. He's behaved extremely well, after all. He could have sued you. He does have that signed confession of yours, and he protected you from the police when you killed Tony. I admire him a great deal, and I won't have you scheming against him anymore. The past is done."

"The past is never done."

He was standing behind her chair in the drawing room of the Washington Square house. Now he pulled the gun from his pocket. Adelaide didn't see him.

"I've given a great deal of thought," he went on, "to how I can best revenge myself for his pushing me out of my company."

"How can you speak of revenge?" she said with annoyance. "Let's put all that behind us and lead the rest of our lives peacefully."

"It's not quite that simple, Adelaide. In the first place, this tic is so painful I can't possibly live with it much longer. And in the second place, I'm not the kind of man who turns the other cheek. Justin has taken everything from me that I hold dear except my children. And *you* took them away."

She caught the odd tone in his voice. She put down her petit point and turned to look at him, still not seeing the gun.

"What in the world are you talking about, Sylvaner? What's going through that peculiar mind of yours?"

"You think my mind is peculiar?"

"It's certainly become so. Your hatred of Justin has warped your brain. You can't hate someone all the time without becoming twisted. Francis has noticed it. He said to me the other day, 'Why is Father acting so strangely?' I told him it was your tic, but it's more than that."

"I don't give a damn what Francis thinks, the little brat!"

"You used to love him."

"Not anymore: he's not mine!"

"Dear God, can't you put that out of your mind too? He's still a darling boy!"

"He knows I hate him!" He came around the chair and Adelaide saw the gun. Her eyes widened.

"Sylvaner," she whispered, "put that gun away. . . ."

"I drink because of the pain, and because my life is so miserable I can't stand to be sober! *He* gave me the tic—he, Justin!"

"He's become an obsession with you. . . ."

"It's because he's *won!*" he shouted. "Can't you understand? He's won—everything! Everyone admires him, even you! The children—all they talk about is Cousin Justin, the pirate, the hero, the this-that-and-the-other! Everyone laughs at me behind my back because he outsmarted me! My every waking thought is how can I pay him back? How can I destroy him? The problem is, if I murder him, he becomes a martyr. So I'll have to murder someone else."

Adelaide put down her petit point and rose from the chair, a look of alarm on her still-handsome face.

"What are you talking about?" she whispered, staring at the gun.

"Can't you guess?" He giggled. "Have your wits become addled, my dear? I'm going to destroy Justin by committing such a horrible crime that the Savage name will be forever despised, cursed, spat on—loathed! A crime of such monstrosity that a hundred years from now, people will still be speaking of it! Justin's great-grandchildren will cringe with shame that they are Savages!"

She backed to the mantel, a terrified look on her face.

"What are you going to do?"

Again, he giggled. "Murder you and the children. And then murder myself. It will be the crime of the century."

"Sylvaner, you're mad. . . ."

"That's what Tony Bruce said before I shot him!" he screamed. *"Your* Tony, your lover—you cheating bitch!"

She was sobbing, backing around the other chair.

"Please not the children . . . kill me if you must, but not the children . . . Oh, God, you couldn't be so cruel. . . ."

"But if I just kill you, it's not a monstrous crime, is it? It would be just another tabloid wife-murder—there's dozens of them. Oh, I suppose because we're Savages, it might cause some attention. But in a few days, people would forget. But if I kill the children too—ah, that's something else, isn't it? That's a monstrous crime! That's a crime of Shakespearean dimensions! No, the children must die too. But first, my dear, will be you. Farewell, Adelaide, you cheating bitch."

As she screamed, he pulled the trigger.

But nothing happened.

Looking confused, he fired again.

Nothing.

Adelaide, screaming, ran to the door and opened it. Francis was standing outside. "Francis, run and get a policeman!" she cried. "Take Georgie with you—your father's gone mad!"

"He can't shoot you, Momma," Francis said. "I hid all the bullets."

"Little monster!" his father roared, rushing at him. "There are other ways to kill!"

He grabbed Francis and started choking him. Adelaide ran to the fireplace, grabbed the brass poker, ran back to Sylvaner, and smashed it down on his head with all her strength.

Sylvaner fell to the floor.

"Darling, are you all right?" Adelaide cried, dropping the poker and throwing her arms around Francis, who was gasping.

"Yes. . . ."

"He was going to kill us all. . . ."

"I know. I heard him. And I saw him playing with the gun a lot of times. He'd been acting so funny lately, I thought I'd better hide the bullets."

"Thank God you did. Where's Georgie?"

"Hiding in the basement. I sent her down there when I heard him yelling."

"Darling, put on your coat and galoshes and go get a policeman," she said, picking up the poker from the floor. "I'll guard your father."

"I know he's not my father," Francis said, looking at Sylvaner, whose mouth was slightly open. Blood was beginning to trickle from it. "I heard him say that too. If you want to know the truth, I'm glad he's not. Was Mr. Bruce my father?"

Adelaide hesitated, then sighed. "Yes, dear."

"And Georgie's too?"

"Yes, but let's not tell her till she's older."

"Did he kill Mr. Bruce?"

"Yes, he did. Now, go get the policeman. Hurry, before he wakes up."

"He's not going to wake up, Momma," Francis said. "But I'll go get the policeman."

As he left the room, Adelaide knelt and felt Sylvaner's pulse.

It was gone, as was Sylvaner.

46 JUSTIN SAT ON HIS HORSE surveying the scene of desolation that stretched before him. He was atop a low hill with his escort of Bannermen and the Chief Eunuch An Te-hai. The Bannermen had met Justin's ship in Tientsin and escorted him to Peking, where An had joined them. An had told Justin that the Dowager Empress wanted him to see the ruins of the Summer Palace, the great Park of Radiant Perfection that had been looted and burned by the English and French the year before. An led the party to the west of the city where, near the Fragrant Hills, the great park had once stood, a place of ineffable beauty. Now it was a park of destruction.

"All the wooden buildings burned," An Te-hai said, mounted on a horse next to Justin's. "What you see are the blackened ruins of the stone 'European' palaces. The Bronze Temple escaped destruction, as well as a few of the bridges, like the Jade Girdle Bridge. But everything else was destroyed. Invaluable art treasures were stolen by the westerners, who auctioned them off with no regard to their artistic value. Her Majesty doubts that anyone will ever know how much was lost." He pointed. "Over there was the Garden of Crystal Rivulets . . . there the Hall of Joyous Longevity . . . there the Pavilion of Auspicious Twilight. Now all is gone. Knowing that you love China, Mr. Savage, Her Majesty wished you to see what the westerners did."

There were tears in Justin's eyes as he looked at the littered ruins.

After an hour inspecting the ruins, they returned to Peking and rode to the Forbidden City where An Te-hai led Justin into the Hall of the Coromandel Screen, where he and Ben had lunched with the Dowager Empress years before. Now the table they had dined at had been removed, and the only furniture was a thronelike gilt chair standing before the many-paneled black and silver Coromandel screen.

"Wait here," An said. "I will tell Her Majesty you have arrived."

He disappeared behind the screen. Justin, who was wearing a black western-style suit, took off his bowler hat. He was edgy. He had brought a million dollars in gold from America and deposited it in the British-owned Bank of Shanghai before traveling to Peking on one of the Savage Line's steamships. The million was an enormous sum. Rich as Justin had become, it was stretching him financially. Many of his friends and business associates had told him that he was crazy doing this. No child could be worth so much.

But Justin was determined to get Julie. He owed it to Chang-mei; and he couldn't allow Julie to be raised in the dissolute court of the Forbidden City. Besides, how could anyone evaluate the worth of a human child?

His nervousness increased when a line of green-robed eunuchs emerged from one side of the Coromandel screen. From the other emerged a number of concubines, elaborately gowned in the peculiar Manchu style. There were twelve of each. They filed out and took positions on either side of the throne, the eunuchs to the left, the concubines to the right. To Justin's confusion, they were whispering to each other, pointing at him and tittering with laughter. Once again, he felt like a freak.

My God, he thought. Bring Julie and let me get out of here! I want to go home.

But he knew enough about the Chinese character and their obsession with "face" that this had all been arranged by the Dowager Empress, that her intention was somehow to humiliate him before her court. He told himself to ignore the stares and titters. He might be an "ugly barbarian," but he would stand straight and tall.

Finally, after an interminable wait, a distant gong was struck and An Te-hai emerged from behind the screen, followed by Tz'u-hsi. The Empress was in full fig, her face made up with the turquoise eye shadow, the pink cheek rouge, and the cherry dewdrop on her lower lip. She wore one of her most elaborate dragon robes and moved slowly on her pearl-encrusted shoes elevated by the central wooden platforms. She obviously thought herself the epitome of elegance and beauty. As the eunuchs and concubines kowtowed, she came to the throne and sat down, turning her basilisk eyes on the young American.

An Te-hai came to his side and whispered, "Kowtow."

The western dignitaries might have fought furiously against this humiliation, but Justin wanted his daughter more than his dignity. He got on his knees and banged his forehead three times on the marble floor. Then he stood up.

"We are the most powerful woman in the world," the Dowager Empress announced in Mandarin, which An Te-hai translated into Cantonese for Justin. "Even Queen Victoria is not as powerful as We, for she has Parliament to contend with. What a silly notion, Parliament. Here, in the Celestial Empire, Our word is law. Do you understand that, barbarian?"

"Yes, I understand," Justin said. "However, parliaments and congresses seem to work."

"We are not interested in your political views. To Us you are an insignificant worm," the Dowager Empress went on, her cold eyes boring into his. "You are not only a barbarian, you are a man. Did you see what your fellow barbarians of the male sex did to Our Summer Palace?"

"Yes, Your Majesty. I am ashamed that westerners behaved with such brutality."

"The problem is that men rule the world, not women. Men cause wars and bloodshed. Men are violent brutes. We women care not for violence. We women wage peace, not war. We shed tears of compassion, not blood. That China is now ruled by Us, a woman, is most fortunate and auspicious. We will inaugurate an age of peace and prosperity. Did you bring the million dollars?"

"It is deposited in the Bank of Shanghai, Your Majesty," he said, pulling an envelope from his jacket. "I have here a letter authorizing it to be transferred to your representatives when my daughter is released to me. May I see Julie?"

"Do not push Us, barbarian. Bring the letter to Us, An."

The eunuch took the letter from Justin and brought it to the throne. The Dowager Empress took and read it. Then she whispered to An Te-hai, who returned to Justin.

"Her Majesty says the million dollars is not enough," he told Justin.

"We made a deal!" he exclaimed, telling himself not to lose his temper.

"True, but since then the Dragon Throne has suffered enormous humiliations. Not only the destruction of the Summer Palace, but the westerners have forced Her Majesty to give in to their every demand. China has been made to look like a weak fool before the world."

"That's not my fault! I regret it, but I can't be blamed for it."

"Nevertheless, you are here, in the power of Her Majesty."

Justin frowned, looking at the throne. Tz'u-hsi was watching him, a slight smile on her face. He had brought no weapon. Had he walked into a trap? Was she going to kidnap *him* and hold him up for more ransom?

"For many years, I was a concubine," the Dowager Empress said, dropping for the moment the royal "We." "I was a toy to satisfy the lusts of the late Emperor. I had to call myself 'this slave' in accordance with court etiquette. Do you know how humiliating it is to call yourself a slave, barbarian?"

"No, Your Majesty. But I have to protest this. . . ."

"Silence!" she thundered. "Do not interrupt me if you want your daughter alive!" Justin shut up. The threat to Julie was worse than the threat to himself. "Female concubinage," the Dowager Empress went on, "has been the custom in this kingdom for hundreds of years. It is a custom created by men to humiliate women, because men had the power. Now *I* have the power, and I wish to humiliate *you,* a barbarian and a man. An Te-hai, take him to the Red Chamber and tell him what he must do if he wants his daughter."

"Follow me, Mr. Savage," the eunuch said. He started toward a door opposite the throne. Justin looked at the Dowager Empress a moment, then turned and followed An. The concubines and eunuchs were tittering.

As Justin reached the door of the Red Chamber, their titters turned to laughter.

The Red Chamber was, not unexpectedly, painted red. In the center of the small room lay a red silk carpet.

"What does she want?" Justin asked An Te-hai after the eunuch closed the door.

"When Her Majesty was a concubine," An explained, "if her name was chosen by the Emperor, she was undressed, then rolled up in this carpet and carried by the Chief Eunuch to the Emperor's bedroom. There she was unrolled onto the floor, as is the custom. Naked, she crawled to the Emperor's bed and kissed his foot. The Empress wants you to do the same thing for her."

Justin grew red in the face. "Tell her to go to hell!"

"Then the half-breed girl called Julie will be strangled by the Imperial Guards."

Justin exploded with anger. "This is an outrage! I made a deal with her! I've come halfway around the damned world and lived up to my end of the bargain, and now she's upped the stakes? This isn't honest or fair!"

"Nevertheless, the Empress wants to avenge her years of humiliation by the late Emperor by humiliating you. She also told me to instruct you to raise your posterior in the air and wiggle it provocatively as you crawl to her throne."

"No, dammit! I'm a banker, not an ass-wiggling male concubine!"

"You may snort with indignation all you wish, Mr. Savage. But the Empress is determined to have her way. If you want your daughter alive, I would advise you to start taking off your clothes. The Empress does not like to be kept waiting."

"This is childish and stupid!"

"True. The Empress has a childish streak in her. She can also be very cruel."

"Of all the goddamn . . ."

"It won't take long. I will instruct you what to say."

Fuming, but realizing there was no alternative, Justin began taking off his jacket.

Twenty minutes later he returned to the Red Chamber and got dressed. It had been the most humiliating moment of his life. He would never forget the howls of laughter from the court as he crawled across the Hall of the Coromandel Screen. He would never forget the way the Dowager Empress rocked with laughter on her throne, clapping her hands with glee. He would never forget his shame as he kissed her pearl-encrusted shoe and said, "This slave wishes to pleasure Your Majesty," as An Te-hai had coached him. The Dowager Empress had scratched his red hair with her nails and called him her "lapdog" as the concubines giggled and the eunuchs cawed.

God, what a nightmare, he thought as he straightened his tie. But I did it and it's over and I sure as hell hope the Dowager Empress is satisfied that she's gotten her own back.

It was then he heard the screams. A girl was crying, "No, please! Don't make me go—the barbarian will eat me! Please!"

The door opened and An Te-hai led Julie into the Red Chamber. The girl was sobbing. When she saw Justin, she started screaming again.

"Here, Mr. Savage, is your daughter," the eunuch yelled.

Justin held out his hands, saying, "Julie, I'm not going to hurt you."

"Stay away—please!"

"I'm your father."

"You're an ugly barbarian who's going to eat me!"

"No I'm not. Who told you that?"

"All the concubines! They say barbarians eat Celestials!"

"They don't know what they're talking about. Here: let me hold you. I love you."

He picked her up in his arms and tried to kiss her, but she continued crying, pounding his face with her fists. "Let me go!" she screamed. "I hate you! You're an ugly barbarian!"

The Dowager Empress, who was listening in the Hall of the Coromandel Screen, smiled. Justin had made her day.

"Julie!" Justin cried, "please listen to me. I'm going to take you to your new home in America. We'll be there in time for Christmas! Christmas is a wonderful time for children. . . ."

"What's Christmas?" she asked, lowering her voice, curiosity getting the better of her.

"That's the birthday of Jesus Christ."

"You mean the brother of the Heavenly King?"

Justin looked momentarily confused. Then he remembered the strange "dream" of the Heavenly King, and his version of Christianity.

"Yes, that's right," he said. "In America, we celebrate the Christ child's birthday, and it's a wonderful time of year. There are Christmas trees with candles and toys, and lots and lots of presents for good little boys and girls . . . like you."

"Presents?" Julie asked. "You mean, dolls?"

Justin smiled as he bounced her gently up and down in his arms.

"Oh, all the dolls in the world," he said. "And sleds and doll houses . . . and it will be snowing and everything will be beautiful."

She looked at him, trying to gauge his truthfulness.

Finally she said, "You promise you won't eat me?"

He laughed and kissed her again.

"I promise."

47   THE SNOW WAS FALLING HEAVILY on Fifth Avenue as the carriage pulled up in front of the Savage mansion. The top-hatted man inside looked out at the strange architectural mishmash, which rather reminded him of his own home, although this New York version was much smaller.

"Wait for me," the man said to the cabbie as he stepped out onto the sidewalk, which had just been swept.

"Yes, sir."

The man was wearing a black overcoat with a collar of bear fur. He climbed the steps to the front yard, then went down the walk to the house where a few lights were already turned on. It was Christmas Eve, and the days were short. All of New York was in a bumptious holiday mood. The long, bloody war against the South finally seemed to be turning in the North's favor, and holiday shoppers were out en masse buying gifts in record numbers with the enormous profits the war had brought the Northerners. Contrary to many expectations, the war had turned out to be good for business after all.

Northern business.

The man rang the bell and waited, his breath misting in the icy air. It was turning out to be a beautiful Christmas: the city was a winter wonderland. A half block away, strolling carolers were singing "God Rest Ye Merry, Gentlemen."

In some ways, the man reflected, New York was reminiscent of London.

The door was opened by a young Chinese butler. "Yes, please?"

"Is Mr. Savage in? Mr. Justin Savage?"

"Yes, sir. Mr. Savage decorating Christmas tree."

"Might I see him? Here's my card."

Outside, the snowflakes came down in wintry profusion; but inside, all was warm and cozy—if one could call a fifty-foot drawing room "cozy." In the pseudo-Gothic stone hearth a fire roared. And in one corner, next to the leaded glass oriel, Justin stood on a ladder affixing an angel to the top of the twenty-foot tree.

"Who invented Christmas trees?" Julie asked. She was sitting on the floor next to the ladder, playing with the decorations. She looked irresistible in a merry red dress trimmed with embroidered holly leaves.

"I think the Germans did," her father answered from above her. "The idea was made popular by Prince Albert."

"Who's Prince Albert?"

"Queen Victoria's late husband."

"Is Queen Victoria like the Dowager Empress?"

"Well, sort of. Queen Victoria's nicer."

"The Christmas tree smells so nice," Julie said as she overturned a box of tinsel, making a mess. "You were right, Daddy. Christmas is fun. When am I going to see my presents?"

"First thing in the morning, after Santa delivers them. And try and get the tinsel back in the box."

"All right." Julie's English was still rather singsongy, but she was picking it up with the speed of a child. Justin had hired her the best tutor in New York. "Is Uncle Ben getting married?" she went on, putting the tinsel back.

"Yes, next week."

"Is he marrying a nice lady?"

"Yes, very nice."

Justin climbed down a rung on the ladder to hang some more ornaments when he saw his butler come in the room, carrying a silver tray. He had brought Po-han, a cousin of Ah Pin, from Canton when he returned from Peking with Julie because he thought having another Chinese with her would ease her fears of the strange new world she was entering. "There's a gentleman to see you, sir," Po-han said. "He gave me his card."

Curious, Justin climbed down the ladder and looked at the card, which was engraved: THE EARL OF SAXMUNDHAM.

Justin saw Percy appear in the door. He had taken off his hat and was brushing the snowflakes from the shoulders of his coat.

"Daddy, who's that man?" Julie asked.

"An old acquaintance. Po-han, take Julie up for her nap."

"Yes, sir." He took Julie's hand and said, in Cantonese, "Come, little one. We go upstairs."

He led her out of the room as Justin came over to Percy, extending his hand. "What are you doing in New York?"

He had no idea what their relationship was at this point—friendly or unfriendly—but he decided to opt for friendly. Percy took his hand and seemed disposed to friendliness.

"I've been posted to the Legation in Washington," he said. "I just arrived in New York this morning from England. Samantha asked me to give you this."

He pulled an envelope from his jacket.

Samantha. A thousand memories swirled through Justin's mind. Samantha, his first love. "How is Samantha?" he asked.

"You haven't heard?"

"Heard what?"

"No, of course you'd have no way to know. Her obituary was in the London papers. . . ."

"Obituary?" Justin whispered. "She's dead?"

"Yes, it happened six weeks ago. She had developed a heart condition during her last *accouchement,* and during a particularly nasty spell of weather in November she caught a cold. It developed into pneumonia and . . ." A look of pain crossed his face. "And we lost her. The children, naturally, were devastated."

Justin's mind was reeling. "The children . . . ?"

"Yes. We had two boys and a girl. They loved their mother very much, as did I. The curious thing was that even though our marriage got off to a bumpy start, what with my uncle trying to get rid of Samantha, after he died we became very close. She was a loving wife, even though"—he hesitated—"I knuh . . . knuh . . . knew her first love was always you."

The two men stared at each other. Justin wondered if there was a hint of resentment in his eyes.

"At any rate," Percy went on, "she wrote this letter two days before she died. She asked me to deliver it to you. I haven't read it. She asked me not to."

Again, the note of resentment. Or was it hurt? Justin took the envelope, which was marked, simply, "Justin."

"I'm being a bad host," Justin said. "Would you like a drink?"

"No thanks. Actually, my cab is waiting. I have to get back to the hotel. I wouldn't want to leave the children on Christmas Eve, especially the youngest. He's only three. Cute little beggar. Oddly enough, he has hair very much your color. Samantha loved him the most, I think. She named him Justin."

"Justin. . . ." He looked anguished.

"Well, then, I'll be going. Things turned out quite splendidly for you, didn't they? Roaring success on Wall Street, China hero . . . all that sort of thing. Samantha used to follow your career in the papers."

Justin was only half listening. He was seeing a beautiful young girl on the deck of the *Sea Witch*.

"I can't believe she's dead," he said, almost to himself.

"Yes, it came as a shock." There was an awkward pause. "Well, I'll be saying good-bye, Savage. And merry Christmas."

"Yes, good-bye. . . ."

Samantha dead. It didn't seem possible. She was his age, barely twenty-seven. . . . How rotten, how unfair. . . .

Po-han showed Percy out the door as Justin went back in the drawing room. He felt numb, sick. He sank into a chair and stared at the envelope.

Po-han appeared in the door.

"When you expect *Tai-tai* back from shopping, sir?" he asked.

"She should be home soon. Is Julie asleep?"

"Yes, sir. So is Number One Son."

Po-han bowed and left. Outside, the strolling carolers were singing "Hark! The Herald Angels Sing."

Justin opened the envelope and pulled out the note. The paper was delicate, as fragile, he thought, as life. It was dated November 20, 1864.

> *My dearest Justin,*
>
> *Percy will have explained to you my situation when he delivers this to you, so you will know that by then I will be gone. How strangely life has worked out. Much to my surprise, Percy has been a kind and loving husband. I have been happy with him, as I hope you have been happy with your wife. There was a time when I could not have said that, but now I can with all my heart.*
>
> *The French have a saying: "The joy of love is short, but the*

pain of love lasts all your life." Alas, that has been true for me. You were the great love of my life, Justin, and the fact that our paths never united has never ceased to pain me, deep in my heart. I know it is no one's fault, but that has not eased the pain. When you came to Saxmundham Castle, I said terrible things to you, for which now I ask your forgiveness. I could never wish you harm, Justin. Far from it: I could only wish for your happiness.

So when you think of me—if you ever do—think of me as someone who loved you from the first moment I saw you. You once said perhaps we would meet in the next world. It remains my fondest—and final—wish.

I bid you farewell, my darling. May your life be long and happy.

Your Samantha

Justin put the note down, staring into the fire.

There were tears in his eyes.

Fifteen minutes later Fiammetta came in the house. After giving three large packages and her fur-lined cloak to Po-han, she went into the drawing room.

"Well, the shopping's done—finally. I got a whole battalion of toy soldiers for Gianfranco and a doll's house for Julie . . . what's wrong? Your eyes are all red . . . *Anima mia,* you've been crying!"

She hurried to him and hugged him.

"Samantha's husband was here," Justin said in a hoarse voice. "He delivered this note. She's dead."

"Dead?"

"Yes. My God, she named one of her children after me, and I never even wrote her. I was cruel to her, Fiammetta. And I suppose I was selfish. I was only thinking of myself . . . and us." He forced a sad smile. "That enchanted rose of yours really worked: I did forget her." He frowned. "But she never forgot me."

"You did love her, didn't you?" Fiammetta said softly.

"Yes. She was my first love. I suppose you never really forget your first love."

She took his hand.

"I can see you're devastated," she said. "I suppose in a way I should be hurt, though how can one be jealous of a ghost?"

"There's no need to be jealous. I love you: you know that. But I loved her once. The funny thing is, love was a mystery to the Chinese. I suppose in a way it's a mystery to me." He took her in his arms and kissed her.

"Who understands love?" Fiammetta said. "You simply *feel* it, and it's the most marvelous feeling in the world. I know you're sad, my darling, but life goes on. *We'll* go on. We, the magnificent Savages." She kissed him again. "Merry Christmas, my darling Justin."

Outside, on the snowy sidewalk, the carolers burst into "Joy to the World!"